Praise for *The Chess Garden:*

"With a richness of invention that makes the worlds of Lewis Carroll, J.R.R. Tolkien and C. S. Lewis seem impoverished, Uyterhoeven creates imaginary scene after scene . . . filled with images of astonishing invention and beauty." —*Boston Sunday Globe*

"These tales form an allegory not only of the Doctor's exemplary life but also of the wisdom that he has gained in it—a quietude and a benevolence that in today's world really do seem fabulous." —*The New Yorker*

"Mr. Hansen is a storyteller with a feel for the gently uncanny, a sense of drama both quiet and accurate." —*The Washington Times*

"A wonderful novel, rich and strange, certain to delight lovers of storytelling and lovers of games." —*St. Petersburg Times*

"A masterpiece of surreal storytelling . . . A writer with a rare gift for evocative description, Hansen deftly weaves allegory and history in this compelling narrative." —*Library Journal*

"Original, complex, and ambitious . . . Brooks Hansen has created a lasting and enlivened image of a universe we have not seen nor imagined before." —*Village Voice Literary Supplement*

"Vividly described . . . quirkily brilliant." —*Locus*

"Startling . . . strange and fascinating." —*South Bend Tribune*

"Highly absorbing and endlessly inventive." —*The Times* (London)

Also by Brooks Hansen

BOONE
(with Nick Davis, 1990)

THE CHESS GARDEN

OR THE TWILIGHT LETTERS OF GUSTAV UYTERHOEVEN

BROOKS HANSEN

WITH ILLUSTRATIONS BY MILES HYMAN

RIVERHEAD BOOKS, NEW YORK

Riverhead Books
Published by The Berkley Publishing Group
200 Madison Avenue
New York, New York 10016

Book design by Rhea Braunstein
The passage on pages 402 and 403 is taken from *The Aquarian Gospel of Jesus the Christ*, by Levi. Reproduced with the permission of the publisher, DeVorss & Co.

Farrar Straus Giroux edition published 1995
Farrar Straus Giroux ISBN: 0-374-16015-5
First Riverhead trade paperback edition: November 1996

The Putnam Berkley World Wide Web site address is
http://www.berkley.com/berkley

Library of Congress Cataloging-in-Publication Data
Hansen, Brooks, 1965–
The chess garden, or, The twilight letters of Gustav Uyterhoeven / Brooks Hansen ; with illustrations by Miles Hyman.
p. cm.
ISBN 1-57322-563-0
1. South African War, 1899–1902—Fiction. 2. Physicians—South Africa—Fiction. 3. Dayton (Ohio)—Fiction. I. Title.
PS3558.A5126C48 1996
813'.54—dc20 96-1480
CIP

Printed in the United States of America

10 9 8 7 6 5 4 3 2 1

To my mother and father

CONTENTS

PART ONE
The First Three Letters

PART TWO
The Study of Effects, 1823–1867

PART THREE
The Fourth, Fifth, Sixth, and Seventh Letters

Whatever is here, that is there; what is there, same is here. He who seeth here as different, meeteth death after death. By mind alone this is to be realized, and then there is no difference here.

—from the *Kasha Upanishad*

The spiritual world in external appearance is quite similar to the natural world. Lands appear there, mountains, hills, valleys, planes, fields, lakes, rivers, brooks, springs of water, as in the natural world . . . Paradises also appear there, gardens, groves, woods, and in them trees and shrubs of all kinds bearing fruit and seeds; also plants, flowers, herbs, and grass . . . Animals appear there, flying creatures and fish of every kind.

—Emanuel Swedenborg, *Divine Love and Wisdom*

What matters won't change. What changes don't matter.

—A vandal pawn from Scarecrow

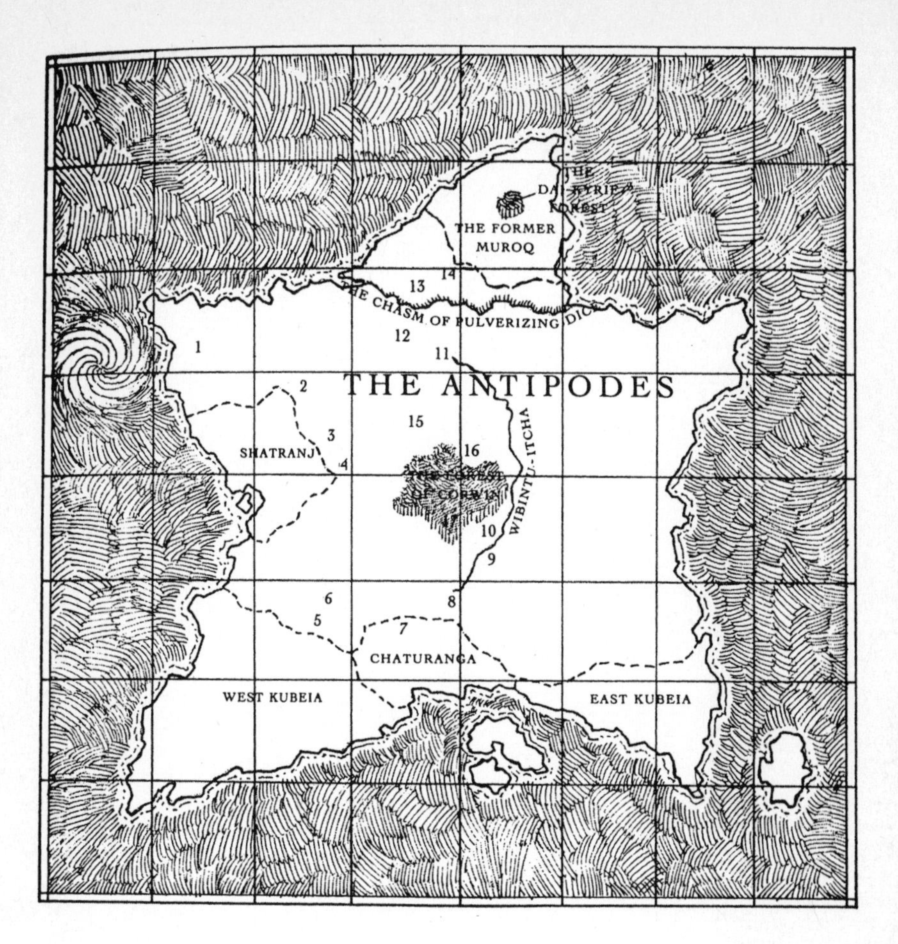

THE MAP

PLACES OF NOTE, IN ORDER

1 *Ludo, first port*
2 *The Candletree*
3 *Scarecrow*
4 *Raggedy*
5 *Macaroni*
6 *Eugene's Rook*
7 *The Camp of the Limestone Totem*
8 *Gwyddbyl, the "tipping" site*
9 *Pelagia's Monastery*
10 *Quigley*
11 *Orzhevsky, home of vandal bishops*
12 *Bumbershoot*
13 *The Chasm Bridge*
14 *The Three Carriage Bridges Po's Tapestries*
15 *Chimeroo*
16 *The Ruins of Hlique, original board of Eugene and Teverin*
17 *Teverin's Cabins*

PART ONE

The First Three Letters

ONE

THE GREAT DAYTON FLOOD

At some time near dawn, on March 25, 1913, there came a loud knocking at the front door of the Uyterhoevens' home in the Dayton View section of Dayton, Ohio. Mrs. Conover was upstairs beside Mrs. Uyterhoeven's bed at the time, trying with limited success to wade her way through the revelations of Hildegard of Bingen. She had assumed that the person at the door must be her brother, Dr. Reeve, coming to check on Mrs. Uyterhoeven again, but it seemed awfully early. Her brother had said that he wouldn't be back until 7:00 or so, and she could see the sky was only barely light. Besides, the knocking sounded too urgent for her brother. It had grown almost frantic by the time she reached the first landing, so much so that she'd looked through the border windows first, just to be safe, just to see who could be making such an awful commotion at such a quiet hour.

It was Andy Fox, standing there in his rain gear, shifting anxiously from foot to foot. Mrs. Conover opened the door just a crack at first. "Andy?"

Andy lowered his hood. "Mrs. Conover." He looked momentarily startled to find her at the door, but it did not distract him from his duty. "It's the rain," he said, thumbing the sky. "The water's up past eighteen feet in the levees, and I'm not sure they'll hold. I just wanted Mrs. Uyterhoeven to be aware.''

Mrs. Conover tried to be polite. She smiled, but this wasn't the first time she'd met Andy under such circumstances. It had become something of a neighborhood tradition, in fact: anytime there was a heavy rainfall, Andy would come by in his coat and boots, rattling all their doors with his warnings. He'd been doing so since he was a little boy. Chicken Little, they called him.

''Is Mrs. Uyterhoeven all right?'' he asked.

''Mrs. Uyterhoeven passed away just a few hours ago.''

Andy's whole body seemed to pause and then he bowed his head. ''Mind if I pay respects?''

Mrs. Conover opened the door, but with a twinge of regret that her brother hadn't come first, or Mr. Patterson, or someone like that. It didn't seem quite right that Andy Fox should be the first to hear, and now the first to see. Still, she led him, dripping, upstairs to Mrs. Uyterhoeven's bedroom.

The day before, Mrs. Uyterhoeven had asked for her blue silk dress because it had been a favorite of her husband's. The black velvet collar was still peeking above the covers where her body lay. ''She doesn't look so different,'' said Andy. ''Most people look different, don't they?''

Mrs. Conover nodded. ''I wouldn't have known if I hadn't been holding her hand.'' She spoke with a hint of pride.

Andy knelt down beside the bed and said a silent prayer, and then stood up to leave. He nodded solemnly to Mrs. Conover, but then he was stopped short. On the mantel was a cherrywood drawer, one half of a companion set for the top of a dresser, but here alone. ''Those the doctor's letters?''

Mrs. Conover nodded curtly. ''She took them down last week.''

Andy walked over to the mantel. The drawer was sitting lengthwise along the top. Andy turned it square so that the sleeve faced out. ''The pieces in here, too?''

''You know they are, Andy.''

Andy touched the knob, which was plain and round. Above it

there was a skeleton keyhole, so he tugged gingerly just to feel the lock, but the drawer pulled out. He looked up at Mrs. Conover, startled. "I didn't mean," he said, but he didn't close the drawer right away. He looked down inside.

Mrs. Conover stepped to the door and touched the latch. "Haven't you others you need to warn?"

Andy's head snapped to attention. "You're right." He pushed the drawer closed and turned it back around on the mantel lengthwise. He went to the window and checked the sky, which was only drizzling. "It's the thaw as much as the rain," he explained. "Ground's already sopped."

"I'll keep an eye on it, Andrew."

"Do. You got help if you need it?"

"Dr. Reeve is coming."

This seemed to satisfy him. He pulled his hood up over his head and, with a final, ominous nod, left.

Mrs. Conover waited to hear the front door close before taking the drawer and setting it back inside Mrs. Uyterhoeven's closet, on the high shelf. There was no need for the letters to be out now, tempting people. Then she resumed her place in the wicker rocking chair by Mrs. Uyterhoeven's bed and opened the Hildegard book again.

She'd chosen it from the doctor's library the night before for no particular reason other than the name, and she'd been struggling with it all night, in and out of sleep. She returned to the passage she'd been reading before the nap that Andy had interrupted, something about a tent in someone's chest that Mrs. Conover wasn't able to make either heads or tails of. She tried plodding her way through the first few sentences again, but the combination of Hildegard's obscurity, Mrs. Uyterhoeven's rocking chair, and the sleeplessness of the last several days took little time to get the better of her.

She was awakened two hours later by a second knocking, which also sounded as if it was coming from the front door. She bolted up and scolded herself in a single reflex, but, with a glance at Mrs. Uyterhoeven's expression, relaxed. She straightened her dress, and then went down, prepared once again to deliver her brother the news.

When she opened the front door, though, she let out a small gasp. The entire front lawn and the street beyond was underneath a good six inches of water, and there was a bucket clanking stubbornly against the first step of the porch.

She was not overly alarmed. She'd seen water on the streets many times before. It had come up a full six feet back in 1889, when she'd been midwifing the birth of her nephew, but the rain hadn't seemed nearly as hard this week as it had back then. Still, Good for Andy, she thought, and then she wondered if her brother would know where to find his fishing boots.

She took the pail and set it inside the door, then crossed to the back of the house to check on the garden. She could see from the patio doors—all of it was submerged, right up to the terrace. The water had yet to crest the top step, but she went to the linen bench for some sheets and towels to jam beneath the doors, just in case.

She'd been kneeling on the kitchen mat, stuffing a linen under the crack, when she heard a windowpane shatter somewhere in the neighborhood, and that was what officially started her nerves. As soon as she'd secured the doors, she began going from room to room, checking the sky from every window. Morning was several hours old now, but the cover was still dark and gray. She wished her brother was there already, the sounds were so disconcerting—the clunks and rasps of loose debris hitting porch posts and trees and picket fences throughout the neighborhood. The water seemed to be carrying the sounds and leavening them. In the living room she could see there was a legitimate current running down Middle Street for Holt now. A tree limb came floating by and she wondered if her brother would be coming at all. He'd have to soon. She'd gauged the water level against the cross-hatch trellis of the grape arbor, and she could see it was rising fast—three hatches since she'd come downstairs—and when it began to slide across the terrace, she thought perhaps she should start moving the valuables upstairs—again, just to be safe.

She went to the dining room first and chose what was most fragile and portable to begin. She took all the plates from along the walls, the Chinese set from the ledge above the wainscoting, the blue Delft from the top of the oak bench, and the Roman pair on the mantel. She stacked them on a serving tray and carried them upstairs to Mrs. Uyterhoeven's sewing room.

The window there faced the garden, but all she could see was the smooth surface of muddy brown water sliding through. It was just as well that Mrs. Uyterhoeven hadn't had to see this. The crocuses had just come up, but they were drowned now and more than likely done for the year. The privet and honeysuckle along the hedge, all set to open for spring, were weeping meekly. The pickets of the south fence looked like a row of whale teeth sticking up. The marble chess benches were entirely gone from view, and the tiled checkerboard tops of the black iron Parisian tables looked almost like rafts. Here and there little swirling eddies appeared and then vanished. All the pieces in the bins would be lost, she thought, which she supposed wasn't so dire. She just thanked heaven that Dr. Burns hadn't returned the sets to the games shack at the back of the garden. He'd taken them all up to the attic before the February snow because the shack's roof was so rotten. He had reshingled it himself and done a good job, but with Mrs. Uyterhoeven's falling ill, he'd never gotten around to taking the sets back down, and all Mrs. Conover could think was, Thank heavens. The shed was so low on the property, at least half of them would already have been ruined by now.

Then she remembered the doctor's cane. It was out at the back of the garden, too, hanging from the limb of the apple tree. The water could well have been four feet deep back there, and there was so much downstairs to get to, she decided she didn't dare risk it. Really, it occurred to her, there were respects in which the Uyterhoevens' was the very worst place she could possibly have found herself during a flood, for all there was to save.

When she returned to the first level, she saw the water had pushed the towels from the door and was already seeping across the kitchen floor. She took off her shoes and put on a pair of boots from the front closet, and then she went to work on the rugs, which meant moving some tables and chairs. She rolled up the Aubusson in the living room and pulled it up the front stairs by the fringe, then the two Turkish runners in the hallway and then the Bokhara in the library. The others were simply under too much furniture, so her next few trips she devoted to the crystal in the oak bureau, the silver, and the tea service. She took the Japanese platter that Mrs. Uyterhoeven used as a coffee table, two silver cookie salvers, two dainty ashtrays, the silver teapot, a sugar basin, the creamer, and a spoon box made of mother-of-pearl. She took a brass chafer and the brass theewater kettle, and then Dr. Uyterhoeven's cigar stand. She set them all in the sewing room with the plates, and by the time she was finished, the water had begun to creep in through the front foyer, so her next trip she took up the baskets of fruit, just as a precaution—and some cider and fruit cakes that the neighbors had been bringing ever since Mrs. Uyterhoeven had taken her turn for the worse.

Her next trip down, she went from room to room to make sure all the gas lamps were out. The floor in the parlor was already under an inch of water, and owing to the house's natural slump, the front hallway was even worse off. The driest room on the floor was the library, but clearly the next order of business. The bookcases were a formidable sight. They covered the walls almost entirely, and there were four free-standing shelves as well, so for the sake of inventory, she began with the card catalogue. She took it up drawer by drawer, then the terrestrial globe, the celestial globe, the doctor's telescopes, the microscope, the kaleidoscopes, and only then the books.

She started with the doctor's personal shelf, all the volumes that he himself had translated. She recognized the names on the spines from so many years of seeing them in Dr. Uyterhoeven's lap out in the garden. With all respect to the living, they were his best friends—Julian of Norwich, Teresa, Eckhart, Ruysbroeck, Pseudo-Dionysius, Gregory the Great, Augustine, Anselm, Philip Neri, and Hans Denk. And of course none had occupied a more prized place, either in the library or in the doctor's hands, than the Swedenborgs. She took them up first, two whole shelves' worth, and then the rest. Then as soon as all the doctor's own books were safe and sound, she applied herself to the remainder of the library, the hundreds and hundreds of books that the doctor's guests had brought him or sent as gifts. She stacked them in the sewing room with all the rest, and when the sewing room became impassable, she used the guest room.

It took her the better part of an hour going back and forth, carrying armload after armload, and each time she came back downstairs, she could feel how much higher the water had risen. It started at her ankles, then came to her knees, then hips, then waist. By the time she'd come down for the last of the books, the water was up to her ribs. She wasn't sure how many more trips she'd be able to make. So much still remained. So much was already ruined underwater, all the tables and chairs. What she chose and what she didn't seemed arbitrary now.

She waded her way into the front living room to see if there were any paintings on the wall she should take, but just then she heard a great collision out by the front door, and something thumping desperately. She looked out the front window and saw it was a horse, bracing itself against the current by the porch beams, and then she recognized the white star on his forehead—it was Ben Kilmer's old plow horse, Cow. Poor thing looked terrified, so Mrs. Conover went quick as she could to the door and led him in. She slung an old raincoat around his neck, and then, with her dress and petticoat billowing up about her waist, guided him up the front stairs, which was no easy trick. She had to wait nearly five minutes for the fool horse to come, while another six inches of the Uyterhoevens' belongings were swamped.

By the time she'd gotten him up into the front guest room, he was shaking like a leaf, more from nerves than the cold. Still, Mrs. Conover took some linens from the upstairs bench and began drying him off, to soothe them both. From the window she could see little bits of neighborhood floating down Middle Street like the images of some awful dream. She saw animals thrashing by in the current—livestock and squawking chickens and dogs whose barks she recognized. The water was sweeping away everything that was not bolted. There were sounds of more glass shattering, poles thumping and crunching through windows and porch beams. Steele dam must have broken, she thought. The whole levee must be washed away, because there just didn't seem to be anything keeping the town from the river.

Mrs. Conover went out to the landing as soon as Cow was calm and dry. Even if she'd wanted to, she couldn't have gone back down. The water was already lapping on the third stair from the top. She got down on her knees to see what she could. The cups of the bronze chandelier in the foyer were scraping the ceiling. The Venetian mirrors had been lifted from their hooks on the molding, and she could hear the large furniture beginning to thump about in the current. She thought of the piano drifting a-kilter, ruined. Everything ruined.

Just then, though, as she was considering the possibility that the water might not have the courtesy to stop at the first floor, she heard a man's voice calling over. It was George Tremont from the house next door, but it might have been an angel for the relief it brought her heart, just to be reminded that she was not alone. He was calling from his own bedroom window where it faced the Uyterhoevens' hallway. Mrs. Conover went to the sill and there he was, standing not twelve feet away, with a crate in his arms, near enough for them to speak without having to raise their voices.

''Mrs. Conover, how are you doing?'' he asked.

''I'm all right, George, but you should know Mrs. Uyterhoeven passed away last night, before all this.''

''That's what Andy said.'' George nodded, and his wife, Sylvia, appeared at the window next to him with their daughter in her arms, Virginia. She was no more than five or six years old, but looking younger at the moment, wrapped in a thick wool blanket and with her head tucked underneath her mother's chin.

''Your brother there?'' asked George.

Mrs. Conover shook her head. ''Didn't make it.''

''Oh, I'm sorry, Mrs. Conover.'' George put down the crate in his arms. ''If I'd have known, I would have come over and helped, but this all came so fast.''

Virginia yawned and shivered, and that seemed to make his point: first things first. ''I understand,'' said Mrs. Conover.

''You all right, though?''

"I'm fine, but we have a guest. Kilmer's horse."

"Cow?"

"Swept right up onto the porch, but he's all right. Just a little frightened."

George let a proper moment pass, and then, to register his apologies for even asking, scratched the back of his head. "Dr. Burns didn't ever get round to returning the chess sets to the shed, did he?"

"Thank heavens, no. They're still in the attic, high and dry."

George heaved a sigh, and for a moment their attention fell upon the water between them. Virginia whispered something in her mother's ear, to which Sylvia shook her head doubtfully, but leaned out the window nonetheless. "Virginia's wondering if you managed to get Dr. Uyterhoeven's cane."

Mrs. Conover touched her chest for forgiveness. "Virginia, I'm very sorry. I did think of it, but it was too late." Virginia nodded bravely. "It may still be there tomorrow, though, or whenever this drains."

"But she'll understand if it isn't." George cupped his daughter's head. "All that means is the doctor left with Mrs. Uyterhoeven."

"That's right," said Mrs. Conover, impressed by George's quick poetic sense.

For vague consolation, Virginia rested her head against her mother's neck, but just as it touched, there was the sound of an explosion. All four of them jumped.

"That's downtown." George set his crate on the sill and leaned out. Mrs. Conover looked out as well, and they could both just barely see a trail of smoke climbing into view from across the river. "Somebody must have left their gas on," he said, pulling back in. He shook his head mournfully, and then Sylvia gave him a nudge, which he acknowledged willingly. He looked back out the window. "Mrs. Conover, you think if this keeps up, we might consolidate our efforts?"

Mrs. Conover looked at him, uncertain. "How do you mean?"

"We've got the water at our feet already, and there's just no telling where it's going to stop." He glanced above her. "I was thinking we might climb some things over and use the doctor's attic."

''Well, certainly, but how do you imagine?''

''Ladder. I got a ladder here I think we could put between the windows. There's just some things from Sylvia's family we'd like to save.''

''Oh, absolutely. If you can.''

George had the ladder right there waiting, and when he extended it, it was more than long enough to reach the Uyterhoevens' sill. He tied a rope around Virginia's waist and she came across first, on her hands and knees, then Sylvia, and from there George did most of the hauling. Mrs. Conover took Sylvia and Virginia into Mrs. Uyterhoeven's bedroom to see the body and say a prayer. They paid a visit to Cow, and then went up the attic stairs to begin clearing space.

The Uyterhoevens' attic was low but otherwise fairly commodious, child-sized. Dr. Burns had stacked all the games and chess sets in front of the street-side window, and there was a set of six small school desks as well, a standing blackboard, a bucket of wooden train tracks, and a large dollhouse. Sylvia and Mrs. Conover moved what they could over to the garden window, next to a porcelain tub, to leave as much space in the middle of the floor as possible.

George continued bringing over Sylvia's family heirlooms, box by box, and by the time he was finished, the flood was calf-deep on the Uyterhoevens' second floor and still rising, so the four of them made a fireman's line. George handed all the books and plates and boxes, the globes, scopes, and everything else to Mrs. Conover on the attic stairs, and she passed them along to Sylvia and Virginia, who piled them where they could. Fortunately, the water had begun to slow, so they managed to get most of what they wanted upstairs before the level on the second floor had reached George's hips, which was also very near to the height of Mrs. Uyterhoeven's bed. Mrs. Conover suggested to George that perhaps it was time to take up the body, and he agreed. He lifted the body in his arms, covers and all, and carried it out to the stairs. Mrs. Conover followed with Mrs. Uyterhoeven's pillow.

As they emerged into the attic, Sylvia was busy making sure that nothing was stacked precariously high and that there was enough space. Virginia was sitting by the chess sets, drying the base of one of her mother's favorite brass lamps, but when she saw her father carrying Mrs. Uyterhoeven like a bride, she fell suddenly still and silent. George crossed over to the school desks and laid the body down next to the dollhouse. Mrs. Conover straightened the blankets, set the pillow back beneath Mrs. Uyterhoeven's head, and then George went back to the stairs and down.

As soon as he was gone, Virginia started over. She walked slowly but directly to the school desk nearest the body, knelt on the seat, and stared. Mrs. Conover asked if she'd prefer the face be covered, but Virginia shook her head no, so intent upon Mrs. Uyterhoeven's pale, serene face that Mrs. Conover was compelled to look down herself and admit the same apparent mystery, that here was Mrs. Uyterhoeven's body but evidently not Mrs. Uyterhoeven.

George's voice broke their spell. He was calling up for help. Mrs. Conover took Virginia by the hand and they joined her mother at the top of the stairs to see what the trouble was. Cow was standing at the foot with a rope tied around his neck and a blanket over his eyes. He looked awfully as if he were about to be hanged. George tossed Sylvia the loose end of the rope, and they all pulled together, but the horse wouldn't budge. George kept slapping him on the rear, and Mrs. Conover and Virginia and Sylvia began cheering him on as they tugged the rope, but it wasn't till the floodwater kissed his belly that finally Cow clambered up in two bounds to join them.

It had been an awkward and slightly frightening ascent. Cow had bumped his head on the attic ceiling, which was too low even at the middle for him to stand straight up. He had to stoop as if he were grazing, and looked so unhappy that Virginia suggested that they beat a hole in the roof for him to stick his head through. The rain had lifted, so George agreed. He took one of the bricks from a pile that lay by the chimney column, and as he started beating through the ceiling boards, Virginia took Mrs. Conover's hand again. She began pulling her, quietly but with force, back to where Mrs. Uyterhoeven's body lay beside the dollhouse. She climbed back onto the nearest school chair and, with Mrs. Conover there beside her, resumed her first examination of death. Mrs. Conover didn't dissuade her. She stroked her hair calmly, as if to soften the sound of George's blows against the ceiling.

Sylvia came over with a pile of clothes in her arms. "Virginia, I have a nightgown for you." Virginia did not look up, so Sylvia simply pulled the wet gown over her daughter's head. "Do you have anything dry to wear, Mrs. Conover?" she asked. "We have plenty."

"Thank you," Mrs. Conover smiled, "but I actually have to make one more trip downstairs." She squeezed Virginia's shoulders gently and kissed the top of her head, then returned to the stairs one more time.

The water was still only just above her waist on the second floor. She waded her way to Mrs. Uyterhoeven's bedroom and went straight to the closet. Sitting on the sweater shelf was the cherrywood drawer, right where she'd put it after Andy Fox had left. With both hands she took it down from the shelf and walked it back to the hall, then when she reached the attic stairs, tilted it safe against her chest and climbed up for the last time.

As she came into view, Cow was standing upright with his head disappeared through the roof. George was at the tub busting up the wood boxes they'd brought over for kindling. Sylvia was kneeling in front of Virginia, who was still in her chair, now in a clean dry nightgown. Sylvia was wrestling a pair of socks onto her daughter's feet, but Virginia's attention was still focused on the body.

"I have something for Virginia," Mrs. Conover announced from the top of the stairs. She held up the drawer for them all to see.

Virginia did not look over, but when Sylvia saw, her eyes flared with surprise, relief, and then gratitude. "Virginia," she shook her daughter's ankle. "Look what Mrs. Conover has brought you."

Virginia turned her head distractedly, and then her eyes lit. "The letters!"

Mrs. Conover walked toward her. "And the pieces," she nodded, holding out the drawer like a birthday gift. Virginia climbed down from the chair and took the drawer in both arms over to the small clearing her mother had arranged in the middle of the room. She set it on the floor and sat down Indian style, with Mrs. Conover, Sylvia, and George all standing above her, watching. She touched the knob, but before pulling it open, looked up at Mrs. Conover once more to make sure. ''May I?'' she asked.

''Of course you may,'' said Mrs. Conover.

Virginia slid open the drawer and they all leaned over to see inside. On top was a goatskin checkerboard folded like a satchel. Virginia lifted it out carefully, and they could all hear the click of what was inside as she set it down gently on the planchment. She did not unfold it, though.

''You don't want to see the pieces?'' asked Mrs. Conover.

Virginia shook her head. ''Not supposed to yet.'' She looked back inside the drawer again, where there were just the letters now, in all their notebooks and small pads and loose stationery. On top was a sheaf, bound by a white ribbon. Virginia took it out and held it up to her father.

''Well, I don't know,'' he said warily.

''Oh, go ahead, George,'' nudged Mrs. Conover. ''I'm sure we'll have time.''

George took the pages from his daughter and examined the top almost like a jeweler. ''It's the doctor's own hand.'' He turned to Mrs. Conover. ''Would you want to read it?''

Mrs. Conover smiled. ''But it looks as if Virginia would like you to.''

Virginia looked up at him pleadingly, and George scratched the back of his head. ''Well, maybe soon as I get a fire.''

''Well, then do,'' said Mrs. Conover.

George handed the letter to Sylvia for her to see, and then returned to the last of the boxes they'd brought to bust them up. The ladies went to get the baskets of food, but as soon as the fire was golden inside the tub and they'd all changed into warmer, drier clothes, once some fruit had been sliced and some pound cake, and they each had one of the Uyterhoevens' china cups in front of them filled with cider, Sylvia gave the pages back to George. Then George took a seat on the school desk nearest the window for light and began reading aloud to them—loud enough, at Virginia's reminder, for Cow to hear as well—the first of Dr. Uyterhoeven's letters from South Africa, of his adventure in the Antipodes.

TWO

THE MERCENARY

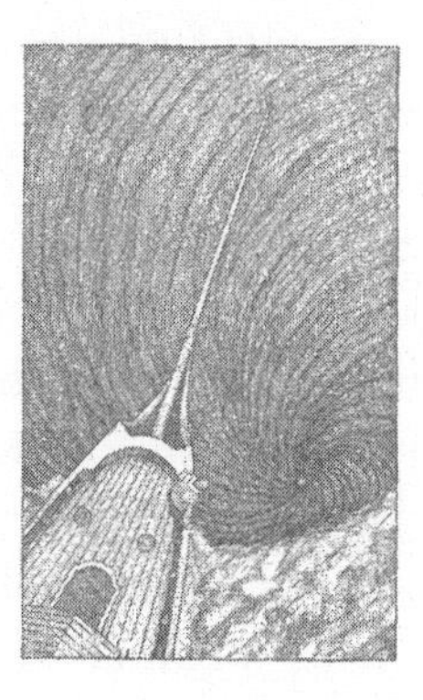

The First Letter

October 7, 1900

Dear Sonja,

Please extend my apologies to everyone that it has taken so long coming, but my news for you and the children is very good, I think, and actually quite astonishing. I am well. I miss you all very much. I wish that you could be with me now and share in all the things I am seeing, but you shall have to take my word. I shall have to make it clear, for there is much to tell.

Before coming to the details of the journey which has led me here, I want first to ask you to keep your eyes open for a visitor. I think you'll find him somewhere nearby the Williams Street Bridge. He will be in a dinghy and I suspect he may be asleep, lying on his back along the bottom. If he is, you needn't wake him. Take him in and read him this as he sleeps, for though I am writing with all of you in mind, I should like to share some of what I have discovered with him as well.

I have no way to be certain how long it may have taken these words to reach you, but my voyage here, I know, has occupied the better part of two months. As planned, the first leg carried me uneventfully across the ocean to Portugal. I spent a short while in Lisbon, two days, and then finagled a bunk on an aged supply ship called the *Vestima*, which was headed down the west coast of Africa, bearing English soap and towels for the Boers in their refugee camps. Our first destination was to be the Cape, then the *Vestima* would carry guns and ammunition up to Delagoa Bay and the port of Lourenço Marques, which the Portuguese currently hold ransom from those interested in the South African conflict. I myself had hoped to leave off at the Cape and there catch a third ship across the Indian Ocean, preferably one with as southerly a route as I could find, in hopes that somewhere along its course we might cross paths with the Antipodes.

I had as yet learned nothing more of its actual location. No one on any of the ships that I boarded or the ports where we stopped had been of any help, and on the *Vestima* I gather I may have made a nuisance of myself, requesting nautical books from the captain and passing my tattered map round at meals to see if anyone recognized the shape. No one did. Some repeated Mr. Patterson's theory, that the Antipodes were not a place at all but rather the name given to whatever lay the far and most opposite side of one's present position. For this reason I was several times compared to a dog chasing his tail—and derided therefor—but I remained determined nonetheless. I set my sights equally upon the Cape and upon the horizon, perchance that somewhere off the African coast I might glimpse a spit of land that had somehow escaped the notice of all the trade ships and fishing boats which chart those waters.

As it turned out, I was able to conduct an only very brief survey, however, as my fifth day aboard I was overwhelmed by a combination of severe nausea and vertigo such as I can only compare to a bout of yellow fever. By the ship's doctor—who was no doctor at all, in fact, but a cook—I was subsequently confined to the sick bay and subjected, by way of remedy, to an extremely upsetting diet of raw onions, radishes with lime and pepper, and lemon water, which I was only permitted to suck through an old swabbing rag. I was to be kept there, so nourished, until we reached the Cape—not for the sake of my health, I don't believe, but rather for the sake of the crew, to subdue me, as I gather they'd come to some agreement about the bother of my constant interrogations.

Now, nearly the whole time I was in the sick bay, there lay across the room from me a very well-built gentleman, who I could see was a soldier. He lay above the covers, and was fully dressed but for his hat, which hung from a hook in the wall, and his boots, which were black and tall, and which stood at the foot of his bed beside a lumped holster and a belt of bullets. His rifle lay beneath the bed. There was a leather satchel there as well. He wore tan jodhpurs, a jersey, and a twill coat which appeared to have been stripped of decorations. Around his waist was a thick leather belt with pouches that he seemed to have emptied on the floor—there were sticks of jerky, a jar of apple butter, all sorts of peanuts, sunflower seeds, oats, and raisins.

Though confined like me to the ship's sick bay, he did not appear to be the least bit ill. His hair was thick but so close-cropped that I couldn't quite tell its colour. He had a strong neck and lantern jaw, and his features were handsome and capable, as I would come to find, of great determination, though in sleep they lay so placid as to come upon deathliness—an effect which was all the more encouraged by his position upon the cot. He lay supine, perfectly flat and straight, hands folded at the belly, feet approximately seven inches apart at the heel, eleven at the toe. Indeed, all there was to indicate that I was not in the company of a corpse was only the barest indication of breathing upon the level of his chest, and the constant blush of his complexion, as of a child just come in from sledding.

Now, the reason that I know so well this man's appearance has first to do with the fact that I had very little else to occupy my interest but to examine it, and second, that he did nothing at all for the first five days of our companionship but maintain the one and same position that I have described, for he did nothing in that time but sleep. Five days he slept without break. He did not stir. He did not snore. Some breaths he drew, I can attest, lasted full minutes in themselves. In fact, I had chance to observe one hour when this gentleman across from me inhaled and exhaled only twice.

My fifth day below—my tenth, then, aboard the *Vestima*—was the first he awoke, and he did so in like manner to his sleep, with military efficiency. One moment he had been prone and silent, with his hands folded over his belt, and the next he was upright. He swung his legs round to the floor and sat straight up. ''How long has it been?'' he asked, and his voice, at least, was rusty but deep. ''How far from the Cape?''

''Two days,'' I replied.

He looked at the wooden tray next to my bed. There were the skins of some onions, radishes, and lemons, and a rag on the lip of my water bucket. ''That will make you sick, eat that all day,'' he said, and he did not look at me but kept his eye nostalgically on my tray. ''They served that in the Turkish camps.'' He shook his head. ''Felt better in Mexico.'' He stood up and looked out the porthole.

''You are a soldier?'' I asked.

He nodded, but his eyes were resting on the horizon outside.

''With whom? Are you English?''

He shook his head and walked over towards the stairs that led up to the deck. ''No one right now,'' he said, lifting the hatch. He stuck his head just out of sight and called to one of the crewmen. ''Salt?''

I don't know that he received a reply, but when he descended I offered him the pepper from my tray. He came over with long, heavy steps, and I was aware as he approached of his immense breadth, though he was lean as well, the sort of man to have about for lifting children up to high apples. He tongued the pepper in the cup of his palm and took it back to his sack, from which he then pulled three oval shells. Whether they were fruit, egg, or vegetable I could not determine—only that he was able to pull them open with his fingers and dump the contents with an audible plop into the back of his throat.

When he was finished he sat back down on the bed and seemed to wait for the globs to slide down to his belly.

"Are you going to the Cape," I asked, "or all the way round to Delagoa?"

"Delagoa," he replied, then he swung his legs up and resumed his sleeping position.

"And where have you come from?" I asked, trying desperately to engage his company, but he had no sooner rested his head upon the thin grey pillow than he was back asleep, his breathing slow and deep again.

So there was an opportunity lost, leaving me more than a bit frustrated, not just at being left alone again, but also at the ease with which this fellow passed the time. I had even begun to consider, as compensation for my relative difficulty, invading his privacy. His leather satchel was open now and tempting, and all I really wanted to know was his name, but just as I was debating whether I should risk sneaking over—I had in fact sat up in my bed to gauge my strength—the hatch door opened and a body came plunging down the steps, limp as an infant, and then smacked chin-first bonk on the floor.

This was Diggery Priest, one of the more peculiar members of the crew, in look as well as trait—a fellow of scrawny, bowlegged build, wild thin hair, no teeth to speak of, and a broad mischievous expression which, it appeared, in time would see the end of his nose actually touch the tip of his chin for good (it is able to do so now, but only at the request of shipmates). Much as he may have looked the part, Mr. Priest was not, however, a sailor, but by trade a horse thief, who'd only come aboard the *Vestima* for the sake of asylum and a quick escape from the most recent consequences of his knavery.

A scoundrel, then, tried and true, but one in whose defense I feel compelled to say at the outset of this—his troubling introduction—also was possessed of one very redeeming quality, particularly for a person so prone to finding himself in unfamiliar and isolated quarters. I speak of an unrelentingly enthusiastic disposition. It was Mr. Priest's saving grace, if I may be so bold—a sense of childlike, and very childish, abandon with which he approached the prospect of each moment, and which his tumultuous entrance to our sick bay that evening did nothing to dispute. There at the foot of our stairs he took just a moment to register the violence of his descent. A thin trickle of blood ran down from his mouth—but never mind, he sat up with a happy cackle and awarded himself a nice long drink from the flask of sour mash which he kept a fairly permanent resident in his breast pocket.

Only then, when he'd sounded his contentment with a loud smack of the lips, did he finally turn round to me. "Well evening, Thir." His eyebrows jumped as he looked down to inspect the tray of food beside my bed. "And how are the radisheth treating you?" I did not reply. I let him have his laugh, and in return, when he was done, he offered me a drink from his flask. I refrained, needless to say, and so without offense Mr. Priest turned his attention to the opposite side of the quarters, where lay my sleeping mate, still utterly undisturbed. "Zzzzzzzzzz-shshshoooo! Zzzzzzzzz-shshshooooo. All day, all night. Isn't that it?" Diggery looked back at me and winked. "He wake up?"

"Just now for the first time," I said. "But only to eat some of those." I pointed at the sticky red shells. "And now he's back to sleep again."

"Not very hothpitable." Diggery reached into his pants pocket and pulled out his fingers, pinched. "I brought him his thalt." He beamed at me, tossed a few grains over his left shoulder, and then turned back to the sleeping soldier with defiance. "Zzzzzzz-shshshshsooo!" he brayed again, and then he started over on his hands and knees, snoring all the way until his bleeding chin was only inches from the placid features of the soldier.

"Who is he?" I interrupted.

Diggery looked back, surprised. "Never heard of Merthenary?"

I shook my head.

"Oh well, you've got yourthelf quite a mate here, Doc. We're the lucky ones to have Merthenary along for the ride." He looked back at the sleeping soldier as if he were an exotic bird in a cage. "Yes, indeed. Captainth'll draw lots to have this boy on their boat."

"Where does he come from?"

"Comes from a fight, I'll bet." Diggery grabbed the sack and started rooting through. "Yethiree, Merthenary and I have crossed our share of paths, but I never theen him when he wasn't either coming from a fight or headed there. Last time in Turkey, right after a thcrap with the Russians, but he's been everywhere. Look here." He pulled out a black book from the sack and with an almost admirable lack of compunction spilled out all its papers on the floor. "Mexico. North Africa. Thays he just come from Ethiopia, and before that Liberia, and before that let's thee—Crimea, Thuez, Taiping." Diggery turned around to examine our silent companion with a mixture of wonder and annoyance. "Merthenary's run for the thound of every gun of God's green, and look at him—Nary a thcratch from shaving."

"It is remarkable, if it's true," I said, thinking he looked awfully young as well. "What's his name?"

Diggery shook his head. "Doesn't use one, far as I know. Just Merthenary."

"Mercenary." I considered the mission. "I wonder what compels him."

"To fight, you mean?" Diggery was back at the satchel again, rummaging through like a frustrated scavenger. "Well, I'll tell you one thing, it ain't for the money. I thaid to him once he could let me have his share, but he won't even touch the stuff."

"You mean he asks no compensation?"

"Nope." Diggery put down the satchel in annoyance.

"Well then, he's not really a mercenary," I said, to Diggery's utter indifference. "But how does he know which side to fight for?"

Diggery shrugged. "Whoever needs it most, I th'pose. If it's a hundred to one, Merthenary thides with the one. Thimple as that." Diggery just then noticed the seeds on the floor and by instinct stuffed a handful in his mouth, chewed once, and then spit them out in disgust.

"But that's very brave, then," I said.

"Very brave or tetched." He took a swig of mash to clear his palate. "But that's why cap'ns want him on board, thee. They figure, man cheats fate like that enough, he must be blethed."

Diggery took another moment to examine the mercenary, treated himself to another pull from his flask, then directed a most sly expression back at me. ''Like to thee thomething, though?'' His tongue flicked in and out of the gap in his front teeth, inadvertently swiping at the blood on his lip.

''What?''

''Thee thomething about his thleep, about his dreams.'' His eyebrows jumped invitingly.

''Well, I don't want to bother him.''

''Won't bother him. We won't wake him.''

''Well.'' I was still uncertain. ''But then, what is it?''

''It's he's got thomeone inside him, praying.'' Diggery couldn't suppress a giggle.

''Praying what?''

''Well, you have to lithen.'' He waved me over.

I wasn't at all sure I should, but it had been so long since I'd any diversion and Diggery seemed so delighted by the prospect. I crossed the room and joined him next to the mercenary. ''Now you got to lithen close, Doc. You got to put your ear right up to his mouth and lithen 'cause it's very thoft at first.'' I did as he said, and Diggery began speaking hypnotically into the mercenary's ear. ''Merthenary,'' he whispered. ''Merthenary, we're lithening but we can't hear you . . . Merthenary . . . Merthenary.''

As Diggery kept on with his petition, I began to feel the mercenary's breath brush faintly against my ear, and his tongue began moving ever so slightly in his mouth. Diggery paused. ''He thaying anything yet?''

''He is, but I can't tell what.''

''Hear that, Merthenary. Doc can't make out what you're thaying. Have to thpeak up.'' Diggery put his mouth yet closer to the mercenary's ear and spoke more softly. ''Thpeak up. Thpeak up, we can't hear you.''

Very gradually then the mercenary's breath began to take form, enough that I discerned he was repeating something like an incantation. The words ''rest'' and ''heaven'' I heard, then ''peace'' and "heaven," and then "my son." "Rest my son's soul in heaven," he was saying. "Rest his soul in heaven."

Diggery nudged me. "Hear?" This time I nodded. "About the thon?" he asked. I nodded again and Diggery's face twisted with delight. He hooted and beat his knee. "Thee? I told you. He's got thomeone—"

"Whoooooooooooo?" came the mercenary's voice, and both Diggery and I jumped back—not just because this outburst was so sudden, though, but because this voice was not the mercenary's, or not the voice I'd heard him speak before. *"Who is there?"* he spoke again, and it seemed to issue from a foreign region of his throat—older, higher, and more fragile. *"Where is my lamp?"* He sat up with one hand against his chest, and his eyes were open now, a much lighter blue than I remembered, and lost. *"Show yourself."*

"But we're right here," said Diggery, his face directly in front of the mercenary's.

"I can't see. Who is there?"

"Oh, don't worry now," soothed Diggery, his left eye nearly popping from its socket, so thrilled was he by this transformation. "Nothing to be frightened of. Just some thpirits floating by." He winked at me. "Heard a prayer in passing, wondered if we might have an answer."

At this point I moved to object, but Diggery raised his hand to stop me and deflected my attention back upon the mercenary. "Now, what was it you was thaying?" he continued. "About your son, was it? Praying he's in heaven?"

"Who are you?" came the strange voice again.

"Told you," said Diggery. "Just some thpirits, thought we might be of thervice. 'Course, if you aren't interested, we can move along, help other Christians find their little boys."

Diggery waited, and I prayed the mercenary would find another dream somewhere, but he sat up in the bed, his frantic eyes still searching the room for the image of this demon. *"Do you know him?"* he asked.

"That mean you're interested?"

The mercenary's head nodded uncertainly.

"Well, that's fine, but now you understand, we'll be needing thomething in return."

"Diggery," I tried again. "Stop."

"Shshshshs, Doc. Only fair. Tit for tat." He turned his mouth back to the mercenary's ear. "Isn't that right, Merthenary? Only fair? Only tho's you can trust us." The mercenary did not answer. "So what'll it be? What have you to offer a couple friendly ghosts?"

The mercenary shook his head. *"I . . . I don't—All I have are flowers."*

"Flowers?" Diggery looked back at me with glee and mouthed the word. "What kind of flowers?" he asked.

The mercenary reached out to his side for something which wasn't visibly there, but then held it out in front of him.

"What's that?" asked Diggery.

"Tulips," the mercenary replied.

"Tulips?" Diggery scowled. "Don't like tulips."

"Diggery!" I tried again.

"What, Doc?" He looked back at me. "You like tulips? Well then, I 'th'pose you can give your flowers to the doc." The mercenary held his empty fist out farther, waiting. "Take 'em," Diggery urged, and I didn't feel I'd any choice, the mercenary looked so helpless. I accepted the invisible tulips from his hand. "Very good, then." Diggery leaned in towards his victim's ear. "I 'th'pose we can help you now, but you'll have to tell us—how do we reckonize this son of yours?"

The mercenary hesitated, but then in a voice still fragile but touched with pride and sorrow—*"He was a little boy."*

"A boy, eh?" Diggery scratched his chin. "Well, I think I might have theen one of those. In fact, just the other day, I theem to recall theeing a little boy. But now what exactly did yours happen to look like?"

"He had a shield," said the mercenary.

"Did he?"

The mercenary nodded. *''Yes, and a pot cover, and a wooden sword.''*

Diggery gagged with laughter. ''Pot cover and a wooden thord? Well, what a coincidence, because in fact the little boy I saw had a pot cover and a wooden thord.''

''Where?'' The mercenary's head turned anxiously.

''Well now, don't let's be getting your hopes up. Remember, there's lots of little boys out there with pot covers and wooden thords—but now tell me if this helps, because I theem to remember this one—'' Diggery looked over at me now, only barely able to contain himself. ''This one had a little cape tucked in the back of his collar as well.''

''Where is he?'' The mercenary sat forward.

''Well, I can't exactly remember is the problem— Thee, I been doing so much traveling about lately, but where was it? Where did I thee that little boy with the cape and shield?'' He closed one eye to think. ''Thee, I'm not even sure what I could have been doing in thuch a place, but I think . . . I think I'm fairly sure there was thmoke.''

''Smoke?'' The mercenary's eyes lit with fear.

''Yes, I most definitely remember thmoke. And fire.''

''Fire?''

''Yes, thmoke and fire—but where was that? Where would I have theen that little boy in all that thmoke and fire?''

The mercenary was sitting straight up in bed now, with both hands to his face. He was beside himself, but before I could think how to end this horrid antic, Diggery snapped his finger. ''Oh, that's right!'' he said.

''Where?''

''Well, you're sure you want to know now?''

''Yes.''

''Well, I believe . . . I think I'm fairly sure it was''—he leaned over the cot until his face was only inches from the mercenary's— ''it was in the belly of a dragon.''

The room fell still and silent. The mercenary's eyes looked out into the black, confused, and then he began shaking his head. *"No,"* he said. *"No, that isn't true,"* and with that Diggery fell back onto the floor, kicking his legs in the air and laughing. *"It isn't true,"* said the mercenary again, his eyes still searching the space in front of him for some shape or answer. *"It can't be!"* he cried.

"It isn't." I grabbed hold of his hand, which felt strangely delicate. "It's completely untrue," I said into his ear. "He is only teasing you."

The mercenary looked out towards me, and I could feel his heart pounding. *"But who are you?"*

"I am no one," I said. "No one who should have disturbed you. Just know that he was fooling, the other man. There's no belly of a dragon."

"There isn't," the mercenary repeated.

"No," I said. "No fire."

"And no smoke?"

"No smoke. He was only teasing."

The mercenary's head descended to the pillow, and I could feel his body begin to relax, but then again he turned towards me. *"But where is my son, then? Have you seen him?"* He looked at me and his eyes were pleading. *"Is he in heaven?"*

All was silent. I looked at Diggery. I looked at the mercenary. "I don't know," I said. "I'm sorry."

With that, the mercenary let go my hand, and his attention drifted from me, for better. His trembling quieted. His eyes fixed upon the ceiling, and very faintly his lips began to move again. His voice was gone, but still I could read his breath, which was one with the prayer: *"Rest my dear son's soul in heaven. Rest his soul in heaven."*

Quietly as I was able I returned to my bed. Diggery looked up as I passed. "Only fooling, Doc." He smiled. "You can ask him when he wakes, when we reach the Cape. There's no little boy."

I said nothing. I was beginning to feel ill again, so I pulled undercover and tried as best I could to fall asleep, while the faint whisper of the mercenary's prayer drifted up like smoke and dispersed across the ceiling above us.

(October 8, 1900—
continued the next evening)

The morning after the mercenary's nightmare, I was awakened by the sound of bodies tumbling up above me on deck, as if a tremendous fight had broken out among the crew. I sat up in bed to listen and suddenly became aware that something very strange was happening around me.

Diggery was up and gone already, and the mercenary was still asleep—he was in his usual position, on his back, hands folded above his belt—yet everything else in the room seemed to have gone suddenly mad. The hanging lanterns were swaying from their hooks as if some invisible ghost had clanked its head on them, and all the peanut shells and sunflower seeds were swirling about the floor as if this same ghost were now sweeping them with an invisible broom. A great crash sounded from upstairs, and then the radishes and lime halves which had been on my towel the night before all appeared from underneath the mercenary's cot and scurried across the room to mine. Another great pounding smashed upon the ceiling, the lanterns clanked wildly, and in the next moment the peels appeared again, followed by the mercenary's sticky shells, all tumbling into the starboard wall.

Now, the explanation for all this might seem perfectly clear to you—that we had encountered a storm which was simply playing havoc with everything in the room that was not bolted down. To me, however, this was not so obvious, since to me the room felt utterly still, more as if we'd run aground. What is more, the nausea which I had been suffering the previous five days, and which the night before had shown no sign of desisting, seemed to have vanished in my sleep.

As quick as I was able, then, while the skins of our food continued racing each other from one wall to the next, I dressed in my warmest clothes. I put on my boots and coat, and then, with more balance than I had felt in weeks, made my way to the stairs and up.

How to describe my bewilderment as I lifted the hatch and looked through. The whole world seemed to have lost its bearings. All the crew were flying every which way, tumbling into the sides of the ship like playing dice. Great waves of ocean were curling over us and smashing down; behind, the horizon was tipping back and forth as if the whole sea were a spinning tray and I its single axis, for this was the strangest thing—not the sudden fury of the ocean—but the fact that I, in the midst of so much pandemonium, could not have been more perfectly at ease. I felt the wind and water, of course, but my balance was such that I might have been standing on a flat, firm seashore. It was stunning, and as I looked round, I could surmise but one possible explanation (which strikes me now as less an explanation than one more description, but there it is): that the pitching and turning to which the tempest was presently subjecting the *Vestima*—and in turn the *Vestima* me—must have been compensating with such flawless accuracy the pitching and turning of my vertiginous condition, that the resultant effect upon my sense of balance was one of perfect equilibrium.

Would that the rest of the crew had been so afflicted. As I climbed to the deck, I could see they'd more or less given up the fight. The sails had been dropped and the men were struggling for hiding places and hatches, tying themselves to brackets and clinging to the rigging. I passed through them to the portside rail, that I might better observe our predicament, and there came face to face with as menacing a sight as one could ever dread encounter: the sea, in its madness, had managed to produce no fewer than seven enormous whirlpools, all deep enough to swallow a redwood tree plunged tip first, and all hovering round us with the unpredictability of seven spinning tops. The men were right, I thought. Not even the most masterful sea captain and crew could possibly have negotiated us safely through the tangle of undertows as was now beginning to spin us.

But then it occurred to me: there was a passenger aboard, sleeping peacefully down below, who—if the stories told of him were true—had demonstrated an instinct for survival that we might all do well in this instance to rouse. Surely in all the battles on all the battlefields the mercenary had endured, he must have faced straits as dire as this—or close—so I made haste back for our hatch and presently descended to the sick bay.

Now again, as I entered it, the room seemed perfectly serene to me but for the clanking lanterns and the continued sprints of our discarded rinds and peels across the floor. I rushed to the mercenary's bed and began jostling his shoulder. "Up!" I cried, in as unhypnotic a voice as I was able. "Wake up!"

And it was as if his dreams had been shielding him from the influence of the morning's tempest, for the moment the mercenary opened his eyes to mine, he was hurled against the wall beside his bed, as by the hand of an invisible giant.

"Can you battle storms as well as men?" I asked.

He looked back at me, at my physical calm, with a combination of fierceness and regard—in his eye was no memory of the previous night's torment—but before he could answer me, he was thrown again, this time from the bed down onto the floor at my feet. "It's a tempest outside," I explained. "And we appear to be in the midst of seven or eight rather large maelstroms."

Without a moment's delay or need to question my condition, the mercenary gathered himself in. He put on his boots and buckles while the boat kept lurching him back and forth, and then we headed up—I with absurd ease, he struggling gamely.

I came out on deck as before, but the mercenary paused in the hatch frame to assess our situation. Clearly the only factor playing to our advantage was my balance, so first thing, he set about harnessing it to our collective purpose. "Bring some rope," he called above the ocean's roar, "as much as you can find."

I'd no idea where, and as I scanned the deck, I realised I'd get little advice from the crew. Those in view to me were all looking back with round eyes and mouths agape, clearly terrified—not just by the storm, but by me, by what had become of the bothersome old man with the apocryphal map, and the fact their hopes should now so firmly rest upon his—my shoulders.

Thank heavens, I saw Diggery Priest next, over by the main mast. His head was peeking out from the top of a fish barrel, mouth opened wide and laughing. "Rope?" I called, and with a delighted beat at the barrel rim, he pointed me back towards the stern. I hustled past the ogling crew, and there by the dinghies I did indeed find a loose heap of halyard, which I gathered up in my arms and delivered back to the mercenary as fast as I could, though still unclear as to his purpose.

There in the hatch, he tied a bowline around his waist, then handed me the other end. ''To the rail!'' he called, pointing at the starboard side. I took my end of the rope and wrapped it three times round the crossbeam. Then as soon as I'd tucked it tight, the mercenary began pulling his way over, hand over hand. He was literally being flogged against the deck like a worm on a hook, but there seemed little I could do. I was about to go and see if I could help brace him, when suddenly there came a giant, thunderous boom out to the starboard side.

I looked over the rail, and there in the distance I saw that a most remarkable thing had happened: two of the whirlpools had apparently just spun into one another. They'd become one, I mean, so much larger than all the others that I could already see—all the rest, which up until then had been hovering round us like a team of cautious predators, now were sliding over in the direction of this much larger, much faster spinning hole. They were being lured in, and then as they came near, they, too, were being swallowed up. The giant maelstrom gulped them down one by one, and with each feeding, the wind lashed out like a whip, the sky cracked with another thunderous boom, and this hollow beast opened its mouth that much wider, spun that much faster, and pulled with that much more craving at the whole sea surrounding.

The mercenary, in his struggle, was aware of none of this. By the time he'd pulled his way to the rail, all the smaller whirlpools had been consumed already, so that out before us now, though still perhaps a knot away, was just the one: a single swirling canyon of sea which I would estimate must have been at least a mile in diameter, its circumference lit the whole way round by a shimmering spray that whistled off the rim, and which from our perspective looked like nothing so much as a spinning silver crown. It hovered out in front of us, waiting in confidence, curling downwards in a counter-clockwise spiral, stirring the ocean round and round till we could actually see a whorling tide appear upon the surface, and then begin crawling out towards us. It smoothed the sea as it expanded, and I could feel the very moment that its farthest tendril tugged upon our keel—a force of such casual might, I knew we'd no hope of escape. Our little boat bobbed, spun round, and then started slowly, innocently, along the curling tide towards the giant hole in the distance.

Credit to his nature, the mercenary looked out upon the churning beast that lay in wait with nothing but defiance. With a quick hook and a hitch he tightened the knot I'd tied to the cross rail, slipped the bowline from his waist, and handed it to me. "To the helm!" he called, and so again I did as ordered. I hustled our line to the wheel and hooked it to the stanchion, though it seemed madness to me, the idea there was anything he could do from the helm to save us. By the time he pulled his way over, the *Vestima* was coasting like a splinter of driftwood towards the rim spray; the wind was like an ice mask slapped against our faces, then suddenly all was a howling silver—no ship, no mercenary, no hand before my face—then I felt us begin to tip. My stomach rose up to my mouth, and down we went.

We did not instantly tumble, though, thanks to the mercenary. He held to the wheel so fast that our rudder kept flush with the keel and we stayed upright, locked to the prevailing current as upon a track, or more like a speeding ball on a very large, very deep roulette wheel. It was quite an achievement on his part, but even so, still it seemed to me one that would only prolong our certain demise. All roulette balls do inevitably fall, after all, and so I took it as done—that our end had been cast as an agonizing, spiraling descent down to the pit of this horrid screaming beast.

Fortunately, the mercenary was not as easily discouraged as I, and he perceived in the sheer size of this maelstrom precious time, and in that time, chance. "My rifle!" he barked. "And an axe!"

I had to think. His rifle was down in the sick bay, but as for the axe, I'd no idea. I went and asked Diggery, but he only shook his head. "Knives in the mess," he suggested, and so I hurried down. The mercenary's rifle was just as I'd remembered, underneath his bed, and in the kitchen I found a butcher's knife standing in its block.

When I returned with it to the helm, the mercenary looked at me, none too pleased. He'd loosed his bowline from the stanchion and was tying it back around his waist, but when he saw the knife, he fired me a stern look. "It was all I could find," I explained, and so with time of the essence, he proceeded. He took the rifle and jammed it barrel-first through the spokes of the wheel—to bolt it, I surmised—and then with the butcher's knife clenched between his teeth, he began swinging himself by our rope across the deck, rappelling his way to the stem.

I followed on foot, feeling all the more awkward and useless for the ease with which I did, for I'd still no sense of his intention. Once at the prow, he straddled the bowsprit between his knees, then took the butcher's knife from his teeth and began hacking at the base. It looked a hopeless undertaking. The timber must have been a good two feet in diameter, but to my amazement he cleaved a good bite with a mere dozen swipes of the knife; he hacked and hacked, and very soon he was far enough through the spar to take it in his arms to begin twisting it off.

It was an awesome, if inexplicable, display. With one mighty wrench he cracked the timber free and hauled it onto the deck. He sheared off all the rope and rigging, save for the jib down near the end, then with only the most superficial assistance from me, he pulled himself back up to our original position at the starboard rail, with the giant spar beneath his arm.

The *Vestima* had completed somewhere between three or four full circuits inside the maelstrom by now, and fallen twelve or so fathoms in the process. We were still fairly high along the slope, less than a quarter of the way down, but our circuits were only tightening the farther we fell and accelerating our descent. Thank heavens, here is where the mercenary's plan finally took effect. Like a harpooner, he lifted the bowsprit onto his shoulder and rammed it sail-first through the rail posts, so that the long spar was almost like an oar and the cross beam a lock. At the far end, the great canvas wing hovered just inches above the speeding surf, a waiting blade. The mercenary looked at me. "You might want to hold on to something," he said, and I did, but only so as not to seem presumptuous. Then with a fury to match the morning's tempest, the mercenary called out at the top of his lungs and plunged the sail into the water.

The *Vestima* lurched violently, and the mercenary was slammed into the rail. From round the ship came cries of hidden sailors, thinking that we were all about to tumble down the maelstrom slope, and yet from my calm vantage, I could see quite the opposite—with the sail plunged into the current, the *Vestima* was now actually carving its way *up* the wall of the vortex.

We gained perhaps a fathom before our flank began to shudder against the current; our splintered stem was pointed treacherously skyward, and I could feel that we were on the verge of toppling over, when just then the mercenary recovered, grabbed hold of the bowsprit beneath his arm, and thrust down with all his might. The jib pulled up out of the water, and almost instantly the boat swerved round straight again, the current took hold of our keel, and once again we resumed the course of the roulette ball, now a full two fathoms higher.

I looked at the mercenary in amazement. He was bent over the bowsprit, pinning it to the deck to keep the sail above the surf. He looked as if he'd just taken a kick in the chest from an angry mule. "The cook," he gasped, "and Jebsen. Bring them here."

"You're all right?" I asked.

"Go!" he barked, and so I went.

They were together, actually, both tangled in the main rigging like two great porpoises—the cook, who was far and away the heaviest member of the crew, and Jebsen, its acknowledged strongman. When they saw me coming, though, walking upright on the slanted deck, they both cowered like pups. The cook covered his face and Jebsen tried climbing farther up the rigging. It wasn't until I told them I'd come at the mercenary's behest that they collected themselves. I think they understood the mercenary was their only chance, so they descended warily, but they would not take the rope from me to pull their way. They crawled on their hands and knees instead.

By the time they reached the rail, we'd turned another full circuit and lost the two fathoms we'd just gained. The mercenary looked to have recovered, though, and wasted no time putting the men to service. He had them cling one each to his legs—that was all—then as soon as they were set, he plunged the mast a second time.

A second time it worked. The *Vestima* climbed up the rushing slope, up and up until we broached, whereupon the mercenary thrust the sail back out of the surf, and once again we resumed the steady downward spiral.

Oh, but what an excruciating labor, for now, with his two human boots to brace him, the mercenary took the full brunt of the snag against his chest and shoulders. A more terrible means the Devil himself could not have contrived, but a means no less, to which it now appeared we were committed: to drive the bowsprit as often as the mercenary could bear, to keep us as high along the slope as possible for as long as this tireless maelstrom chose to run its course. A labor fit for Heracles, it seemed to me, and yet as I looked at our oarsman, I felt what seemed an almost blithe confidence that he could outlast any test that nature chose to fling at him. By our fifth circuit and his fifth stroke, the strain upon his shoulders was such that he had ordered Jebsen and the cook to bite into his calves before he plunged the mast, as only in such pain as their piercing teeth inflicted could he summon the rage required to raise the sail again; but summon the rage he did. Again and again, they gnashed into his legs, he clung to the spar as to the neck of a raging bull, and we were spared.

It was frankly more than I could bear to watch, and also I considered there might be better uses to which I could put my good balance. I went to see about the rest of the crew, to tell them of our situation. I found them in every little nook and cranny—clutching white-knuckled to the rigging, clamped in cubbyholes with their fists clenched against their foreheads in prayer. I told them they shouldn't fear the boat's periodic lurching, that it was the mercenary raising us, and that I trusted in watching him that we'd be well—but their reactions were much the same as Jebsen's and the cook's. None would so much as look at me to listen. Some shrank back at my approach and others spat, I am afraid to say, which I did my best to understand. One could hardly blame them for thinking me possessed, but I did not fully appreciate their enmity till coming in my rounds to Diggery Priest, the only one among them who would speak to me.

He'd summoned me from his barrel to ask if I'd refill his flask of sour mash, and as I returned to him, he was looking down at my feet as though I were wearing a handsome new pair of shoes. "Look at you, Dr. Uyterhoo. You should have told me you was a witch doctor."

I bowed to my boots for him. "I would have if I had known, but this has taken me as much by surprise as anyone." I gave him his whiskey. "Thank you, though, for not holding it against me."

"Ah, don't you mind the others, Doc," he toasted. "I'm sure they're just a little peeved is all. They'll get over it." He took a rather long pull and then offered me a drink, which I refused. "It's just they didn't warrant when you come aboard that we'd all be running you quite such a nasty little errand."

I didn't understand. "How do you mean?"

"Well, Doc, this whirligig ain't just thittin' thtill in the ocean. If it don't thwallow us first, it's going to take us thomewhere, and I'm with you betting the merthenary won't let us down."

As if on cue, the boat lurched upward, and Diggery's head disappeared inside the barrel. The mercenary carved us all another fathom's worth of life from the maelstrom's slope; then when we'd regained a steady line, Diggery's head appeared again, open-mouthed and exhilarated.

"But you're not suggesting you know where the maelstrom is headed?" I asked.

Diggery smiled. "Ain't a navigator, Doc, but I ain't a fool neither. I take a look at you, making your way about like the God of all thea-legs, and you'll excuse me for putting the two and two together: wherever this thpineroo is headed, I thay you're the one it means to take, and all the merthenary was ever doin' aboard was making sure you'd get there thafe." He offered me another drink from his flask, which this time I accepted.

His assessment was not without its reason, after all. What a curse I must have seemed! What an albatross! I hadn't even considered—not just as home to this unperturbable demon, but one with the impertinence to pirate the services of their boat and then subject them all to such horrors without apparently suffering me the peril.

For Diggery was quite right—we were rolling through the sea like a cyclone across the prairie, so fast the nighttime sky spread above us like a starlit blanket. But then I think we must have changed our course, for that night lasted much too long, it seemed to me. How much so, I cannot say, for my pocket watch had stopped, but still I think we must have been running a good race against the planet's spin to stay as long upon its shadowed half as we did. The crescent moon and every star were swept into our vortex, turned 'round like rice in a great black cauldron, and then flung off again, but all I could think as I looked up at them was what Diggery had said, and how true it would seem from their perspective—if any of these stars should chance to look earth's way when light finally carries out to them the spectacle of our little predicament; if they could squint and see us there, barreling through the ocean, would our eddy not appear to them a vessel? Could one blame them for confusing its course and speed for motive? And presuming that these stars had lenses thick enough to observe the splinter turning round inside, would it not seem just as obvious to them that the old man standing so impassively on its back must be the subject of that motive?

It was a dizzying thought, enough apparently to preserve my balance the remainder of that interminable night. I tried to make myself as useful as possible. I delivered the crew what food I could find—fishcakes, herring, and bourbon—and I summoned the heavier members for duty at the mercenary's legs, but otherwise I stayed close to Diggery. I sat beside his barrel quietly. I listened to him sing his drunken sailor songs, and I watched the mercenary plunge his oar, but never once did I forget the whirling moon and stars, or the questions they turned round and round in my weary brain: what on earth? how on earth? and then the one which I'll confess did tender hope—where on earth?

Now, in the simple fact that you are reading this, it should be clear that our journey did end finally and that my question has found its answer in whatever place has provided me the means to write you. At the risk, then, of taking the mercenary's inexpressible heroism for granted, I shall burden you no more with the recollection of the *Vestima*'s captivity, except to say that it did not see dawn. With the night still high above us, we entered a haze so thick as to obscure the stars, and then with nothing else to herald it, a great spit of water came up from the sea floor like a spring. The maelstrom's current began perceptibly to slow, and the center of the vortex rose up and up until once again it was at the level of sea surrounding.

Only then, as we floated off on the dying stream, did the mercenary finally put down the mast from his aching shoulder. The crew emerged from their places to man the ship again, and I took the mercenary down to our quarters, to dress the wounds along his legs and calves, which now were caked with blood.

All I could find to work with was a bottle of bourbon and some old rags, but he didn't object, nor did he say a word until finally I asked him if he'd any idea where we might be.

"Don't know." He looked over at the portal window. "I'd guess still southern, though." I poured a swig of alcohol into his wounds, but he did not flinch. He looked into my eyes keenly. "You mind my asking, sir—was the Cape your final destination?"

I gathered his point—it was the same as everyone else's on board—but I told him no. I said I hadn't been sure exactly where I was headed, that I'd found a map in my home, and that I was looking for the place it pictured.

"You have the map with you?" he asked.

I went to my duffel and gave it to him.

His face was determinedly expressionless as he studied the shape. "And where is your garden?" he asked.

"Dayton, Ohio," I said. "Have you seen this place before?"

He did not respond, but handed back the map. "You should rest, Dr. . . ."

"Uyterhoeven."

"Uyterhoeven," he pronounced.

Just then I began to feel very dizzy, as if all the tribulations of our evening had finally caught up with me. I wanted to tell him that he should rest as well and keep his legs up, but it was as if I'd been thrown back to my bunk and smothered by exhaustion. All I remember before I closed my eyes was the image of the mercenary there across the room, seated on his cot, with his legs all bandaged, his back against the wall, and a look of great concern on his face. Then I was driven to sleep by my reeling, whirling brain.

Just how long I slept I'm not exactly sure, but my sense was of its being only very brief—minutes at most—before I was awakened by a now familiar voice and rank breath.

"Up and at 'em, Dr. Thea-Legs!"

I opened my eyes and there before me was Diggery's face and toothless grin. "What is it?" My head was still spinning.

"We've arrived!"

"We've sighted land?" I could see the pink light of dawn just peering through the window.

"Have indeed, so get your things ready. We'll be docking thoon."

"But does anyone know where we are?"

"Nope." His eyes beamed at the mystery.

I sat up and looked over at the mercenary's bed to see if he was yet awake, but the morning light slanted flat across his sheets and blankets; they'd been pulled tight and tucked. The floor was swept. There was no bag, no boots, nor gun. "Where's the mercenary?" I asked.

Diggery looked round and smiled. "Guess he'd had it with saving us. Jumped a dinghy."

"Jumped—" I was stunned. "But is he headed for land?"

Diggery shook his head. "Other way."

"Away?" I asked.

Diggery nodded. "Didn't want no part."

"And you didn't try to stop him?"

"Know better than to get in the mercenary's way."

Quickly, angrily, I wrapped my blanket round me and climbed up on deck. All the crew were out, but none turned to note my emergence. They were all lined up against the portside rail, looking out towards the horizon, where a low and groggy morning hung in the mist, and a vague sliver of grey divided the sky from the sea. Land.

I turned my back and made for the starboard rail, to see if the mercenary was still in sight. The whole blue ocean rose and fell, with night still high and ripe above—I couldn't see. I looked and looked, and then finally the crest of the near swell came and lifted us high on its back, and there in the churning valley of blue I thought I saw a struggling speck, like a little bug. I looked closer and there he was, wrapped in blankets, his oars turning at the sides like splinters. But why? I wondered. Could his engagement with the Boer possibly be so firm, or was it this place behind us?

Diggery came up beside me. Apparently the crew had drafted him as their envoy to me, the demon. He said they'd sighted what looked like a beacon and port, and that the captain had determined that the ship would stay two days at most, long enough to get some food in our bellies, repair the damage to the ship, and store up for the trip back. He said that I would have to stay, though, or find another ship. I told him I understood, and then with a rather kindly pat upon my back, Diggery let me be. I stayed at the rail until the mercenary was gone from sight, sent off a prayer for him, and then descended to collect my things.

When time came to head for shore, the crew set aside a dinghy just for me. Only Diggery offered company. He took one oar and I the other, and we rowed in together, just the two of us. We docked at the longest pier and found it led directly to the main street of what appeared to be a small whaling village. There was no one to be seen, though, and we were both exhausted, so we found ourselves an inn first thing. It was right there on the main street, a two-story colonial inn called Winkler's, distinguished by two very handsome horse busts framing the entrance and an equally well-wrought tobacconist Indian standing just inside the door with a box of cigars. There was no one at the desk. Some ten minutes we waited before Diggery suggested we simply avail ourselves now and worry about the booking later. I was too exhausted to object, so we lifted a room key from its hook, left a note for the clerk, and made our way upstairs.

No sooner had we set our bags upon the floor than both of us fell to our beds fast asleep, and that morning—my first morning here—I was visited by a most intriguing dream, one I think might make a good stopping point, at least for the time being. For though the story of my arrival is as yet unfinished, I can sense from a certain stiffness in my wrist that perhaps some of the children's eyelids have begun to flutter, or worse, perhaps they haven't, and I'd imagine it's time they should.

So my dream was this, and it is as vivid to me now as if I had just awakened from it: I dreamt of the mercenary in his boat, lying in its small hull with his hands upon his chest. I dreamt that the ocean currents had carried him across the sea and up into the Gulf of St. Lawrence, that he'd floated down the river there to Lake Ontario, and then to Erie. I saw him on the Maumee and passing through Defiance, and from there he drifted along the Auglaize farther down—I suspect it was to Wapakoneta; but there a black stream carried him underground to our Wolf Creek, which delivered him straight to Dayton, to nuzzle at the banks of the Williams Street Bridge and wait.

That is where my dream ended, too soon to know if anyone has found him there. If not, I'd be obliged if you would go and look, and if he's there, remember you needn't wake him. Take him in, but let him be, and when you meet next time to hear the rest of this, let him sleep among you, for in what I was to discover upon waking from my nap, there's news for him as well as you.

I miss you all very, very much.

Good night,
Gus

THREE

THE FIRST READING

Sometime in early August of 1900, the map of the Antipodes made its first public appearance on the dictionary stand in the Uyterhoevens' library. It was made of goatskin and cotton cloth, cross-hatched in a checkerboard design—it looked to be a chessboard, in fact—except that someone had drawn the outline of what was very clearly a land mass across the top, of a shape that some of the guests compared to a ghost in flight and others to a windblown star.

The doctor claimed to have found the map in the games shack at the back of the garden. He said that he'd been cleaning out the dresser there—which many considered the least credible part of the story—and that he'd found it folded up behind a panel in one of the top drawers. From there he'd taken it straight to the library and set it in the dictionary's anointed place for all the guests to see. He'd even moved the terrestrial globe over to stand beside it, in hopes that someone might be able to find a shape somewhere on the globe to match the one on the map.

The doctor himself claimed to have had no luck. He'd suspected that the seams of the cross-hatch design might represent lines of longitude or latitude, but they hadn't been marked, and there was no ledger either, so it wasn't even clear how big the place was, whether it was continent- or more island-sized. Judging from the topology, by what appeared to be several anonymous rivers and a mountain range across the southern part, the dimensions looked to be somewhere in between. Aside from that, however, there'd been very little else to go on—just the shape and the name, which had been written in thin capital letters, in an arc across the face: T-H-E A-N-T-I-P-O-D-E-S.

The doctor gave the guests several weeks to ponder the question. A number of the children had suggested that the Antipodes might be somewhere in the Pacific, as there was so much room there and so many islands. Several of the older guests had pointed out that the Antipodes had long been an alias for Australia, which the doctor knew, of course. He failed to see the relevance, though, since the Antipodes on his map were clearly not Australia. John Patterson, a close friend of the doctor's and head of National Cash Register, offered that the only reason Australia was called the Antipodes was that it lay on the opposite side of the earth from England, and that this was all the word ''antipodes'' referred to literally—not to any specific land at all, but to the point opposite one's present position on the globe. The doctor appreciated Mr. Patterson's input, but still observed that whatever the name, the land pictured on the map had a specific shape, and if it had a shape, it must have a place as well, which remained a matter of simply locating.

By the last week of August, however, it was clear that no one at the garden had been able to do so, and a consensus was reached that these Antipodes must therefore be uncharted—other of course than by the negligent author of this mysterious map.

That settled, questions of greater weight had come in greater number: if the Antipodes were, in fact, unknown, what was life like there? What were the animals like? What were the trees and plants and people like, if there even were people? Numerous different parties of children had discussed it over lemonade at the garden. In particular, they'd wondered what sort of games the native Antipodeans might play, whether they were at all like chess or checkers—as the map itself had seemed to suggest—or whether their games had different rules altogether.

Of course, the only way to know for certain was to find the Antipodes, and the only way to do that—in the absence of any geodetic assistance—was to go look. So that was why the doctor was said to have left. He was going to search for the Antipodes. He insisted on going alone, because he wanted to travel light, but he said that he would be taking a chess set with him as well, so that in the event he did find the place pictured on the map, he would have something to offer the natives as a gift, in return for which he hoped they might provide him a game of theirs that he could send back to the garden, along with whatever explanation of the rules he had been able to glean. So armed and so determined, the doctor left on September 3, bound for the opposite side of the world—in deference to Mr. Patterson's observation—somewhere in the middle of the Indian Ocean.

There was no word for some time, and the children had been predictably impatient. The doctor had been gone less than two weeks when they started asking Mrs. Uyterhoeven if anything had arrived in the mail. Every day they came and asked, and every day she explained to them that finding an uncharted continent or island was no easy business, and even if the doctor had succeeded, there was no telling how slow the postal service of such a place might be.

Several more weeks' worth of eagerness and frustration passed before the children finally grew tired of waiting. They stopped pestering Mrs. Uyterhoeven. The garden established a rhythm in the doctor's absence, and only then, once the children's patience had all but worn to forgetting, did invitations finally appear in all their mailboxes, the second week of November.

Henry Gray's invitation had been standing proudly on display on the foyer chest since the day it arrived.

Mrs. Gustav Uyterhoeven requests the presence of
Master Henry Gray
in the chess garden, 6:00 on the evening of Nov. 17, 1900.
The doctor has written us a letter.

The brevity of the note had been almost too much for Henry to bear. He was seven and one-quarter years old, and he had questions. Had the doctor said where he was? Had he sent any new games? Henry had asked his parents, but they were no help. His father acted as though it were something he had not considered, which Henry knew wasn't true, and which only served to intrigue him all the more, since this shoulder-shrugging dumbness was a manner that his father adopted only three times a year: on Christmas Eve and Easter, and on Henry's birthdays. Surely the doctor had sent something, but when Henry went to ask Mrs. Uyterhoeven about it, which he was by no means alone in doing, she was stubborn as usual. She'd said it would be easiest to hold his questions until the reading, and perhaps the doctor's letter would answer them.

So Henry waited anxiously until Saturday the seventeenth. He thought of little else all that morning at school, and the afternoon was just as slow. Dinner at the Grays' was a brisker affair than usual. They skipped dessert, since there was bound to be food at the garden. Henry's mother had baked crullers for them to bring. She gave them to Henry to carry, and a bag of powdered sugar. Henry's father took a bottle of something beneath his arm, and off they went, all dressed in their best clothes and good shoes. Henry didn't say a word the whole way there—down Euclid, left on Monument, left on Broadway, and then across the bridge.

There were several other families already there when the Grays arrived. The Stiverses, the Beauchamps, and the Tollivers. They were all on the patio underneath the grape arbor, and Mrs. Uyterhoeven was gently directing traffic. Henry's father went straight out into the garden to help Mr. Tolliver and Mr. Beauchamp bring over the iron chairs from the games tables. The benches had been carried over already, and the parlor chairs were out as well. Henry's mother gravitated to the food table, to splay the forks and spoons, to set cups on saucers, and to make sure there were enough tumblers and wine-glasses. Mrs. Beauchamp tapped powdered sugar onto the crullers and a plate of waffles that were already out. There would be puffball biscuits and jellycakes as soon as Mrs. Connoly arrived, and brandy peaches. There would be shortening bread and grape jam, cheese and maple molasses, and for those with a sour tooth, there were cucumber pickles and sweet pickles and pickled onions. There would be pears and plums and pistachio nuts, fudge and washed grapes. Mrs. Uyterhoeven had told the children to help themselves while they were waiting, and the fathers poured themselves brandy. The strains of the piano came drifting out from the parlor, which meant that Mr. Pierce had arrived, and when Mr. Patterson came around the side path, the children moved from chairs down onto the patio brick. Henry sat next to his best friend, Will, and they gorged themselves with puffballs while all the bodies slowly crowded in around them.

Henry hadn't expected so many people. None of the faces was unfamiliar; he'd just never seen them all together at once. All the students in his class were there. The Wrights were there, and Jason Tolliver and his cousins Meredith and Helena. Peter Federman walked up, scuffing the soles of his shoes as usual, and took a place on the blankets, as did Penny Langenkamp, who always walked on her toes and was ruining her arches, according to Henry's mother. Then Robert and Oliver and Sam, who always monopolized the armored pieces. Then Andrew Quigley, who was one of Henry's playing partners, and Heather Mckinnon, to whom Henry had been engaged for two days when he was five; and Millicent Fredericks and Jimmy Bickford, who did not seem to take much notice of each other at the time but who would eventually marry.

Will Rubicon sat down next. It looked as if all nine of the Rubicons had come down from their farm, including Will's older brother Morgan, who was fifteen, and who had scraped all the skin off his back last year racing a wagon down Belmont Hill. He was talking to Elizabeth Raintree, whose golden hair and perfect posture had convinced Henry to begin associating with girls again just as soon as they all turned thirteen, like Elizabeth. Normally Peter Willicker would have been talking to Elizabeth and Morgan as well. They all went to Steele High School together, where Henry would someday go, but Peter was not there, which was strange, since he certainly came to the garden more than Morgan ever did, or Elizabeth. Peter Willicker had blue eyes, and a slim face with slim features—as opposed to Henry's, which was young and round—and Peter was very slender, with loose brown hair that covered his right eye when he read. But Henry couldn't see him anywhere.

He saw Father Wilder, though, and Monsignor Lott. And Miss Steele was already on the patio, sitting in the chair that Mr. Beauchamp had made for her, since she had a problem with her nerves and never stood up. Horace Pease and Mrs. Ramsey were talking about their greenhouses. Mrs. Stevens was smoking her pipe at the edge of the garden next to Mr. Peck, who once lived with Blue Jacket Indians on the Ohio River when he was eighteen. He was talking to Mr. Barney, who made the railway cars. And Dr. Burns and Mr. Dunbar were talking to Captain Stivers, who'd brought his violin, but no one was asking him to play because he'd lost his hearing. And there was John Black and Mr. Morrison, who'd given everyone tombstones for presents last year, and Thomas E. Thomas. Auntie Boydd was standing by the food table, with the lump in her pocket that Henry knew was an Irish potato she kept there to ward off rheumatism. Mrs. Davis was choosing her seat already—she had let Henry play with the pots and pans when Helena was born—but her husband, Mr. Davis, was still out talking to Mr. Garrett and Harrison Holt, who'd given Henry all his books when his family moved to Virginia.

There were more guests than that, many more whom Henry couldn't see from his knee-high perspective on the patio brick, but it was fairly clear—everyone was there. Even the older chess players—Theo, the Greek, and the two Russians—and people who'd moved away, like the Eackers and the Holts. Everyone, except for Peter Willicker.

Then there was the sound of a bell. Mr. Patterson was out in the garden walking around the outside of all the guests, shepherding them in with a cowbell. Mrs. Uyterhoeven came in through the patio doors and took her chair in the middle of all the children's blankets. Mrs. Kunneworth followed behind with a footstool she set at Mrs. Uyterhoeven's feet, with a stack of handwritten pages on top. Everyone found a place to sit, all crammed in together as close as they could get, except for some of the men, the fathers, who stood around the outside. Then when they were all settled and could hear, Mr. Patterson stepped forward and stood next to Mrs. Uyterhoeven—his shoes were right in front of Henry's knees—and on everyone's behalf, he thanked her and the doctor for inviting them.

She accepted their gratitude with a quiet nod, but offered no words of her own. She took the stack of pages from a footstool beside her and set it on her lap. She sat straight up, with her knees and feet together, then lifted the top page from the stack and held it out in front of her, so high that her chin lifted slightly. Then she began: "Dear Sonja."

Her voice was clear and steady. She made no attempt to emulate her husband's, which was of a more dramatic contour. She read at a slow, steady pace that seemed to still the surface of the doctor's prose, and her movements were equally calm and firm. When she came to the end of a page, she laid it facedown on the stool beside her, straightened her back, and then took up the next. Every page made the same journey, at the same pace—from her lap, to her eyes, then down onto the stool. There was a patience and a tolerance to the way she told the doctor's story that seemed to welcome the children's minds to wander but pierced their distraction nonetheless, so that in the days to come and the years to follow, Henry's memory of that first reading would be an easy mix of things imagined alongside things felt and seen: of the sleeping, hardly breathing mercenary on his cot; of Mrs. Uyterhoeven's free hand resting still upon her lap; of the blood on Diggery's chin; the bugs flicking against the garden lanterns; the cook and Jebsen gnashing their teeth at the mercenary's legs; the sound of Auntie Boydd behind him, fast asleep and snoring; and finally the mercenary in his little boat, floating all the way to Dayton.

When at last Mrs. Uyterhoeven set the last page from her lap down on the stool and said good night for the doctor, everyone slowly emerged from their various levels of quiet attention. They stood and stretched. Parents picked up their sleeping children, and Henry assumed they would all be going home now, it was so late. Some of his classmates ran out into the garden for one last sprint, while the mothers all started in with the food and dishes and the fathers returned the chairs and benches to their places. Henry and Will went out to the oak swings and agreed that first thing in the morning they'd go to the levee together to look for the mercenary.

When their fathers came out to collect them, Henry had been surprised by how many people were still there. They were all milling about the patio; then Mr. Patterson led them around the side of the house to the street, even Miss Steele—Mrs. Conover was pushing her in her wheelchair. Mrs. Uyterhoeven came through the front door with a bundle of candles in her arms and passed them out to all the children. Henry's father and Mr. Beauchamp handed out some lanterns to the grownups; then when Mr. Patterson had checked to make sure that everyone was present and accounted for, they all turned and started down Middle Street in the direction of Wolf Creek. Henry didn't know exactly why, and didn't ask, but he'd never been in a pack of so many people walking. It was like being in a parade, except at night, and he'd certainly never been out so late, but he felt safe in the midst of all the lanterns—safe and yet defiant, as though for just this once, after so many days ending in night, so many scary dreams and frightened moments in the shadow of his room, here this evening, banded together with all the guests of the Uyterhoevens' chess garden, they would conquer the darkness.

At Negley Street they all turned left along the creek, and then at the Williams Street Bridge Mr. Patterson split the group into several search parties. Henry's father was head of one, and Captain Stivers, Mr. Thomas, and Mr. Patterson each took one as well. The children were told to pair up and hold hands, and Mrs. Uyterhoeven came round and lit all their candles with her own. Then when everyone was set, all the groups headed off in their own direction. Mr. Patterson's headed left along Negley toward Sunrise, Mr. Thomas's headed for the Summit Bridge, and Captain Stivers and Henry's father led their groups across the Williams Street Bridge to check the far banks.

Henry wasn't sure which group he'd been assigned to. He assumed he was in his father's, but he'd paired up with Will, and Will was in the captain's group. In all the confusion, he lost Will's hand, his candle blew out, and he was set adrift. Not lost. He could see the others. Out across the creek the candles of his father's and Captain Stivers's parties were bobbing and dancing like two swarms of fireflies, and he could hear their voices very clearly—but with no light of his own, he felt invisible. It was as though he'd disappeared, all still and quiet.

Then a voice called out, "Who is that there?" It was Mrs. Uyterhoeven. She was standing on top of the levee with her back to the river. She was holding her long candle at her waist like a rose, and he could see her face by the light of its bloom. "Who is that little boy?" she called in a whisper.

"Me. Henry."

"Henry Gray? Come up here with us." There was someone standing next to her, silently, but Henry couldn't see who. They waited for him, but the levee seemed so high in the darkness, Henry couldn't move. "Do you need help?" asked Mrs. Uyterhoeven, and when he didn't answer, she gave her candle to the figure beside her, who started down the levee toward him. It was a man, but Henry still couldn't tell who it was until he came to the flat and the light of his candle touched his face—Peter Willicker, smiling faintly. He extended his hand to Henry. Neither said a word, and together they climbed back up the levee.

When they reached the top, Mrs. Uyterhoeven asked Henry how he'd lost his group, but his heart was thumping too loud to answer. The three of them just stood there, looking out. Across the creek Henry could see his father leaning over the bank by the Williams Street Bridge, holding out his lantern and looking underneath as if it were a cave, and he began to feel sorry for Mrs. Uyterhoeven, because there seemed to be no boat and no mercenary. It seemed a great deal of stake to put in the doctor's dream, for them all to have come so expectantly. The doctor hadn't even said how long the mercenary would take, but Henry wanted to tell her that they could come back tomorrow. They could come back every day, he thought, but just as he turned to tell her, something caught his eye, something bumping up against the bank right there where they were standing.

He peered at it through the darkness. ''What do you see, Henry?'' asked Mrs. Uyterhoeven. She grabbed hold of his shirt collar as they both stepped closer to the bank. It looked like a tiny canoe, no bigger than Mrs. Uyterhoeven's shoe, fastened to the banks by a string tied around a little stick. ''What is it, Henry?'' Henry got down on his knees and Mrs. Uyterhoeven transferred her grip to his belt loop while he leaned over and unfastened it.

It was a boat. He took it from the water and showed them. Mrs. Uyterhoeven held the candle up to it for them to see—there was something inside, a figure no more than four inches tall and carved out of wood, covered by a tiny blanket, lying on its back with its hands crossed over its chest. Henry touched the shoulders with his fingers.

''Don't wake him,'' said Mrs. Uyterhoeven. ''Peter, go tell the others—Henry has found him.'' Henry looked up at them both, confused. He hadn't been sure himself what he'd done until Mrs. Uyterhoeven said so. The figure didn't look like he'd expected the mercenary to, but before he could say so, Peter was already crossing the bridge to tell the others.

Together Mrs. Uyterhoeven and Henry looked closer at his discovery. The boat was like the ones from whaling ships, with oars and screws, much as Henry had imagined, but the figure inside had slimmer shoulders, and its hands were small. ''But it's a boy,'' he said.

Just then from across the creek he heard some of the children squealing. Peter had told them, and others were groaning from disappointment. He'd heard his father's voice too—''Henry?'' Then he could see the little blots of light all race down the bank to inform Captain Stivers's group, and soon everyone was calling out to each other that Henry Gray had found the mercenary. They all came back across the bridge and down the banks to see, and when Henry showed them, they all reacted the same—quietly, so as not to wake him. They passed the boat around gently from hand to hand, and nearly everyone agreed—it appeared to be a boy. Even Mr. Patterson allowed there was no good explanation for it, nor for the fact that he appeared to be so small and wooden. Mr. Thomas wanted to know where exactly Henry had found it, and Henry pointed to the spot, while everyone kept patting him on the shoulders and telling him what a good eye he had. "Thank goodness for Henry," Mrs. Conover had said. "Who knows how long the poor thing might have had to stay out here in the cold."

Finally, after everyone had a chance to see and they were all saying good night, Henry took his mother aside. He asked her if they were going to take the boy home with them, but she said she didn't think so. She said it might be best if Mrs. Uyterhoeven took him for now, for safekeeping. But they could go tomorrow, she said, and so they did. Henry even brought his own pillow for the boy to sleep on, and they went the day after that as well.

Then on Sunday, the second of Dr. Uyterhoeven's letters was read. Again, all the same guests came over after an early supper, and as reward for being the one to find him, Henry was allowed to sit beside the boy while Mrs. Uyterhoeven read. He sat right beside them both, so he had felt it more keenly than the others, and more so that first year than ever afterward, that Mrs. Uyterhoeven was really reading the stories to the boy mercenary, and that the rest of them were only being allowed to listen.

FOUR

THE MYSTIFIC AND MRS. ANNA

The Second Letter

October 10, 1900

Dear Sonja,

I hope the mercenary has shown. At least I shall write in such faith, that the library is warm with little bodies on mothers' laps and fathers' knees and pillows, and that the mercenary is there as well, eyes closed and hands folded above his belt. I hope he is sleeping, and that your voice shall carry my words inside his dreams, and that he might remember when he wakes.

It was nearing twilight when I awoke my first day here. I didn't know the time precisely. I'm afraid my pocket watch didn't fare well in the maelstrom, but I could tell I had missed the day. The sun was falling already and I was very hungry. Diggery was still curled up in his bed, though, snoring, and I didn't think it right that I should go foraging without him. So, to let him sleep a while longer, I pulled up a chair to the window to see what I could see.

The street was quiet at first and undisturbed by traffic. Every so often a red or black dish would come rolling by, which struck me as odd certainly, but I supposed there must be children somewhere beyond my view, pushing them. It even occurred to me that such dishes might make a good gift to send you, as they seemed very good rollers—but the greater share of my attention was focused upon the few passersby who did make their way beneath my window, in particular because of two attributes they all shared. First, they were all headed in the same direction, but separately, from my left to my right, back towards the pier. Second, and much more intriguing, they all appeared to be in costume. In the time I sat there at the window of our room, I saw a man dressed as a sultan, in fine purple silks and green sandals. I saw two gentlemen dressed as militia from the American Revolution, with their hair tied in ponytails under tricorner hats. I saw an armored knight on horseback with red and gold plumes dancing from his helmet. I saw a team of huntsmen with bows and arrows; a seventeenth-century Frenchman in an enormous white wig; a monk in brown sackcloth tied at the waist with rope; and two Oriental soldiers with triangular breastplates and long wispy moustaches.

There may have been others who've escaped my memory. More and more kept entering from the side streets, but every one of them in costume, and every costume rendered with a level of ingenuity and determination such as I have rarely seen outside the opera. Indeed, as they all paraded beneath my window in the direction of the pier, I felt something like a king up on my balcony, and they the players in some marvelous historical pageant.

So I had been quite content watching them when Diggery finally stirred. He awakened with the croak of just a single word—"Huuuungry."

"Yes," I answered regretfully, "and it appears that someone's having a costume ball down towards the pier."

''Food, you think?'' asked Diggery, joining me now at the window.

''I'd imagine.''

''Well then, let's go.''

''But we haven't been invited,'' I said.

''It's a costume ball, Doc. No one'll know.''

''Yes, but we haven't any costumes.''

''Wha'bout those?'' Diggery turned round and pointed back at the beds. ''We could take the sheets, go as ghosts.'' To demonstrate he returned to his bed and threw the top linen over his head. ''Just cut holes in them for eyes—and mouth tho's we can eat.''

As I looked at Diggery, besheeted, and my stomach grumbled its endorsement of the plan, I wondered at my susceptibility to the contagion of his lawlessness. And yet I had to admit that I was also interested to see from closer range the costumes on display at this ball, so very quickly, in order to get there while most of the food was still out, Diggery and I tailored two ghost costumes just as he'd described, with holes for the eyes and mouth, and then we headed down.

There were perhaps five or six new guests on the street as we joined in—one dressed as a bishop, two German burghers, a bear, and a Norseman—and down among them I could see more clearly, it wasn't only by attire that they had achieved their remarkable effects, but by makeup, and expression, too. Much the same as with their dress, the visages of those beside me appeared almost overly characteristic, set with expressions that did more than merely reflect the spirit within, but actually accentuated it. Indeed, everything around me seemed to have taken on a certain, brighter emphasis. I suppose it may have been only that I was a touch lightheaded from hunger, but the street seemed very colorful to me, very vibrant and clear and fragrant. And I'd even felt a twinge of shame at the comparatively meager contribution that Diggery and I were making to the parade, except that no one seemed to object in the slightest, and that I actually felt quite invigorated there beneath the slick-slack of my bedsheet—at once safe and very daring.

Indeed, so stimulated did I feel by my new surroundings, I considered I might celebrate the mood with a good smoke. I remembered the cigars in my pocket, the ones I'd nabbed from the Indian at the door of Winkler's. I took one for myself and the other I gave to Diggery. Unfortunately, neither of us had a light, so at first we did without. We strode along the avenue with our two cigars protruding lustily from our mouth holes, and we'd gone perhaps a block when I noticed, much to my pleasant surprise, a young man seated on the curb smoking a similar cigar to ours—or rather, he was staring at his cigar in one hand and holding a match in the other. It appeared that he had momentarily withdrawn from the parade for this purpose, though what sort of persona this gentleman meant to convey I couldn't quite recognise, save for that of a man somewhat distracted. As we approached I could see, in addition to the bewildered attention he was giving his match and his cigar, that one of his shoes was unlaced, both his trouser pockets were pulled out, and his vest had been mis-buttoned over a homemade sweater, which he appeared to be wearing backwards. Also, there was a string tied round the index finger of his left hand.

"Excuse me," I said, taking the cigar from my mouth to show him. "Have you another light?"

The young man looked up at us as though I might be speaking to someone just over his shoulder, but then engaged the two of us with a bewildered squint I found instantly, and strangely, poignant.

"A light?" I repeated, and from the breast pocket of his vest he extended us a box of matches. Diggery snatched it up, and the young man watched with much the same expression as Diggery offered the flame to my cigar and then his own—a look of uncertain uncertainty, as if what stood before him must be utterly beyond, or utterly beneath, his reason. He stirred as if about to say something, but stopped him-self.

"Yes?" I urged, handing him back his matches.

"You are a ghost?" he asked warily.

"I am." I spread my arms proudly and turned for him. "A ghost named Gus, and this is my friend Diggery Priest." Diggery, who'd turned back round and was observing the parade, howled indifferently from over his shoulder. ''He is a ghost as well,'' I said. ''And you?''

''Me?'' The young man seemed unprepared for the question.

''Yes, what are you going as?''

He looked down, confused, and touched the buttons of his vest vaguely. ''I'm not sure.''

''Oh, but you should definitely come along,'' I said. ''It looks as if it's going to be quite an affair.'' I felt the poke of Diggery's impatience from behind, that we should go, but for some reason this young man's bewilderment had sparked a strange sympathy in me. I considered his rumpled attire. ''You could go as a young professor of pathology.''

He failed to see the humour in this, understandably. Again he looked down and felt the neck of his sweater—I'm not sure he'd been aware—and when he looked back at me, the slight smile on his face seemed lonely. ''I'm afraid I'm not very good with answers.''

''Well, that's all right,'' I said. ''Diggery, what do you say?''

Diggery looked round impatiently. ''Thay about what?''

''What do you think he should go as?''

Diggery considered briefly. ''How 'bout a fella has to bring a dozen eggs home to his missus?''

The young man looked up at Diggery, equally as confused by his suggestion as by mine.

''I believe,'' I said, to clarify, ''that he's referring to the string tied round your finger.''

The young man opened his hand to consider it. ''What do you mean?''

''That it would remind you to pick up some eggs for your wife.''

The young man looked at me straight and with the barest hint of offense. ''But that is not what it's for.''

''I understand, but Diggery was only suggesting—'' I paused, arrested by the utter innocence of his expression. ''What is it for?'' I asked.

''It's for when I lose my way,'' he said. He held up his hand to view, and there was a glint of recognition in his eye. ''It reminds me to find the canals.''

Diggery poked me in the ribs again for us to go and leave this poor fellow, but I stood fast. ''But you're not lost now, are you?'' I asked.

The young man considered this. ''No,'' he said finally, looking back at me absent even a trace of irony. ''But thank you.''

''All right, then.'' Diggery swooped round and took my arm as if to unsnag me. ''S'long as you know where you are, then Doc and I'll be headin' along. Thanks for the light and good luck with your other shoelace.''

I nodded my farewell, and Diggery began pulling me away, but just as we were about to rejoin the procession, the young man called, ''Excuse me.''

I turned round to find his countenance changed; it had taken on an almost calculating aspect. He motioned with his cigar. ''Ghosts can speak to other ghosts, can't they?''

There was a pause. I wasn't quite sure of his meaning, but Diggery looked up at me, and though it was difficult to gauge his expression from beneath the sheet, the single bounce of his cigar seemed to indicate that if indeed this strange young man was to take up any more of our time, it would not be at the expense of Diggery's entertainment. He took a step forward and bowed. ''Why, thertainly,'' he said. ''Doc and I do it all the time.''

''No, but I mean to other ghosts, too.'' The young man sat forward with much too credulous an expression. ''You can find each other and talk to each other.''

''Absolutely.'' Diggery leaned in closer, sensing prey. ''Who'd you have in mind?''

''Well, I've a friend—''

''Excuse me,'' I interrupted, as it had occurred to me finally the confusion that Diggery was already prepared to seize on. ''You are aware that these are just linen.''

''Doc!'' Diggery stepped back from me in mock surprise, and then with a wink challenged me for claim of the young man's trust.

''Don't offend our friend here. He knows ghosts when he thees 'em. Isn't that right?'' He glanced quickly at the young man, who returned a fully blank expression. I was overmatched, I knew, but in the name of mercy I stepped up.

''Sir,'' I said, as frankly as I was able. ''You'll have to forgive us. We don't mean to tease. *I* don't mean to tease. We're simply both very hungry, and my friend here, Mr. Priest, is only—''

''Is only trying to be honest.'' Diggery poked his sheeted head round my shoulder. ''Honest to a friend in need. All it is is, Doc here don't like to frighten folks, but I can thee you're not given much to fright, am I right?'' The young man shrugged. ''Truth is, we both just come from the ocean floor. Giant maelstrom thucked us down like thtones, so we're fresh, it's true, but it's thomething the doc'll have to get used to. Now, tell us, who was it you wanted us to talk to?''

The young man looked pitifully confused, but he'd at least understood this last part. ''Well, I've a friend,'' he said, ''Mrs. Ann—''

''Sir,'' I interrupted again, and this time I actually held out my bedsheet for him to touch. ''We are not ghosts. These are only linens from the inn where we are staying, Winkler's just down the street. They are costumes, and we—Mr. Priest and I—were simply on our way to attend the costume ball down near the pier in the hopes of finding something there to eat.''

''Costume ball?'' The young man's face knit with bewilderment.

''Costume ball?'' Diggery echoed with tenfold dismay.

The young man looked down in the direction of the pier. ''That''—a sad laugh interrupted his words—''that is not what I'd thought at all.''

''Well,'' I said, ''I know, and it's perfectly understandable. It is very confusing with everyone dressed up this way, but that is what we are doing here. We are just visit—''

''Look, look, look.'' Diggery stood beside me and assumed a reasonable air. ''We don't need to settle this here. Why doesn't our young friend just come along with us. We'll all go down to the pier, and if there is a masquerade, as Doc here seems to think, then our friend'll thee that we're not really ghosts. But if there is no masquerade''—he leaned in and winked confidentially at the young man—''as him and I know there won't be, then we'll know that Doc's the fooler here—'cause he and I are ghosts, as couldn't be more clear—and we'll be glad to thpeak with anyone you like. That seem fair?''

I looked at Diggery, utterly nonplussed, wondering if he'd any purpose in life but to make a mockery of things, but he returned my glare with twinkling eyes and then gave notice of his purpose. ''And I'm sure that in exchange for our service, our friend with the matches here might thee his way to giving us a bite to eat.''

The young man looked at me to see if I had any objection to these terms. I offered none. Given Diggery's mood, it seemed like the simplest resolution. Also, as I glanced behind us, a man dressed as a pilgrim looked back at me and actually pointed to the pier as if time were wasting. ''Very well,'' I agreed.

The young man stood up then, but before we started, he held up his cigar to clarify our terms. ''So if there is no costume ball at the pier,'' he said, ''then you two will come back with me to Mrs. Anna.''

''Mrs. Anna cook?'' asked Diggery.

The young man nodded. ''I caught a rabbit this morning.''

''Well, all right, then!'' Diggery clapped us both on the back and ran up ahead, hooting and spooking the other guests, much as I suppose he imagined ghosts behave, but leaving behind the young man and me, and my great concern for his perilous gullibility.

''You really shouldn't mind Diggery,'' I tried assuring him, and was going to explain that it was simply his idea of fun, to tease, but the young man's expression as he looked back at me was so leery, I realised that any attempt on my part to be frank would only be construed by him, in light of our contract, as a manipulation. So I invited him to the road beside me and switched to a topic which might incur less suspicion on his part, and at the same time instruct my concern.

I gestured to his finger. ''Do I take it that Mrs. Anna is at the canals?''

He nodded warily.

''She lives on a boat?'' I asked.

Again he nodded, but with his eyes set firm upon the road in front of us, as if my questions might otherwise have the power to topple him.

''And you live there as well?''

He nodded more surely. ''I pull it for her.''

''Really. For how long?''

The young man thought, but as mine was a question not particularly well-put, nor one which he could answer by simply nodding or shaking his head, he struggled—hardly out of stupidity, though, for I should be clear: though innocent, though gullible, though somewhat muddled and wary, this gentleman's bearing was actually a quite intelligent one, really more over-burdened by consideration than under-. I could actually see him wander the labyrinth of his reason for an answer and become lost. ''I'm sorry,'' he said. ''I have forgotten the question.''

''Perfectly understandable.'' I let the matter pass. ''But do you mind my asking: This confusion of yours''—I gestured again to the string on his finger—''is it a chronic condition?''

He looked at his hand, and there was a glint of self-effacing humor in his eye. ''Yes,'' he said, ''but getting better, I think.''

''Well, I hope I'm not prying, but I am a doctor. Now, did this problem develop suddenly, or over a period of time?''

''Over a period of time,'' he answered, with a sudden lucidity I counted as reward for my frankness. He looked at me almost confidentially. ''I actually cultivated it.''

''On purpose?''

He nodded with a faint smile. ''I was a member of a temple,'' he said, ''a Temple of Mystifics. The mystifics' purpose was to see the world as new, and it was during that time, while I was studying with them, that this''—he turned his hand over in observance of the string—''developed.''

I thought. ''So you're saying that your confusion developed as a result of your efforts to see the world as new?''

He nodded.

''Do you mind my asking how?''

He looked at me, surprised at my interest. ''Well,'' he said, ''at least as I understand, at other temples—no matter if one is studying numbers or rocks or stars—the purpose is always to know more and better, and to remember what one knows. With the mystifics, though, because it was our goal to see the world as new, the purpose really was to un-know''—he looked at me—''to forget.''

''Hm,'' I considered. ''So you're saying that you became disoriented in the course of learning to forget?''

''Yes,'' he said assuredly.

''And do you mind my asking—how did you learn to forget?''

The young man's eyes narrowed, but not without amusement. ''Do you mind my asking why you are so interested?''

''As I said''—I looked him square—''I am a doctor.''

The young man shut one eye and gauged me with the other. ''Well,'' he said finally, ''I had a very good teacher. He believed that for everything there was a way of knowing, there must be a way of un-knowing. You simply had to find the way, and that is what he did. He found many different ways, which he showed to me, and together we practised them.''

''And what were they, these ways?''

One final time the young man looked at me to make sure of my sincerity, then gave over to the topic more fully. ''In general, my master's way was always to turn our attention from what we recognised about something to what we didn't. With the sky at night, for instance, instead of looking at the stars and the shapes they suggested, my master and I would try to look at the space in between.'' He looked at me. ''Does that make sense?''

''It makes sense,'' I said. ''It also sounds as if it would be extremely difficult to do.''

The young man nodded. ''It isn't easy, but there were simpler things. Words. For instance, if you said a word to us—'cobblestone'—instead of thinking of this''—he gestured down at the street in front of us—''we would just try to hear the sound—*cobblestone*—and really that wasn't so hard. All we had to do was repeat it often enough. *Cobblestone, cobblestone, cobblestone.* If you hear a word often enough, you'll forget what it means fairly quickly.'' He looked at me with a most certain nod.

"Yes, I suppose that's true, but now let me be clear, your purpose was to do this with everything, correct? Not just words or the sky, but everything surrounding you."

"Yes."

"Because when you'd forgotten everything, then presumably you would see the world as new?"

"Exactly," he said.

"Hm." I considered the prospect. "And you were actually able to do this?"

The young man shrugged. "The truth is, once you've managed to forget one thing, it's not so hard to forget another. Most of what we know depends."

"Yes. I suppose I can see that." I looked at him—they seemed to me to have been a most reckless pair, this young mystific and his master—and of course it was no wonder he'd become so disoriented. "Was it fun?" I asked.

"Oh yes, at the beginning." He looked at me with great assurance. "The things we forgot turned out to be so much more beautiful than the things we remembered. The colours were more colorful; the sounds were like music. My master and I could spend a whole day forgetting a pair of shoes, and they'd be the most beautiful, the most delicious pair of shoes we'd ever had."

"You actually ate them?"

"Well, we tasted them. Or sometimes we could spend hours sitting by the temple fountain, holding teacups to our ears and listening." The young man had taken on a nostalgic air. "I remember one morning, we'd been given a broom to sweep my master's room, but instead we plucked out all the straws and scattered them across the floor, and then the light came in his window. It looked as if the sun had fallen down in splinters." The young mystific looked at me, face flushed and pleasantly dazed. "It was wonderful."

"But . . ." I said.

"But." He nodded sadly. "But then I guess we forgot too much, or forgot the wrong things."

"Yes, but now I'm wondering, were you able to sense this—when the trouble began? Were there any symptoms, I mean."

The young man nodded. "Well, it happened to my master first. He was much more adept than I obviously, so the trouble began for him before it did me. He was becoming lost. We would be walking together, then all of a sudden he would forget where we were and what we were doing. And that wasn't even so bad, but then sometimes he wouldn't know who I was, or how we'd gotten there. He couldn't express himself, and he couldn't understand what I was saying. He would shrink of fear."

"That must have been very disconcerting," I said.

"Yes, it was, but at first they were just like spells. They passed. I could bring him back and then he would understand again. The problem was, he kept forgetting more. He couldn't help himself, and the more he forgot, the more he forgot, so the spells kept getting worse. He was becoming lost more and more, until I'm not sure he was ever really aware of where he was or who I was. He stopped talking, and then he stopped taking care of himself. I had to bathe him and feed him. I had to make sure he swallowed his food, because otherwise he'd just hold it on his tongue. He'd spit out water if I gave it to him, but he'd put pebbles in his mouth, and candles, and he'd just sit in the tub for hours and hours, mumbling things I couldn't understand."

"Awful."

"It was awful. And what made it worse was when I began to feel the same thing was happening to me. I was having spells myself. Whole stretches of time were passing that I couldn't remember. I'd find myself in places I didn't recognise—and not colorful places, but strange and grey, and I didn't know how I'd gotten there, or how to get back. I'd try asking people, but I couldn't understand what they were saying, and I couldn't make myself understood. I'd find sand in my pockets, and sticks in my hair, and I didn't know if I should take them out. I didn't know what I should do or what I should pay attention to, because everything I did, it just seemed like I was getting more and more lost.

"The only times I wasn't lost—the only time I knew I was where I should be, doing what I should be doing—was when I was with my master, feeding him and bathing him. But that only frightened me more, because I could see how much worse he was getting. He didn't walk anymore. He never left his chamber. He just knelt there with his head on his chair watching the light pass across the floor, across all the dirty broom straw.

"And then he stopped watching the light. I could tell. I could see in his eyes. All he was doing was breathing, because that's all he could remember how to do. And I would look at him kneeling there, and I would be terrified, because I knew if I didn't somehow learn to control all this forgetting, it was going to leave me the same as him. I was afraid that soon someone was going to have to take care of me, and bathe me and feed me, and soon it would take all of my energy and attention just to breathe, just like my master."

"My word," I said. "And what did you do?"

The young mystific looked back at me frankly. "I asked him."

I stopped. "You asked him what?"

"If I was right," the young man said. "I went to his room one day to bathe him—I didn't know if he heard me. I doubt if he even knew I was there, but I told him that this felt like a disease to me, this forgetting. I said that he seemed ill to me, and that I thought I was becoming ill too, but I didn't know, so I was asking: Were these feelings of being so lost and mistaken ever going to get better, or was this just a sickness growing worse?"

Again the young man paused, of distraction with the memory of such dire emotions.

"And did he answer?" I asked.

The young man shook his head blankly. "I don't know."

"He didn't hear you?"

"I don't know."

"He did nothing?"

The young man looked at me. "He died."

"While you were bathing him?"

The young mystific nodded gently.

''How awful,'' I said, but the young man did not so judge. He gave a shrug. ''And so what did you do then?'' I asked.

''I buried him, and then I left the temple. I had no purpose there anymore, and I knew purpose was my only hope, so I left.''

''And that is when you found Mrs. Anna?'' I asked hopefully.

''No.'' He smiled vaguely at his folly. ''That is when I became very lost, and Mrs. Anna found me.''

''And she took you in?''

The young mystific's expression warmed. ''She was very kind to me. She gave me a meal and listened to my story. When I was through, she let me stay the night, and in the morning she asked if I would pull her barge for her down to the next village. I did. I was grateful for something to do, but I hadn't wanted to impose, so when we came to the next town, I thanked her again and said I should go. She didn't try to keep me, but before I left she cut a piece of string from her ball of twine and tied it around my finger, and she told me I needn't fear being lost anymore. She said that if I should find the world becoming strange and unfamiliar, I only needed to look at the string on my finger and be reminded that I had use at the canals, to find her barge and pull it for her, as she could always use the help. Then she let me go, as she has always let me go, and soon enough I was lost again. I have been lost many times since, but every time I have been reminded by the string on my finger of Mrs. Anna's promise, which she has always made good. She has always given me food and a place to sleep. She keeps a bed for me now and lets me drag her barge. I have dragged Mrs. Anna's barge throughout the lowland, and I do believe by this labour, slowly, my mind has begun to heal.''

He looked at me with hope and confidence that this was so, and I was not quite so worried for him as I had been. ''It sounds as if you were lucky to have found Mrs. Anna.''

''I am.'' He nodded, but then his expression darkened slightly. ''But she has been haunted by ghosts of late. I have heard her speaking to them in her room, telling them to go, and I would like to help her as she has helped me.''

My linen turned to lead at the reminder of his errant purpose. "And you would like Diggery and me to speak to her."

As he nodded his answer, I didn't know whether to begin preparing him for imminent disclosure of his mistake or whether to let the masquerade simply and evidently surround us. We were by now almost upon the pier. All the people were congregated near the end, so I supposed that the latter would have to do, but then suddenly I was seized by dread, for there was Diggery coming back toward us in his sheet, shaking his head. "Nope," he was saying. "No ball. Let's go have some rabbit stew."

No ball? I went past him, to be sure, to see how this could be. Everyone was down as close to the end of the pier as they could be without spilling into the bay—perhaps a hundred in all, whose diversity of appearance was all the more remarkable now that they were all together. Monks, knights, horses, bears, bishops, Arabs, Chinese warriors, and a host of other figures culled from throughout the world and history, and yet Diggery was right. Beyond their costumes there was no other sign of festivity. No food or music, and no one was looking about for the sorts of acknowledgement which one so desperately needs in masquerade. In fact, they were all looking out beyond the pier at the setting sun. Even the war-horse stood and watched the low sky, and it was a beautiful sight, I'll allow—well worth the attention—but what, I thought to myself, was this all about, then? Was this a stop on the way to the costume ball? I looked round for someone to ask, and there to my left was the tobacconist Indian, standing there with the cigar box now tucked beneath his arm! My mind began to reel. Could I have been infected so quickly by the mystific's disease? My eyes fell next upon an English king in front of us, on whose face I saw a king's experience inscribed. Behind him the men who'd carried his throne waited with their heads bowed, not daring to look upon the same object as their monarch. There was no pretense to their behaviour, or in the countenance of anyone else surrounding me. The monks wore their bald crowns with utter humility and poverty. But was I to believe these figures were not in costume, then? Was I to believe that those were actual bears over there and not men in bear costumes? Were there no buttons or seams in their coats? But how?

Standing directly beside me now was a sultan, all wrapped in his cloaks and turban. He was staring very seriously at the horizon, where just the very tip of the sun was clinging, but I leaned over nonetheless and in a tone of confidence I asked, ''Why are we all dressed this way?'' He did not answer. He remained face forward, arms crossed, intent upon the sky. ''Excuse me,'' I tried again, but now as the sun disappeared from view, he turned round and headed back down the pier, followed ten paces behind by seven veiled women.

A bit away, I could see that a man dressed as a bishop was looking at me, smiling. He had a long black beard and was wearing what I recognised to be Russian Orthodox attire. He seemed to be taking humour in my perplexity, but a kind humour. His twinkling eyes invited me to his side, and when I reached him, discreetly he leaned over and whispered in my ear, ''I don't think the Arabs can hear you. The turbans cover their ears.''

''Really?'' I said. ''But I seem to have offended him.''

''No,'' the bishop smiled. ''They never stay long past the sun. They only come for the colours.'' He paused. Several other figures, including the bears, were turning now and making their way back towards the main street.

''And what brings you?'' I asked.

He pointed to his ears. ''I come for the ocean as well. You?'' I nodded from underneath my sheet, and we both swayed on our heels as the tide drew in, shushing the beach. ''Did you come for more than the colours and the tide?'' he asked.

''Actually,'' I said shamefully, ''I came to eat.''

He looked at me most pleasantly. ''A ghost came to eat the sunset.'' He considered it and smiled again, shaking his head. ''I saw a marble totem here the other night, another bishop,'' he said. ''From Tibo. I'd love to have known what it was doing here.''

He looked out now and I felt myself beginning to grope. ''There isn't one here now?'' I tried. ''A totem?''

The bishop looked round. "I don't see one. But what would an abstract be doing at a sunset anyway?"

"Not much, I suppose."

"No eyes," he shrugged.

"Absolutely." I drew on my cigar and he looked on rather admiringly.

"I saw a cluster of them outside Untilleflu not so long ago," he said. "All together."

"Really."

"All floating up in the air." He raised his hands to imitate their hovering. "I went and stood in the middle of them." He looked at me. "Nothing."

"Hardly surprising," I offered.

The bishop nodded. "Only fair, though, I suppose. We do have the sunset."

I pointed to my ears. "And the ocean."

"Indeed." He nodded. He raised his finger. "And our tongues."

"Yes. To say nothing of our noses."

"I hadn't wanted to presume." He indicated my covered face.

"Oh, I have an excellent nose," I assured him.

"And you, sir, Mr. Ghost," he said, stepping back, "can eat the sunset."

"Yes, I can." I took the cigar from my mouth, sensing the possibility of escape. "And it has been delicious. Will you excuse me?"

"Certainly," he bowed. "A pleasure talking to you."

"And you as well."

I turned and headed back to Diggery, who was tapping his foot impatiently, and the young mystific, who now had my most profound sympathy. He was looking out at the horizon as if he'd found its disappearance disturbing, and then he looked at me without so much as a hint of gloating. "Shall we go?"

"Indeedy," Diggery interjected, and an audible growl from his stomach punctuated the sentiment.

We had little choice, as I could see. I felt awkward about continuing to mislead the young mystific, particularly in light of his condition, but frankly I was so confused I didn't feel that I was in any position to dictate our course of action. So I conceded, trusting Diggery to negotiate us through whatever awkward pass might await.

The mystific started us in the right direction. We found the canal at its mouth where it fed the bay, and Diggery led to keep us brisk, but again I engaged the young mystific, this time to clarify not his confusion but rather my own.

"Was that what you'd been expecting at the pier?" I asked. "The sunset."

"I'm fairly sure it happens every night," he said, "and I suppose the pier is as close as the people can come."

"Yes, but have you any idea why they are all dressed so differently?"

He looked at me curiously. "Well, they're not all from Ludo."

"But still," I said, not comprehending. "What do you mean?"

"I mean that Ludo is a port. Lots of people come through."

"Lots of people wearing costumes?" I asked.

"Lots of people from different teams."

"Different teams? You mean teams of people who are dressed alike?"

"Well," he looked at me curiously, "yes." He reached into his pants pocket and took out a map. "The Arabs come from here." He pointed to one of the towns. "And the bears here, in Yarmuk; the monks here—" He kept on, but as I looked over his shoulder at the figure on his map, I stopped listening, so thrilled was I by the shape—it was the windblown star of the Antipodes!

"This is a map of where we are?" I interrupted.

He nodded. "And I know there are Indians here—"

"Then these are the Antipodes?"

He looked up at me, impressed, and a touch boosted that my own bearings had turned out to be worse yet than his own. "Yes. How lost are you?"

"Not at all," I said. "Quite the opposite. I have been looking for this very place." I took out my map from beneath my bedsheet to show him. "See. I have been searching for this place, to send my friends at home the games."

"Well," he nodded at the comparison, "here you are." He pointed to the northwest corner, to the town of Ludo. "But I don't know where the ghosts come from."

"Oh, you needn't worry about that," I said. "But now you're telling me the towns are populated by all these different types we've just seen?"

"Well, not *just* them. There are many teams."

"But that's very strange, don't you think?"

He nodded, but with a shrug, as if to say that it was no more strange than anything else he saw.

"But what's the explanation?" I asked.

"Well," he thought. "I only know what I believe, and what I believe could certainly be mistaken, but I think it's as you say: games."

"Games?"

"That's all I've seen since coming here." He looked at me very sympathetically. "You all look like games pieces to me."

"IS THIS THE ONE?" Diggery had stopped up ahead and was looking back at us. He was standing beside a bright red barge, not so very large, trimmed with green. At the prow above him was a handsome woman in a blue dress, with her hands resting where the two rails met, her hair silver in the moonlight, gathered behind to frame a face of perseverant wisdom and beauty. As we approached, she tipped her head gently at the young mystific and offered smiles to Diggery and me, and whatever reason we had come to her home so attired.

This was Mrs. Anna. The young mystific introduced us from the shore, perceptibly more nervous now, much in the manner of one about to give a very thoughtful gift.

We all climbed aboard and Mrs. Anna directed us out to the foredeck; then she drew the young mystific to the side for a moment. She placed her hand on his cheek. "Why have you brought them?" she asked quietly.

"They are ghosts," he said proudly. Diggery howled as evidence, but she looked round at us with doubt. She came and stood directly in front of me, and as she peered through the holes in my sheet, into my eyes, I was suddenly seized by her expression and the form it took upon her brow. I thought to myself, I have seen these eyes before—a grey-blue, lit from within, and their countenance, so true and firm and searching. I know these eyes, I thought, and though I couldn't think of where, I still was filled with contrition that we had come on such false pretense. She opened her palm to me and I gave her my hand from beneath my sheet, prepared to extend my most profound apology and to assure her that we intended no harm, but she spoke first: "I am very sorry."

Upon hearing this, the young mystific turned abruptly and faced the water, nearly sick with the realisation that once again, for all his good intention, he'd been mistaken. My heart ached for him and for shame.

"No," I said. "*I* am sorry. It should never have come—"

"There was talk of food," Diggery interrupted.

Mrs. Anna looked at him with a stern curiosity at first, which gave way to an only cordial grin. "Of course," she said, and I was smitten by the familiarity of her voice as well. She turned back and stilled me with her luminous eyes. "And you?"

"If it wouldn't be too much of an imposition."

"No," she shook her head.

"But will your friend join us?" I nodded towards the young mystific, who was hunched over the prow as if he'd just been clubbed in the gut. Mrs. Anna shook her head doubtfully, and then directed us to the afterdeck.

There was a table and two benches. I removed my linen, and she lit candles for us. She set out bowls, and then as I watched her ladle us both ample helpings of hasenpfeffer, I tried again to think of where it was I could have seen her, but she left us too quickly; as soon as we'd been served, she excused herself to go console her friend.

But for my hunger, I'm sure I wouldn't have been able to down a bite, I felt so awful—but the stew was delicious. Diggery and I gobbled it up like two beasts, or two scolded children finally permitted the meals they'd been deprived for their roughhousing. Diggery poked me every so often from underneath his sheet and chuckled at our fortune as we sopped up all the broth with Mrs. Anna's bread.

When we were through, she returned with a bowl of fruit, and she brought me a large map of the Antipodes as well, nearly the size of our table. She said the young mystific had mentioned my interest, and then she excused herself again. She said that she'd been having trouble sleeping lately, and she was now going to prepare for bed.

Her graciousness was a torture to my profound compunction; her eyes and bearing an equal torment to my memory—but I did make use of her map, not knowing when next I'd have the opportunity of such detailed reference. So while Diggery devoured some of the native fruit, I made note of all the rivers and towns and forests, and I shall send you all a copy as well with this, so you may keep better track of my whereabouts.

As you can therefore see, it took a bit for me to finish, but when I was through, I excused myself from Diggery and, quietly as I could, made my way round to the foredeck to see if the young mystific was still at the prow. I wanted to apologise for having taken such advantage of his condition, but as I crept along the side rail, I passed a small window at my feet. It was open just a crack to let in air, to a room in which I could see a single candle was lit. The light it shed was nearest upon a vase of tulips, which stood upon a table next to a bed, and on the bed I saw Mrs. Anna. She was lying on her back, looking up towards the ceiling. Her white hair was spread against the pillow beneath her head. Her hands were rested at her heart, and I was stopped just long enough by the beauty of this image that I could see her mouth was open and moving faintly. She was praying, and suddenly my heart began to race, for though the movement of her lips was faint, and the light extremely dim, and though the night air was hushing my ears, still I could hear the words, for I remembered them. They were a prayer to her son, a prayer that his soul might rest in heaven—and I knew now where I'd met her blue-grey eyes before: in the mercenary's, and that I'd heard her voice in his as well, within his dreams.

I nearly fell from the side of the boat, but quick as I could, I staggered to the front. The young mystific was sitting dejectedly in a chair at the prow, staring out at the canal.

"Excuse me," I said, breathless, but he did not turn round. "What is the dream that haunts Mrs. Anna?"

At first he did not answer.

"Please," I said.

"You've had your meal." He spoke to the water disgustedly.

"I know, I know, and I am sorry. I am very sorry you were misled, but I think you may have done remarkably well in bringing us here, better than you could possibly have hoped. But you must tell me—how is she haunted?"

The young mystific turned and his face looked ashen in the blue night. "Is it during the lie or after that you most enjoy mockery?"

"But I swear to you, I am not mocking. I think I may have seen her son."

The young mystific looked back out at the canal. He looked for a good while, and I'm sure he wished that I would simply go, but in my answer I do believe he perceived the chance of helping his kind caretaker, and this was too much for his own discouragement to thwart. So finally he spoke, but still as to the water. "She lost her son when he was a little boy. He went skating off after the men to fight the Vikings when the cold trapped their boats in ice, and he never came back. She's been searching for him ever since, but in her nightmare a spirit came to her and told her he was burning."

I gripped the rail. "Yes, but he's not, you see. I have just come from him."

The young mystific looked back at me with a pained, uncertain expression. "Why are you saying these things?"

"I'm saying them because they're true. He saved our lives."

His eyes softened. "And is that what you would tell her?"

"I would. I certainly would."

"And would you tell her he was well?"

I looked at him and I was stopped short. Could I tell her he was well? I thought of the last I'd seen the mercenary, a bug on the ocean, rowing away. I thought of his deep sleep and endless battles, and I wondered if such news would be more welcome, if the thought of him in his tiny boat out amidst the mountains and valleys of the cruel and untamed sea was any better than the thought of a little boy in a dragon's belly. "No," I said.

The young mystific stood up. "Then I'd ask you to leave." For a moment he seemed almost threatening. "And take your friend."

I could hardly blame him. I turned and made my way back around to the dining area, dazed at the onslaught of so much revelation and my utter helplessness to put a single shred of it to use. The light in Mrs. Anna's bedroom was out, but when we reached the afterdeck, Diggery was still sitting at the table, still in his sheet, gnawing away at the stringy core of something like a pear. He looked up when he saw us. "Boo."

"Diggery, we've been asked to leave."

He nodded expectantly and stood up. From beneath his sheet his hands stole two more pears from Mrs. Anna's bowl, and then we made our way out to the banks, with the young mystific following behind.

There we parted. Diggery looked off in the direction of the pier. "Th'pose I should be headed back to the boat."

"Yes."

"Looks like you've found yourself quite a place to visit, though."

"So it seems."

"Well, that's good, then. Heck of a time getting here, after all." He swiped at my elbow and then saluted, and then he toddled off, giggling, a little bowlegged ghost. As I watched him go, my feelings were oddly bittersweet. Such a rascal he was, such a scoundrel, and yet if not for Diggery . . . none of this.

Behind me, the young mystific had taken the warp round his waist and was starting down the bank, hauling the barge behind. I came up beside him. "I want you to know," I said, "I understand your resentment entirely, and I am very sorry." The young mystific kept walking as if I weren't there. "I have given you an unkind turn, I know, but I wish you would believe me when I say: I *have* seen her son, and I know that he hears her prayers when he's asleep." The young mystific still did not look at me, but I persisted. ''And I am going to make you a promise, though.'' I tore a loose thread from the fringe of my bedsheet. ''Do you see? I am going to tie this string to my own finger, and I shall keep it there to remind me of you and Mrs. Anna, that I owe you, and that if I should find a way to make it up to you, I shall. I promise: If I should discover anything more about her son, anything to put away her nightmare, I shall be reminded, by this string round my finger, to go to the canals and wait for you.''

The young mystific did not seem to hear. He kept walking silently, and I knew that I should let him go. I stopped and he plodded off like a grave and gentle ox, with the barge floating obediently behind, and Mrs. Anna warm inside—asleep, I hoped. I said a prayer that she should sleep well tonight and never mind the ghosts again, or the two scalawags who'd so abused her hospitality.

Then, of perfect puzzlement, I found myself a place on some soft grass beside a tree. I tied the thread round my finger, and then lay back beneath the slow, serene stars to rest my weary mind. I thought of you, and how far I had come. And then I cannot even tell you if it was a dream or not, but that if it was a dream, then it has yet to end, of four glass marbles rolling up and circling my body like the eyes of two wise cats, wondering as they gazed upon me lying there, ''But what sort of a piece is this, then?''

The young mystific is right. Games. But I will let you know as I learn more.

Good night,
Gus

FIVE

THE LAAGER AT BLOEMFONTEIN

(The Origami Knight)

All twelve of the letters that Dr. Uyterhoeven sent Sonja to read to the guests of the chess garden were composed in South Africa. He wrote the first at the Cape. He wrote the second three days later in Beaufort West, and the final ten were all composed in the Orange River Colony, at the refugee camp near Bloemfontein, where he had gone to serve in a nominally medical capacity.

The doctor's interest in the African subcontinent was long-standing and visceral. The blood being spilled there at the turn of the century was like his own, primarily Dutch and English, and it was also there, thirty-three years before, in Griqualand West, that his scientific career ended for all intents and purposes, and he embarked upon a life of faith. Ever since then, he'd kept a close eye on the conflicting interests of the Boers, the native Africans, and the British government, relying mostly on reports and editorials that friends would send him from London, since the coverage provided in the American press was scant.

He had not been surprised, therefore, when hostilities between the Boers and the English flared up again in 1899, nor was he convinced of their ostensible cause, having to do with the franchise rights of British residents of the Transvaal, or *Uitlanders,* as the Boers called them. It was no secret that Britain was becoming increasingly threatened by the challenge that both the United States and Germany posed her global economic supremacy. The quickest fix clearly was to bolster the Bank of England's dwindling gold reserve, and there was gold in South Africa.

Unfortunately for the British, the current owners of the land in which this treasure was buried—that is, the Boers of the South African Republic—were not a people of great capitalist or imperialist ambition, and were not inclined to undertake the measures necessary to get at the deeper reserves which were known to lie within the hillsides. This, went the common wisdom, would require a more concerted effort between prospectors and local governments. There would need to be highly complex engineering, which meant more capital and more labor, which meant better transportation, sewage, and police; in other words, a fairly thorough restructuring of society in the region, for which the local governors—already fat from the sale of transportation, alcohol, and dynamite monopolies—saw no need. So emerged the sudden British concern for the suffrage rights of their expatriates, and war was effectively contrived.

The British were not wrong to have expected victory. Theirs was still the premier military power in the world, while the South African Republic had a mere militia. The British mistake, which Dr. Uyterhoeven noted in several letters to friends in England and Europe, was to have expected *easy* victory. The notion that Paul Krüger's knees would buckle at the mere flex of British military muscle was "tragically naïve," in the doctor's opinion. "The Boers are nothing if not obstinate, and I have the sense that Mr. Krüger is just as hungry for this brawl as all of England's coffers.''

This was true, and the Boers did, in fact, turn out to be tenacious, if not fearsome, foes. War was officially declared in the fall of 1899, and by the late spring of 1900, the Boer ranks had been effectively whittled. They were strewn about the veld in small uncoordinated bands. Their main supply routes had all been intercepted, but they remained defiant, resorting to guerrilla tactics—ambushes, train derailments, and an assortment of other subterfuges which, though they posed no great threat to the British, were definitely a nuisance, and also impossible to combat.

In the Astral winter of 1900, then, in hopes of hastening the now embarrassing conflict to its inevitable but elusive conclusion, the commander in chief of the British armed forces, Field Marshal Lord Roberts, instituted a policy which again, upon learning of it, the doctor found extremely dubious, ''both degenerate,'' in his phrase, ''and ill conceived.'' By Roberts's order, the British were to begin burning the homes and property of all the Boer commandos who remained in the veld, on the theory that with their land, livestock, and families under siege, the guerrillas would have no choice but to come in and surrender.

Unfortunately, this again both over- and underestimated the Boers, in the doctor's opinion. ''They are still essentially squatters and frontiersmen,'' he wrote, ''stubborn, resourceful, and completely unafraid of the veld.'' Far from devastating their spirit, Roberts's slash-and-burn policy only hardened the Boers' posture of resistance. They remained, as the doctor put it, ''like their host, the mosquito—small, annoying, and insuperable.''

By late winter the British were forced to face the consequence of Roberts's miscalculation—the legion of homeless Boer women and children. Plans for the first refugee camp were first reported in early August. A week later, the map of the Antipodes appeared on the dictionary stand in Dr. Uyterhoeven's library, and three weeks after that, on September 3, the doctor left for the Cape.

He had not expected much difficulty finding a place to make himself useful. The camps, or laagers, as they were called, were administered through the two new colonies in the Transvaal and the Orange River, and staffed primarily by civilians. It is true that, as he was both Dutch and English, his loyalties were unclear, but in a war as generally welcoming to mercenary interests as this one, Uyterhoeven had not imagined there being much objection to the services of another doctor. It is also true that he was old—seventy-seven years, and a good half century removed from the sort of medical practice required at the camps—but he was to all appearances still a remarkably fit specimen and, as his letters home would indicate, possessed an alert, if peculiar, mind.

Even so, his first application, to serve at the Mafeking camp in the Transvaal, was denied because of his age. He applied next to the Orange River Colony administration, to the office of Colonel Hamilton Goold Adams, and even there his application was not accepted until first a letter of recommendation and then a second, of reprimand, arrived from Lloyd George's own office in London. Uyterhoeven was assigned to the camp at Bloemfontein in early October.

The laager at Bloemfontein was the largest of the ORC camps, a village of white-bell tents, numbered in military style, spotting the southern slope of a brown-baked kopje just outside the city proper. Not much thought had been put into its design. Like all the laagers, it had been modeled after the military encampments of British battalions. The British military camps, however, were never intended to remain more than a week at a given location, and were always reasonably clean and well aired as a result. The laagers, on the other hand, were situated permanently, to fester in the sun, overcrowded and defenseless against disease. When Dr. Uyterhoeven arrived at Bloemfontein, there were nearly eighteen hundred refugees at the camp, and epidemics of all kinds were rampant—measles, whooping cough, enteritis, diphtheria, typhoid, pneumonia, dysentery, bronchitis, and malaria. Rations were scarce. There was no milk for babies or children, and no vegetables, just meal, and occasionally, to reward those families whose fathers had come in from the veld to surrender, meat. There was no soap, no tap water, inadequate latrines, scanty fuel, no forage, and too few brick boilers for drinking water. On top of all this, the staff were pitifully undermanned. In addition to Uyterhoeven, there was only one other doctor at Bloemfontein, named Peter Sullivan, aided by three nurses and one superintendent. Dr. Uyterhoeven had not expected much better, but upon his arrival, he wrote his old friend Rudolf Virchow: "I can see already, my purpose here shall be more to minister death than save life."

The doctor's daily regime was simple, then: to visit as many tents as he was able and be a consoling presence. There was little he could offer in the way of medicine. He brought quinine when it was available, and reminded the Boer mothers to keep the flaps of their tents open during the day, to boil their water before drinking, and to eat only the food the camps supplied. When his day was through, he would return to his own tent to read from the small collection of books he'd brought with him, to pray, and to conceive the stories he would send back to Dayton.

Of the eleven letters Uyterhoeven composed at Bloemfontein, only the last two bear his own hand. Two were transcribed by James Thaibes, a colonel from Major General Pretyman's office; two by a minister, Sylvan Berthol, and two by one of the laager nurses, whose name has been lost.

The first of the doctor's amanuenses, however, was a fourteen-year-old Boer girl named Alexandra De Villiers. Her family's experience that year was sadly common among the refugees. The De Villiers had lived in a farm just outside the town of Reitz. In the fall her father had left to become a commando and fight the British. She had neither seen nor heard from him since then, and in mid-August, she, her mother, and her brother had been forced to flee their farm in the light of British torches; they were, in fact, among the first victims of Roberts's policy. For one month they'd traveled out on the veld in a caravan of other displaced Boer families, headed east. On several occasions their party had been harassed and looted by marauding bands of Africans, and in May they were picked up by a British column. They spent one week among animals in an open truck at a railway siding near Kroonstad, and then were transferred to Bloemfontein the first week of September. Since then, Alexandra's family had subsisted on meal and water. They had eaten no meat, at first because there was none to be had, and then because her mother had refused the portions they were given, to protest the implication that her husband had been captured or was dead.

Dr. Uyterhoeven came to know the De Villiers because Alexandra's brother, Beno, had contracted malaria soon after their arrival at the camp. He had suffered remittent fevers at least twice per week since, so the doctor had come by as often as he was able to check on him and to bring them all quinine. During one of Beno's less severe fevers, the doctor had shown him how to fold a sheet of paper into the shape of a crane. The crane, he'd said, would bring good health, and it appeared to do just that. Beno took to origami with a fervor that seemed, for the time being, to supersede the malaise of his illness. The doctor brought him whole stacks of British military stationery to practice on, and showed him several other designs as well, boats and birds with flapping wings. Beno's inspiration was to attach them all to strings, tie the strings to sticks, and hang them like mobiles from the struts of their tent.

Beno's sister, Alexandra, had availed herself of the stationery as well. She and Beno were among the better educated of the Boer children. Their mother had been a teacher at one of the English-speaking schools in Reitz, so they spoke fluent English. Alexandra in particular was an avid reader and writer, and she asked the doctor if he had pens as well as paper, as she wanted to keep a journal of what had happened to them since being driven from home, to save and then give her father when he returned from the bush. Better than just a pen, Dr. Uyterhoeven brought Alexandra a diary of her own, whose first entry is October 17, 1900, Alexandra's fourteenth birthday. Her brother gave her a butterfly.

According to her journal, Beno was no longer content with just winged creatures, though. His great ambition was to make a paper man, a commando to fight the British. The doctor knew of no such design, however. The closest figure to a man for which the doctor knew the folds was that of a cow. He had shown it to Beno, and Beno had studied the problem over the course of several weeks, trying different folds, altering the design little by little in hopes of somehow turning a paper cow into a paper man. He worked on it every day, and every day the doctor came by to check and see how he was coming along.

On October 25 Beno was apparently closing in. It was that evening that the doctor asked Mrs. De Villiers if he might borrow her children until bedtime. He said that he needed their help to send his friends at home a gift.

Beno and Alexandra had been to the doctor's tent several times before, with other children at the camp, for tea and to play his phonograph. His tent was the last in their row, and though it wasn't any bigger than theirs, it was the doctor's alone. He had his own grate for boiling water and a trunk for clothes, a shelf of books, a small stack of phonograph records, a desk, a rocking chair, a standing kerosene lamp, a lantern, a painting of a man in a rowboat which he'd suspended in midair, and a small picture frame with a photograph in it, of a beautiful woman with blond hair, dark brow, and light, wide-set eyes, and a little boy beside her, who he'd said were his wife and son, long ago.

The doctor offered his guests quinine, as usual, and took some himself, in combination with gin he'd had sent especially from England, since the Johannesburg liquor was well known to be undrinkable. He let Alexandra crank the phonograph. She picked a piece with voices singing in Italian, and then sat down in the doctor's rocking chair, to listen and sip her tonic, while the doctor and Beno conducted one final examination of the paper commando. The two of them were like surgeons, going over all the folds and discussing the changes. Finally, then, after six or seven more sheets of stationery had been torn square and subjected to some final experiments, the doctor and Beno had more than a passable commando—in their opinion, a hero.

Alexandra conceded that now there was at least more trace of man than cow.

The doctor asked Beno to fold one more commando by the same design, and then he turned to Alexandra. He said that he wanted to send a letter to his friends at home, a story which he'd begun the night before but which he'd had to interrupt because his hand had grown too weak. He showed her how it trembled, and then he said that several days before he had chanced to see her penmanship. He'd observed that it was of a very high and handsome quality, and wondered if she would be kind enough to help him end his letter. He said he suspected that his wife would be much obliged.

Alexandra said she certainly would, and the doctor thanked her in advance. Then he produced several handwritten pages from the drawer of his desk and turned his chair around. He said he thought it best that Alexandra and her brother hear the first part of his letter, the better to understand the second. So Alexandra remained in the rocker, and Beno continued folding his commando on the bed, while the doctor read them what he'd written the night before.

The Third Letter

October 24, 1900

Dear Sonja,

How is one to know, I wonder, if a backgammon counter is sleeping or if it is only resting? If it is dreaming or daydreaming, and what of its dreams—what must they contain? Beside me lies the answer—polished red, round, and perfectly still—a young counter and my newest friend. Still, I haven't the faintest idea if it is napping now, or listening in as I compose my thoughts for you.

There is so much here to understand. It's one of the reasons I've been slow to write. I haven't wanted to commit any of my impressions to words, for fear that I might round the next bend and find something there which overturns everything I'd thought I understood. For this is a more astonishing place than any of us had anticipated—more astonishing by far—though as to its essential nature, I will admit that for all I've seen since I last wrote, I cannot improve on the young mystific's assessment in Ludo: the Antipodes are indeed a land of games, strewn with every different kind of piece one can imagine, looking much the same as normal pieces do, except that here they all have life, are of life-size, and move and will and think.

But even as strange as this may be—and I assure you, it is most strange—it is also my observation that once one has come to accept this single local convention—that one's company is comprised entirely of pieces—the rest all seems to follow naturally thereof. The rules of society and conduct all make perfect—I am even tempted to say common—sense. Is it not common sense that darts should fly through the air alongside sparrows, that black fields of clover should shine beneath the sun like tar? That checkers stack, that backgammon counters roll, that dice tumble, that playing cards travel in hands or packs, and that cribbage pegs scissor down the street like stilts?

It is all, that is to say, very much as you would imagine, and the same holds true of one's impressions. I mean that my opinions of the various pieces here are the same as they have always been. The dice I observe to be an arbitrary creature. They tumble wherever they like, guided by no particular purpose; not the sort upon whom I'd stake much value or place much trust. The marbles are sleek and knowing. The playing cards are bullies, swindlers, and bluffers who, as I understand, generally inhabit the southern province of Katalin, which for that reason I shall be trying to avoid.

I have tended, as you might guess, to gravitate towards the chess pieces, who are as ever an exceedingly trustworthy ilk, duty-bound, forthright, guided by reason that I recognise and discernible calculation. And yet it isn't only this that finds me so often in their company. There is also the fact that among the chess pieces—and only the chess pieces—are what are here called "effigy" or "representational," as opposed to "totem" or "abstracts"—a fairly essential distinction to keep in mind, and which for that reason I am afraid I must take a moment to explain.

When I say "effigy," I refer to those pieces that look like something other than just a games piece. All the pieces I saw on the pier in Ludo, for instance, were effigy. They were effigy of Arabs, if you will recall, bears and monks and so forth, but I have since seen a great number of other varieties. I have seen effigy of elephants, scythed chariots, Asian foot soldiers, castles, towers, jesters, runners, buccaneers, troubadors, and Roman soldiers. Really, a chessman may be an effigy of almost anything, just so long as in addition to the appearance which it conveys, of man or beast or even god (for I have heard of these as well—teams of Greek and Roman gods!), it is also identifiably either a pawn, a bishop, a rook, a knight, a king, or a queen.

The effigy do more than just resemble other things in appearance, however. They do so in behaviour as well, thank heavens. That is to say, if a piece looks like an elephant, I have found that it probably will call and eat and act like an elephant. Likewise, the more a piece resembles a man, with human eyes and ears and arms and legs and so forth, the more it will behave like a man, and the particular man it most appears to be. If a Viking, then a Viking—and he shall live among other Vikings in a Viking's way. Again perfectly reasonable, but of inestimable comfort to me, since I cannot deny, particularly as I find myself in such an unfamiliar place, that I do derive a certain amount of reassurance from being among those who, despite the plumage of their costume or the exaggeration of their features, do at least resemble me in species. So let me simply admit that though the landscape belongs to pieces of a seemingly infinite variety, it is the map of the most civilised effigy (by which I simply mean those which most resemble man) which I have been touring, their society in which I have tended to circulate, their place-names I use; it is their world, in other words, that I have entered into—if for no other reason than because it is most like the world from which I have come.

But now let it be clear that though the effigy have predominated my experience, they are nonetheless very much in the minority here, the majority of pieces being what are called "abstracts," or "totem," which denotes the fact that they do *not* appear to be anything other than what they are. Totem simply are what they are. Dice are totem, then. Dominoes are totem. I am told that marbles are the most ancient of totem. Checkers are totem, and many chess pieces are totem as well, as you yourselves can attest. A Staunton pawn, for instance, does not appear to be anything other than a pawn (aside perhaps from a bedpost), so it is regarded as a totem as well, as are a great variety of other chess pieces. The glass set that Professor Virchow recently sent from Bruges, as another instance, would here be recognised as totem, since none of the pieces in that set could truly be mistaken for anything but what it is, which is a chessman.

Of course, it is precisely this selfsame quality of the totem which has hampered my getting to know them better. I simply don't feel that I have much in common with them, at least as compared to the effigy. Totem have no eyes, after all (with the exception of the chess knights, who almost all look like horse busts, officially qualifying them, I should think, as effigy, and yet I don't believe they are), likewise (with the exception of the knights) none of the totem has a mouth to speak with, or ears to hear, or a nose to smell with. I assume they can touch and feel, since they can move, but that seems very little on which to forge real sympathy or communication. So, notwithstanding the perceptible influence which they can exert on a room—and the chess totem in particular have a way of making one feel slightly crude and foolish—most of the totem remain fundamentally enigmatic and inscrutable to me, which may help explain why it was not till yesterday that I truly befriended my first, and was rewarded by the extraordinary events which have finally compelled my pen back to paper.

But before coming to them, and at the risk of seeming a bother, let me simply offer a chart of pieces myself, on the chance that my prose has served better to obscure than to clarify.

We have, then:

THE ANTIPODES
which is populated entirely by
ALL GAMES PIECES
which may be distinguished as either

EFFIGY	OR	TOTEM
whom I believe are only chess pieces, and only those which look like something other than a chess piece: e.g., man, beast, plant, edifice, etc.		which denotes any piece, including certain chess pieces, which looks like what it is and nothing else: e.g., marbles, dice, checkers, cribbage pegs, Stauntons, etc.

So. If I have had any purpose in my travels here other than to explore, it has been to find you all a gift. I know I promised you the native games, but given the circumstances which abide here and the effort which it would therefore require to make good this pledge—of packaging an entire continent and shoving it through the ocean to you—I trust you will forgive my reneging.

Still, just because I cannot send you games per se, that is no reason that you shouldn't have something to show for my presence, so as I have been making my way from one board to the next—''board'' being the name by which most civilised sets refer to their townships, fittingly—I have been casting about for suggestions as to where I might find something distinct and local to send you. More than once, I have been referred to the establishment—a rook actually—run by a pawn named Eugene, who is said to have a good eye, and apparently collects all different sorts of goods from round the land. Eugene's rook is just outside a town called Macaroni, which, as I believe you can see on your map, is located south of Ludo and farther inland. So I have been wending my way, with as many interruptions as whim and curiosity dictate, in a southerly direction.

Specifically, I had been on a road called Triboli yesterday, passing through the province of Shatranj, when a red backgammon counter came up from behind to join me. To the naked eye, it may have seemed an indistinct piece—a flat red marble wheel is all—but such are the limitations of the naked eye, for my more intuitive appraisal of this counter was of an individual every bit as distinct and idiosyncratic as any piece or person that I have come across, of an open, playful, and generous nature which I would also contend, if asked, was youthful.

Naturally, being a disk, the counter was more swift than I, and so as we became acquainted, it tended to roll all about the road, tracing figure eights and twisting wreaths; it would circle back behind me and then race ahead, and was even able, if I lengthened my step and slowed my gait, to slip between my legs, in and out like a puppy.

So we made our way, without much mind of time or destination, until at a certain spot along the way, and marked by no sign or fork that I could see, the counter rolled off the road into the ditch and stopped. I stopped as well, thinking that perhaps my friend had lost its way. I waited for it to climb back up, but it remained. I beckoned it to return. I actually called to it as if it might hear, but it answered by turning two more rotations away from the road, then stopping again—waiting, it seemed, for me.

Well, among the greatest pleasures of being here, I find, is that I've no appointments to keep, so I did follow the counter into the ditch and through the brush. We traveled into the countryside, I the happy subject of what seemed to be the counter's whim, and soon found ourselves in an orchard of lemon trees and another tree whose fruit I would compare to certain descriptions I have read of the avocado. On we ventured, so far and long that even our shadows began to stretch and yawn for evening, until finally we came in view of one particular tree, so distinctive and arresting I knew when I saw it that we'd come to our destination.

It rose up three lengths higher than those surrounding and was the size and shape of an oak; at first glance, as fine a tree for climbing as one could hope to find, with strong outstretched limbs shrouded everywhere by leaves which were thick and dark and waxy like magnolias. But as I came closer, I could see what made this tree so magnificent was neither its foliation nor its physique, but its bloom, which was not a flower or a fruit but candles; candles everywhere throughout its crown, on every limb and elbow, high and low; candles, all ivory-colored and standing up the length of human hands, each one slightly tilted to its own attitude but yielding a straighter line of hardened candle drip beneath, traced on every leaf or twig which interrupted the descent of its melted wax; everywhere the stalks hung down like icicles, and as we passed through the last of the orchard trees, I saw that down beneath them, all across the moss and twisted roots that surrounded the base, were hundreds upon hundreds of amber dripcastles—an entire kingdom there, rising up no higher than my hip, the colour and translucence of honey, and comprised entirely of candle drips, layer upon hardened layer, each applied with such whim and patience I recognised the hand of nature and not man.

I wanted to go to see them and walk among them, but I wasn't sure I should. The red counter had stopped just outside the edge of this golden kingdom, and a certain boundary was suggested by a ring of seven stone benches which encircled the umbrage, save for where a small creek ran along the far side from us.

I looked back at my friend to see if it might give some indication whether I was free to invade this perimeter, but there beside him now was another counter, and two more a bit farther around—one green, one white, one brown. They'd come up through the orchard and taken their places alongside my friend with an equally meditative aspect. I thought perhaps I should do the same. I took a seat on one of the stone benches, and as darkness descended, I watched as more and more counters emerged from the landscape. I could just barely see them rolling in from the trees, shadows floating up the creek and tumbling up the banks, and all dutifully taking their places around the tree. They seemed to be waiting, though I'd still no sense what for, until—out of thin air—a candle on the nearest bough above me lit. How so, I hadn't the faintest, but then another on the far side did the same, and then another, and another. And as more of the counters settled in their positions, more of the candles began to light. One by one the little flames ascended higher and higher up the boughs, their excitation here and there declared by the scamper of squirrels, or the chirp and brief round flight of birds who made their nests nearby.

Here the doctor paused and put down his pages. Beno had long since finished folding the second commando. It lay beside the first on the cot. The doctor asked which one Beno preferred. Beno chose the first, so the doctor put it aside for him and took the second back to his desk. Beno and Alexandra both came up behind him to watch, and an air of concentration descended. The doctor lifted the glass from his lamp, wet his fingertips in his drink, and then very carefully put the tip of the commando's left arm directly to the burning wick. As soon as it caught, the doctor held the figure out away from them. Then, just before the flame reached its torso, he waved it out, then dabbed the paper dry. He said nothing, and Alexandra and Beno watched in silence as with equal care the doctor lit the commando's right leg. Again he held it up, and again, before the flame could reach the torso, he blew it out and dabbed the cinders with his fingers.

The commando was barely recognisable now, with just one arm and a leg. The doctor laid it down in front of him, and proceeded to unfold what was left, until the paper lay open and crumpled, burnt at opposite corners.

Next, the doctor removed a pocket watch from his vest, a silver-cased watch with a chain, and opened it on the desk. He took a handkerchief from his jacket and wrapped it around the face. In his desk jar was a letter opener, whose duller tip he placed against the covered watch face. He asked Beno to hand him a book from his shelf. Beno chose one of many called *Arcana.* The doctor took it in hand and very swiftly, very abruptly, spiked the letter opener. They could all hear the crystal of the watch face break. The doctor removed the cloth, turned the watch over, and tapped the shards into the cup of burned paper.

Finally he turned to Alexandra and asked if she was ready. She said she was, so the doctor stood up and gave her his chair. He took the burned paper and glass shards and placed them carefully on the cot for Beno, then set a stack of stationery in front of Alexandra—it was military issue, from the office of Major General Pretyman, military governor of Bloemfontein. Alexandra took her pen, set the well in its place, and readied herself. The doctor poured another glass of gin, straight, and sat back in his rocking chair. Then, while Beno lay on the cot awaiting his next instructions, Dr. Uyterhoeven recited the rest of his story, and Alexandra wrote it down as fast as she could, just legibly enough for her to read the following day, when she would copy the whole thing over for the sake of the doctor's wife.

He continued:

As I sat watching this luminous twilight bloom ascend the tree, I was suddenly startled by a movement in the boughs, of something larger than a bird or a squirrel rushing up through the branches. I couldn't see it well, it moved so quickly, but it was dark and very agile, and much larger in size than its lightness on the boughs would have suggested. It looked almost human, sitting there quietly like an Indian. What is it? I wondered, and was close to calling up when just then the flicker of several more candles drove it even higher. It climbed as high as the tree would allow, and just barely in my sight.

All the candles appeared to have lighted now, and darkness had descended about most of the sky. I wondered if this creature might be trapped there all night, but just as I stood to call up, I was stopped short again by the splash of something coming across the river—or two things actually, which were not counters at all, I could tell, for I could hear their lumbering footfalls coming up the banks. I sat back down and held my breath as two great bears entered the glowing, golden kingdom of dripcastles. They each wore crowns askew on their heads, one with points—who was the queen—and the other with a velvet top—who was the king.

Together they sat down by one of the larger dripcastles and began licking the two highest spires, bobbing their brown heads up and down, lapping away as though these minarets were made of rock candy, or maple sugar, or something very good, something very very good and sweet, for it wasn't long before their craving got the best of them and they each broke off the castle towers with their paws. They started chewing on them like dogs with biscuits, grunting with pleasure, chomping on their cones. They lay on their backs, so lost in honey reverie that they did not even notice as now a fourth character joined the scene.

It quite startled me, in fact, as I'd not heard it coming. It entered from the orchard, through the circle of counters—a figure all of white, with white face and hands; a knight, I recognised, of human build and proportion, but for some difference which I couldn't yet discern, he was moving so swiftly.

He passed the bears, actually touching them both hello, then made his way straight to the trunk. He looked up into the boughs with something of a craftsman's purpose, intending to climb, and apparently unaware that anyone was watching. Like a squirrel, then, and just as fast, he scrambled up the bark and out upon the lowest limb, lengthwise peering at the nearest candle. The branch strained not at all beneath him, though, even as he reached out to coax the candle from its cup. Something was very strange about this fellow, something strange and marvelous, but I couldn't tell what it was until he'd plucked the candle from its stem and raised the burning wick up near his face.

He blew gently at the flame, teasing it to flicker, but I could see his features by its golden light, so creased and straight, so flat and smooth, and by his reverence for the flame: he was made of paper, folded of a single sheet, like rice or tracing paper—an origami knight. He reached to coax a second cup and candle from their place, and I could see better—a more exquisite creature never was, in gesture as well as feature. Every move he made, the turn of his wrist or tilt of his neck, was perfectly enunciated by the flex of some tiny crease or fold. And so I watched in awe as now, with candles in each hand and all the grace of one who has no weight to sprain his landing, he dropped from the bough like a leaf.

At the foot of the tree, the bears had been munching away at their spires in happy oblivion. The origami knight approached them again with a distinctly chivalrous air, plucked one of his candles from its cup, and offered the leafy saucer to the queen. The king seized it first. The queen groaned that he should share, but the king would not. He licked the dripping from the white knight's paper hand, then rolled onto his back with the cup in all four paws and poured its warm syrup into his mouth. The origami knight plucked the second candle and once again offered the cup to the queen. She accepted graciously. She sipped from it as though it were tea; then when it was dry, she gently plucked the petals and chewed them one by one like the leaves of an artichoke.

The origami knight, meanwhile, had taken his two candles over to one of the dripcastles—one closer to me, in fact. He'd knelt down and was melting the wax with his flames, holding them against its highest spire, and I understood not even so much from his actions as from his manner that something must be hidden inside. He worked anxiously, several times looking over his shoulder as he passed the small flames over the yielding surface. Twice he looked in my direction, but apparently from within the glare of the candletree he could not see out.

Nor did he see, up in the tree itself, the shadowed figure lurking there. It had descended from its perch. In fact, from the moment of the knight's appearance, it had been crawling down branch by branch, and was now paused midway, peering through the leaves and candles at him.

I could see him better now. It was distinctly the shape of a man, and he had something long and thin in his hand. I wasn't sure what, but then he pulled something from over his shoulder—a long tinder—and suddenly I became alarmed, for as he reached out to light its end by the nearest candle, in the sudden flare of light I could see this was an arrow in his hand, and that he'd a bow as well.

I couldn't think what I should do, whether I should make my presence known, but at this very moment the king bear stood up and made his way over to the trunk. He had no notion what was taking place above him; he and the queen had finished with their cups and simply wanted more of the tree's confection. The queen was standing now as well, with her mouth turned up expectantly, and the king was taking measure of the tree trunk like a wrestler. I looked up at the dark archer. He'd stretched his arrow against the bow, and now was training its fiery tip upon the hunched back of the unsuspecting knight, but just then, just as he took his final aim, the king bear wrapped his giant paws round the trunk and started tugging back and forth. Instantly all the leaves began to tremble, the candle flames all wavered, and everywhere throughout the canopy there began a light rain of candle drip.

Then suddenly there was a mad thrashing up in the boughs. The queen gasped as a flaming arrow came whistling through the leaves and spiked the castle next to the white paper knight, who turned up just in time to see the dark assassin come tripping down the branches like an ornament falling from a Christmas tree. He struck at the king bear's feet like a kernel of popped corn, and I could see very clearly now—he was precisely like the white knight, made all of paper, but the sheet from which he'd been folded was the colour of coal.

He scrambled to his feet at once, drew a second arrow from his quiver, and lit it by the nearest candle in the boughs. Both the king and the queen bears recoiled from the flame, and with a single sweep of his thin torch, the black paper knight was rid of them. They bounded off on all fours, howling into the orchard.

Slowly then, the black knight turned to address his white opponent, who now was standing before his melted castle, holding his candles out like two stilettos.

"Timothy."

"Odin," replied the white knight.

The black knight—Odin—pointed to the melted castle with his flaming arrow, and his voice was thick and dry, like whispers. "What is inside?"

Timothy stepped back for him to see—as yet only a simple wooden handle was exposed. Odin gestured for Timothy to continue, so Timothy knelt down again and applied his two flames to the wax.

Slowly it began to melt away. Odin stepped closer to see, and suddenly Timothy flung one of his candles at him. Odin dodged it easily and, unoffended, bowed. ''Now take it out,'' he said. Timothy, unashamed, obliged. He took the handle and pulled it from the syrupy wax.

I could not see what it was at first, but as Timothy ran the flame of his remaining candle along its edge, the shape came clear: it was a hand mirror.

Odin held out his hand. ''Give it to me.''

Timothy shook his head.

''It's no use.'' Odin extended the tip of his burning arrow, but Timothy only began to circle slowly. He held the mirror behind his back and I could see how heavily it hung from his delicate paper hands.

Odin did not wait. He swept his flaming arrow at Timothy like a swordsman, but the white knight jumped and tumbled towards the tree trunk, mirror still in hand. Odin lunged again, and this time caught Timothy's hand. The flame licked up to his arm before he rolled behind the trunk and frantically beat his limb against the ground to put it out.

Odin spoke as to the tree, which stood between them now. ''I don't mean you harm. Just leave the mirror there.'' Timothy did not move. ''I'll tell no one you were here. I'll tell them I found it, and I'll show them where.'' Odin waited, but Timothy's reply came not in words. With his one good arm, he tossed the mirror up into the air, then scrambled up the trunk to catch it upon the first limb.

Odin looked up at him with both pity and admiration. ''You are a fool,'' he said, but Timothy only crept farther out along the limb, the mirror now swinging pendulously from his good hand.

Odin began to laugh, but then without warning leapt up with his arrow still aflame. Quick as a flash, Timothy scrambled up to the second branch, and again they stared at each other, for a moment perfectly still. ''Very well,'' said Odin, and which of them moved next, I cannot say, the other answered so quickly. Like lightning they bolted from their places and raced through the candletree after each other, faster than the light from Odin's arrow could follow. Birds flew squawking from their nests. Whole stalks of wax came falling down onto the castles below, but neither knight ever teetered or was unsure. For the briefest moments they would pause to taunt each other, poised on the very fingertips of boughs. Then they'd dash up or down while all the burning wicks yearned after them.

Then, three-quarters of the way up the tree, all stopped. A last candle stalk fell and broke softly on the moss, and this time it seemed that Odin had finally won. He'd chased Timothy out onto a high branch from which there appeared to be no escape. Timothy's chest was heaving from the burden of the mirror, but he had one last plan in mind. Very deliberately he took one more step. The branch bowed heavily. "What are you doing?" asked Odin. Timothy held the mirror out into the darkness as far as he could, gripping it by the fingertips of his one good hand. "Don't!" came Odin's cry, but Timothy only looked back at him, nodded, and then tossed the mirror high up into the darkness.

Before it left Timothy's hand, Odin had already dropped his arrow and flown down the tree. Out into the orchard he dashed, to try to break the mirror's fall, but whether he arrived in time I could not see, it was so dark. My eyes remained on Timothy, who'd no sooner let the mirror go than plucked a candle from its cup and then himself jumped headlong out into the blackness, down towards the spot where he knew Odin and the mirror would meet. Down plunged his tiny flame into the night, and where he landed, I could see only the tip of his candle, thrashing round and back like a furious lightning bug caught in a jar. Then for an instant it seemed to disappear. All was black and silent. I heard a gasp, and suddenly a great conflagration burst out, the shape of a man consumed by flame. It staggered into the orchard, arms and legs ablaze, then fell to the ground and was gone. All was dark again but for a grey cloud of smoke which rose into the sky, and just beneath it a fragile ashen bracelet floating up and up, hovering there above the trees, and then falling down like a feather.

Whoever had survived was still in the brush. I could hear him gasping for air. Quickly I stood up from my bench and stepped into the lightshed of the tree.

"Hello," I called out. "Hello, do you need any help?" I listened, but there was only the wind in the orchard. I took a step towards the brush, and then, at the light's edge, an arm appeared, all black and charred. I went to help. I lifted him up, and I could see now, it was Timothy—but how light he was, he might have blown from my arms. I carried him beneath the tree and laid him on the levelest surface I could find. His left arm was all ashes. He'd lost his right leg entirely, and he was having difficulty breathing. "Is there anything I can do?" I asked.

He looked down at his injuries and shook his head, then turned away slightly. He extended his blackened arm and clenched his fist. A terrible low gasp issued from his paper mouth, and the entire limb collapsed on the moss in ashes.

I heard him whisper, "The mirror, please."

It was still out in the orchard. I could see the flame of his candle flickering on the ground, and found the mirror just to the side—a very plain mirror, with a round face and a handle made of wood. I brought it back beneath the tree.

"Is it broken?" murmured Timothy.

"No," I said. "It seems to be perfectly intact."

He nodded, then looked out into the black orchard as if others might be out there waiting for him. "A favor?" he asked.

"Yes?"

"Break it."

For a moment I hesitated; it seemed like a strange desire after so fierce a battle.

"Please," he whispered.

I took the mirror over to the creek and dropped a heavy stone three times on the glass before it shattered. Then I brought the mirror back to Timothy. He looked at the fractured reflection of his face and his whole body seemed to ease.

"Now." He looked up into the boughs of the tree, and his voice was just the breeze now, guided through his body and out his mouth.

''I need you to cup away my cinders.'' He reached down to touch where his hip was burnt open. The edges were all puckered, flaked, and ashen.

I took my kerchief and wrapped it round my fingers to pick a shard from the mirror frame, then with its sharp edge I sliced all the black and useless paper from Timothy's body.

When I had finished, he looked down at his open hip and shoulder and nodded his thanks. Then he extended his good arm out to the side, opened his hand, and stared at it a moment. The main seam of his palm flipped open, the fingers unfolded, and the whole of his hand lay creased and open like foil.

He looked up at me, and his voice as he spoke was weaker yet. He had to wait for the breeze. ''I am going to unfold now,'' he said, ''and try to find another form.'' He paused again, then as the limbs creaked above us, he instructed me in whispers: ''When I am opened, place the shards upon me and stay the night. If I've not returned by morning, take the last burning candle from the tree and set the page afire.'' He laid his head back gently on the moss.

''Very well,'' I said, and I waited. The whole night and every candle in the candletree waited, and then it began. Like the petals of a flower opening, the seams came undone at his elbow and at his shoulder. I looked down at his good leg and the same became of his paper foot. His ankle and calf opened, his knee unfolded. All the intricate pleats which had provided his agility, the origami knight spread out by will, until the only features of his body that remained were his torso and his head. One last time he looked straight up to see the glowing tree above him, lest he not return, then laid his head back down, and with only the sound of paper scuffing against itself—no cry or whimper—his chest opened out, his neck and then his face unwrapped, and he was gone.

I looked down at the paper now—an envelope torn brutally open, with nothing inside. As he'd asked, I placed the shards of the mirror on top, then sat and waited, unaware of how long it should take for his life to leave or to return. All around me, the candle drips began to fall on their own, down along their stalks and onto the castles below, and though I'm sure that every night they do the same, this time they did seem to be weeping for Timothy please to come back.

I did what I could to pass the time. I studied my map; I prayed (without petition); I swept the ashes of Timothy's arm and sprinkled them in the creek, but still the paper did not move. I went out to the orchard for food. I picked two avocados and a lemon. For drink, I filled one of the candlecups at the creek, and for dessert, I had a small stalk from one of the dripcastles, which tasted like honeycomb and butter. Still the paper did not move. I returned to my map, and prayed some more (this time, with petition), but found no answer. The page lay flat beneath the weeping tree.

I am afraid that my exhaustion then got the better of me. I fell asleep, I don't know for how long, but it was nearly dawn when I awoke. Several warm pats of candle wax came dripping down upon my forehead to wake me. First thing, I looked at the paper next to me to see if it had changed, but it was just as I'd left it. I could see the daylight was ready to begin its slow ascent from the horizon. Some of the counters had already begun to stir, as if waking from a slumber. All the candles were desperately low in their cups, and some were flickering out already, streaming up thin trails of smoke.

I looked for the tallest. I stood up to inspect the lowest branches, and from the corner of my eye I thought I saw the paper's edge move ever so slightly. The wind, I thought. I could hear it stirring the orchard. But then one of the corners rose higher, and all at once the paper came to life. Its two sharp corners reached out over the shards of glass to meet, and then, as if some invisible hand were there to flatten it, a crease appeared along the edge. The page opened and closed again, rose up like a diamond, then narrowed its lower tips, which turned up inside themselves. One of these reversed again, as the two top corners both pulled down, and I could see that they were wings, and that by this very simple dance, this half-consumed white sheet of paper, which the night before had rendered such an exquisite paladin, had transformed before my eyes into an origami crane.

He awoke with a gentle flap of his wings and lifted forward sluggishly. He bent his head to see the form he'd taken, and beat his wings a second time, but the dripcastles were in his way. I thought he'd need a clearing, so I went and picked him up.

By now an orange glow was creeping up the sky. Every candle in the tree had gone out. The counters had all awakened and were rolling off into the orchard, all but my red friend, who was standing out by the rows, waiting. I brought him the crane in my arms, and we turned and followed the others through the trees. They kept circling round behind us, begging us to hurry, and the crane was struggling in my arms. He beat his wings in protest, and I could hear the shards of glass slide inside his belly, but I held fast until we came to the orchard's edge.

There was a bluff beside the sea, covered in a thick blanket of white flower. The counters raced out ahead, all bumping up and down, appearing and disappearing underneath the white and leaving thin trails behind. But my red friend remained with me. Together we walked the crane out into the middle of the meadow, and as we felt the winds sweep round us, I let Timothy free from my arms.

He dropped down at first. His belly whisked the tops of the flower, but then a breeze swept underneath him, and with another strum he rose higher. Higher and higher, he beat his paper wings. He turned a wide circle above us, and as he flew out beyond the cliff was met by stronger winds, which threw him straight upwards, so high and far I knew he wouldn't be returning to us. He soared out above the ocean, and from the bluff I stood and watched him grow smaller and smaller until he disappeared entirely inside the morning blue sky. Where he shall land, where he shall fly his precious shards, I suppose I'll never know.

I miss you all. I think of you. Now go home and sleep, and say a prayer that Timothy lands among friends.

Good night,
Gus

Three days after the reading of the doctor's third letter, a paper crane with a slightly burned tail and little shards of glass in its belly was found by Mr. Thomas E. Thomas. It had apparently landed on his lap while he was enjoying an afternoon nap on one of the sunny benches by the Holt Street fence.

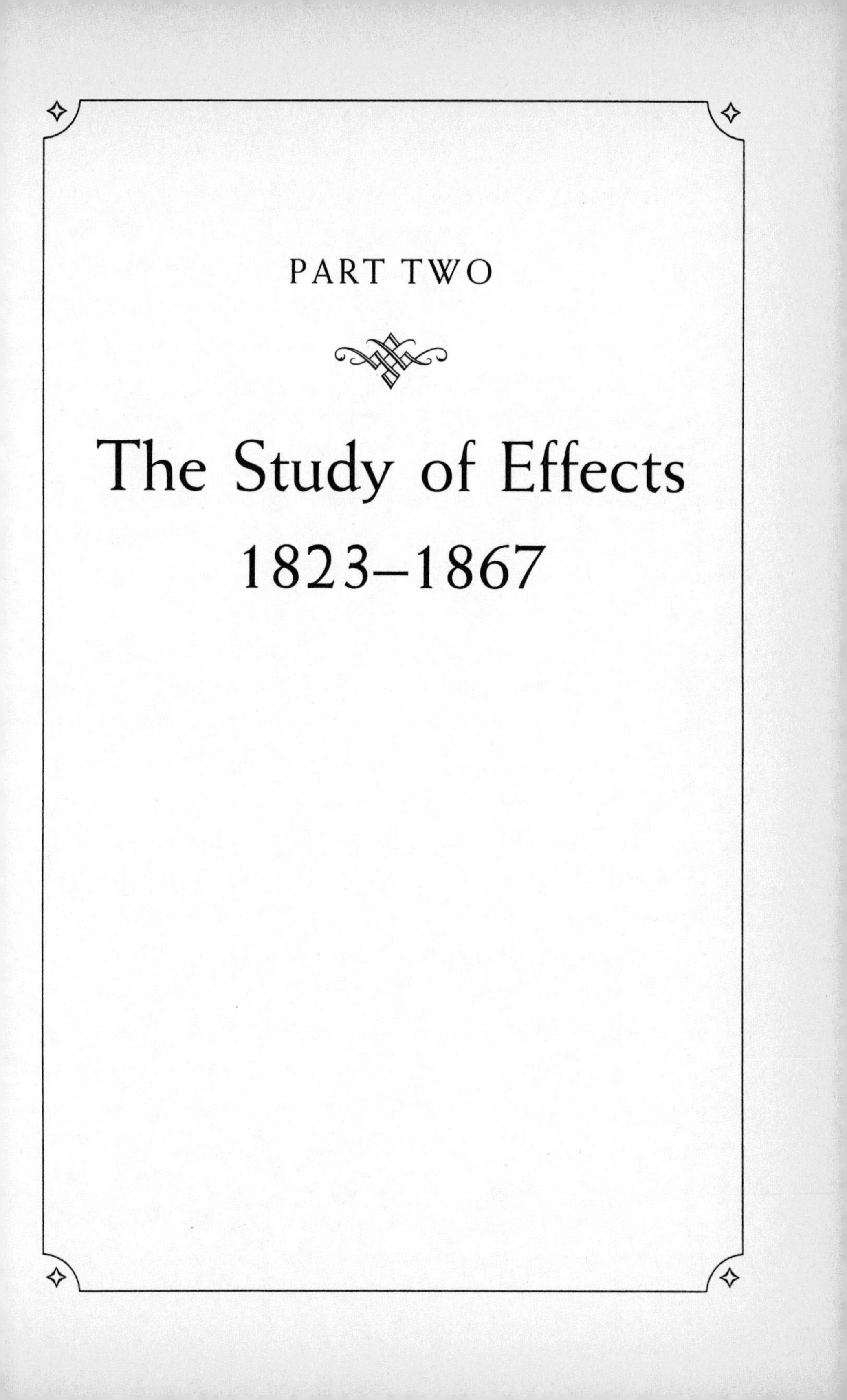

PART TWO

The Study of Effects 1823–1867

SIX

YOUTH AND COURTSHIP (1823–1855)

The Uyterhoevens did not come to America until 1869. Previously, they'd lived in London briefly, and in Berlin for nine years, and before that in the Netherlands, which is where they both were born and raised, and also where they met, at a church fair in Groningen in the winter of 1853.

Gustav was twenty-nine at the time, having just returned from twelve years abroad, spent first in school, then in Germany's medical academia, and then in London. Sonja was nineteen—although the exact date of her birth was unknown even to her. She had grown up on the canals, a member of the canal population, or *woonschuitschippers,* who were not a people much concerned with records or the individual marks they left after them. Gustav once wrote: ''I suspect that whatever questions the *schippers* have about the course or the value of their lives are more than satisfactorily answered, or washed away, by the turns and flow of the canals.''

It is known that Sonja's family, the Bruyns, were among the oldest of the *schippers.* They had been touring the aqueducts of Holland since the 1200s in a succession of twelve barges, or *tjalks,* all of which bore the same set of brass plates along the bulwarks, and which the

Bruyns always made sure to keep well polished. The *tjalk* on which Sonja grew up was painted green with red trim, and served as home to herself and her sister Mirjam, her father Koos, and her mother Neeltje, who custom-made and decorated funeral biers. When Sonja was twelve, her mother died in childbirth. The child was lost as well, so Sonja had just her father and her sister after that. They kept a garden on board and an aviary as well, and they owned two dogs to help pull their loads along the shore—freights of cheese, peat, vegetables, and timber. Their routes generally remained on the North Sea canals, but sometimes they dipped as far south as the Rhine. Sonja was familiar with most of the Northern European landscape as a result, but before coming to know Gustav, she had never ventured more than six miles inland. Sometimes she and her sister sold preserves at church fairs, and on occasion she attended school among the other children of the *schippers,* to learn reading and arithmetic, but most of her time she spent either on the canals or near them, and so her most influential teachers were the ropes and dikes, the locks and levees, the fat green landscape of the lowlands, and the water which kept pushing them by.

More is known of Gustav's youth, as he was born to a more materially fortunate class that was very much concerned with the traces it left. He was born on January 7, 1823, in The Hague, the son of Jacob Uyterhoeven, a successful tradesman of Dutch and German extraction, and Isabel King-Wood, a proud and cool Englishwoman. The elder Uyterhoevens enjoyed a highly cultured existence. They attended the symphony, the theater, bazaars, balls, the opera, and all court functions, but nonetheless remained aloof from their society, for the most part because Isabel never completely accepted Holland as a home. The Hague she tolerated, and also Arnhem, because they were both crossroads and therefore relatively cosmopolitan, but otherwise she found the Netherlands much too provincial a place for her ever to feel anything more than welcome. To compensate her this, Jacob took her with him on most of his business trips, near and far. They dedicated at least a quarter of every year to travel, sometimes with

Gustav, but more often depositing him in England—in Windsor, where Isabel's father had a manor.

In addition to having been an excellent businessman and an attendant servant of Isabel's heart, Gustav's father, Jakob, was also, according to all who knew him, a man of untold and untested brilliance. He spoke nine languages fluently, and was invited to the equivalent of graduate study in seven different fields before entering business, along much the same trail as his father. His weekly salon, or *kring,* was the most coveted in The Hague and entertained a more vast array of intellects than any in Holland. He was a keen critic of science and of philosophy, and could well have doubled his considerable income by charging for the political and financial advice he offered his many friends and associates.

The remarkable facility of Jakob's intellect was also, however, its curse. He considered the mind to be an ultimately accommodating instrument—a host, really—and the unearthly ability of his own to entertain any idea was seen by most to proceed at once from both an intellectual fearlessness and a disturbing want of personal stake. Whether he lacked conviction, as some thought, or was simply disinclined by the breadth of his sympathy to take any stand or action, the result was a man of extremely liberal opinion, achingly conservative practice, and a seemingly inexhaustible set of ideas which all suffered the same stigma, of having been spun by one who could just as easily, and probably just as willingly, unspin them. So went the popular complaint, if Jakob Uyterhoeven had only been able to find a single perch from which to sit and view the world, there would have been no limit to his vision, and probably his contribution. Unfortunately, it was not in his nature to slight the other perches. Wrote his son the year following Jakob's sudden death of cholera in 1849: "When I think of my father's mind, I think of the God who made a stone so large that even He could not lift it."

Isabel considered her husband's burden to be a matter ultimately of heritage—the very worst combination of German comprehensiveness and Dutch graciousness—and therefore grudgingly accepted it as bound. She was not so resigned about her only child Gustav, though, and encouraged in him her independent view of their surroundings.

Perhaps the most decisive step she ever took in this regard was to withhold him from the Dutch school system and enlist the services of a private tutor. She did not choose an Englishman, as would have been her preference, but, to conciliate her husband, appointed an occasional guest at his *kring,* a Mennonite minister named Menno Vanryckheghen.

An austere man in public and with his contemporaries, Vanryckheghen was also, however, a grand intellect and eloquent example of Anabaptist principle, which stood for spartan living, pacifism, higher accountability, and therefore, much to Isabel's liking, a certain detachment from the passing concerns of popular society. Vanryckheghen was also, fortunately, a more warm individual in private than public, and so, in addition to being Gustav's principal companion in youth, also became his best friend.

His tutelage was comprised of three parts. The first was purely academic and entailed an imposing curriculum of sciences, history, geography, mathematics, and classical languages. The second, which neither of the Uyterhoevens had commissioned but did not discourage, involved chess. Vanryckheghen was a master—it was the one extravagance he permitted himself—and took as compensation for his academic tutelage the opportunity to mold a player from early childhood. Every day, when their lessons were through, he spent at least an hour across the chessboard from Gustav, rooting the game's patterns and strategies into his pupil's still impressionable brain.

The minister had been strictly forbidden to exert such open influence on the boy's religious development, however. By Jakob's explicit instructions, Gustav was to study the Bible as a matter of cultural inheritance, but without any lingering reflection, and certainly not as a matter of faith. Vanryckheghen was therefore compelled to disguise his ethical teachings inside tales that he and Gustav conceived together, and which ultimately came to represent the third prong of his instruction. With almost the same regularity as they played chess,

Menno and Gustav returned to their tales, the vast majority of which were serial—some taking whole seasons to complete.

Among those which survived Gustav's youth, at least in summary, was a legend of spiritual readiness which—according to a eulogy the doctor was to give nearly sixty years later at a New Church in Urbana, Ohio—"my tutor and I, over the course of my tenth year, disclosed to one another the deepest darkest sins of an entire town."

The name of the town was Afgunst, which, for the sake of those who do not know, I should perhaps make clear is the Dutch word for "envy." Afgunst was situated on the coast of a small island called Cupertin, which was itself the peak of an ancient mountain poking up through the sea. Our village sat on a small plateau where the sea met the land, and kept the ocean tides at bay by a thorough network of canals, which all flowed into Cupertin by tunnels and ducts.

Afgunst was a comfortable home, and the people of Afgunst were generally a contented people, but for the usual strife which civilized living entails, and also for the belief, handed down from generation to generation, that on the far side of Cupertin was another village called Nut, whose residents were said to have discovered a panacea for all ills and unhappiness. (I should perhaps mention here also, for those who do not know, that *nut* translates in Dutch to mean "usefulness.") As I say, the people of Afgunst were not so badly off, but they could certainly imagine a lot preferable to their own, so they envied the people of Nut. They dreamed of Nut. They coveted the secrets of Nut. Some had even become so obsessed by the notion of this happy town that they led expeditions by ship around Cupertin to see if they could find it, but these parties never returned and were thought either to have been swallowed up by the sea, by sea monsters, or seduced by the happiness of Nut, and thought better than to come back and share its secret.

Now, in a town such as Afgunst, strewn with so many canals, it only made sense that among the pedestrians there should live boat people as well, one of whom was a man named Peter, who owned a gondola like those in Venice. Peter was a tall, quiet man who delivered goods from place to place and whom everyone knew to be helpful and dependable.

What they did not know was that Peter was an explorer, too, a man of yearning and bravery, who was not satisfied to dream and trade stories of Nut. Like so many voyagers past, he wanted to see it. Unlike those voyagers, however, he thought better than to go around Cupertin and tempt the ocean's appetite. In his gondola, with just a lantern at his prow, he went every night to explore the canals which entered the mountain, to see if somewhere in the labyrinth of aqueducts within Cupertin he could find a route to the other side. Sometimes he'd be gone for days, but the people of Afgunst could only wonder where, for he told no one of his efforts, until one day he appeared at the crosswaters at the center of town. He called all the people there together and announced to them that he had found a way through the mountain. He had seen the sun set in the ocean, and seen Nut there. They asked him what Nut was like, and he told them he could not describe its beauty and the happiness he'd felt there. He said that he'd been tempted to stay himself, but that he wanted all of them to feel the same as he, so he'd returned along the route he'd discovered and lit the walls with torches to guide him back.

Of course, all the villagers of Afgunst who heard this wanted to go. Word of Peter's discovery spread quickly through the streets and down the canals. Soon everyone was rushing to hear. "Lead us, Peter," they said, "and we shall follow you in our boats." But Peter said no. He said that his gondola was only barely slim enough to pass certain of the channels on his route, and that none of their boats was as slim as his. He said that he'd be happy to take as many of them as wanted to come, but that they would have to go seven at a time, as his gondola could seat only eight, including himself.

So seven villagers were chosen to go first. The mayor insisted he should be one, and then the bravest of his guard, for protection, lest anything untoward occur. An election was held to see who else, but when the ballots were counted, it turned out that everyone in town had received one vote, save for a milkmaid, who received two, and her husband, a merchant, who received none. So, out of shame for all their greediness, it was decided that these two should be allowed to go, and then by lots, a doctor, a minister, and a teacher. That made seven, and so the rest of the town was made to wait.

So these seven set off with Peter at the helm, and none but Peter had any notion of the mountain's size, or how circuitous was the route to the other side. Peter brought an hourglass, though, which he placed in the doctor's charge, so that they could keep track of their journey's length. He told them that the doctor should not have to turn the sand glass a dozen times before they came to Nut.

Upon entering the mountain, all the passengers were amazed by the beauty of the cave. They marveled at the colors which every turn revealed, that such beauty should have remained hidden so long, that such grand chambers, like church cathedrals, should have known no worshippers until now, and that such delicate passageways, like the tiniest alleys of Venice, should only now admit, but barely, their first gondola.

Still, when the doctor had turned over his glass for the sixth time, he spoke up. ''I am half finished with my assignment,'' he said to Peter. ''Would you say you were with yours?''

Peter did not turn, but answered, ''I believe,'' and so they all returned their attention to the hidden wonders of the mountain cave.

But as they entered deeper into the labyrinth, they began every so often to pass torches which had gone out, and so for certain stretches their only light was Peter's lantern hooked to the prow, which cast the walls a dimmer, less beautiful, less comforting hue. The shadows grew deeper and larger, and at times the current beneath them would meet with currents from other passageways which were too strong for Peter to master, and they were forced to enter unknown corridors.

Peter showed no sign of panic, though, and so the passengers had no cause to admit their fear. He always seemed to find new passages back to the trail, and every time, when the passengers spied the flicker of light coming around a corner, they would look at each other with nervous smiles, thanking heaven for Peter their guide.

Still, when the doctor had turned over his hourglass another six times and there remained no sign of daylight, the mayor spoke up. ''It has been twelve hours,'' he informed Peter. ''Pray, how much longer, do you think?''

None had feared what he might answer, but when Peter turned around this time, he showed a face so grim and pale they all fell suddenly breathless. ''I confess,'' he said, ''the journey is taking much longer than I remember.''

''Well, but we have been doubling back,'' the minister reminded him nervously. ''I should not even be surprised if we had turned a circle or two, so it's no wonder we should be delayed, just as long as we keep to the trail which Peter has set.''

The rest looked to Peter to see if he was equally assured, but his expression remained solemn.

''He is thinking something and not telling us,'' said the milkmaid.

Peter shook his head. ''Only that I have made this journey twice, but I do not remember any of the chambers we've been passing through.''

''Then we are lost?'' cried the milkmaid.

''No,'' scolded the mayor. ''No, if we were lost, there would be no torches to guide us. Peter has simply forgotten.''

All the passengers looked at Peter again. ''Is it possible you have forgotten?'' the doctor asked.

Peter shook his head. ''It is possible, but I don't think so.''

''What, then?'' asked the merchant. ''What are you saying?''

Peter spoke slowly, with his eyes on his passengers' now

trembling feet. ''I am saying that I don't believe that these are the tunnels of Cupertin anymore.''

''But what do you mean?'' asked the guard. ''You mean we've found another island?''

''But that's impossible,'' said the teacher. ''We'd have had to pass beneath the ocean floor for that, and that cannot be.''

''What are you saying to us, Peter?'' demanded the mayor.

Peter shook his head faintly. ''I am saying that it is my belief that one of these currents has taken our lives without our knowing, and that now we are being carried to our eternal home.''

The seven passengers all held their breath and looked at Peter in horror as he continued: ''And though I cannot speak for you, I know for myself that since the first unlit tunnel we passed, I have felt the Devil's weight sitting on my prow, and I know that this boat shall be taking me where I deserve, to a darker place even than this.''

There was quiet. Now the cave walls which had seemed so beautiful before looked grim and silent. ''But you have been a good man, Peter,'' the mayor said nervously. ''We all know you to be kind and helpful.''

Peter's gaze continued, blank, on their feet. ''But I have lied in bringing you here.''

''What do you mean?'' The teacher looked up fiercely. ''You have not found a way to the other side?''

''I did,'' said Peter. ''I did. I saw the sun set in the water, but there is no town there. There was no one. I have lied. I have brought you here on false pretense, and now I fear I shall be made to pay.''

Again there was silence, till again the mayor spoke out. ''But hold,'' he said. ''You are not the only one in this boat, Peter. Where you are being taken, so are we all, and yet I know, I have been a leader of men. I have served Afgunst my whole life. I could not be headed your dark way.''

At this the minister, who had been sitting behind with his head bowed, merely touched the mayor on the shoulder, and the mayor fell silent in the knowledge that he had admitted such sins in the minister's confessional as would earn him a seat on any doomed boat.

"I confess," spoke the soldier for the first time on the journey, "I belong on this boat with Peter." And he proceeded to tell why. He confessed to them all the things he'd done, of lies he'd told and children he'd bullied as a little boy.

Unfortunately, we haven't the time here to remember the rest of his sins—nor those of the doctor, the teacher, the merchant, the milkmaid, the minister and the mayor—though this is precisely what my tutor and I did. Let it suffice here to say that as Peter's gondola continued through uncharted tunnels, where death seemed not imminent but already upon them, each one of the seven passengers was compelled to admit that it was true and just that they were all in the same boat, for seven different sinful reasons.

When the last, who was the minister, had confessed his sins and all were convinced how well he deserved his seat with them, the current then picked up and carried them to a larger channel, at whose appearance Peter could not help but smile. A light shone in through the tunnel mouth—not the light of Peter's torches, or the fires of hell, but the natural light of day. They emerged from the innards of Cupertin, and it was as Peter had said. There was no town of happy people; just a stretch of land like that from which they'd come, but that where Nut would soon arise, the river cut through wider fields and the sea embraced the sun. And all the passengers were so thankful at the sight of their reprieve, they were not angry with Peter but grateful. They sent him back to fetch the others, and likewise suggest to them, boat by boat, that the waters had taken their natural lives and would carry them to some eternal home, prepared for them by all their thoughts and deeds.

The legend of Peter, Afgunst, and the gradual population of Nut was not the only one of Menno and Gustav's tales to feature boatmen.

In fact, most of them did, as Vanryckheghen was a great admirer of the *schippers*. His own grandfather had lived on a *tjalk*, and so he had always esteemed the inherent simplicity of their lifestyle and their independence from the mires of society. Whenever possible, he took Gustav to the markets set up alongside the canals, to buy cakes or watch the men unload timber or stones to repair the dikes, and in time Gustav acquired his tutor's high regard. He wondered at their children, and envied their simple clothes and brightly colored boats. "A people neither rich nor poor," he later wrote,

> but of a wholly different kind, who never went to school, never stayed long and never left home, and who for these attributes assumed a quality of such wisdom and magic in my eyes, they were like fairies to me, or angels, so much so that when I first learnt of my own mortality, such as I was able to comprehend it, I had assumed it was a condition related to my own mooring, and not something to which the *schippers* were therefore subject.

However binding and lethal it may have seemed to him at the time, Gustav's own schooling proceeded at an accelerated clip. To see that his social skills were not neglected, his parents had enrolled him in the Gymnasium at the age of twelve, but the teachers there were unable to keep pace with the momentum of learning that Vanryckheghen continued to oversee in the afternoons and on weekends. By age thirteen, Gustav was speaking English, Swedish, German, Latin, and Greek, in addition to his native Dutch, and he would go on in subsequent years to add Spanish, Italian, and French. By age fifteen, he had read Sallust, Cicero, Virgil, and Sophocles, and perhaps most impressive, he could boast a chess game equal to his tutor's.

His keenest interest, however, owing in part to the fact that it was the one subject he and Menno approached on an equal footing, was the natural sciences. For three years he and Menno plowed their way through instructional books that they selected together out of curiosity, but when Gustav turned fourteen he apparently outstripped Menno's aptitude, and Isabel enlisted the help of a second tutor, a German biologist and graduate of the Friedrich Wilhelm Institut in Berlin named Heinrich Schleide. They studied together for two years and then, at the age of sixteen, Gustav entered the university at Utrecht to study biology.

He did not remain long. The Dutch university system seemed listless by comparison with the intensity of his private education, and after just one year, Schleide arranged for Gustav to meet his former master and current director of the Friedrich Wilhelm Institut in Berlin, Johannes Mueller. Mueller was a man of broad interests and sympathies, in fact, a student of mysticism as well as a leading proponent of exact science, and it was under his stewardship that Berlin was just beginning to wrest the reins of clinical medicine from the "romantic" physicians of Paris. He recognized a similar broadmindedness in the young Uyterhoeven, and in 1841 personally expedited his transfer to the Institut. Soon thereafter he introduced Gustav to a widespread community of scientists in Berlin, those of a somewhat more ecumenical perspective, such as Gustav Fechner, but also and in particular those at work in the field of physiology and pathology—a group which included Ludwig Franke, Emil von Behring, Benno Reinhardt, Johann Lukas Schönlein, Ernst Brücke, Friedrich Löffler, and Hermann Helmholtz, all of whom were to play important roles in the mid-century revolt against "old science."

Uyterhoeven was not the first undergraduate to have enjoyed such special treatment from the Institut's director. The year before, Mueller had provided many of the same introductions with much the same eagerness to a young Pomeranian named Rudolf Virchow. Virchow, too, was a student of immense aptitude and potential, and in the years to come would grow to be Uyterhoeven's closest friend and greatest intellectual influence. "Rudolf was the teacher from whom I learned what I myself believed," he wrote years later, "and I deem it my contribution to medicine—for better or worse—that I may have done the same for him."

Both entered research as undergraduates, and from the very start were pitted against one another, not because they were so similar, but rather—as Uyterhoeven's comment suggests—because their minds and manners were so unalike. Some at the Institut even alleged that part of the reason Mueller had been so quick to assign them near-celebrity status so early in their careers was that he recognized them as emblems of the hostile poles at play within himself. There was the one, the lean and elegant philosopher of serene bearing and perennial concern, and this was Uyterhoeven; and then there was the other—shorter, powerfully built, politically minded, and passionate—and this was Virchow. When Mueller spoke of Uyterhoeven, he referred to "gifts" and "insight," and to his "instinct for the natural forms and rhythms of nature." With Virchow, on the other hand, Mueller spoke of "craft," "rigor," and "precision." Virchow worked in the morning, while Uyterhoeven preferred the late afternoon and evening. Virchow's approach to research was strict and regimented. He believed firmly that good science consisted in good methods, while Uyterhoeven was more spontaneous in the laboratory. He treated his instruments with an almost deliberate irreverence, for fear that the formal approaches tempted one, in his own phrase, "to lose sight of the matter at hand, that our subject is flesh, and flesh beneath lenses." For these reasons, Uyterhoeven was thought to have been the more prone to discoveries and breakthroughs, while Virchow's contributions—no less significant—were expected to address the more procedural elements of their work, and in fact, Virchow did devise many laboratory techniques that are still in place today, though even there, he was forced to share some of the credit with Uyterhoeven. "Rudolf would never have known so well what the rules should be," wrote Emil von Behring, "if he had not spent so many years watching Gustav mock them."

For all the differences between the two, or more probably because of them, their careers progressed as one. Both passed the state exam in 1846. Both served as company surgeons at Berlin's Charité Hospital, where they continued their studies in microscopy and biochemistry, and both demonstrated pathological anatomy in the dissecting laboratory of Froriep.

Their influence upon each other through all this was much the same as it had been at the Institut. Like siblings, they continued to cultivate their ways and visions in contrast to one another. In both private and public debates, they delighted in taunting each other, Virchow with his clench-fisted harangues and reproaches and Uyterhoeven with his traps and calm circumventions. If Virchow praised the spread of democracy and the rights of individual men, Uyterhoeven would reply that cultures had rights as well, that they should be allowed to grow at their own pace, and that premature democracy could represent as great a tyranny on certain peoples as any king. If Virchow spoke warily of the threat which new technologies might pose nature, Uyterhoeven pointed out that man was a part of nature, and that whatever havoc he managed to wreak would therefore be perfectly natural. In one of their better-known exchanges, as recorded by Mueller himself, Virchow had been positing the Copernican revolution as the pivotal moment in the conflict between science and religion—"the first ascent of rationalism into the mind of modern man, the first great decline of religion's influence." Gustav replied that it represented no such thing, of course, and that simply knowing that the earth revolved around the sun did nothing to refute the much more vivid, and much more "religiously significant impression that the universe continues to revolve around every individual man."

Like so, and like rams, they went at each other tirelessly, and although to most it appeared that their debates had been staged as nothing more than a form of mental exercise, occasionally bordering on the absurd—Uyterhoeven defending the virtue of the flat as opposed to round world—the players themselves observed that they were more and more often taking the same opposed positions for the same opposed reasons, which at the time they saw as boiling down to a pair of fundamental and related disputes: the first having to do with the impetus of the universe and the second with the impetus of humankind.

Simply, Virchow was a determinist. He believed that life could ultimately be reduced to a set of physical laws, like mechanics, and that man's reason could therefore someday penetrate and explain all its mysteries. Consequently, he regarded the course of human history as being one of overall enlightenment, and he desired both as a scientist and as a political thinker to be a part of that process, of finding out what was true and ridding from men's minds what wasn't.

Uyterhoeven, on the other hand, was a vitalist. He recognized life to be a fundamentally spontaneous and creative phenomenon, subject to no law beyond an apparently indomitable will to grow and to expand. Physics and chemistry did well to record her habits, in other words, but provided no explanation as to the vital force which still evidently charged the universe. Accordingly, he didn't see the history of thought and knowledge as being a record of enlightenment so much as a parade of constantly changing and constantly competing grids and schemes, none of which had ever managed to frame one insight without at the same time obscuring another. What Virchow called scientific progress, Uyterhoeven preferred to think of as "the persistent articulation of human experience," which he accepted as inevitable and indefatigable—and therefore, he supposed, necessary—but not an obvious improvement. He admired the new periodic table, for instance, but he did not see that it possessed any more truth than the ancient table of four elements, and he felt somewhat the same toward most antiquated notions: that they'd passed from favor not so much because they'd been wrong or ignorant, but rather because history had simply lost its use for them. "Truth is truth," he once wrote Mueller. "Like the moon. It only seems to wax and wane as our perspective changes."

The overall evolution of Virchow's and Uyterhoeven's ideas was fairly clear, then, and very much in keeping with Mueller's original estimation: in less than a decade, his two chosen prodigies had managed to forge in one another a perfect philosophical complement. In their master's own words: "Virchow is the political and Uyterhoeven the perennial thinker; Virchow the champion of what is correct, Uyterhoeven the proponent of what is true; Virchow the advocate of what should be, Uyterhoeven the notary of what is so" (1847). It was an almost convenient partnership, and yet because each could so plainly see his own limitations in the other's strengths, over time their differences engendered conflicting measures of reliance, respect, and resentment. By his own admission, Virchow spent the whole of his third decade, "in constant fear and faith that my ideas were outflanked on all sides by [Gustav's]—that however broad the view I possessed, he possessed the one yet broader." Alternately, Uyterhoeven envied the passion of Virchow's convictions. "The world and history are changed by such men as Rudolf," he wrote Vanryckheghen, "and only witnessed by men such as me."

Inevitably, by 1848, signs began to emerge that each was growing tired of the other's ballast. Virchow had acquired some celebrity that fall, as a result of an article he'd written for his own medical journal, *Medizinische Reforme,* concerning a typhoid epidemic that both he and Uyterhoeven had gone to study in Upper Silesia. In brief, he'd warned that if Europe was to have any hope of combating the contagious diseases sweeping her cities, diet and medicine alone would not do. There would need to be fundamental political and social reform, not only to improve the standards of sewage and hygiene, but in general to promote education, prosperity, and freedom—all ideas which in the restive year of 1848 had gone over very well. For having incorporated them into his medical view, Virchow was praised throughout the Continent as champion of the new democratic health regime, and in the coming year was inspired to more and more crusades and yet bolder political pronouncements.

Uyterhoeven took care not to begrudge his friend's quick public ascent. When Virchow's pay was suspended in 1849 as result of his agitations, Uyterhoeven offered neither support nor censure, preferring, as he put it, to "render unto Rudolf what is Rudolf's." Late in the year, however, Virchow may finally have overstepped his bounds. In an essay entitled "The Struggles for Unity in Scientific Medicine," he cast his now very prominent hat in the philosopher's ring, attempting, in essence, to define the boundaries of knowledge. In an early, simple distillation of a soon-to-be-prevalent opinion, he argued that while "transcendental possibilities" certainly existed, faith must necessarily begin where science left off. Needless to say, the piece was well received by all—all, that is, but the one whose opinion Virchow held in highest esteem. In a private letter, Uyterhoeven responded:

They are, as ever, ideas well formed to the moment, and yet at the risk of seeming contrary, I might ask you to consider the opposite possibility: that obviously science can only begin where faith leaves off . . .

But it is a pretension even to argue. My greater concern—or my wish, I should say—would be that you stop concerning yourself so much with the map and please return your attention to the ground.

The friendship was given little time to degenerate from there. In the winter of 1849, Jakob Uyterhoeven fell suddenly ill from cholera. Gustav returned to The Hague to help care for him, but his father's condition was already too advanced. He died in February. Gustav remained through the early spring to settle his father's estate, and then escorted his mother back to England. He planned to stay only a month or so, long enough to see her safely into the hands of her sister in Windsor. Then he would return to Leiden to take up a position he'd been offered at the university.

During his first week in London, however, Uyterhoeven was introduced to Dr. Scott Geddes, a leading proponent of alternative medical therapies, who was presently at work developing new treatments for cholera. His approach was basically homeopathic, vested in the understanding that the body could not support two similar fevers at once, and that therefore an effective means of treating certain diseases was basically to wean the patient of his or her illness by administering drugs that produced symptoms similar to those from which the patient was suffering. Geddes invited Uyterhoeven to observe his therapies at work, and Uyterhoeven was impressed, not so much by the theory at first as by the results. Geddes's treatments for cholera were boasting a demonstrably higher rate of success than any of those currently in favor on the Continent. So Uyterhoeven decided to defer his position at Leiden and join forces with Geddes, to learn more about his methods, to help him with research, and also, of course, to help treat his patients.

His apprenticeship turned out to be less constructive than he had hoped, for the simple reason that his father's death had been more overwhelming than he first had realized. Over the next eighteen months, his belated grief chose two addictions in which to express itself, the first of which had seemed perfectly innocuous to begin. In the summer of 1850 Uyterhoeven began to frequent several chess clubs in the West End. At first he went just two or three times a week, aware of the game's appetite for good players. His old tutor Menno had always warned him of its dangers, and he could see in the pale, sallow faces of his opponents the years they'd lost in front of chessboards. Still, he flirted with the game more and more recklessly, until soon he was going to one or two clubs a night. He began playing for money, both blitz and natural games, often with odds, and for a brief time was considered, in these slightly shadier circles, one of the coming players in all of London.

Whatever reign he did enjoy was severely curtailed, however, by the second of his addictions, which developed as a direct result of the work he'd been doing with Geddes. In order to match as faithfully as possible the symptoms from which their patients were suffering, it was necessary to keep a catalogue of the effects which given medicaments induced in healthy people. Geddes and Uyterhoeven had therefore conducted a great variety of what were called "provings," wherein they did just that, administering small, safe amounts of medicine, or "specifics," to healthy subjects in order to record the symptoms they incurred.

Among the specifics that Geddes had been proving was opium, various preparations of which had long been thought to relieve symptoms of gout, constipation, neuralgia, and "female complaints." Uyterhoeven had himself taken part in several of the opium provings, which posed no real danger in themselves, since the dosages administered were so minuscule. He did, however, maintain many of the contacts he'd made in Fens, while searching for as pure an extract as he could find. The purest had come from a Chinese apothecary named Liu, who was one of roughly one hundred Chinese then living in London, the notorious opium dens still a good twenty years off. Liu was a keen chess player, as it turned out. Uyterhoeven introduced him to the competitive circles to which he'd recently gained entrance, and in return Liu provided him a more thorough education in the arts of opium eating and smoking.

Under Liu's tutelage, the course of Dr. Uyterhoeven's addiction was brief and not very harrowing, relatively speaking. He was what was called a "moderate addict." His plateau dose was low by comparison to those around him, and never so high that he couldn't pay his way with his chess earnings. He never completely stopped working with Geddes, and he also continued to see his mother at least once every two weeks, but his existence did lose focus for a time. In his later years he would come to name the roughly eighteen months between the fall of 1850 and the spring of 1852 his "lost year"—not because he considered it wasted or cause for regret, but simply because, as it had drifted further back in time, "it has all found the same remote place in my mind that I suspect I keep old dreams. A murk of crudded chess and perfumed rooms, sleepless nights spent playing games of gibberish; runny noses, broken clocks, goose pimples, cravings, chronic euphoria, and chronic despair."

It wasn't until the spring of 1852 that Uyterhoeven was moved to right himself. By then his dreams and waking life had begun to bleed into one another to the point that he was having trouble telling the difference between them. Worse, he'd begun to suffer recurrent nightmares, which he knew were at least in part the opium's doing, and recognized that for the sake of his own sanity he should probably remove himself from any further temptation. His mother certainly encouraged his leaving. "This extent of grief, she says, should not continue," he wrote Menno, "and she is right." So, in July of 1852, Dr. Uyterhoeven bid Liu and Geddes and the chess junkies of London goodbye and returned to Leiden, now a full two years later than he'd initially intended.

His first weeks back on the Continent he suffered "a good bout of penance," as he put it to Menno—"appalling abdominal pain, sweats, and profuse diarrhea. Still, a light sentence for my indulgences of the past year." Soon after, he contacted Virchow. It had been almost two years since they'd last corresponded, and Virchow had lost track of his whereabouts. It was known he'd gone to London, and there was a rumor he'd done some consulting on sewage systems there, but he'd published no articles, no research, and occupied no academic post. He was thought basically to have vanished, in other words, and so when his note arrived from Leiden, Virchow had been both surprised and relieved. He was at the University of Würzburg now, the first ever professor of pathology in Germany, and he invited Uyterhoeven down immediately. He'd wanted to show his friend the series of microscopic investigations that he and a Parisian pathologist named Hermann Lebert had begun just that year. In fact, he urged Uyterhoeven to join him at the university, even offering to create a chair for him.

Uyterhoeven was tempted. He agreed that Lebert's research was promising, but he was wary of the expectation that he and Virchow would be able to pick up again so easily. Much had happened in the time they'd been apart, and he also felt that if Virchow and Lebert were truly on the trail of something, it wouldn't hurt for the three of them to approach it from independent perspectives, with the assurance that they'd keep each other abreast of all their findings. So it was agreed, and in September, Uyterhoeven returned to Leiden to honor his commitment at the university there.

As it happened, this decision would turn out to be the most consequential, and fortunate, of Dr. Uyterhoeven's life. Professionally, the triangulate investigation that he, Lebert, and Virchow were to pursue over the course of the next three years is widely considered to have marked the dawn of modern pathology, and would therefore earn Uyterhoeven a place of permanent and pivotal importance in the development of Western medicine.

More important to him personally, if Dr. Uyterhoeven had not returned to Leiden that fall, he would not in all likelihood have met Sonja that winter. The second week of December, he had been visiting his old tutor Menno Vanryckheghen in the village of Ijilst in Friesland, and that Sunday he had gone to pick up some food for dinner at the local kermis. Menno had asked that he get a yard's worth of a long, tough bread called *ellekoek,* and Gustav had been choosing among the loaves when he noticed the elder of two sisters selling preserves at the next stand over. She had golden hair beneath her cap, and dark eyebrows poised decisively above ice-blue eyes, and Gustav was so taken by her—not just by her beauty but by her bearing, which seemed at once fierce and serene—that though he had never favored the particular jam they were selling, a preserve of black currants, gin, and sugar called *boerejongens,* he gathered the courage after rounding the market twice to buy two jars from her in silence.

Their eyes no more than glanced, but that night after he'd returned to Menno's, Gustav fell asleep with her in mind, and the following day, near dusk, he returned to the kermis, prepared to buy a third and a fourth jar, if need be—but the stand and the young woman were gone. The man from whom he'd bought the *ellekoek* was still there, though, and Gustav asked him if the two young women with the *boerejongens* had returned that morning. He said no. Gustav asked their names, and the man said he wasn't sure, but that they were Koos Bruyn's daughters. Their mother had died years ago, he said, but they both still lived with their father. Their *tjalk* was green with red trim, and hammered brass along the bulwarks, and he said that Mr. Bruyn could almost always be found sitting at the tiller with a church warden pipe in his teeth. Gustav asked if there was any way of knowing where they were headed next, but the man with the *ellekoek* said he didn't know. He offered to take Gustav to Sneek the next day, if he liked, as he was headed there himself, but Gustav declined. He returned to Menno's, thwarted, and slept so poorly that night that the next morning he rose at dawn and went to see if he could catch the man with the *ellekoek.* He did, just, and they boated to Sneek together. There were no green barges there, though, nor word of the Bruyns' having come through, so that afternoon Gustav returned to Ijilst with nothing to show or tell, and the following day made his way back to Leiden and his laboratory.

He tried to put the young woman out of his mind after that, but his mind did not comply. She entered his dreams, always in silence, standing with people all around them. In the day, when he was at the university, his thoughts would return again and again to the only image he kept of her—handing two jars to him across the counter, and the wolfen color of her eyes. He often imagined her somewhere on the canals, on her *tjalk.* He pictured her father at the tiller, a long pipe in his teeth, and she standing near the rail. And the more she haunted his dreams, his memory, and his imagination, the more he cursed himself that he had not done something more in Ijilst. He wasn't sure what it could have been, except to tell her, if he could possibly have known, that he would be powerless in the coming year to forget her.

He began taking lunch at the markets along the canals every day, and whenever he had an appointment or an errand to run, he chose to walk along the water. When he traveled far, he always went by boat. Even in Germany, when he would go to Würzburg to compare notes with Virchow, he always came back along the Rhine, as far out of his way as it was. Several times he did come across boats that were close to fitting the description of the Bruyns', and he would wait discreetly by the ties to see who lived inside, but it never was the young woman he'd seen in Ijilst. She remained ever elsewhere, so his memory subsisted on the mere cordial purchase of two jars of black currants, while the young woman and her father's *tjalk* continued to explore his dreams and his imagination. As months passed to seasons, he even began to wonder if it was she that he was thinking of anymore, or if perhaps his recollection had given way to some figment of his imagination. Sometimes he even feared that if he ever were to find her, she would pale by comparison to what his mind had conjured in her absence. He found himself at the banks less often that summer, and when the weather began to cool again without a sign of her, Gustav all but abandoned the hunt. As if they were a mirror he'd resolved not to look at, he stopped going to the canals. He traveled overland to and from Würzburg, and when Menno invited him to Ijilst for the November holiday, he vowed to himself that he would make no effort to attend the kermis where he'd seen her the year before.

His third night in Ijilst was a Saturday. Menno had invited an old friend of Gustav's father for dinner, an accountant for the Dutch East India Trading Company named Kerboesch. The three of them stayed up late. Kerboesch and Gustav shared port, cigars, some pears and cheese, split a bottle of eau-de-vie, and at some point well after midnight devoured the two jars of *boerejongens* in Menno's cupboard. They both became sick soon thereafter, and then retired for the night, but the following day, which started late, Menno sent Gustav back to the kermis for more.

He found her in the same place, at the same stand, with her sister beside her. Her cap and dress were the same, if a year more worn, but her bearing was a year more wise and restless, and when Gustav saw her eyes again, he realized it was his imagination that paled. He went straight to her. He made no gesture for the jars, but asked if she would share dinner with him that night when her stand closed.

Much earlier in the year, Sonja had been told on several different occasions, by several different *schippers,* that there was a young doctor from Leiden asking after her. They said he never stated his purpose, other than to know where she was, and some offered that he was smitten, but Sonja was not flattered. She did not allow herself to be. This doctor had never shown, and people from the city, the *stadsliedens,* didn't ever take such interest in the *schippers.* The *stadslieden* did not understand the *schippers.* This was something her father had once said when she was a little girl. He had been treated badly by a dry-goods man in Rotterdam, and Sonja had heard him tell her mother that the *stadslieden* looked upon them as fools and servants, when, in fact, the city folk were the fools, because they all lived in prison and didn't even know. "We are their jailors," her father had said, and there had been as much pity as anger in his voice, but it was the only time that Sonja had ever heard him speak ill of another, and so she had always remembered it.

Of course, she could not simply discount the idea of this young doctor from Leiden, and when in Ijilst the gentleman emerged from the crowd with such kind and clever eyes and asked her to dinner, she remembered him from the year before, knew that this must be he, and accepted as if their meeting there again had been expected.

She told him the kermis would be through at dusk, so he excused himself to let her finish her day's work. He bought a basket, some sausage and cheese, fruit and bread, some wine and flowers. Then he went to the Mere, to see which *tjalk* was theirs. He saw her father in his hat and beard and pipe, sitting in a rocking chair by the tiller. Two dogs sat faithfully on either side, and every so often he would scratch their heads, but otherwise he was still and silent, just as Gustav had been warned.

He returned to the kermis at dusk, but Sonja refused his help taking down their stand. She asked him to wait while she and Mirjam carried their jars and table back to the barge, and then she alone returned.

Gustav took her to the rectory of the Old Church, where the monsignor was an old friend of Menno's. He built a fire, and as they sipped their wine, they listened through the door to the choir practicing for the next day's service. They said little and ate only the fruit and cheese he'd brought. Then, when the choir was through, Gustav walked her back to the marketplace, and there they said good night. Gustav told her he would not be in Ijilst long and asked if they could meet again tomorrow, but Sonja said she couldn't, as her father had planned to leave for Workum at dawn.

Gustav spent the night at Menno's, but the following morning boated down to Workum. This time, he waited by the ties of the Bruyns' *tjalk* for Sonja's sister, Mirjam, to give her a note for Sonja asking that she come meet him in town later that day. She did, and they spent the afternoon together, touring the cemetery. Sonja told Gustav of her family and of the biers her mother used to make, and Gustav recounted the stories that he and Menno had imagined when he was a boy. Then they parted at the cemetery gate. They made no mention of whether they should meet again. Gustav only asked where her father was to make his next delivery, and she told him, in Hindeloopen.

Thus were the terms of their courtship set. The following week

Gustav went to Hindeloopen and spent a day with Sonja. Thereafter, all the way through to the summer of 1853, not a fortnight passed that Gustav did not find the Bruyns along their route and meet Sonja in secret, at a mill, a market, a church, a field, or a tree. When he was not with her or in his laboratory at Leiden, he was either plotting his next dash across the countryside or was already on his way, either on foot, or by boat or carriage. He would leave single flowers for her to find, and notes with Mirjam or with the other *schippers,* telling where she should meet him, and always she did. She would make excuses to her father about mysterious errands she had to run or ill friends to attend to; then Gustav would take her in carriages farther inland than she'd ever been, to restaurants where they ate partridge from plates which looked to her like prizes. He took her to museums and to halls where orchestras played and chorales sang, and every time when their days or evenings were through, the doctor would walk her back until they were just beyond sight of her father's boat, and she always said good night to him with restraint, as though it were for the last time.

She never expected that she would see him again. If her sister asked, Sonja would tell her about the places they'd been, the food they'd eaten, and the music they'd heard. She would describe the dresses she'd seen and the silver and crystal. And if Mirjam asked about the doctor, Sonja would say that he was a good man, a man who looked upon everything surrounding him with humor and delight. She told Mirjam about the little microscopes he carried with him, and she said that he was an admirable man in this way, for being so eager to know and understand, and she said he was handsome man as well, and kind, and that everyone to whom he introduced her respected him highly, and treated her nobly for simply being at his side, when otherwise they would not have looked her in the eye.

But then when all her sister's questions were through, Sonja would try with all her might not to think of him again. She would hide all his notes and flowers, and return her attention as best she could to the canals and to her father's work. She'd thought it would be vain to expect the doctor to return, so she would pull the *tjalk* herself sometimes, with their two dogs, and try as best she could not to let her father know that anything had changed.

Of course, Koos had been aware that his elder daughter was being courted. He had recognized that her errands were contrived, that she took much too long to complete them, and he could see the blush in her cheeks when she returned. He did not mind, though, because he thought her suitor was another of the *schippers,* a young man named Matthijs van Kroon, whom his girls had known since they were infants. Koos approved of Matthijs, and tested his ardor by simply keeping to his schedule and seeing if Matthijs kept up. He seemed to. Sonja's cheeks continued to flush, and so Koos had been very pleased, until the early spring, when they came to The Hague.

A spring ball was given in The Hague every year in one of the loveliest halls in all of Holland, the Riddarzaal. Gustav had wanted to take Sonja, and he bought her a dress for the occasion. He had never given her such an intimate gift, but he had seen that the dresses she wore were not hers, and he had wanted her to have one of her own. He bought it in Leiden—a simple dress, he'd thought, that he had happened to see in a clothier's near his laboratory. It was made of blue silk, and had a black velvet collar and cuffs and black onyx buttons. He also bought a basket in which to hide the dress and took them both to The Hague before the Bruyns arrived. When they did the morning after, he met Sonja's sister, Mirjam, in secret to give her the basket with the dress folded inside, and she left it on Sonja's bed.

Sonja did not return to their room until that afternoon, but when she saw the basket, she knew it was from the doctor, and as always when his gifts would appear, all her bridled hopes took wing. She thought that they would have a picnic that evening or tomorrow, and she imagined carrying preserves to the markets in her basket and how happy this would make her, but when she looked inside the basket for his note, what she saw confused her. It was the finest silk she'd ever touched, and the softest black velvet. The blue was more luminous than any color she had ever seen. It was a more beautiful gown than she had ever dreamed of, but she could not imagine wearing it herself. Such gowns were worn by the women in Gustav's world, and though Sonja had been happy to visit there with him, she had never considered entering it herself, as a gift of such extravagant beauty seemed to bid her. The dress inside the basket frightened her, and so she did not even read the doctor's note. She left the dress out on her bed deliberately, and took his basket with her to the wood, where she remained all day, cutting the flowers and crying.

Her father discovered the dress that afternoon and was no less dismayed than his daughter. He knew that this was no gift from Matthijs. Only a man from the city would intend to see his daughter in such a gown. He took the dress, folded it, and placed it in Sonja's trunk. He said nothing to her when she returned at twilight, but when they'd eaten their supper and Sonja and Mirjam had both gone to bed, he awoke the dogs and dragged the *tjalk* with them all the way to Haarlem, two days without stop and without a word.

The night of the ball in The Hague, Gustav waited for Sonja by the fountain in front of the Riddarzaal until dark, then went to the canals to see if something was wrong. When he saw that the Bruyns' boat was gone, he did not know what to think. Sonja had never failed to meet him before and he wondered if he had misinformed her of the place or the time. He wondered if she'd even received his gift, but there was no way of knowing, so he returned to Leiden the next day and waited, uncertain.

When three days had passed he received a brief letter from Sonja.

Dear Dr. Uyterhoeven,

My father has found your kind gift, and no longer will tell us where we shall be making our deliveries. I shall always think of you in the places we have been.

Sonja Bruyn

Gustav was stunned. The note was too quick, and he knew that her father was not to blame. The dress was to blame. He wrote Menno: ''It is my fault for having been so bold, but I fear that she has mistaken my gift as something more than a very innocent desire on my part—to show the most beautiful rooms and people of my society true beauty.''

It was a misunderstanding that betokened the great differences between them, he knew, and the intent of her note had been quite clear, yet he had never been more certain of his own desire. He would not presume to defy her request, therefore. He would refrain from pursuing her, but he made certain that if she ever did turn her head in his direction again, as he prayed she would, he would be ready. He bought her a ring, a simple band of gold, which he kept in his pockets at all times, and he befriended the lumbermen with whom Koos did business as well as the boys at the locks. He asked if they would watch for the Bruyns. He described the *tjalk* for them and entrusted them with notes to give the elder daughter if she should ever come through, but weeks passed with no word. He began bringing flowers to the canals every morning and giving them to the boys to pass on to her, but day after day she did not come, and flower upon flower died waiting.

A month passed without a sign, but then one day in May, he came home from the laboratory to find a note from Sonja saying that she would be at the steps of Pieterskerk that evening.

He left directly. He brought the ring and all the hopes he'd been defending since he'd returned from The Hague. His first glimpse of her was from across the canal. She was wearing the dress he'd given her. He saw the blue of the fabric and the gold of her hair, which was up—she wasn't wearing her cap. She was standing straight and still at the foot of the steps, waiting. She did not see him until he had crossed the bridge, but her dark brow and light gray eyes took such hold of his, all he could think to ask when he finally reached her was why had she come back. She said that the canals felt like prison now. Then she asked if he had been thinking of her, and he answered by taking the ring from his pocket. She offered him her hand, and together they walked from Pieterskerk to where her father had berthed the *tjalk*.

Koos had not been expecting to meet his daughter's suitor that evening. He had been sitting at the tiller as usual, watching night fall when he saw Sonja coming up the bank in the blue silk dress, and he understood that the gentleman beside her, clearly a man of wealth and education, was the one who'd given it. He waited for them to climb aboard, and then, as the young man greeted the dogs, Koos saw the ring on Sonja's finger. Without a word, he passed by them both and went below.

For five days he did not speak, but the barge remained in its berth. Then the sixth evening, he went to Sonja. He said that the coming season he would be delivering timber with Luka van Maaren, and that there was room on van Maaren's boat. If the young man she'd brought to meet him was earnest in his desire for her hand, he would spend a season with them on the canals.

When Sonja told Gustav of her father's wish, he accepted more as if it had been an invitation than a demand. The spring session ended that June, and he joined them two days after. Then, from June through August, Gustav saw the Netherlands, as he had only ever dreamed of doing, from the canals. He took a bunk on van Maaren's boat, helped the Bruyns and van Maarens deliver their timber, shared meals with Sonja, Koos, and Mirjam at least once a day. He introduced them all to Menno, came to know their dogs, their garden, their birds, and slowly but surely persuaded Koos of his devotion to his daughter. Then, when the summer was through, Gustav and Sonja were married in Ijilst, with Menno on hand and Koos's blessing. Sonja said goodbye to her father and her sister for the first time, and she and Gustav returned to Leiden.

SEVEN

THE FRIEDRICH WILHELM INSTITUT (1855–1867)

In a lecture series he was to deliver years later throughout Europe, England, and then America, Dr. Uyterhoeven described the research triangle that took shape in the early 1850s among himself in Leiden, Hermann Lebert in Paris, and Virchow in Würzburg as being founded in "a mutually guarded reliance" that recent advances in medical technology—particularly those which followed in the wake of the microscopic lens—promised "more than merely to expand the catalogue of known physiology." "We believed—or at the very least took inspiration from the idea—that the new lens, in offering a more intimate view of nature than man had ever seen before, might shed light on more nagging perennial questions, having to do with the place, the origin, and the impetus of life itself."

The irony, of course, was that Virchow and Uyterhoeven had never agreed on such matters, and that their positions had only grown more remote and intransigent during the years they had been apart, while Uyterhoeven was living in London. In that time, Virchow had become Germany's most vocal and ardent determinist, attributing all the individual phenomena of life to physical laws and the conditions of what he called "a purely physico-chemical order"; while Uyterhoeven was more than ever convinced that life, though certainly reducible and describable by the schemes and formulae of physics and chemistry, was still evidently charged by a vital force for which ''such schemes did not even pretend to give an account.'' ''Nature does not heed physics,'' he wrote his first year at Leiden. ''Physics heeds nature.''

Having sensed the growing intensity of this dispute, Uyterhoeven had found extremely disconcerting, therefore—but also in a strange way thrilling—the realization, first gleaned in 1853, that despite the stark differences that existed between them philosophically, and despite the deliberate sequestering of their investigations, they had all three—including Lebert—begun to bear in on the same conclusion. Throughout the next year the three doctors worked in closer and closer contact, until in the spring of 1855 their diverse perspectives did finally converge upon one and the same object of understanding, an insight which would forever change the course of Western medicine and the contemplation of physical life in general: that all cells stem from other cells.

Virchow was the one to stand and tap his glass, actually, to inform the rest of the world, in Latin. Of the three, he turned out to be far and away the most energetic salesman of cell life, in large part because he appeared to have been most excited by its potential medical consequence. Up until then, after all—and going back for nearly two millennia—health had been understood in the West to consist more or less in the regulation and well-being of blood and whatever other fluids comprised organs. With the discovery that cells possessed life independent of the larger organisms surrounding them—that cells were, in fact, the basic building blocks of life—Virchow, Lebert, and Uyterhoeven had in effect drawn to a close the prolonged reign of humoral pathology. Now the health of all living things, including human beings, could be understood to depend more precisely upon the health of their cells. This at least was Virchow's understanding, and it was following on this ''decidedly rationalist opinion,'' according to Uyterhoeven, that Western medicine would evolve into ''the overwhelmingly technological industry it is today'' (1869).

At the time, Dr. Uyterhoeven had not been thinking in such terms. His first impressions at observing cell formation hadn't so much to do with the mechanics of health as with the conduct of life. In another letter to Mueller, written in 1855, Uyterhoeven stated: ''We have reached a next threshold in the hunt [for life]: we have stepped from what had seemed a well-manicured glade back into the woods again.''

His reasons for feeling so were visceral, he admitted. They had come from the observation itself—of seeing one cell, of its own apparent devise, become two. He wrote Mueller:

> Are we to find it more troubling or heartening that the apparent behavior of life changes, depending upon the distance from which one observes it? Hadn't we supposed that this behavior would be the same from magnitude to magnitude?—and yet, no. Looking skyward, at the largest, farthest parts of heaven, the movements are elementary and metric, consigned to what seems an endless repetition, over and over again, like nursery rhymes. From the compass of human eyes unaided, nature continues to play a relatively formal game, something like billiards, so predictable and measurable in its demeanor as to provoke the effort of the physicist to proscribe it with law . . .
>
> And yet at closer, microscopic range, the performance is quite different—it opposes what we'd thought was intuition: addition by division; life not bound by law, but clearly spontaneous, unrepeatable, unaccountable, free and strange . . .
>
> Our choice appears to be a personal one, then, which range we find most consoling and beautiful—that heavenly lullaby of things remote and immense; the machinations perceived in a casual glance; or the anarchy of the near view. For myself, I cannot help the feeling that life itself is somewhere in the chaos, untraceable, like heat in fire.

Virchow had not been so moved, obviously. He referred to his old friend's unabated penchant for citing life's inherent vitalism to ''accounting for the color of the sky by its blueness.'' The appearance of spontaneity in cell formation was nothing more than that, in Virchow's view—an appearance, which was easily attributed to what he called ''excitability'' or ''irritability,'' which simply meant that cells, when they divided, were only reacting to external stimulation, and only then within the confines of physical law.

Of course, Uyterhoeven considered ''excitability'' an even more tautological notion than vitalism—''a rationalist sleight of hand,'' he called it in another letter to Mueller. ''It simply begs the question once again—whence excitability?''

Whatever the answer—and Uyterhoeven did not believe there was a good answer—one thing was clear. The expectation that the ''closer view'' would help resolve his old dispute with Virchow had apparently been mistaken. In point of fact, the greatest medical breakthrough of the century had failed to persuade either of them of anything he hadn't already believed, which, in the end, Uyterhoeven accepted as only fair. He wrote Gustav Fechner: ''How disappointed would I have been if our dispute had been resolved by the mere unveilings of technology? I think we should admit—or resign ourselves to the fact: there shall be no resolution.''

The viability of this position—the agreement to disagree—between two such close and influential friends was soon put to the test. In 1856 Mueller retired, leaving vacant the directorship of the Friedrich Wilhelm Institut in Berlin. Virchow had been the obvious pick for successor. He was German. He had proven himself to be a leader, an administrator, a shaper of opinion, an innovator, and now, with the patenting of cell law, a visionary as well. His appointment had been so indisputable, in fact, that he used his leverage to set two conditions on his acceptance: first, that an institute be built devoted exclusively to pathology, the first of its kind; and second, that his friend and esteemed colleague Dr. Uyterhoeven be lured from Leiden at any cost to sit on the faculty and help oversee the new building's design and construction.

The FWI agreed without hesitation, but Uyterhoeven was wary. That pathology was entering an exciting new phase he understood all too well, and that the most powerful seat of the new regime would rest in Berlin was equally clear, particularly now with Virchow's appointment. And yet the prospect of actually working with Virchow troubled him. As fond as he was of his old friend, and as formidable as their track record now was, he could not help thinking that their disputes would at some point down the road come to haunt them. In answer to the Institut's first bid, he wrote Virchow that they should "perhaps take heed of recent events, and the never more conspicuous demonstration of our biases . . . and let the discovery (of cell succession) stand as a happy and perplexing coincidence of our interests, but now carry on with their own investigations, as we have been doing, separately."

Predictably, Virchow disagreed. He conceded their views were hostile, but that was the point, in his opinion. Had it not affirmed the authenticity of their recent work, that again and again their findings had matched even despite the conflict of their perspectives? "It is as difficult for me to admit, as I am sure it is for you, my friend, but no less true: the practice of an ardent methodist and an ardent empiricist, provided they are both suitably ardent—prove to be shamefully compatible. Come."

Uyterhoeven was not entirely convinced, but what finally tipped the scales were more personal considerations. His and Sonja's first two years together had not been easy. Gone was the romance of their courtship, the trysts and secret notes. Gone the suspense and the exultation of their first glimpses in the markets. Gone most of all, for Sonja, was the flow of the canals. "She has lost color," Gustav wrote his old tutor Menno in 1854. "I have begun to fear the bolted existence does not suit her."

Also, of course, Gustav's attention had been more devoted to his work than ever. These were the years of the hunt—the hot pursuit of cell life—and so whereas before, during their courtship, Gustav's work had seemed admirable to Sonja, and exotic, now in Leiden she could not help feeling that her husband's laboratory was a fierce rival for his attention, and one which she felt absolutely helpless to contest.

Through the whole first year of their marriage, then, her father's doubts were never entirely put to rest. They drifted only as far as the canals could take them—in winter, the Rhine; in spring, Friesland or Groningen; most of the time they hovered just outside the windows of their home, whispering to her that she and Gustav were much too different, that she was not meant for this settled life, was not one of these people. In the spring of 1854, near the time of their first anniversary, Gustav wrote Menno: "She is no better. I look at her and wonder sometimes if she is drowning in the still air."

With the start of their second year, they began to rest their hopes on having a child, in faith that a son or daughter would anchor Sonja finally, happily, and unite them. Sonja became pregnant in November of 1854. She was due in August, but it was a difficult period for her. At the same time as Gustav was fast closing in on what seemed the most significant moment of his professional career, Sonja was haunted by her mother's death in labor, and in July she lost her child, a girl.

By the following winter, Sonja was pregnant again, and was showing five months when the FWI came bidding for Gustav in early May of 1856. That summer, a year to the week from her first miscarriage, she lost her second child, another girl. Gustav wrote Menno: "The air which before had seemed merely stale now smells like poison." In July he accepted Virchow's invitation, and the following month he and Sonja packed up their possessions and moved to Berlin.

The professional gamble paid off quickly. There was much to be said for placing oneself at the center of things. On the basis of the work he'd begun in Leiden in the area of plant forms of disease germs, pneumonia, and lung disease, Uyterhoeven re-established himself as one of the Continent's most progressive thinkers and physicians, now a pioneer of bacteriology as well as cell life. By the end of his first year, he had taken rank among the Institut's best instructors, and his ministrations at the new pathological facility were equally well regarded. Also, Virchow appeared to have been right about their "practical compatibility." In matters of design, curriculum, and facilities, they were in almost complete agreement. They sparred on occasion, of course—when Virchow publicly denounced the blastema theory of Schleide and Schwanne as "speculation," Uyterhoeven countered that it was merely "bad speculation"—but such spats were seen as a harmless diversion, offered up more to satisfy the faculty's expectation than to vent any real strife. In point of fact, their collaboration was, by 1859, a much heralded success. The new pathological institute was universally acknowledged to be in the vanguard of Western medicine, and its two principal architects had to all appearances fulfilled their destiny as the most celebrated physicians in Europe, the pride and private cadre of the new German school.

On the private front, Gustav and Sonja were called upon to exercise a good deal more faith and patience. The house upon which Gustav had insisted in his negotiation was conspicuously large—enough to accommodate a sizable family—but its rooms remained still and quiet throughout their first four years in Berlin. Sonja suffered no miscarriages. She simply did not become pregnant, and as one year passed to the next, she and Gustav began to wonder if they were even capable of children, and if they were not, what purpose they had together. "There is a horrible temptation," Gustav wrote Menno in 1859, "to admit that a union of such ill fate might possibly have been ill conceived."

He was not alone in his uncertainty. Sonja found Berlin a more restrictive and hopeless place than even Leiden. She didn't speak much German, the Institut was that much more demanding of Gustav's time and attention, and that much farther removed from her true home, the lowland canals. By 1860 her restlessness and detachment had grown so severe that in the late summer, she broached the subject of returning to the Netherlands, just herself and just for a brief period. Her sister, Mirjam, had recently married Mattijs van Kroon, the young man whom Koos had first believed was Sonja's suitor. Now Koos was alone on his barge, and Sonja wanted to help him during the harvest season, when there would be more to deliver. Gustav agreed. He was aware of her unhappiness, felt largely responsible, and let her go, frankly uncertain what the future held for them.

In November came the best answer imaginable. Sonja sent word from Friesland that she was with child. Gustav left to see her at once and, upon reaching her in Smilde, wrote Menno: "I admit that in hope as great as mine the insinuation of dread is that much more distinct, and yet on seeing her, only faith. She has not looked so well since the summer of our engagement.''

Gustav stayed with her just three days, but they agreed that she should not leave the canals for the remainder of her pregnancy. That winter and spring, just as he had the year of their courtship, Gustav traveled back and forth between his laboratory and Sonja, only now from Berlin. It was far from a convenient arrangement, but with each return he was more convinced that so long as Sonja remained on the water, their child would be well.

In Sonja's absence, though, alone in the great house on Friedrichstrasse, Gustav was moved by solitude and by the new promise of his marriage to face the fact finally that all was not quite so well at the Institut as he had been pretending. Over two years before, he had begun a letter to that effect to his old master Mueller, the former director. Mueller had died that spring, however, so Gustav had let his anxieties fester until the second month of Sonja's pregnancy. He finished the letter in December of 1860, wrote another, and another to follow that. In all, he wrote four letters, all dedicated to the recently departed Mueller, and all addressing his general concern for the state of medicine in Berlin, and in particular the philosophical mooring of the pathological institute.

Uyterhoeven had been under no false pretense when he'd decided to return to Berlin, of course. He'd known ever since his undergraduate days that Berlin was the capital of European rationalism, but in the past he had always been able to tolerate the local outlook on a case-by-case basis, as he'd done with Virchow, deeming it a matter of what he called ''unfortunate personal inclination.'' What he had not quite been prepared for was the cumulative effect of rationalism's now almost universal acceptance within the academic community. He wrote in the first of his letters to Mueller: ''It is the basic assumption of everyone with whom I work, including my students, that the temper of nature is obviously mechanical, that science has somehow proven this, and that to think otherwise demonstrates a latency of superstition . . . It is the current rage, I mean, to think that life is dead.''

The reasons for the unprecedented prevalence of this view were hardly difficult to deduce, in the doctor's opinion: they had basically to do with technology, and the fact that it had managed to yield such groundbreaking insights in the past decade. Anytime a man-made instrument came along to reveal some unforeseen wonder, Uyterhoeven allowed that there was bound to follow "a swell in the rationalist breast . . . It becomes very difficult, in light of such revelations—even those as enigmatic as ours, apparently—to imagine that there could possibly exist a mystery which lies beyond the power of man's reason, man's instruments, and man's ingenuity to solve. Silly us, we have been more taken by the window than the view."

Of more personal concern to the doctor was the role he perceived that his own institute had begun to play in disseminating this misguided conceit. He observed that pathology in general had come to assume a significance, in its new cellular phase, that it hadn't ever enjoyed before, and as the first genuine home of such study, the pathological institute had come to serve as a "galvanizing force"—none of which the doctor minded in itself. There was no shame in "looking as close as one can," or in conferring influence upon those who had dedicated themselves to doing so. The mistake, wrote Uyterhoeven, was in "assuming that by looking closer, we have somehow learned to see better . . . The mistake is in letting the advantages which technology has provided our study somehow revise our stated objective." And yet this is precisely what had happened. As the magnitude of their lenses had increased, the definition of pathology had inexplicably transformed. It had changed from what Uyterhoeven had always understood it to be—which was the study of the effects of disease—"to what is now the popular understanding—that it is somehow a study of causes."

And this, of course, was the classic rationalist foible. This was the great offense, in Uyterhoeven's opinion—"the casual conflation of cause and effect." He wrote: "There seems to be a subtle but profound confusion which plagues all those of the determinist, methodist, and rationalist persuasion, between the desire *to observe* the animation of the universe—which is perfectly admirable—and the desire *to explain* it—which is patently absurd."

Of course, there was nothing radically new in this complaint. Uyterhoeven had noted this error many times before during his battles with Virchow at the Charité. What he had not before identified, however, at least in so many words, was the particular oversight which he believed permitted this confusion: the failure, as he now put it, to acknowledge "the eternal and unfathomed ellipsis which exists between every effect and its cause."

> I suppose what needs to be understood, and always borne in mind, is that ultimately every causal relation, even the most rudimentary—the relation of gear to gear, of rainfall to puddles, of fire to smoke—is as mysterious as that grief should cause tears to fall from a man's eyes, or that irony should cause his cheeks to rise in smile: I believe that these relations are true. I know this from experience, but is it not clear that somewhere in the logical chain which would attempt to link the one to the other—link the departure of a loved one to tears, for instance—that no matter how precise our study of glands and tear ducts, no matter how sensitive our appreciation of men's fears and consolations, there shall be one link missing?—the one, I would suggest, that actually connects them . . .

The point, in Uyterhoeven's view, was that "all the links are missing," and that it was not in the capacity of reason or technology to find them. Technology could only reveal what was there to be seen in the first place, and all that could ever be seen were effects: "that whatever we are given to apprehend in the present moment is the result of something else which has made it so."

> But hold, the question comes, are we not able in retrospect to identify certain of these effects as causes, too? Could it not be said, for instance, that blood loss—no doubt the effect of Madame Corday's having stabbed him in his tub—was also the cause of Marat's death?
>
> Certainly this could be said. It could be said on what seems

at first a very acceptable standard—that which measures cause by the reliance of a given effect upon it—for it is true, if not for an excessive letting of blood, Marat would not have died there in his tub.

But could it not also be said on this same basis that Madame Corday's zealotry *caused* him to die as well, that her butcher's knife *caused* him to die, that the Girondists, the Revolution, and Monsieur Marat's own skin condition *caused* him to die? For it is no less true of these—if not for any one of them, Marat's death, such as it occurred, would not have.

But now it seems that we have trivialized the point, for it is our desire in determining Cause to be as specific as possible, is it not? To say that the Girondists, Madame Corday, the butcher's knife, blood loss, and scabies *all* caused Marat's death is tantamount to admitting that none really did so in itself. It is, in fact, to admit that these various factors are not Causes of Marat's death so much as Antecedents—relevant antecedents, I will allow, but causes? No. The true cause of Marat's death—that force specifically responsible for rendering the living Marat dead in his tub, and therefore by necessity at play in all of the preceding conditions which made that demise possible—that Cause . . . I do not know. I have no idea. And I would hope this doesn't brand me a skeptic. I only mean that there is nothing to which I could ever have pointed and said, "There. There is the cause of Marat's death," because no such thing ever encroached the plane of human apprehension; only signs of it.

Uyterhoeven was literally overwhelmed by arguments which he felt made this equally clear, as well as innumerable examples, all present at hand—"in the burning wick of my candle; as I drop a coin upon the floor; as I boil water for my tea, or spread jam upon my bread"—each and every one of which seemed to him incontrovertible evidence of the same simple fact: "What makes things so, ultimately and definitively, *is* so. The True Cause of each effect is in effect, I mean, and since it is in effect, is not itself shown so much as indicated; is present, and yet by nature inscrutable.''

> What to make of this Unshown Force, how to recognize, acknowledge, and treat it, are all worthy questions which I far from protest, but insofar as they all pertain to a subject *which will not show itself*—no matter the degrees of genius or magnitude we employed in searching for it—and insofar as this force, Cause, and God could well be thought the same, I would confer its study upon those of religious temperament.
>
> . . . As for the scientist, as his remain an essentially empirical endeavor, he should have to content himself with what *is* shown. That is his assignment: to study life and nature such as it *can* be apprehended, moment to moment—as an effect, for instance, of rain, which antecedes an effect of puddles, which antecedes an effect of mud-tracked rugs. This is as much as may be said.

Never before had Uyterhoeven taken his views quite so far. Indeed, upon finishing the last of his letters to Mueller in April of 1861, he had more or less confirmed his permanent exclusion from the intellectual fellowship of his colleagues—in the first place because he was the only member of the Institut engaged in such abstruse ruminations; and second, because by their lead he had come to refine a perspective which had confounded and then summarily dismissed the most prized device of the rational mind—that being induction.

Of course, the temptation had been there to publish a cleaner, more diplomatic rendering of his argument—to point out that when his colleagues spoke so casually of cause, they were in fact engaged in metaphysics, in ''anti-science.'' His old friend Gustav Fechner certainly encouraged him to, but in the end, Uyterhoeven decided to keep his opinions to himself—perhaps understandably. He still valued his position at the Institut and felt no particular need to antagonize the rest of the faculty with objections he knew they would find, in a word, semantic. The fact remained, for all the fault he found with the motives and assumptions of his colleagues, he still did not recognize any great practical difference between his work and theirs. Virchow's view continued to hold, in other words. ''Whether an effect of rain, or the cause of mud-tracked rugs, a puddle is still a puddle,'' Uyterhoeven wrote Fechner, in refusing.

> As long as this remains the case—or until such time as I find my colleagues' applications egregiously at odds with my own—I can see no benefit in divulging any part of the confidence that I have so enjoyed this spring, with the memory of our friend, my dear master Mueller.

On August 7, 1861, on her father's barge and with Gustav in attendance, Sonja gave birth to a boy. Her labor was long and difficult. ''He will be our only child,'' wrote Gustav in a letter which he never sent his mother. ''But his first breaths have extinguished my yearning for any other, ever to have been or ever to come. He is the one who joins us.'' They named him Larkin, the family name of Gustav's grandfather's footman in Windsor.

Isabel came over from England to meet her grandson in The Hague. It was the first time she'd met Sonja as well. Gustav had never sought his mother's approval in marrying Sonja, for fear, as he put it once in a letter to Menno, that she might

> object to the inclusion in her tree of someone who, but for the curiosity of having grown up on water, would otherwise be thought a peasant, and therefore of peasant stock. If I could but be sure she'd recognize, the curiosity is of essence, and has bestowed Sonja precisely the worldly disattachment which Mother would have wanted for herself, but for her being English, and therefore English.

He apparently needn't have worried. Isabel stayed with them two weeks and, upon returning to England, wrote her son:

You have underestimated us both. She is a most extraordinary creature; the two of you an extraordinary pair, now with that dear child, a family.

The first evening of his tenth week, while still on Koos's *tjalk,* Larkin developed a fever. Gustav had been preparing to take him and Sonja back to Berlin, but for the next several days Larkin's temperature continued to soar until, on the fifth, Gustav diagnosed him with cerebral fever, or meningitis.

There was very little that either Gustav or Sonja could do. They took shifts sleeping so that one would always be with him, and Koos remained by his grandson's crib day and night. When the fever was nine days old, Mirjam arrived with her newborn daughter, Elsa, and that evening, while Mirjam held Elsa outside Larkin's window, Larkin's fever finally broke. His father wrote: "In our hearts, we shall always be grateful to his cousin Elsa."

In the beginning of September, Gustav and Sonja finally took Larkin to his home in Berlin, relieved but wary. They moved his crib into their bedroom, but Larkin showed no ill effects of his first fever until February, when he suffered another bout of meningitis. Gustav wrote Scott Geddes, the homeopathic physician with whom he'd worked in London. He described Larkin's second spell as "a spasm of the first—less severe to him, I think, and perhaps his mother. Still, I am concerned about an increased proneness to seizure."

Geddes answered that calomel, camphor, and *Juniperus sabina* might serve as a preventative. It is not known whether Uyterhoeven followed the prescription, but in the coming months peace returned, and with it, slowly, confidence. Then in November Larkin was stricken a third time, now by scarlet fever. Again Gustav wrote Geddes, describing the fever as "meeting in severity all the strength he's gained back since February."

Geddes suggested wraps of castor oil, glycothymaline, and "ultramolecular doses" of belladonna. Gustav administered all faithfully, and within days Larkin's fever normalized. In fact, his health returned so quickly that Gustav observed in a letter to Menno that his son "seemed almost stronger for it, as if he were now an old hand." He continued:

> I have heard there is sympathy within the faculty that I have been given such a sickly child. It surprises me. Am I to think him sickly for having suffered so much of his first two years? Mine is quite the opposite impression—that to have weathered so much malady, as to have entered life so willfully, he must be a person of exceptionally strong will, tempered by three fevers now to be sooner like his mother than I could ever have imagined. Calm but vigilant. Like her, he welcomes one to every moment. The humor in both their eyes is at always being made to wait. Of the three, I am the one left ragged by these trials, but with this last come and gone, I can feel a weight has been lifted. Last night, for the first time since returning here, we all three slept at once.

❧

Not long thereafter, Sonja spoke to Gustav for the only time in the marriage about his work. In a letter he wrote Menno to mark the occasion, Gustav claimed that she had been quiet for several days, more so than usual, and in his estimation "cross." Finally, he had asked if there was anything wrong, and she answered with "a proper scolding."

> She asked how it was that a man who takes such pride in his ideas, and who had come to Berlin for the express purpose of sharing them, should after four years in this community still not have established a single associate whom he would trust to consult in the event of his own son's illness, but rely instead upon "this Geddes man from London."

It was a question well worth an answer, and the doctor offered a very public reply later that spring—or at least the beginnings of a reply. He did not explain his particular preference for Geddes's prescriptions or even mention his son's illness—on the contrary, he took care to frame his argument in as purely analytical terms as he was able, for fear that any direct association with ''alternative'' schools would only serve to marginalize what he believed was a central point. Still, to those familiar with his son's recent ordeal, he left no doubt as to why he'd waived the services of the most highly reputed physicians in all Europe.

An article had appeared that April 1863 in Virchow's *Archiv für Pathologische Anatomie* by Rudolph Buchheim, who was one of Germany's leading pharmacologists. Buchheim had been extolling the virtues of animal experimentation in helping to determine what he called the ''physiologic effects'' of given drugs, and Uyterhoeven took the opportunity to offer in response what he called ''A Brief Caveat'' regarding the allopathic scheme which compelled such aggressive—and, in his view, ''impertinent''—research in the first place.

The allopathic scheme was the conventional therapeutic approach of the rationalist school, not coincidentally, and therefore the prevalent doctrine being applied throughout Berlin and most of the Western medical community. As Uyterhoeven characterized it, the first recommendation of the allopathic approach, in the face of a given illness, was to distinguish between ''insignificant'' or ''superficial'' symptoms and those which represented ''more relevant morbific and internal physiological change,'' the point being to identify what was called either the ''proximate cause'' or ''primary disease.'' The ''primary disease'' then functioned as a kind of a target for the pharmacologist, a chief offender to which he could subject a heavy bombardment of ''oppositive'' drugs—that is, drugs which had been proven to yield effects opposed to those of the offending ''cause.'' If the ''primary disease'' was found to be *hot,* for instance, allopathic theory recommended that the remedy administered be one that effects a *cold* reaction.

Uyterhoeven tried to make clear that he did not reject such thinking outright. He allowed there was benefit to distinguishing between morbific, sympathetic, and idiopathic symptoms, and in those cases where it had been proven that oppositive drugs did contribute to the patient's recovery without an overabundance of extenuating complications, they should by all means be administered.

He pointed out, however, that very often this approach of "contesting the effects of certain illnesses" served only to complicate the body's own healing process, by setting off other imbalances which in turn needed treatment. This alone was cause for a careful review, but Uyterhoeven went on to offer that the reason for the "clumsiness" of the approach and the intrinsic failing of the whole allopathic scheme was that it was premised upon a fallacy: simply, that there existed a demonstrable cause or "disease itself."

Empirically speaking, reminded the doctor, there did not. All that could be shown were symptoms, and any line which one attempted to draw between those symptoms which were "mere effects" and those which represented "disease itself" was inherently arbitrary and deceptive, since disease itself—if by this one meant to specify that which had caused the anomalous symptoms—could not be shown, or therefore directly contested. The "Caveat" ended:

> Disease cannot be seen or dealt with but by its effects, which are symptoms, the same as one cannot see the wind but by observing its effects—which might be swirling leaves, for instance. If one were for some reason annoyed by swirling leaves, one could certainly rake them, put them in a sack, and burn them, but such a person would not be understood to have defeated the wind. Such a person would be understood to have generated some smoke.

Uyterhoeven was not in Berlin when his "Caveat" appeared, in July. Larkin was well enough by then that the Uyterhoevens had gone to the Netherlands to spend the summer on the canals with Sonja's family. Gustav had not necessarily been expecting a response to his piece. He had assumed that if there was one, it would most likely come from Virchow, as Virchow had always in the past been the one to rebut his published opinions.

In this instance, however, Uyterhoeven had overestimated his friend's willingness to involve himself in debates outside his area of expertise. Virchow had never been a particularly enlightened student of therapeutics or pharmacology—he remained a proponent of older methods such as purges, vomitives, and laxatives—so he had offered the opportunity for rebuttal to a close friend of Buchheim's and another of Germany's leading pharmacologists, Karl Mitscherlich.

Mitscherlich had been reluctant at first. In truth, he hadn't wanted to dignify Uyterhoeven's essay with a response, but after some coaxing from Benno Reinhardt, the journal's other editor, he finally relented and that July submitted an extremely caustic rebuttal, which Virchow had no real choice but to run, for fear he might be accused of protecting a friend if he did not.

In short, Mitscherlich advanced the view, on behalf of the German pharmacological community as a whole, that when it came to therapeutics, the esteemed Dr. Uyterhoeven should kindly mind his own business. All that philosophical hand-wringing about cause and effect may have been fine within the halls of the pathological institute, for old friends to squabble over what they were and were not doing, but therapeutics was not a field to be guided by epistemological principles, especially ones which intimated spiritualism. After all, if disease did not cause morbific physiological change—that is, if causes didn't cause things—what alternative did Dr. Uyterhoeven leave? All Mitscherlich could think of, only partly in jest, were "ghosts and guardian angels."

Earnest or merely political, Mitscherlich's mockery succeeded in trivializing Uyterhoeven's comments, and when the doctor returned from the Netherlands for the fall semester, he was surprised to find his "Caveat" the subject of more derision than reflection—"smirks and exasperated glances," as he put it to Fechner. "Particularly vexing is to have been deflected as mystical," he went on. "I am not the one claiming to see things that I cannot. Let history note—we've apparently reached a juncture where methodist conjecture passes for science, while the most orthodox empiricism can be dismissed as metaphysics."

Not one to let the open perversion of his ideas go unchecked, the doctor did, however, respond. That November he submitted a second piece to the *Archiv,* this one slightly more to the point and therefore slightly more revealing. He began by expressing his regret for not having made himself more clear in the first pieces, and "for leaving to suggestion certain indications which could apparently be so easily misconstrued." His purpose in calling attention to the fallacy of "primary disease" had not been to focus therapeutic attention on "first cause," which he continued to insist was an unknown. His purpose had been to prompt a re-examination of "the increasingly and unnecessarily hostile relationship which the allopathic scheme encourages between malady and remedy." After all, if it were allowed, by common sense, that what physicians such as the Professors Buchheim and Mitscherlich were so anxious to call a disease was really, demonstrably, only a complex set of symptoms, then a whole world of other possible therapeutic schemes was opened up, the majority of which were not so combative, since without "disease itself" there was nothing necessarily to fight. There was only a process to be observed, and assist. He wrote:

> The primary purpose of every living organism is to grow and at the same time maintain a balance with the environment. Symptoms, which is to say, all that we can observe, are merely and significantly an indication of that effort. Aggravated symptoms, or anomalous cell activity, indicate an imbalance and are not either to be dismissed as physiologically irrelevant or to be opposed as "disease itself." They are each and every one of them to be understood as an attempt, or as the indication of an attempt, at reattaining this balance—in other words, healing.

The gist of Uyterhoeven's argument was simple, then: the body, with respect to the physician, often knew best what it was doing. Bombarding symptoms with oppositive drugs was, in certain instances, tantamount to "massacring the messenger" or, worse, foiling the patient's own attempt at righting him- or herself. "There is, to be sure, a time and place for thwarting symptoms, but there is also a time for encouraging symptoms on their way; for recognizing that who, in the allopathic scheme, had been the hero—the physician—should become the student; and who had been the villain—the symptom—should be acknowledged as the teacher.''

❧

This time, Buchheim was the one to respond, though not in the *Archiv*. During a talk he gave in Dorpat that winter of 1864, he was asked about Dr. Uyterhoeven's defense, and responded with an observation which was far more damaging in its way than merely to accuse his adversary of sophistry or spiritualism. Rather, he pointed out that Uyterhoeven's empiricist finger-wagging had begun to sound ''patently homeopathic.''

Buchheim was right, of course. He'd had no knowledge of the work that Uyterhoeven had done with Geddes in London, nor of the remedies the doctor had employed in treating his son two years before, but when Uyterhoeven alluded to ''encouraging symptoms on their way,'' he had tipped his hand. All Uyterhoeven had really done, said Buchheim, was rederive the law of similars, which at that time in Germany was almost like coming out in favor of leeching. Indeed, homeopathy was by then popularly thought to be the very lowest breed of empiricism, so concerned with the brute efficacy of its treatments that it neglected the more lasting goal of medicine, which was to understand how the body worked. Homeopathists preferred to play tricks on the body, luring it to health with comically diluted potions, pathetic trial, and constant error. In these respects, their practice was closer kin to witchcraft than science, and for Buchheim to have smelled its principles lurking somewhere in Uyterhoeven's reasoning was taken by many, as no doubt had been intended, to be a rather blunt impugnment of Dr. Uyterhoeven's scientific integrity.

Uyterhoeven was aware of all this. That was part of the reason he'd tried to couch his argument in empirical, rather than specifically homeopathic, terms—and he still believed that his position should be considered on its own merits—but he frankly didn't think it was a good idea to place any more of his credibility at risk by offering up yet another defense. He had his research to consider, research that he knew was vulnerable to just the same sort of misinterpretation. That winter he'd begun recording the symptoms yielded in healthy tissue at the cellular level by both homeopathic and more traditionally allopathic drugs. It was an effort whose benefit even Virchow had conceded in principle, but the damning association had already been made once. When Lebert had seen his work in December, he'd dubbed it "cellular homeopathy" in a letter to Virchow. "If anyone is capable of such a thing, it is Gustav, but in all seriousness I don't believe our instruments are yet apace with such a subtle venture."

Uyterhoeven did not share his friend's skepticism, obviously. He was very excited about his work, and therefore, in hopes of being left alone to pursue it, he decided to let Buchheim's slur pass, and for the moment withdrew from the society and intrigue of the community.

This did not go unnoticed. Many interpreted Uyterhoeven's quiet retreat as a *prima facie* admission of guilt, that he had indeed been trying to smuggle homeopathy back into the therapeutic debate. Still others took his silence as one more indication of his growing indifference to the opinions of those with whom he was supposed to be working. Ever since the birth of his son, Uyterhoeven was seen to have become more aloof. At first this was forgiven on account of Larkin's recurrent illness, but now that the boy was apparently well, Dr. Uyterhoeven seemed more distant than ever. When Buchheim wrote Reinhardt to ask if "the Dutch wizard" had yet offered a response to his recent observations, Reinhardt returned that Uyterhoeven "appears at the moment to be more interested in fatherhood than medicine."

An argument was to be made. That winter, the canals up in Friesland had frozen, and Uyterhoeven had spent the entire month of February shuttling back and forth between the Institut and Ijilst because Koos had insisted Larkin learn to skate with his cousin Elsa. From Hoogeveen Gustav sent his mother a drawing of Sonja and Larkin standing together in their skates. "And here is the beast that greeted me," he captioned, "all wrapped in coats and scarves—two-headed, four-legged, and with blades on all its feet—and whose smaller half, at seeing me, released itself and skated very well in my direction, growling, with curled mittens and arms outstretched. I am hoping the frost has reached Berlin by the time we return.''

The rest of the doctor's letters bear out Reinhardt's observation almost as vividly. His longest at the time was a five-page essay to Menno comparing the relative drawbacks and benefits of subjecting his son to chess at such an early age. Larkin was only four years old at the time, but had apparently gravitated to the game on his own, out of attraction to the military pieces in the window set of a local chess shop—his weakness for all things military having already been established. ''It appears we may have a soldier on our hands,'' Gustav wrote his mother soon after Larkin's birthday in 1864, in thanks for the set of lead soldiers she sent from London.

> His only difficulty is not knowing whose side he should join. Your gift tipped the balance toward England for a good month, but his ambivalence has returned. I am afraid that he asked his mother the other evening, before heading into the parlor for one of his candlestick fencing matches, whose side he should fight for. She suggested he fight for whoever needed it most. I don't believe England has fared quite so well since. This week his cape is black and red—I suspect Rudolf may have mentioned something to him about the Turks.

Most of the rest of the doctor's correspondence he composed with Larkin actually—not letters so much as tales, which they conceived together, just as he and Menno had when Gustav was a boy. Larkin brought more of an illustrator's mind. He had begun drawing soldiers one rainy afternoon on his grandmother's hearth the summer before, and not many days had passed since that he hadn't taken up a pencil, a pen, or a crayon and done the same. Every evening when Gustav came home, Larkin would show him the pictures he'd drawn that day. Then they would sit together at the desk in Gustav's study, bring out one of Larkin's pads, and instead of Larkin drawing, Gustav would, as Larkin described the picture he wanted to see. ''He prefers the lines not be broken,'' Gustav wrote Menno. ''He prefers a drawing of as few lines as possible. If I could manage one of just a single line, I am sure that would be his favorite.''

The period of quiet isolation that Dr. Uyterhoeven had sought for the sake of his research—and peace of mind—did not last very long. The summer of 1864, less than six months after Buchheim's derisive comments in Dorpat, there came to the attention of the German medical community a satirical chapbook entitled *The Delusions of Sobriety: A Cognitive Homeopathic Remedy to Opium Addiction in Londoners.*

Published nearly eleven years before in England under the name Bishop John, *The Delusions of Sobriety* had been intended for private circulation among the patrons of a dilapidated chess club–turned–opium den in the West End called Branaughts, and then also, as demand required, among other circles of a like sensibility throughout London's opium-eating community.

The purpose of the chapbook, as stated in its subtitle and then again in its preface, had been ''to effect a weaning from opium addiction, in obeisance of Samuel Hahnemann's law of similars.''* The

*The preface continued:

. . . Pending the discovery of that chemical medicament which renders the symptoms of opium addiction innocuously, and also pending the ability of science to secure in direct correspondence the abstract element of thought, or thinking, to its commensurate coagulant expression—or brain-state—it has been conceded that of these two, the only traceable symptoms of such chemical addiction as opium is known to cause, are of the former type: of mind, thought, idea, and word. So the text in hand has been conceived as a specific, to exercise by words the intellectual and imaginative function of the reader in such a way as to render a brain-state symptomatically like that effected by extended exposure to opium, ingested at a minimum of 160 grains, or 4,000 drops, per day, every day, for at least the period of six months.

For those of such dependence, and only those, the text may be ingested at whatever pace the reader sees fit to bear, in reliance that his illness, previously satisfied by the chemical opiate only, shall be cured by the similarity of illness which these pages have been contrived, and subsequently proven, to effect.

The question remains, without empiric answer yet, whether such brain-states are more precisely and beneficially rendered by attempting to comprehend certain images and concepts (''The skyclad, death-marked emperor said I see, that air is breath of leaf, but death of rock . . . and earth of space''; from *All Elements Are Like to Like,* p. 17) or whether the state of such likeness may be achieved more accurately and reliably by the mindless in-taking, and repetition, of words chosen for their sound and shape, as opposed to connotation (*Ebre-Dama Teke-Chiju Gara-komine,* p. 43). Our text, in absence of any certain answer, presents both possibilities, as reason it had come to light in Berlin, however, had little to do with the German appetite for either satire or hallucinogens. The rumor was that ''Bishop John'' was a pseudonym for their very own Dr. Uyterhoeven, a claim which, if true, would cast two new shadows upon the doctor's credibility—the first having to do with his apparent erstwhile addiction to opium, and the second of which could be traced to the telling homeopathic fluency that the chapbook displayed. Though obviously satire, *The Delusions of Sobriety* had clearly been written by someone familiar with homeopathic theory, practice, and repertory. If this turned out to be Uyterhoeven, it would, as Reinhardt put it, ''confirm suspicions in many minds that the doctor's renegade interests are more long-standing and probably more inveterate than he has led us to believe, and shall therefore cast his grievances of this previous year—as well as any more to come—in an even more dubious light.''

Despite this, Uyterhoeven was hardly evasive when confronted with the matter. In fact, he appears to have taken the reappearance of the chapbook as an opportunity to come clean finally. He admitted having penned it, and to having worked as Geddes's apprentice while in England. He furthermore confessed to having administered and taken part in several provings there, and had as a result come to observe that the law of similars was borne out in practice. As to whether this qualified him as an adherent, he did not feel in a position to say, but acknowledged that though his first reasons for becoming interested in homeopathy had to do with its high rate of success in treating cholera, which had taken his father's life the year before he'd gone to London, he had grown in the years since to appreciate more and more the consonance between many of the underlying principles of Hahnemann's theories and his own medical, epistemological, and even ontological convictions. Homeopathy was an influence, in other words, for which the doctor made no excuse and expressed no shame.

---

the reader shall see, on facing pages throughout . . .

Know, too, the text following has been intended for the Englishman's brain, taking into account its unique proclivities and resistances, and should not yet be administered, without a tutor present, to those of continental mind, even if addicted, for fear of some result or madness as yet uncharted.

In fact, that fall of 1864, he actually began integrating homeopathic theory and history into his lectures. Virchow had strongly recommended against this, but the doctor persisted. Especially in light of recent events, he felt it would seem spurious for him not to include the full breadth of his learning and experience into his instruction. Furthermore, he contended that in as close-minded an atmosphere as the Institut was becoming, it was imperative that the alternative schools at least have a voice. To that same end, he even proposed teaching a course on what he dubbed ''the divided legacy of Western medicine,'' that winter submitting a full syllabus and bibliography culled from the contemporary writings of resident faculty such as Virchow himself, but also extending all the way back to the works of Galen and Celsus.

The course was not approved, needless to say, and on the whole it would be fair to suggest that Uyterhoeven was not well served by candor. His efforts to expand the curriculum were perceived as more chafing than constructive, and over the course of that academic year, there ensued a muttered but still distinct backlash against him. His lectures were the subject of almost constant surveillance from curriculum committees, his research came under more and more scrutiny, and his name was frankly scorned. In drawing rooms, laboratories, letters, and libraries throughout Germany he was called variously a ''poet,'' a ''cynic,'' a ''fanatical Humean,'' a ''romantic,'' an ''anachronist,'' a ''hypocrite,'' and finally, merely, ''the Dutchman.''

By the spring of 1865 the doctor's stock had fallen so low that Virchow had urged him to publish some of the research he'd been conducting in the area of pneumonia and lung disease, just to remind their colleagues of his value, but Uyterhoeven refused. He had embraced the role of apostate, and in May, he chose instead to open the books of his pharmacological research—his ''cellular provings.'' Then the subsequent fall, in what was widely perceived as retaliation for the faculty's having rejected his historical survey course, Uyterhoeven actually began to conduct more conventional homeopathic, albeit moot, provings with one of his graduate-level classes.

Again, Virchow had been steadfastly against such demonstrations, but Uyterhoeven held his ground. He assured Virchow that he was not administering any untested substances, and that the provings were for no research purposes. His intention was simply to compare the subtlety and unreliability of traditional homeopathic procedure and repertory to the cruder but more certain research that men like Buchheim and Mitscherlich were pioneering in the area of animal experimentation.

The point was lost. When word got out that Uyterhoeven had been using his own students in provings, there was another uproar. The very idea that such barbaric techniques were being practiced within the most hallowed halls of scientific progressivism, not to mention on the most talented students in Europe, was deemed an unforgivable offense, and the clearest indication yet that Dr. Uyterhoeven's scientific and educational intentions were no longer to be trusted. He had become "seditious" in Reinhardt's opinion, "perverse" in Löffler's, and by the spring of 1866 there were as many as five calls from among the faculty for his resignation.

Sadly, Uyterhoeven was tempted. He still felt a vested proprietary stake in the Institut, and was as convinced as ever of the faculty's obligation to entertain alternative views, but he had begun to sense that in light of the portrait which had emerged of him—as sophist, spiritualist, opium addict, and closet homeopathist—he might do more harm than good to whatever school of thought he chose to represent. Worse, he was finding it impossible to teach or pursue his research in an atmosphere of such constant scrutiny and suspicion. Finally, in May of 1866, he wrote Virchow that he had begun to entertain the interest of other universities. "Know, dear friend, that I have been aware and grateful to you for your constant faith and patience, but the time has come for us to admit that I have failed to make myself clear." The same week he wrote his mother: "I have finally worn out my welcome in Berlin. Just as well. Who wanted a German son anyway?"

The Faculté des Sciences had been courting Dr. Uyterhoeven for some time, in fact, and that June he finally reciprocated. The second week he went to Paris to meet with the head of appointments. Sonja and Larkin were to come later in the month to spend the summer, and then depending upon how his negotiations turned out, they would stay or return to Berlin.

Before he left, Gustav wrote nine stories for Larkin, one for every night they were to be apart. Sonja read them to Larkin before bed, and for each one, Larkin drew a picture to show his father when they rejoined him later in the month. The seventh night Gustav was away, June 14, Sonja read Larkin a story about a boy who for his birthday was given a jacket which let whoever was wearing it fly. The boy flew over London and saw the Tower of London and London Bridge. Then over Windsor he saw Grandmother in her gardening hat. He flew down, and they had tea and biscuits in her garden. Her footman brought them out a birthday cake, and then the boy flew home again.

When Sonja was done, she left Larkin his pad and pencils as usual, and went to bed herself. That night she had a dream that she and Gustav were looking at a house by the seaside which the water had flooded to its windowsills. In the morning she awoke later than normal and went to Larkin's room. She found his newest drawing on the nightstand, of a boy flying over London Bridge, but when she turned down his blanket to wake him, only his body was lying there.

PART THREE

The Fourth, Fifth, Sixth, and Seventh Letters

EIGHT

EUGENE'S ROOK

Seven weeks elapsed between the reading of the doctor's third and fourth letters. The letters themselves had been written just a month apart, but the doctor had chosen a different postal route for the fourth, one less likely to fall victim to the Boers' penchant for blowing up the railway. By pulling a few old strings and exerting his charm here and there, he managed to reserve his letters and gifts a place in packages of official military correspondence, which as a rule were taken by British officers to the Cape, by hand, and from there sent to London, to the office of Major General Pretyman, whose secretary was kind enough to remove the doctor's letters and whatever else he had sent and ship them first class to the United States and Dayton.

It was a safer route, to be sure, but the whole course took roughly six to eight weeks, so it was mid-December by the time the fourth letter reached the garden. On the eleventh, a Tuesday, a chalk-written slate appeared on the inside of the front gate to notify the guests that the doctor's next letter would be read on Sunday, January 16.

That same day, the eleventh, a third piece appeared in the library. Mrs. Uyterhoeven had been keeping everything pertinent to the Antipodes in the library. She'd brought in the top drawer of the cherrywood dresser in the games shack—the very one in which the doctor claimed to have found the goatskin map—and set it on the doctor's desk blotter to keep the letters in. One of the children, Harold Bickford, had made a copy of the map with all the place-names written in, so that the guests could trace the doctor's progress. Mrs. Uyterhoeven put that up on the dictionary stand and laid the goatskin out flat on the candlestick table to use as a board for the pieces as they arrived.

The first had been the boy in the boat, which she put on the king's side knight's square; the second had been the paper crane, which she set in the knight's square on the queen's side; and now, the day the fourth reading was announced, a third piece had taken its place on the queen's side rook: a copper thimble filled three-quarters high with ash.

The Fourth Letter

December 3, 1900

Dear Sonja,

It is evening. I am out on the terrace of my suite in Macaroni with a warm brew of some native root in front of me and a cracker which tastes a bit like mashed black beans and sugar, but which has the image of a Danish pastry baked into its crust. The innkeeper, a German burgher named Montescue, was kind enough to bring them up when he saw me come in late this evening, and I know I should be hungry. I haven't eaten since this morning, but after what I have learned today, in the light which smoulders on the hillside, I find that I've no appetite.

I finally came to Eugene's rook today. I arrived last night in Macaroni, which is the board nearest by. The rook, you will remember, is where I had been told I'd the best chance of getting you all some gift.

I'd expected I might do better, of course—that I might be able to send you something I'd found rather than acquired. Still, I'd kept the rook in mind as a kind of milepost, a way to orient my travels as I attended to the more pressing business at hand, which was simply to see what I could see.

And yet, I must admit, the closer I came to this place, the rook, the more intrigued I was. Not because of anything new I learned; in fact, I came across no information either to elaborate or to controvert what I had been told from the start—that Eugene was a pawn who'd built himself a rook which traded in goods which everyone here seems to think of utmost value. What compelled me, more than what the pieces said, was the way they said it; the way a straw pawn from a board called Scarecrow actually removed his hat at the mention of Eugene's name; or when I mentioned to one of the cotton dolls in Raggedy that I might be headed to the rook, she looked up at me with envy almost, such as her button eyes and stitched mouth could convey, as if I were about to read a favourite book of hers for the first time. Indeed, the pieces here speak of Eugene in tones of voice and turns of phrase that one would normally reserve for saints or prophets. And so it was this that compelled me to the rook with more and more determination, to the point where, I must admit, for the last several days of my journey it has become precisely what I had resolved it shouldn't—an outright destination, and so the distance between us a mere obstacle, a nuisance, a means best undertaken without attention, like the turning of a page.

❧

It was yesterday, then, I came to the penultimate leaf. Macaroni is home to a team of what *appear* to be eighteenth-century German pieces, although they speak English and call themselves by extensive, aristocratic French surnames, which confusion may account for their title: whatever the Macaroni may be, they are plagued by severe Continental pretensions. I've yet to see their royalty or clergy, but their knights are horses who walk on their hind legs, their rooks are great round elephants with tiny native Africans atop their backs, and their pawns all appear to be burghers, with buckled shoes, white stockings, long frilly cuffs, and feathers in their caps. Their coats are either green or orange, but most noteworthy regarding the appearance of Macaroni is that they are much closer to two- than three-dimensional, like playing cards or gingerbread men. As a result, they move about very awkwardly, as if they are forever walking on the ledge of a high building, but for which purpose they all carry very baroque walking staffs, which I will admit to envying them, as I have been having some trouble with my hip.

For this same reason, I had made it my first order of business upon arriving here to find out how far away the rook was—to gauge whether my hip was up for the remainder of the journey, or whether I should take the evening to rest.

I had been headed towards the central square for just this purpose when I was accosted by a passerby. "Don't tell me," he said, pointing his cane at my sternum and striking a rather jaunty pose—a greencoat he was, with long black hair, half-descended eyelids, a thin moustache, and a rather unfortunate habit of covering his mouth when he spoke, which he did with a slight impediment, pertaining specifically to the pronunciation of *r*'s, which from his tongue sounded slightly more like *w*'s. "Don't tell me," he said again, surveying the whole of my appearance and then tapping my chest with the tip of his cane. "You want to know the way to Eugene's wook."

"Well, yes," I said.

"You've come from far?" he asked.

"I've come from an entirely different continent, actually," I said.

"How impwessive." He cocked an eyebrow. "And have you a good you hope to twade Eugene, or are you going to bwowse?"

"I was actually looking for a gift," I said, "to send my friends at home."

"Hm." He smiled coquettishly to veil what I nonetheless perceived to be a touch of disappointment. "How quaint."

"Is it very far?" I asked.

He turned round swiftly, like a weathervane, and once again pointed with his cane to where the Coupra foothills rise from the valley in which Macaroni sits. ''The middle hill is Eugene's,'' he said. ''And the woad is called van Maawen.'' He held up his lorgnette for me to see: what looked like a beaten path wind its knobby way three-quarters up the hill and then stop between two oak trees. ''Between the twees—you will see the wook.''

I did, barely. My hip winced at the distance, and I knew that I would have to rest the night in Macaroni. ''Is it possible I might find one of those in town?'' I pointed to his cane, a slightly overwrought mahogany staff with a ivory dog-head handle. ''I've been having some trouble with my hip.''

His eyelids descended till they nearly shut, and his lips then curled with a mixture of offense taken and privilege asserted. ''If one hasn't a cane, sir, one hasn't a cane.''

I didn't know quite what to say to this and so concluded our encounter by asking if he could recommend a place in town that I might spend the night. I gathered there were a number of possibilities, but in judging me, I know not how, he suggested the inn of Herr Montescue, pointed me in its direction, and then bid me good evening.

Herr Montescue I found to be a somewhat more palatable fellow. I believe I was the only lodger, so he let me have the terrace suite and personally served me dinner in his dining room, a meal which, like the Macaroni physique, was of two dimensions: a cracker the size of a table mat, which pictured a rather appetizing spread of pork chops, carrots, and mashed potatoes in its crust. The cracker was not nearly so savoury as the meal it depicted, but I was at least properly sated, and with some tea I went to my room and slept the night soundly.

In the morning, I was again served by Herr Montescue. He brought up some coffee and a cracker pictured with ham and eggs, which I took out on my balcony, and there Herr Montescue informed me that the gentleman I'd met on the street the night before—Herr Fauntleroy was his name—had apparently come by early that morning and arranged that I be taken to Eugene's by a team of checkers.

I could see them from the balcony. They were actually standing at the door already, in two stacks of four, waiting, and I felt ashamed at having judged my benefactor so harshly the day before. As soon as I finished my cracker, I went down, and Herr Montescue helped show me how I was to ride them. It was very simple, in fact. I took a seat on top of the first stack, strapped onto my head another checker, which the remaining three checkers then mounted—or "kinged" I suppose would be the word. Once in place, we were propelled forward in much the same manner that checkers normally transport themselves, somewhat like leapfrog, but for the fact that I was seated in the middle: one by one the checkers above my cap would hop down in front of us—click, click, click—and when they were three high, my seat-checker would gently hop on top—click. Then, in like fashion, the column of three now stacked behind me would flip up onto my cap very gently, ready to start the whole process over again, as another stride.

This all happened so quickly and with such flourish, it was a bit like being in the midst of a juggler's juggle, and I had some trouble keeping my balance at first. Fortunately, the checkers were patient with me, and once I grasped the rhythm, I found it a fairly pleasant sensation, not unlike riding a horse at trotting gait, but smoother, and also more passive, as I was not called upon to direct the checkers in any way. They seemed to know where I was going.

We had a very pleasant journey, then, and at such leisure as my team afforded, I lit myself a most delicious local cigar and took in the landscape, which is of a contour I would compare to that of a casually tossed blanket, very lovely and also cheering, I think, the ability to point to a destination the side of a hill, see the path that one should take and take it. As the road beneath us turned and rolled, the rook and I kept ducking in and out of view from one another, but when I could see it, I must admit, my feeling was one of . . . I cannot say disappointment, for it was in fact an intriguing thing to behold—but how modest a dwelling it seemed, particularly to have inspired the devotion I'd observed throughout the civilised boards of the land. With each nearer view, its simplicity was even more evident. It was made entirely of wood, two stories, vaguely six-sided, and sloped inwards slightly, like the base of an obelisk, putting me in mind of a lighthouse with no tower.

Also I observed, when the checkers had carried me near enough to see, in the second-story window facing us was the silhouette of a human figure, sitting perfectly still in the frame. Whether it was looking back at me I could not be sure, but it was there the whole of our ascent, until the last of the swells rose and fell between us, in which time the figure had withdrawn from the window.

I observed no other movement from either inside or outside the rook until the road had led my checkers and me directly to its door, which faced east. There, a second figure, of a decidedly different shape than the one I'd seen sitting at the window, came out upon the steps. He was wiping his hands on his apron and seemed an extremely genial fellow, whose physique was something like that of an egg or a porcelain salt shaker, with a bald head, sloped shoulders, and very gentle, wide-set eyes.

"I trust I've found Eugene's rook?" I said, dismounting my team and removing my checker cap.

The egg-shaped pawn smiled warmly and tilted his oval body to affirm.

"Are you Eugene?" I started up the steps.

His expression jumped delightfully at the very idea, and then visibly humbled. "No," he said, looking up in the general direction of the second story. "I am Eugene's scribe, Egbert." He opened the door for me, and I entered to an open and mildly cluttered showroom. "I think Eugene may be upstairs. If you'll excuse me." He turned and waddled across to the far side of the room and up a hidden flight of stairs.

I remained where I was, to take in the atmosphere, which in truth was even less impressive inside than out. The space was nearly desolate. All the windows looked as if they'd been washed with milk, so the air seemed thick and adrift with dust. In the middle of the room, and very clearly its centerpiece, was an extremely large tree stump, perhaps eight feet in diameter, with a flat and burnished top. To the right of this was a more open space for the larger merchandise, which had been set out across the floor, each in its own space, to give the appearance of crowdedness: there was a bassinet, a hat stand, a drawing table, a rent table, a hymn board, a milking stool, a lectern, a dictionary stand, a sled, and what I believe was a cattle prod. To the left of the stump and extending from the back of the room all the way to me were two sets of long wooden shelves, which held an equally random and meagre assortment of goods. In the far left-hand corner was a tall scribe's table, with a large accounting book opened on top. There were some clothes racks as well at the far end behind the shelves, with not much on them—used jackets and pants and a few old dresses. I will admit, as I heard Egbert's footsteps descending the stairs, I felt my expectations betrayed.

"I don't know where he could have gone," he was saying. He stopped at the landing to strike a stumped expression and assume his natural pose, fingers clasped at his belly.

Just then there came a sudden movement from behind me, followed by a dark, lifeless voice. "Why is he here?"

"Eugene!" gasped Egbert, and I turned to see him standing there—a large figure behind the door, still too dark to make out clearly, but whose silhouette was clearly the same as I'd seen in the upstairs window.

"Eugene," Egbert said again, now with calm, to quell the start which this unexpected introduction had given both our hearts. "I would like you to meet Mr. . . . ?"

"Dr. Uyterhoeven." I bowed.

"He has just come up from Macaroni."

Eugene emerged from the shadow—tall, broad, lean, and so far the most distinctively rendered piece I have seen since coming here. He wore the simple clothes of a woodworker or a carpenter—a blue collarless shirt buttoned to his very prominent Adam's apple, overalls of a darker yet more faded blue, and, covering his abdomen, a chairmaker's breastplate. His hands and face were beautiful and monstrous, his features like those of statues set high up on building ledges, strong and square and deep-cut so that the people can see from down below. His hair was thin and short, the colour and luminescence of gunmetal.

He had a broad, straight, and quiet mouth, and his eyes, a gentle blue, reflected less his intelligence than his innocence. His intelligence resided in his hands, which were like creatures wholly unto themselves, with long, strong fingers and scarred knuckles like tree knots.

"Why are you here?" he asked me directly and with such rebuke in his voice that I stammered.

"I wanted to find a gift for my friends."

He looked at me with eyes almost dead with distrust. "Why?"

"Why?" I replied nervously. "Because I am here and they are elsewhere." He waited, almost contemptuously. "It is a small pleasure," I continued, "to know that they will see something I have seen."

"It's true." Egbert came up from behind. "And with the goods especially. They are very good for sha—"

"No gifts," Eugene interrupted calmly. He measured me head to toe, then glanced at Egbert. "You'll come and get me if there's anything else."

"Yes, Eugene," said Egbert. Then the beloved proprietor of this beloved place walked past us both without another word, past the tree stump, and disappeared behind the hidden stairs.

Egbert looked at me to beg forgiveness for his master's behaviour, then gestured to the shelves. "You may look, if you like. There isn't very much, but you never know, and I might be able to talk to Eugene."

He smiled to reassure me, and I started down the aisle between the shelves. Egbert did not follow me, but stood watching the whole while, which I found a touch unnerving, particularly since the merchandise didn't excite much response in me at first. I'd hope no one there would take offence if I compared it to the wares one might find at a neighbourhood yard sale or a church flea market. I recall passing a tea pitcher, a thimble, a kerosene lamp, an atomizer, a pincushion, an alabastrum, a sleeveboard, a nightcap, a sugar shell, a stereoscope, a woman's shoe heel, a compote, a milk-bottle cap, a pinwheel, a sadiron, and a penholder.

There may have been more, but I trust you gather the effect of them together. It was an extremely random collection of no particular distinction, and in this respect a good deal inferior to one of our flea markets. Indeed, as I made my way along, I couldn't help thinking that if such a plain array of miscellany could have inspired the reverence which I had gleaned in my travels, what sort of cult could Mr. Geogheghan establish here for himself by merely cleaning out his barn.

In any event, when I had come three-quarters of the way down the aisle, I noticed that my cigar ash was growing treacherously long. I gestured back to Egbert, who was still watching me attentively at the front of the aisle. ''Have you an ashtray?''

Much too happily, ''Why, yes!'' he said. ''Yes, we do. Second shelf to your right.''

''No, but to use,'' I explained.

''You may use it.'' He smiled.

A rather casual attitude, I thought, but I looked to my right and there it was—a very simple pewter ashtray. I examined it underneath for some original marking, but there was none. I tapped my cigar on the rim. The ash tumbled off onto the plate. I looked at it. How many times in my life must I have seen clumps of ash lying on trays? Since I was a boy, a countless number, I would think—on plates and saucers and mistakenly on tablecloths—and an equally countless number of times I have thought nothing of it, but for some reason this ash on this tray arrested me. How apt they seemed together.

I drew another long draught of my cigar and flicked a second clump of ash onto the tray, and this confirmed my vivid, if unspectacular, evaluation: that for this purpose, the plate in my hand was one well suited. No addition to its appearance would have enhanced its suitability to the task. It neither offered nor lacked anything that one would require of a plate for ash, and in this respect—upon my having used it—now struck me as a very fine ashtray, an ashtray of supreme self-possession and yet modesty.

I looked back down at the shelves, and there was a brass door knocker there—again, the sort of brass knocker which, if one was to find it at a church sale, one would only purchase out of charity. It was very ordinary. And yet in light of my new regard for the ashtray, I couldn't help seeing that the knocker displayed a similar, shall I say, germanity of purpose, an apparent and perfect lack of pretension. I lifted the clapper and let it fall once against its base—not a chime, not a bell, but a perfectly adequate sound to summon a person to his door.

''Do you like it?'' Egbert had come up the aisle and was standing right in front of me now, looking up at me with an exuberant, proud grin.

''Well, I do, in fact,'' I said. ''It's very nice, but I'm afraid I haven't any door at present which needs a knocker.'' I held up the ashtray to convey my appreciation of it as well. ''Does Eugene do all the choosing?''

''Why, yes!'' Egbert nearly jumped with excitement. ''Do you think you might have something?''

There was a look of such hopefulness on his face, I wished I had. I actually checked my pockets, on the chance I might find some simple thing to offer him, but there was only my pocket watch, which I haven't yet managed to fix, and some of the little chess pieces I brought with me, which I've been using for barter. ''I'm sorry,'' I said. ''But do I take it that Eugene will consider anything?''

''He's Eugene.'' The pawn smiled. ''And one never knows. The watering can came in just the other day.'' He pointed down to the end of the shelf and there was indeed a watering can there. I took over the ashtray to see it more closely. It was made of tin and had a curved handle—but perhaps I should refrain from describing it, for I'm quite sure that it looks quite like the watering can which each of you has already conjured in your minds. Here it was. I lifted it up and tipped it as though to pour. A fine watering can—not by any means exquisite, nor by any means deficient, but, like all the other goods at Eugene's rook, an unadorned and unmistakeable instance of what it was.

Again, Egbert had come to join me at the end of the aisle. He was looking up at me, smiling, his pudgy hands folded underneath his belly and wiggling with a kind of piglet glee—watching me with such encouragement I felt obliged to make clear, lest he get his hopes up, that even as much as I admired his collection of goods, there was very little chance I'd purchase one—if I couldn't give it as a gift, that is—as I was travelling and preferred to remain light.

I was on the verge of this very admission, when over his shoulder, standing behind one of the clothes racks, I saw it: a cane. A cane like all the other goods, simple and well wrought. It was of varnished wood with a hook top and a brass ring around its neck. An exceptionally unexceptional example, but oh, has the burn of an image upon my pupil ever so instantly excited my covetousness. My hip throbbed once with longing, and Egbert, observing the desire in my eye, glanced round to see its object. He walked back to the rack and took the cane in his hands. "This?" he asked.

I nodded helplessly.

"Well, let me go ask Eugene." With a bow he excused himself and walked to the foot of the stairs, but he did not go up. He stopped suddenly, and I could tell from the angle of his deference that Eugene was sitting on the steps, hidden from view, and that he had been eavesdropping the whole while. Egbert stepped behind the façade for a moment and they spoke in hushed tones. When he appeared again, he was smiling congenially. He came and offered me the cane to see, then folded his hands politely.

"Eugene would like to know why you want the cane."

"Well"—it seemed an odd question—"to walk with, I suppose."

"You would use it, then?"

"Yes," I said, somewhat confused.

"And you're quite certain you don't mean to give it away?"

"No," I said. "Truly. I have been having trouble with my hip. In fact, that's the reason I came up here on the checkers." I tried to speak up so that Eugene could hear. "One of the Macaroni was kind enough to lend me their service, because of my hip."

At this I could hear Eugene stand up quickly, turn, and stomp up the stairs. Egbert and I both listened, wincing, as he trod above us across the floorboards and into his room. Very clearly we could hear him throw up the sash of his bedroom window and call out, "Away,

away!'' Then suddenly, out the window I saw something come frightfully close to striking my team of checkers—Eugene had hurled a hammer at them, upon which they all scattered and began tumbling back down the hill separately.

Egbert looked back at me apologetically when all was still again. ''I am very sorry,'' he said.

''Do I take it this means I may have the cane?''

Egbert nodded in embarrassment, and I began rummaging through my pockets for one of the little chess pieces. ''I'm afraid I haven't much to give you in return.''

''Oh, there's no charge.'' Egbert looked at me, surprised. ''Just take it.''

''You mean for free?''

''For as long as your hip troubles you, and then when it is better, just bring it back. Come.'' He directed me back to the scribe's table. ''I'll need the spelling of your last name,'' he said, ''as a formality.''

This all struck me as very odd, but I obliged. Egbert sat on his stool and I gave him all my pertinent information, my name and our address, and when we were through I asked him if this was all they did, lend out the goods.

''To whoever can use them,'' he replied. ''That's why Eugene wanted to know. He prefers lending them to those who actually need them, and you, with your ailing hip''—he wrote this last phrase in his ledger as he spoke—''will need the cane to . . . walk . . . with.''

''Yes,'' I confirmed. ''But may I ask what is it you suspect I might do with a cane other than walk?''

Egbert looked warily up at the ceiling. ''Eugene fears you might break it,'' he whispered.

''Break it?'' I tried to keep my voice down.

Egbert's eye closed a moment, out of sympathy. ''This has been a very difficult time for Eugene.'' He looked with heartbreak at all the empty shelves. ''It's hard for him to believe that our customers are just keeping the goods for themselves.''

''So he believes they're breaking them?''

Egbert nodded sorrowfully.

I thought. "You'll have to forgive me," I said, "but I'm not sure that really makes sense to me. What reason could he have to think anyone would want to break his goods?"

Egbert looked at me with a very curious expression all of a sudden.

"But you do understand about the goods, what they are?"

"Well . . ." I considered my impressions. "I'm not sure. They are, as I understand, what Eugene chooses."

Egbert's posture arched slightly; he seemed at once offended and charmed by my ignorance. "They are what Eugene *recognises,*" he clarified, and then he raised his hand to stay me, turned round on his stool, and removed a long wooden object from the wall, something like a stew spoon, except that it was hollow and was bound along the stem by a cloth wrap.

"Have you ever seen one of these?" he asked.

"Well, I think I might have," I replied.

"Do you know what it is?"

It looked a bit like a salad spoon, but the circle at the top was too round. "Not exactly."

"It is called a loon," he said, admiring it. "Do you know what it is for?"

I considered it. I certainly felt that I was familiar with such a thing, and that I had seen something like it in a spoon jug or some such place, but I had to admit that I didn't know quite what I would do with it. "One could probably blow bubbles with it," I tried, "with some soap and water."

Egbert smiled. "Yes, one probably could."

"One could hold a very large egg with it," I suggested.

"Yes. You could," said Egbert again, this time a touch less charmed.

I tried again. "You could serve salad with it."

"Yes," said Egbert impatiently, "but the point is, you don't actually know what it is for."

"No."

"No, of course you don't, and neither do I. Neither does anyone." He turned it over reverently for us both to see. "Anymore."

This seemed to have been his point, so I asked, "What do you mean 'anymore'?"

"Well, I will tell you." Egbert hopped down from his stool and led me by the arm over to one of the northern windows, that we might be as far as possible from Eugene's place upstairs. We both sat upon the sill, and there he proceeded to explain to me in glowing detail the story of the forgotten loon, a most instructive bit of lore which in its course conveyed the history of Eugene's rook as well, which for its pertinence both to my experience and to this land in general, I shall recount to you as faithfully as I am able—if at a mercifully less Socratic pace.

As fully as I can recall, then: Eugene came originally from a team of pieces all like him, of course—surpassingly well wrought, and all expert craftsmen, carpenters, millers, and coopers of the highest order. But as happens to even the most gifted and handsome teams, they had lost their king long ago, and suffered the subsequent dispersal and malaise which normally follows the abrogation of one's primary purpose, which, as you know, in the case of all chess pieces is to defend their throne. Teams which have surrendered their king almost invariably enter into diaspora. The individual pieces become lost and derelict, for lack of use, like a pawn one might find shrouded by dustwillows underneath a parlour couch.

Eugene, however, had been a piece of such apparent distinction and self-possession that he had managed to keep his bearings in absence of his king. He did not wander, then, so much as explore the Antipodes alone, and, upon finding the hill which would someday come to bear his name, chose it as a place where he could live and make himself a home. He built this home from a single oak, the middle of three which stood most prominent on the Coupra foothills, and whose stump I myself could see at the center of the room.

These efforts did not escape the notice of the Macaroni and several of the other nearby teams. This was not normal behaviour—for a lone piece to plant himself on a hillside—and yet upon seeing the quality of his work, they did not object. Quite the opposite, they availed themselves of his apparent talents. Whenever they had need of an expert hand, they would go up to Eugene's rook and ask his help, and he was always happy to be of service. He rewove their seats, shaved their table legs, realigned their bedposts, and fit their bureau drawers better to their slots. He used the stump of the oak tree for his workbench, and upon its broad, flat face he built chairs and desks and chests and tables, and soon he acquired a reputation among all the civilised teams nearby for the excellence of his craftsmanship. For this reason, then, and despite the fact that they could well have taken exception to his odd, lone nature and superior quality, these other teams welcomed Eugene as a neighbour.

One auspicious day, it happened that a pawn named van Maaren, from a distant board called Vanlookerencampagne, came to the rook with a box of old tools and such which he'd found among the ruins of a board that his team had recently routed. Van Maaren was a businessman and so had little use for tools, but he'd seen that some needed fixing, and he had thought he might be able to sell them one by one, so he left the box with Eugene overnight to see what he could do.

Van Maaren's box was filled with all sorts of different things, apparently—calipers and levellers and weights and such—but among them was a loon; not broken, but perfectly fit and simple. Eugene set it aside while he looked at all the rest and fixed what needed fixing. Then when he was done, he took up the loon again. He set it down upon his oak to look at: such a sound and worthy loon it seemed to him, the sort of loon he would have been proud to have made himself. Indeed, it struck Eugene as a loon of such ideal perfection that right then and there he began to build a chifforobe, so that he might offer it to van Maaren as a trade. He took out all his lumber and worked the whole night through, so that by the time van Maaren returned in the morning, the chifforobe was already waiting out on Eugene's porch.

Van Maaren's first concern, of course, was to see if Eugene had been able to fix his tools, and so Eugene went through the box with him, piece by piece. When he came to the loon, however, he asked if he might keep it himself.

"But haven't you loons of your own?" van Maaren asked.

Eugene replied that he did, but that there was something about this one he preferred.

"Very well," van Maaren said. "But what do you offer in return?"

Eugene pointed to the chifforobe.

"The chifforobe?" Van Maaren looked at him suspiciously. "Tell me, Eugene, is there something you deem to be of great value about this loon?"

"Only that it seems to me the sort of loon I would want to have made myself," the pawn replied. "It seems the sort of thing I should be reminded of, and so I would like to give you this chifforobe in exchange."

"But it is so large," said van Maaren. "How would I get it to my home?"

"I would carry it for you," said Eugene. "I will take it in my wagon."

Now, van Maaren was a reasonable man and not bereft of self-interest. He saw the advantage in this trade and so accepted quickly. He and Eugene shook hands, Eugene lifted the chifforobe up onto his wagon, tied it fast, and then, just as he'd promised, pulled it down Coupra Hill all the way to Vanlookerencampagne.

By the time Eugene had returned to the rook and his new loon, word of his trade with van Maaren had already begun to circulate. Van Maaren had boasted of the "steal" to friends, and Eugene was surprised to find certain of his customers coming up the hill to ask if they could see his new loon, to see if it was as plain as van Maaren had said. Eugene always obliged their interest. He kept the loon in a jar on his ledger desk, and he would take it out and show it to anyone who desired, most of whom agreed with van Maaren, of course. As much as they respected Eugene, they could not understand why anyone would trade a whole chifforobe for this. Some would even laugh and say that Eugene had swindled himself, but he did not mind. He said it had been no bother making the chifforobe, and that the better acquainted he'd become with the loon, the more pleased he was with the trade. Indeed, he claimed he would not now exchange his loon for anything.

Anything? the customers would say, grinning sidelong at one another. "You would not give up the loon for a stable of horses?" they'd ask. "Not for oxen, or for land?"

"Well, I suppose I would have to see the horses," Eugene would reply. "But I think no."

"But what about a string of pearls?" they'd ask, and some would even bring their offers up to show him, they took such pleasure in testing Eugene's claim. They brought him jewels and trinkets to compare with the wooden loon, but these and more temptations he refused. "No," he'd say, politely as he was able. "I think I'd prefer to keep the loon."

So, among the boards in the vicinity, there was added to Eugene's reputation as a master craftsman the fact of his strange attachment to his loon; an appreciation which half his patrons considered evidence of some derangement, half considered a kind of obscure wisdom, but which all agreed had seemed to confer upon the loon itself a certain undeniable pricelessness.

At length it came to pass that the King of Orzhevsky heard tell of Eugene's loon. The King of Orzhevsky was at this time experiencing difficulties in his marriage to the queen, and he decided that to express the new extent of his devotion, he would make her a gift of this famous loon. That Eugene had refused all bids, the king well understood, but never had this pawn been posed an offer such as the king was prepared to make. To trade for Eugene's loon, he called his bishop to the throne and handed him his own sceptre. "See if our carpenter can refuse this," he told his bishop.

So the bishop took the royal sceptre in its case and set off with his coterie. They made the trek to Macaroni, and then up to Eugene's rook. Upon their arrival, the bishop stated their business without digression. He said that he had come on behalf of his king, the highness of Orzhevsky, and asked to see the loon. Eugene brought it out for him. The bishop set the loon on Eugene's oak and then removed the king's sceptre from its case. "This"—he placed the sceptre next to the loon—"for that."

Eugene shook his head. "But I've no use for a sceptre."

The bishop looked up at the rook's proprietor, stunned. "But this is the sceptre of our king, you understand. It is more precious than anything you have ever beheld, I can assure you."

Eugene looked at the sceptre with a shrug. "It is a magnificent thing," he said. "But I prefer the loon."

The bishop was speechless. His coterie, however, was not. In fact, they took great and instant offence at Eugene's refusal. They could not imagine such insolence—such impudence! Eugene could only shrug, but several of his customers, who were also there, took up his defence. They returned that the coterie was merely jealous and embarrassed and ignorant. A shouting match ensued. The shouting soon gave way to pushing and to shoving, and then, regrettably, to blows. Not Eugene or the bishop, of course, who both were peaceful men—but everyone else at the rook was soon tumbling about the floor, pulling each other's hair and gouging each other's eyes. Then at some point in the ruckus a member of the bishop's coterie—a pawn named Fedorov, if I remember—grabbed hold of the loon itself and cracked it over the sharp tin head of a Macaroni named Fortescue.

The sound alone stopped all the action, and then from round the room, gasps as all looked down to see: The loon was lying on the floor, split in two. All eyes turned to Eugene, who had seen what happened. He passed through the tangled bodies, through the shame and silence, and picked up the two splintered pieces. He sat down on his stump and tried to fit them back together, but it was no use. The loon was clearly ruined, everyone could see. And yet the look on Eugene's face was not of rage or sorrow, strangely. The look was one of bewilderment, first directed at the splintered wood and then at the company of combatants, all frozen in their positions with their hands still wrapped round each other's throats. Eugene held up the pieces of split loon and asked, "Can anyone remember what this was used for?"

All the customers and the coterie looked back at him dumbly. They thought perhaps he'd gone mad, but he looked at the bishop with earnest confusion. "You, bishop of Orzhevsky, can you remind me what use the loon served?"

The bishop looked at the split loon. "Well, of course," he said, "it is to . . ." He approached Eugene to see the pieces better. "Well, it's very simple, the loon was to . . ." He thought and he thought, but as he thought, he realised he'd forgotten, and he shook his head. "I am afraid at the moment that it has escaped my mind."

Eugene then looked at one of his most faithful customers. "You, pawn Wiggins. Do you recall the purpose of the loon?"

"Why certainly," said Wiggins. "The loon is for . . ." he stammered. "Why, it is for . . ." But just as with the bishop, he could not finish his answer.

"Anyone?" Eugene looked round the room, but no one offered a reply. None of them, who presumably had known very well that morning what loons were for, could for the life of him remember.

Well. Standing there, with the flush of rage in all their faces turning quickly to shame, no one had known quite what to make of this. The bishop of Orzhevsky was so overcome by contrition and dismay that he very quickly withdrew the members of his team from the rook. He took back the king's sceptre and, with a profound apology to Eugene, left. He and his coterie descended the hill in what I gather to have been a stunned silence, but when they reached Macaroni, the bishop went straight to several burghers on the street and posed Eugene's question to them—could they remember what loons were for? They could not, to their surprise. The bishop went from store to store, but there the answers were the same—not a single Macaroni could remember.

Puzzled, the bishop and his coterie started back towards Orzhevsky, and everywhere they stopped, at every town or market or cathedral, the bishop would ask if anyone could remember the purpose of loons, and everywhere he went he met with the same stumped expression. No one could. Even those who themselves owned loons would take them out of their drawers and hold them up, but they could not remember the purpose which these things had served.

And so when the bishop finally reached Orzhevsky, he went straight to the other bishop of the team to tell him what had taken place and to ask if he could think of an explanation. The second bishop pondered the question, and then suggested that perhaps Eugene's loon had been the loon of loons. The first bishop did not understand this—loon of loons—and so the second clarified: Perhaps this loon which they'd broken had been the one which embodied the very essence of all loons. Perhaps it had been the one which preserved their meaning. Why, this would make very clear what had happened: when Eugene's loon was broken in the scuffle and lost its use, of course the same had befallen all other loons.

The first bishop considered this. Indeed, he found this a very convincing argument—not only a fit explanation for the countrywide amnesia, but also an almost perfect elucidation of the feelings which the loon had conjured in him (and that the ashtray, the brass knocker, and the watering can had conjured in me, I would add). It seemed quite right to him (and to me), that this loon had indeed been the loon of loons.

And if there was a loon of loons, the bishop surmised, did it not follow that there must be a clock of clocks as well, a box of boxes, a shoe of shoes? Did it not follow that for all things of use—every trowel and mousetrap—there must be, as with the loons, some example somewhere preserving the memory of that use—some essential instance, which, if it was broken, would likewise render broken the very meaning of all things akin to it?

The answer, of course, was yes, and the dictate equally clear, at least to the bishops of Orzhevsky: These other goods would have to be found, and protected, to make sure that what had befallen loons should never befall another useful instrument of our existence. Equally clear to the bishops was the role that Eugene would have to play in this effort. He had shown the keenest eye, after all—he had recognised the good loon—he would presumably find the other goods. So the bishops of Orzhevsky spread word throughout the civilised boards of the Antipodes that if anyone thought they might have a piece of the broken loon's quality, something of quintessential air, they should bring it to the rook as soon as possible for Eugene to appraise.

Apparently the bishop did not bother to inform Eugene of his campaign, so very much to Eugene's surprise, all sorts of pawns and knights and bishops began appearing at his door with items from their homes, things they'd found in their attics and cellars and dungeons, or sometimes things they'd been looking at their whole life—pillows and jackknives, measuring spoons, kettledrums, saddlebags, jackboots, bookends, candleholders, picture frames—anything which seemed appropriately standard they brought to Eugene's door to ask if it might be a good like the loon.

Eugene was a gracious pawn, fortunately, and obliged them each and every one. Whatever they brought he would take over to his oak stump. He would set it there and look at it and use it for whatever purpose it served, to see if it affected him as had the loon.

In most cases, of course, it did not. Goods are very rare, and so, more often than not, Eugene would have to disappoint his guests and tell them that as handsome a butter churn as theirs may be—or flower vase or crab mallet or whatever the case may have been—it was not a good like the loon.

It was some time, in fact, before the second good was found. According to Egbert, it wasn't until a knight had come all the way from the board of Hevonshire with a ladder on his back. Eugene had taken the ladder and set it by his oak stump. He'd climbed the ladder. He'd descended the ladder, and he had simply known. He had known by using it that this ladder was to other ladders as the loon had been to other loons. He informed the knight of this—that his ladder was a good—and the knight, who rightly considered it an honour to be of service to the rook, let Eugene keep it. Eugene built him another ladder to take back to Hevonshire, and then put the good ladder on display just as he had the loon. This attracted more pieces to the rook, of course, who brought more of their things to be appraised, and gradually more and more goods came to light—the next was a derby, if I remember, then a shoehorn, and these were displayed alongside the good ladder, which in turn brought more visitors and slowly more goods.

Among these early visitors had been Egbert. He had come with a bowl he'd thought might be a good. It wasn't, alas, but when he saw the other goods, and what a burden it was for Eugene to keep everything straight—meeting with all the pieces who kept flocking to his door, assessing their belongings, compensating those who brought goods, keeping track of who'd brought what and when and where—clearly it was not the sort of work that Eugene had been meant for, so he offered to help. Eugene accepted gratefully, and so just like that, Egbert moved in and assumed most of the more administrative, clerical duties of running the rook.

And a good thing, too. He said he frankly didn't know what Eugene would have done without him, the rook soon became so popular. He said one could look down the hill all the way to Macaroni and see pawns and bishops and knights lined up waiting with their belongings to show Eugene. Even kings had come to see them. Pawns would carry kings on their shoulders past the line, and they would bless Eugene or dub him for the good work he was doing, work they deemed to be of such clear and vital interest to everyone throughout the land.

Of course, with so much business, it was only a matter of time before the rook became overcrowded with goods. Soon they covered the whole floor and even upstairs. As hard as Egbert worked to keep them straight, something had to be done, so he and Eugene consulted the bishops of Orzhevsky, and they suggested that perhaps Eugene should lend out the goods as pieces needed them, as one would books from a library.

Eugene was very pleased by this idea. He thought that the goods should be used, and so the rook became like a library, the goods like books, and Egbert the librarian. Eugene continued with his appraisals and his building, but if someone came up to the rook complaining of a dusty floor, Egbert might give him the good broom to sweep it. Or if a pawn had a stopped pipe and the rook had the good pipe cleaner in stock, Egbert would let the pawn borrow it. He simply kept track of who had what and where and why and so forth.

It was a horrendous administrative burden, as I gather, but more than worth the effort, according to Egbert, for it had been a golden time when the goods were all in use, when the shelves and the floor were always full and changing. He said pieces used to come up just to see what was there, to sit in the good captain's chair, to ring the good bell, and just to be near Eugene, to meet him and watch him work at his stump. ''It was a glorious time,'' said Egbert, and I could tell from the light in his eyes, lost in the memory of this bygone day, that it was true.

And yet to look at the rook now—with the floor so bare and Eugene upstairs, sitting alone at his window, the contrast was too brutal not to mention. ''But I gather at some point the pieces stopped returning the goods,'' I said.

Egbert looked at the shelves sadly. ''Some forgot, yes. Some stole them outright, I think.'' He shook his head. ''I tried to keep track. I'd go to them. I still do, to ask if they're finished with the goods yet, to ask if they could give them back, please, so others can have the chance, but they say they lost them. They say they lent them to someone else or they can't find them anymore.'' He heaved a painful sigh. ''As long as they're safe, that's what's most important, but it makes Eugene so nervous. I tell him that they'll turn up, but it doesn't bring him any peace. He says he can feel them, the goods, and he knows they're not being used.'' He looked up at the ceiling. ''All day, all night, he stays up there feeling them.''

''But you said before he fears that they'll be broken?'' I asked.

The pawn took another deep breath. ''Eugene is under the impression that there's a band of pieces working together, hiding them. He believes the bishops of Orzhevsky are their leaders, and that when they have all the goods together, they are going to destroy them all at once.''

''Deliberately?''

The pawn's gaze remained upon the floor as he nodded. ''Very deliberately. The vandals, he calls them.''

"But that's madness," I said.

"I know," the pawn sighed. "I know. But it's what he believes. I suppose it makes it easier for him—to think that there's some plot under way instead of just . . . selfishness."

"Which it clearly is," I said. "Of course it is. No one would be so malicious as to destroy the goods on purpose."

"That is what I try to tell him, but he won't listen. He just sits there all day at his window, losing his mind to grief."

Egbert's expression nearly melted in pity, then he saw the cane on my lap and shook his head. "But you shouldn't mind about that." He pointed to the cane. "You should take that with you, and walk with it."

"Well, but I don't have to," I said, "if it is going to cause Eugene any more uneasiness."

"Oh no." The pawn looked at me plaintively. "If you really need it, there's nothing that would make Eugene happier."

I wasn't sure that this was true, but as I looked down at the simple staff, I did in fact feel a responsibility, and I vowed to myself that I would protect this cane for as long as I was here. "Do you think I could see him?" I asked. Egbert looked at me, surprised and a bit reluctant. "Please," I said. "Just to reassure him."

Egbert pointed to the front of the window warily. "It's the room facing town."

I took the cane and climbed the stairs.

The second level was small and like a priest's quarters. One larger room appeared to be storage space with nothing in it, one room was Egbert's, and in the next I found Eugene, sitting in a simple chair, looking out the window. I knocked on the door frame. "Excuse me." He did not turn, but I took a step in. "I'll be going now," I said, "but I wanted you to know how much I enjoyed my visit, and I wanted to thank you"—I hesitated—"for the cane."

He continued looking straight out at the valley and kept his silence. "I just wanted you not to worry," I continued. "Your friend told me about your troubles, and I want you to be assured, I will use it, and I will keep it safe, and I will see that you get it back. I promise.''

Eugene still did not move, and I realised there was nothing I could say to console him, so I turned to leave, but one step from the door I heard his voice. ''If you're honest, I wouldn't advise going down the way you came.'' He nodded slightly to the landscape. ''They might be waiting.''

I almost wished he hadn't said it, it was so painful hearing him actually speak his derangement. I wished I could have shown him the madness in what he was saying, but as he sat there at his window, casting his forsaken gaze upon the valley, I could see the grip of his suffering was much too fast for me to break. I descended the stairs and said goodbye to Egbert at the door. I gave him my word, just as I had Eugene, that I would make good use of the cane, or as good as I was able.

He took my hand to bid me well and pressed the good thimble into my palm.

''Oh, but I've no use for a thimble,'' I said.

''A gift.'' He smiled gently. ''For your friends at home.''

And there, no doubt, his failure as Eugene's scribe: much too generous. I thanked him and placed the thimble in my pocket. He thanked me, and then I started back along the beaten path for Macaroni, the comfort of my checkers traded for a cane. But what was the pain in my hip, I wondered, compared to that in Eugene's heart? I did not look round to see if he was sitting at his window. I knew he was, and I didn't think I could bear the sight. I hobbled down towards Macaroni, and the splendour of the vista in descending hues of periwinkle was but a fog to me, my thoughts were all so taken by pity for Eugene. Each man knows best his fears, he best conceives his nightmares—but what madness, I thought, to have conjured such a horrible plot against himself. Poor Eugene was all I could think, step after step—poor poor Eugene.

Halfway into my descent, I was coming round one of van Maaren's more pronounced shoulders when I saw, just above its crest, the tip of what appeared to be a golden spear. As I continued, the horizon fell between us to reveal beside the spear a black feather plume first, and then the helmet from which this plume had sprouted; then the épaulière, the breastplate, and the shield of an immense medieval cavalier. He was mounted upon a great steed which was just as heavily mailed and plated as he, and just as still; both waiting there—for me.

Now, who this knight was to be expecting me, I could not evidently see. The armour stirred at my appearance and the gauntlets raised up their reins ever so slightly, but where the visor of his helmet was raised to look at me, I could see nothing but an empty space. The only evidence of tenancy were two recurrent puffs of mist, steaming the cool night air out in front of the hollow.

I tried not to show my alarm. I nodded him a good evening. The helmet tipped slightly in response and turned slowly as I passed. I set my attention back upon the road, but I could hear the war-horse clop onto the path behind me. For a good dozen steps I walked inside its great dark shadow. Then, as we cleared the bend, I saw there was a wagon at the roadside up ahead, and a second piece stepping out onto the lane to meet us.

He appeared to be an English chancellor in full judicial costume—a long black robe, buckled shoes, breeches, jabot, tippets, and a long white wig framing his features, which were of decidedly more substantive and friendly countenance than the knight's. He was a bishop.

"Good evening," he said.

I stopped. Behind me the horse stopped as well, close enough that I could smell its breath. "Good evening," I replied.

"Have no fear of our friend Ganelon." The chancellor glanced up at the figure on the steed, then looked back at me with a nod. "You are coming from Eugene's?"

"I am."

The chancellor examined my attire, head to toe and back again.

"Is there something I can do for you?" I asked.

"You are a distinguished gentleman, I can see."

"That is kind of you to say."

"A distinguished gentleman to be carrying such a simple walking staff. Don't you think a man such as yourself deserves something more worthy?''

''A worthy cane is one which offers me support,'' I answered, ''which this one does very well.''

''As would the staff of my friend Herr Fauntleroy.'' The chancellor gestured back towards the wagon, but in the dim light I could see nothing. ''Herr Fauntleroy,'' the chancellor said again, and suddenly, as if from this air, the Macaroni with whom I'd spoken upon my arrival, the one who'd shown me where the rook was and who'd arranged my transportation, appeared in front of the wagon by simply turning his flat tin body square to face me. ''I believe you two have met,'' said the chancellor. Herr Fauntleroy and I exchanged nods, as the chancellor reached back his hand. ''Your cane, Herr Fauntleroy?''

The Macaroni looked up at the chancellor, aghast, but, as a piece of lower rank, was in no position to refuse. The chancellor's hand remained, and so Herr Fauntleroy sidled out onto the road and, with great reluctance, handed over his cane.

''Now that,'' said the chancellor, extending the staff in turn to me, ''is a cane befitting a man of your distinction, don't you think?''

It was, as I had seen before, a polished ebony with a dog-head handle. ''It is a very handsome piece,'' I said. ''But I am perfectly happy with the one I have.''

The chancellor smiled. He seemed almost charmed by my resistance, if not particularly patient. He looked up at Ganelon behind me and was on the verge, I believe, of conferring the problem to him, when suddenly his eyes flashed over my shoulder. ''Oh dear,'' he said. He looked back at Fauntleroy, who covered his mouth, and then at Ganelon. ''Oh dear,'' he said again.

I turned round, and there was Eugene coming over the bend. His strides were long and determined. He did not look at any of us. His eyes were set upon the wagon. Ganelon and the lord chancellor both bowed their heads in shame and reverence as he came near, but Eugene passed directly through us. He descended the roadside to the wagon, and then threw back the tarpaulin.

I could see only the tops of what was there—a weathervane, a spinning wheel, and an easel. Eugene reached down with his great hand, and as a priest might bless the head of an infant, he touched the rim of a bell-tower bell. He smoothed the track of the spinning wheel with his thumb, and then lifted up a wedding dress, to cradle in his arms as though it were a bride.

Faintly, then, from up the hill I heard Egbert. He was calling out after Eugene, and I turned to see him come waddling round the bend as fast as his little legs could carry him.

When he saw us, he stopped short. "Chancellor Harold?" he cried out, but the chancellor did not look up. "Herr Fauntleroy?" The Macaroni turned sheepishly away. "Dr. Uyterhoeven?" He looked down at me, but I was still too flustered to explain.

I turned back to Eugene, who had placed the gown down on the crest of a birdhouse and now was covering over the goods again. He tied the straps of the tarpaulin firm round their hooks, and then again, without looking at any of us—as if he was too ashamed of us to meet our eyes—he walked back through us and started up the road.

Egbert waited at the bend with his hands upon his mouth, and he winced slightly as Eugene came near. Eugene stopped beside him. He looked up the road towards the rook, with his broad, straight back to us, and then—I could tell from the tilt of Egbert's head—Eugene began speaking. Egbert listened, nodded meekly, and then called down the road in a trembling voice. "Eugene would like you to know," he said, "he does not know how you've come by the goods in your wagon, but he will not challenge you for them. He says that he has no more right to them than you . . . than anyone . . ."

Egbert paused, and Eugene began to speak again. He spoke as if to the hill above him, and once again, when he finished, Egbert called down. "But he asks that you do the same. All the goods that remain at the rook, he says that he shall be taking with him, and he expects that you—all of you—shall leave him be and not come looking."

Eugene touched Egbert's round shoulder for one last word. As Egbert listened, his eyes began to brim; then, with a nod, Eugene started up the hill again towards the rook. Egbert looked back down the road and delivered the last of his master's statement. "He says he wishes for you to know, however, and for you to convey his message to the bishops in Orzhevsky and the rest . . . of your collaborators: he says he will not be of service to you anymore . . . He will never name another good again. The rook has ended, as you shall see when you look out your windows tonight.''

Egbert looked down at us then, for a moment too stunned by his own report to move. His large wide eyes touched mine, and they were swimming with betrayal. He shook his head in disbelief, and then, as best his frame could convey, he hopped in fury, turned round, and waddled after Eugene, with his arms out in front of him and his little legs pumping, struggling to keep his master in sight.

The three vandals did not raise their heads until the road had hidden Egbert from view. Slowly then, Ganelon guided his steed over to the wagon. The chancellor helped fasten it to the horse's bridle, and they began pulling it across the road, off into the countryside.

Fauntleroy was confused. ''But the cane?''

The lord chancellor handed him back his mahogany staff. ''Eugene is right,'' he said. ''The cane is his for now.'' He turned to me and addressed my eye. ''Perhaps in time he'll give it freely.''

''Not much time,'' said Fauntleroy, hastening to climb aboard the wagon. The chancellor did not answer. He looked up at the rook a final time, removed a diamond from his pocket, kissed it, and then he followed the knight and the wagon of stolen goods off into the wilderness of the Coupra foothills.

I continued down the road myself, boggled. By the time I made it back to Macaroni, fire was pouring from the windows of the rook. From the balcony of Herr Montescue's, it was an ember on the hillside, smouldering there like a fallen star. Now at dawn, a trail of smoke. My tea is cold, the cracker hard and stale, but I still have the good cane safe with me, and I shall be sending you the good thimble along with this. Tomorrow, after sleep, I will go back up to the rook to see if there is anything left. What I find, I'll send.

Yours,
Gus

NINE

THE IMPLICATION OF DOMINOES

One morning in the middle of February, Cedric Tomlin and John Wentworth, who were both nine years old, met at the Uyterhoevens' garden to play soldiers. Cedric had already taken down a favored set of lead Vikings from its shelf in the games shack when John arrived. He proposed the lily pond as a venue, and John agreed. The stone ledge was good for setting up the pieces, and also, the lily pond was shielded from most of the chess tables by a great raspberry bush, so they needn't worry about distracting the players.

They'd rounded the bush and Cedric was taking the Vikings from their box when John stopped him. "Look," he said, pointing at the water. All across the surface, where in the summer lilies covered the small pool, were at least thirty black dominoes floating face up, staring back at the stone statue of a boy who as ever stood blind and naked at the edge.

The dominoes looked very comfortable where they were—almost natural—but still the boys thought it worth mentioning to someone. They went to the nearest adult, who happened to be Captain Stivers, who was enjoying the morning newspaper as he normally did, next to the doctors Groth and Geogheghan, who were in their usual places as well for this time of day, in mittens and earmuffs, forehead to forehead over a game of chess.

Since he was very nearly deaf, Captain Stivers did not look up as the boys approached, and Cedric had to excuse himself. ''Someone put dominoes in the pond,'' he said.

Captain Stivers put his ear horn to his ear—''Again.''

John tried this time, practically shouting, but trying his best not to sound angry. ''There's dominoes in the lily pond!''

It was clear to none of them whether the captain had heard this correctly, but he nonetheless stood up, folded the paper beneath his arm, and followed Cedric and John around the brittle shoulder of raspberry stems.

The boys simply pointed to show him. The captain teased the dominoes with the tip of his walking staff. ''Did you tell Mrs. Uyterhoeven?''

The boys shrugged no.

''You should tell Mrs. Uyterhoeven,'' said the captain. Then he turned and started back to the doctors' table to continue reading his morning paper.

Cedric and John followed the captain's order. They proceeded to the house to look for Mrs. Uyterhoeven. She was not there, so they returned to the garden and finally found her near the back by the birdhouse, in gardening gloves. She'd taken the birdhouse down from its pole and set it on a raggedy blanket, and was now scraping the loose paint with an old flat kitchen knife. ''Yes?''

''There's dominoes in the lily pond,'' said Cedric. John stood silent, as he was slightly afraid of Mrs. Uyterhoeven; she could be so intent. It was only when she spoke that he was reminded of her kindness.

''Are there?'' She put down her knife.

Both boys nodded.

Mrs. Uyterhoeven took off her gloves. ''Show me.''

All three of them made their way back to the lily pond. The boys led, and were both very relieved to find the dominoes still there.

''So there are.'' Mrs. Uyterhoeven leaned over the pieces as if they were a type of bug she'd never seen before. ''Tonight will be cold,'' she said. ''We should take them out in case the water turns to ice.''

The boys knelt down on the border stones and Mrs. Uyterhoeven held them both by their collars as they plucked the pieces one by one from the water and put them in the pouches of her apron.

There were only five or so left when John noticed something underneath the water. It was sitting on a rock just beneath the surface. He reached down and picked it out: a small wooden figure of a man, a fat man kneeling over with his hands on the ground and his head bowed, and he had no clothes on.

''What is that, John?'' asked Mrs. Uyterhoeven.

''It's a man,'' John said, handing it to her.

''So it is.'' She squinted, and Cedric was quiet with envy the moment he saw: it was the next piece.

Mrs. Uyterhoeven dried the figure on her apron. ''We should take this in, too.'' She gestured for the rest of the dominoes, which John collected, in a slight delirium at his discovery. Then the three of them walked back to the house. They went straight into the library and built a fire, and there by its light they dried all the dominoes with towels from the kitchen. When all the pieces were warm, Mrs. Uyterhoeven set the candlestick table by the fender and lined the dominoes in a row alongside the goatskin board. The kneeling man she set in the pawns' row, much to John's delight and Cedric's commensurate jealousy—both understood that there he would remain, this plump and humble figure, for all who visited the library to see, and all to know that John Quigley had found, even though it had been Cedric's idea to go to the lily pond in the first place.

Three days later, it was announced that the doctor's next letter had come in the mail, and the following Sunday, February 17, it was read—in the library. All the guests arrived as usual after supper. Mrs. Uyterhoeven had the great stone fishbowl brought in from the front parlor, and she'd placed all the dominoes on the surface of the water.

The kneeling man was right where she'd put him from the start—in his square on the goatskin board—though for modesty's sake, he had been wrapped in a small brown robe and had a tiny white turban on his head.

The Fifth Letter

December 27, 1900

Dear Sonja,

An apology to begin for what follows, and let it be said that I have spent not a brief amount of time contemplating whether I should burden you all with the less happy moments of my travels. But finally I have decided that I should never want to feel that I am here alone. I should want to know that when you think of me, you think of me as I am, as I find myself, and so am obliged to tell you the whole of what I have learned since last I wrote, even as dark as it may be.

I had entered a rather glum period, then, after visiting the ashes of Eugene's rook. This notion of vandals roaming the countryside with goods beneath their coats was frankly more than I liked to think of, and yet impossible to put from mind, for I saw no reason to think that I should be spared the consequences of their actions—if they should succeed, I mean, and destroy all the goods at once. Exactly what those consequences would be I do not pretend to know—that is a great part of what I find so disturbing, in fact, is my ignorance—but the prospect would appear grim, such as I can fathom it: of turning round and finding myself suddenly surrounded by strange objects, objects the purpose of which I have no recollection anymore. I should be quite lost, it seems to me, in a way I might even think comical if it did not seem so frightening, too—for what should I be left with when the purpose of all the chairs and tables, the glasses and watches, door-knobs, bellows, cribs, and flower pots have all been washed from my brain like so many designs drawn along the shoreline? What will become of my memories, I wonder, and of the things I love when everything surrounding them has lost its meaning—the shoes you lace up, the hats you wear in winter, the saucers which hold your cups? Will I even be able to write you anymore, I wonder, or will I have forgotten the purpose of pens and choose instead to scratch myself with their tips, and stare about the room dumbly, ink-stained? I keep thinking of the young mystific, and of his master kneeling in his room watching the light pass across the floor, and I am filled with personal dread.

A grim view, I know, and not the sort I'd recommend to the wayward traveller. The first civilised board I visited after leaving Macaroni was of an elaborately decorated Indian team, the Rajasthani. The bishops were a most remarkable piece, as I think of them—brightly painted elephants with cannon barrels on both sides. It gives them quite a fearsome appearance, actually, and I'm sure I would have enjoyed them immensely had I not just been coming from the rook and my first encounter with the vandals—but alas, that is precisely where I was coming from, and so the appearance of the Rajasthani bishops seemed to me a rather capricious curlycue. I remember one in particular, an elephant rearing up on its hind legs, with its trunk thrown skyward—but all I could think in the presence of this magnificent beast was whether the little Indian atop its back was a vandal or not, and if he was, was he hiding goods somewhere? And where was he hiding them? And how many others on the team were vandals, too? How far along are they, and who shall give the signal when they're done?

All these questions I had, but no real prospect of an answer. I certainly didn't see myself infiltrating their ranks to find out, for what if they discovered my allegiance? Who knew what other sorts of horrors these miscreants might be capable of? And even if I did dare investigate, I wouldn't know how I'd begin. The vandals wear no sashes across their breast, or feathers in their cap. They give no sign of their intention. Indeed, life proceeds from board to board here with a vexing normalcy, a listlessness which one might well confuse for tranquillity if one didn't know the threat which looms. There is a stillness in the air, a certain unspoken complicity in the chat and palaver on the village streets, and the slow, unconcerned roll of the counters down the path. It's the sort of dead calm that I am told precedes hurricanes and tidal waves, and I can feel it even now. We are all of us, whether we have the courage to admit it or not, waiting.

But forgive my dwelling. After two days feeling so racked by dread and suspicion in Rajasthani, I decided a retreat might be in order. I didn't know exactly where or for how long, but it seemed that for the sake of my own sanity I should probably remove myself from the community of those responsible for this frightening state of affairs, whom I took to be only the civilised pieces. I thought perhaps I should go spend some time with the vast majority of others—the marbles and Stauntons, the checkers and dice and so forth, for whom the destruction of goods could not possibly be of interest. Why, if I were with them, I thought—and by them I mean the totem—I might in the hour of the vandals' triumph not even notice the darkness falling about the civilised nooks of my brain. It would be like a candle dying in a remote chamber of the castle.

I ventured off the roads, therefore, and there encountered the totem in much greater number. And yet, for the very reasons I'd long anticipated, found theirs a fellowship not easy to win. All nature is like to like, and totem are no different. They did not shun me, but they did not much welcome me either. Flocks of darts would fly overhead without a pause, and dice would tumble by in pairs too fast for me to follow. If I so much as came near a nest of cribbage pegs, they'd scatter at my approach as if a small tornado had descended.

It wasn't until my third day in the wilderness that I finally chanced upon a team that seemed at peace with my presence. I found them standing by a cavernous rock formation in a region called Chaturanga, a set of limestone chessmen who could not, it seemed to me, have been better suited to my now ascetic purpose, as they could not have been more evidently totem. The pawns were simply cubes; the rooks, rectangles standing on end; the knights were stout columns; the bishops had slightly rounded heads; the queen was a tall cone and the king an obelisk—a surpassingly simple and very self-assured team they were, who perhaps most important of all stayed still, and could not therefore avoid my imposition.

I went and sat with them, and as a matter of simple etiquette tried as best I could to converse in the language of my hosts, which in this case seemed to be utter, utter silence. I did the same in the matter of deportment, and tried to emulate their physical quiet, but I should warn, in case any of you are ever for some reason compelled to do the same: meditating with chess totem is a bit like running laps alongside a racehorse—one, no matter how hard one tries, is simply no match. In the first place, one—if one is as old as I—has trouble sitting in any single position for long, and the ground was out of the question. Eventually I had to take a seat on one of the limestone pawns, which didn't seem to mind, fortunately.

But, of course, even more difficult than the physical demands of their company was the mental strain. I found myself extremely prone to distraction—more so than I would like to admit.

But if I was not a perfect student, I did at least achieve something of my original purpose, which had been to put the destruction of goods as far from mind as possible. After just a day or two, it had begun to seem a quite remote and even slightly mad affair. As dire as I had thought this plot in Rajasthani, I was now inclined to think it almost funny, so much so that at one point, sitting there among the quiet limestone, I actually did laugh out loud at the thought—the destruction of all goods! I laughed, and couldn't help but take the sparkling rain which fell down soon thereafter as a kind of approval; its drumming upon the several pawns beside me sounded so much like applause.

Now how long, left to myself, I would have remained in this state of giddy oblivion I suppose I'll never know, as on my ninth day among the limestone, my mid-afternoon meditation was invaded by a sound—very faint at first—of hoofs and feet and turning wheels beneath the strain of heavy loads, all making their way up and over the silent horizon to cross the very plateau where we were sitting.

I resisted opening my eyes at first, in emulation of my hosts, and I was perfectly prepared to let this vagabond orchestra pass right by, except that it did not. In fact, it grew louder and louder, until I could feel it casting its shadow directly upon us, at which point I could not help myself. I lifted my lids to see, like some mirage, like some grand concoction of my mind's yearning for human company, an Arabian caravan there before me, with camels and wagons and tents and trunks. Agog, I held my position as several pawns descended their camels and billowed towards us—all wrappings and blankets—and without so much as a word began picking up the limestone chessmen in their arms and taking them back towards their carts.

I wasn't sure exactly what I was a witness to—an impoundment or an ambush—and I felt in no position to arrest these intruders, but I did manage to stop one of them by the hem of his caftan. "Where are you taking them?" I asked.

He looked down at me, a large round pawn with bright, smiling eyes and an unexpectedly high, mellifluous voice. "To the tipping in Gwyddbyl," he answered. "Would the gentleman like to come?"

To a tipping? I'd never heard of a "tipping," and I'd still no sense of his or his team's intention, but he struck me from the first as a very friendly fellow, and one who was at that moment carrying away two more of my nearest companions beneath his arm, so, without much more thought than that, I pulled myself up and followed him back to his cart.

He introduced himself as Ali-Uthmar, a pawn in the tribe of Sayyid Umr Ben Abd, their king, who was apparently in the lead wagon of the caravan. "You shall be our guest," said Ali-Uthmar. He arranged a place for me among his pillows, and then as soon as he'd retrieved the remainder of the limestone and the caravan was started on its way, this most kind and gentle Bedouin explained to me where we were headed, and why.

Tippings are a behaviour of the domino, as it turns out, who are a migratory creature, much like geese or ducks. They travel the land endlessly, stopping at fairly regular intervals at certain specific places to their liking. Unlike geese or ducks, however, the dominoes are entertainers of a sort, and will, whenever they come upon a suitably flat and open space, spend the day lining up in all sorts of patterns and then ''tipping'' in much the manner that we all associate with dominoes—with the difference here, of course, that they are able to do so of their own volition, like acrobats. They are in this respect more like a travelling carnival than geese, and theirs is one of the few performances enjoyed by totem and effigy alike. Hence the liberty which the Bedouin had taken in removing the limestone team from their contented place; if my friends had not wanted to go, Ali assured me, his tribe could by no means have taken them.

In any case, the tribe of Umr Ben Abd also enjoy a good tipping. Ali said they considered it great good luck to cross paths with the domino, and that it was his king, in fact, the Sayyid Umr Ben Abd, who'd calculated that the dominoes would be passing through Gwydd-byl the following day.

He was right, as it turned out. I spent a restful night on Ali's wagon, and by morning we were there. Gwyddbyl is more of a strolling park than a town really, with paths and ponds and fountains. The dominoes had arrived at dawn, and we were told that the tipping was already under way at the great terrace fountain. The Bedouin set up their tents what they considered a safe distance away, at the edge of a great sheep meadow, and then when we were all ready, the sheik Umr Ben Abd emerged from his tent to lead us over.

It was the first I saw him. He was an extremely dark and tall figure, a good two heads higher than the rest of us, with a long, slim, rectangular face and skin an almost blue-brown. He had a slight black beard, a long thin moustache, and eyes like ivory slits which rested on high, straight cheekbones. The whole of the way there he walked alone, ten paces in front of us, with his frame tilted forward as against some imagined sirocco, although in fact there was only the gentlest breeze stirring the trees and bushes.

It was a very pleasant walk, actually. The limestone were remarkably light in our arms, and as we came near the exhibition, we could hear the excitement of the spectators rising up to greet us. They sounded almost like an audience at a fireworks exhibition, with the only difference that their oohs and aahs responded not to the reports of bursting powder but a rather more gentle and pleasant whirring.

This was the sound of the dominoes tipping. The terrace was sunk down like an amphitheatre and surrounded by a small knoll, so it wasn't till we came over the top that we could see: the dominoes were everywhere—hundreds and hundreds of them, and the guests were down among them as well; pieces of all different kinds—chessmen of Asian, Egyptian, and European origin, as well as Pente stones, go pieces, dice and marbles, chips, cribbage pegs, and Indian clubs. I gave thanks to Ali at once, for really, I don't think I could have conceived a more pleasant, friendly occasion for my return to civilisation.

We'd come in the middle of the first round—tippings are divided into three normally, the first being more of an acrobatic show. The dominoes had divided into a dozen or so clusters and were conducting separate tippings throughout the terrace. It all seemed very improvisational to me. They circled the fountain, down the terrace steps and through the legs of the taller members of the audience. They created star designs and pinwheels and spirals. They flipped and catapulted each other, and just as entertaining as watching them tip over was watching them set up again, scrambling about the terrace like a low swarm of bats.

Before I knew it, the noon bell rang and there was a brief intermission, with food and music and mingling. I struck up a pleasant conversation with one of our host pieces, the Gwyddbyls, who are what we might call a "bust set," with the head and sternum of fifteenth-century Welshmen set on top of tall, slim pedestals.

When the bell for the second round rang, my friend and I took to the steps surrounding the terrace, and the dominoes all split up into the same teams as before. This time, however, instead of performing tricks, they competed against each other in a kind of tournament of races. They raced in straight lines and circles. They started at opposite ends of the terrace and spilt towards each other, and if the race was to see who was fastest, the King Gwyddbyl would place a bell at the centre for the winner to ring; and if the race was to see which team was the slowest, instead of a bell, the king set down a blue egg.

It was all a great deal of fun, and my friend and I had been commenting to one another how good it was to see the effigy and totem enjoying each other's company like this, when I was stopped short by the sight of my friend Ali-Uthmar over beneath a nearby tree.

He had withdrawn from the circle of spectators and was kneeling down in the shade. At first I thought he must be praying, but then it seemed to me he looked too unhappy. He was drumming his head with both hands and his face looked very sad. Ali was a fellow of such a jovial nature, his face so naturally inclined to delight and benevolence, it concerned me to see this furrow on his brow, so I excused myself from my Gwyddbyl host and made my way over to see what was the trouble.

"Ali." I stood before him. "Is something wrong?"

Ali lowered his hands from the top of his head and moaned. "I have learned a very sad thing just now."

"I'm so sorry," I said. "Is it anything I can help with?"

"I think no, Dr. Uyterhoben. Some gentlemen here from Untilleflu tell me a bad thing has happened to a good friend. They say that his enemies have come and burnt his home to the ground."

"How awful. Had he a family?"

"No family—but a friend. They escaped into the wild together, with just their wagon and what was left."

"What was left?" My heart clutched. "You're not speaking of Eugene?"

Ali looked at me wide-eyed and nodded. "Yes, Eugene," he said. "They say he is finally becoming lost. They say he is all mad and shaggy in the forest with his little friend, the egg."

As if a dam had broken, I could feel all the dread and world-weariness I'd tried so hard to put away spilling back towards me. "You say you are a friend of Eugene's, Ali?"

Ali looked off at the distance with his brow knit. "Eugene is a very great man. I do not know if I can say Ali is a friend of Eugene, but Eugene is most certainly a friend of Ali.''

''How do you mean?''

''Eugene trusted Ali with a gift.''

''A good, you mean?'' I asked.

''Yes, a good.''

''Which one?''

''Was a very simple good.'' His round face warmed at the thought of it. ''Was a jar.''

''A jar,'' I said. ''Well, that would seem to me to be a most coveted good, Ali.''

''Yes,'' he answered with pride. ''Is why he is a friend, and forever will be. For Eugene said to me when he showed me his jar—he said he had enemies who would like to steal it from him, and break it—and Eugene asked me if I would do this, but I told Eugene no. I said if he would give this jar to me, I would treat it as a gift from Allah, and Eugene trusted me.'' Ali continued gazing in the distance, and I was heartened as I looked upon his face by the excellence of his intentions.

''And what have you kept in the jar?'' I asked.

Ali looked at me and smiled. ''I do not keep anything in it.'' His chest puffed out. ''I give it to my sheik.''

''Well, that is very good,'' I said. ''And I am sure that he has found some fine thing to keep in it.''

''Yes,'' beamed Ali.

''And do you know, Ali, that Eugene is also a friend of mine.''

''He is?''

''Yes, and he told me the very same thing as he told you, of those who want to see his goods destroyed.''

''Yes?''

''Yes. But it wasn't they who burnt his rook, you know.''

''No?''

''No,'' I said. ''Eugene himself burnt the rook, so that these others couldn't come and take advantage of him anymore.''

Ali pondered this a moment and then nodded. ''This was wise.''

"Yes, I think so, too. I think he's better off. But do you know, he gave me a good as well."

"He did?"

I lifted my cane to show him.

"Dr. Uyterhoben's cane is from Eugene?" Ali got up from his knees and I handed him the cane so that he could see for himself. He took it and held it up to his face, delicately upon his fingertips. "Yes," he said. "Is from Eugene." He handed it back. "And what will you do with it, Dr. Uyterhoben?"

"I am walking with it," I said, "as my hip has been bothering me."

Ali considered my application and approved. "But you must protect it as well," he said, now suddenly serious. "You must keep it with you at all times, because of those who would steal it and break it." He mimed snapping a stick over his knee.

"I suppose that's right," I said.

"Yes, is right. If Eugene our friend has placed his trust in us, we must be prepared to give our lives for his cane, and his jar." His eyes were wide upon me. "You will spend this night with us."

"But I wouldn't want to impose—"

Ali shook his finger. "No. While you are in Gwyddbyl, with so many types around whom you cannot trust, you will stay with Ali. Ali will see that your cane is protected."

It didn't seem I had much choice, and I had found Ali a more than trustworthy soul, so we headed back to the terrace together to watch the third and final round of the tipping. For this, all the dominoes came together to tip in lines of increasing length, until, for the finale, they all took part in a single glorious spill, initiated by the King and Queen Gwyddbyl.

It was fairly spectacular, in fact, but I am afraid that I was a bit distracted now—disheartened at the sudden return of my uneasiness, and also slightly unnerved by Ali's determination to see that my cane was safe. He stood right beside me the whole while, and when the final tip was through, he escorted me directly back to the Bedouin tents. We dined on chick-peas and pocket bread. He attended my every need, and when time came for bed, he insisted upon standing guard while I slept. There was no convincing him otherwise. He stationed himself at the foot of my mat, facing outward on his knees, ready.

This, needless to say, I found a difficult situation in which to sleep. For the better part of the evening, I lay there painfully awake, pretending slumber but thinking fretfully of the conspiracy again. I desperately wanted to get up and walk, but I knew that if I tried, Ali would only insist upon accompanying me, which I did not want. So I lay trapped on my mat until well after midnight, when I finally saw Ali's head sink down and begin to bob gently with sleep. As quietly as I was able, I rose, took the cane, and exited the tent, out into the early-morning darkness.

I hadn't any particular destination in mind, but Gwyddbyl seemed such a lovely place for strolling, I hadn't thought it would matter much. I headed off in an unexplored direction, and hadn't gone far, when to my very pleasant surprise I chanced upon the limestone team again. I saw them in the distance, lined along the shallow grass slope by the banks of a duck pond, gleaming in the moonlight like a set of tombstones.

I went over to say hello. I took a seat on one of the pawns, and laid the good cane across my knees. The ducks of the pond were all huddled on the strand, asleep in the shadow of the pier, and I was prepared to settle there as well, to see if I could perhaps retrieve the peace and quiet which the limestone had conferred to me before, but just as I was about to close my eyes, something out on the lake caught my attention.

It was the figure of a man, walking upright across the surface of the water. He was wearing a long cloak with a hood and carrying something in his arms, slowly and steadily making his way towards a small island at the center.

I watched him in the silver moonlight. When he reached the island, he set down his bundle on the sand. He took up a small shovel and begin digging; not long. When the hole was knee-deep, he placed his bundle at the bottom, then covered it over again. He tamped down the sand till it was flat, then turned and stepped out upon the water again, as if it were a pane of glass. With slow certainty, and not once sinking below the level of his hem, he walked back across the surface of the pond, moving with such patience and solemnity, I felt myself a witness to some apparition, some pitiable spectre who'd been consigned to this strange and tedious ritual—of traversing this pond by moonlight, to bury treasures in its cay.

He was coming closer to me now, headed towards the pier, at the end of which I now saw there was a chest. I did not move to conceal myself, though. I looked at him openly from the seat of my limestone pawn, and when he'd crossed halfway, he stopped there, out above the blackest depths of the pond, and turned his hooded head to me. I looked back, helpless. He raised his right arm slowly, and as if pulled by an invisible string, I stood up. His cloak opened and then closed again like a great black wing, and I descended to the water's edge with my cane in hand.

He stared at me silently, but I could not see his face beneath his hood, or his feet or hands for the length of his black garment. He lifted up his right arm again to beckon me closer, and again, as if I'd lost rule of my own body, I was drawn along the water's edge and up onto the pier. To be nearer him, I walked down the wooden aisle to its end. Beside me was the open chest, but I did not once take my eyes from the figure waiting out upon the water. He stood but half the pier's length from me now, rising and falling ever so slightly with the water's gentle billow. A third time he raised his arm, to summon me beside him.

I stepped from the pier. I extended my left foot out above the water and then lowered it till I could feel the sole of my shoe just touch upon the surface. And yet as I committed my weight from pier to pond, something emerged from underneath—something solid, as if a small raft had come to catch my foot. I looked down and there were white dots surrounding my boot, faint in the night, but arranged like those on the face of a die—a pattern of five, and next to it a diagonal row of three. A second raft then slid up beside it, a three and four combination at a right angle to the first, and I realised—they were the dominoes. Indeed, as I looked round now, I could see that all across the surface of the pond were hundreds and hundreds of dominoes, all lying on their backs, basking silently in the moonlight.

I still had one foot balanced on the pier, but so sure was the support of the domino beneath the other, and so clear the invitation of its match floating there beside, that very carefully I stepped down from the pier completely. The dominoes accepted my weight without so much as a waver, and so I found myself standing upright on the water—just like the dark figure before me. A third domino floated up silently as if to suggest a next step. I propped my cane upon its face, and in response several more glided up to offer me whichever path I chose.

Leading with my cane, I started out across the water towards the figure in the hood and cloak. My steps were slow at first, but once I trusted the sturdiness of the dominoes' support, I found I could walk much as if I were on a flagstone path. For each step, no matter how casually I dared commit it, a domino would slide underneath to catch me; but better even than the certainty of their support was their domino genius, that if I should step from a piece of four and five, I would land on a five and three, then a three and one. So the dominoes led me on a path not perfectly straight but perfectly stable, and very well played, out to the dark figure who'd summoned me.

He had waited in silence, but looked at me square as I approached, a commanding figure still, despite the fact that his miracle had been revealed an illusion. He was a good two heads taller than I, and when I came to stop in front of him, I recognised beneath his hood was the long, dark face, the thin black beard and straight white eyes of Ali's sheik, the Sayyid Umr Ben Abd.

His voice was as dark as his appearance and as deep as the pond beneath us. "What have you brought?"

I didn't understand. "For your highness?"

"For the lagoon." He turned his head slightly to indicate the island. "Is it that?" He looked down at my cane, and there was a sudden flare of apprehension in the pit of my stomach.

"I'm afraid I don't understand."

"Is the cane your good?"

"The cane is a good, yes," I said warily.

"Then you may bury it in the lagoon. The water will have covered it over by morning."

I still did not understand. "But I have promised Eugene that I would keep this cane for him, and use it."

The sheik stood back and looked at me curiously. "What is your name?"

"Dr. Uyterhoeven."

The sheik took his hand from the pocket of his long dark gown and opened it to show me—in his palm were two jewels, a diamond and a silver stone. "There is no need to deny your allegiance, Dr. Uyterhoeven," he said. "The dominoes have recognised you."

I looked at the gems, confused. They were the same as those I'd seen the chancellor kiss on the road from Eugene's rook. "What do you mean, 'recognised me'?"

The sheik smiled faintly. "You know very well, Dr. Uyterhoeven. Now give me the cane." He reached down towards my hand, but I pulled away.

"Are you saying that you are a vandal?"

The sheik's eyes narrowed from amusement. "As are you, Dr. Uyterhoeven."

"No." I stepped back, and deftly a domino slid beneath to catch me. "But I am not."

"If you were not"—the sheik looked down at my feet—"the dominoes would not have carried you out to me. They would have drowned you."

"You don't know that." I looked down as well at all the floating, basking dominoes. They seemed so gentle. "How can you say such a thing?"

"I can say it because I know. That is what we are doing here, Doctor." He pointed behind. "That island out there is filled with goods—buried in its sand—all the goods I have in my collection, as well as those of others like us. We are keeping them there so that when the day comes, we shall return here, the dominoes will bear us out, and we shall take our goods from the sand and destroy them with all the rest.''

I began to feel nauseous. ''But why?'' I said. ''I don't understand, why are you doing this?''

The sheik looked down at me with concern, and I think that finally he recognised the extent of my ignorance. ''Have you nightmares, Dr. Uyterhoeven?''

''Of course. We all have nightmares.''

''Well then, I'd ask you to think of them. Imagine them as well as you can, because you shall have to get used to your nightmares, Doctor, if all the goods are not destroyed.'' He looked at me and the whites of his eyes cut through the night like two ivory blades. ''There is another piece from Eugene's set—a pawn named Teverin. Teverin is not gifted like his brother to find goods, but he has in his possession the shadow of one thousand nights. He has collected them in jars and jugs in his home, and he will loose this shadow on the land unless the goods are destroyed.''

''He has told you this?''

''He has let this be known, and make no mistake, Doctor—if Teverin does not have his way, there shall be no morning to come and wake us. It shall be as though the sun were choked, and you and I and all of us shall be abandoned to our nightmares forevermore.''

I looked up at him, frankly saddened. ''And this is why you are a vandal, because of a pawn who claims to hold the daylight ransom?''

''I am a vandal because I have entered this shadow, Doctor, and every time I sleep, every time I close my eyes, I am reminded of what I saw there.'' He looked at me, unashamed at this admission, and I could see in his sallow cheeks and sunken eyes his fear of sleep.

''Well, but then you see, I have a problem,'' I said, ''for I myself can imagine no worse nightmare than if all the goods were destroyed.''

The sheik stood still and looked at me, at once amused and affronted by my parry. ''And yet you are standing here.''

''Perhaps you don't understand the dominoes as well as you think.''

The sheik's eyelids descended in contempt, then suddenly flashed white over my shoulder. "Who is that?" he whispered.

I turned round to see someone coming into the clearing at the pond's edge. It was Ali. He was standing beside the limestone, clearly out of breath, and taking support from the crown of the limestone queen. When he saw me standing out on the pond, he stood up straight. "DR. UYTERHOBEN!" he called.

"You know him?" whispered the sheik.

"That is a subject of yours, your highness—Ali-Uthmar."

"DR. UYTERHOBEN! IS THAT YOU?" cried Ali.

"Yes, Ali," I called back.

The sheik spoke beneath his breath. "What is he doing here?"

"HAVE YOU THE CANE WITH YOU?" called Ali.

"I do, Ali." I raised the cane to show him, then I whispered to the sheik, "He has most likely come to look for me, as he has made it his duty this evening to guard my cane from vandals."

The sheik leered towards the shore. "Has he?"

"DR. UYTERHOBEN!" called Ali.

"He has," I continued in a low voice. "He has told me he would give his life to save just one of Eugene's goods."

"DR. UYTERHOBEN!" Ali called again. "WHAT ARE YOU DOING THERE? AND WHO IS THIS BESIDE YOU?"

There was silence for a moment. "Would you prefer I not say?" I asked.

"Allow me," said the sheik, "and we shall see who understands the dominoes."

Sayyid Umr Ben Abd then turned square-shouldered to Ali and pulled down his hood.

"MY KING!" Ali fell to his knees and elbows.

"Ali." The sheik's voice was so resonant he hardly needed to raise it. Ali looked up furtively, and then with the same gesture as he'd summoned me, the sheik lifted his arm. "Come, Ali."

Ali stood humbly and bowed, but he could not help peeking up at us, to be sure of what he was seeing—the sheik and I standing afloat on the surface of the pond.

"Closer, Ali," called the sheik, and Ali approached the water's edge, still bowed.

"Closer." The sheik gave another beat of his black wing, and just as I had done, Ali climbed up onto the pier and walked out to the very end beside the chest.

"Look in the chest," the sheik commanded, and Ali obeyed.

"Take out the sack," the sheik instructed, and Ali did.

"Look inside the sack, Ali."

Ali removed something long and oval. "My king!" he cried. "It is my jar, which I have given to you!"

"Yes, Ali. Now bring me the jar."

"But, my king?" Ali looked down at the water between us.

"Bring me the jar," said the sheik again, and such was Ali's faith that once again he obeyed. He held the jar to his round chest, closed his eyes, and stepped out onto the water, smiling.

The great round pawn plunged directly in. He began thrashing desperately, and I could see there were dominoes surrounding him, but not to help. The ones in front of him slid away, while others came up from behind to knock him in the back. They pushed him out farther from the dock, and there was a great commotion of white froth in the moonlight, from Ali beating desperately at the water as he gasped for air, from dominoes fleeing his grasp, and others which seemed intent upon covering him over.

Horrified, I looked to the sheik, but he stood watching with a mild expression on his face. I rushed to help. The dominoes lined up for me like soldiers, but when I reached Ali, I beat at those surrounding him with my cane. I got down on my knees and tried to shove them away, but the dominoes were too strong, and Ali began slipping beneath the surface. I grabbed hold of the hem of his robe, but it pulled out from the water like rope, and Ali slid down. I plunged my arm beneath the surface to catch him, but he was gone, into the depths of the black water.

The dominoes all calmed. I looked back at the sheik, who stood tall and silent on the surface. "How could you?" I asked.

He shook his head faintly. "*I* did not." Then he started towards me. The dominoes slid a trail beneath him, silently and with perfect grace, straight to where the good jar bobbed innocently in the water.

''But he was one of yours,'' I said.

The sheik reached down and plucked the jar from the water. ''Apparently not.'' He stood back up and looked at me, the ugly beam of vindication on his face. ''Your cane?''

I clutched it to me. ''No.''

The sheik only smiled at my stubbornness. ''Very well,'' he said. ''But I'd advise you learn what you are doing here, Dr. Uyterhoeven, and why the dominoes have spared you, for there isn't much time.'' He slid the jar beneath his coat. ''And if you should fail, then beware your nightmares, Doctor, and know that you've wished them on us all.''

I looked up at him in disbelief: how mad he was, and cowardly. ''But I cannot imagine,'' I said, ''what dream could possibly have frightened you so.''

The sheik stopped one last time and looked straight into my eye. ''That I am not king,'' he said. Then he turned with the good jar beneath his cloak and started back towards the island while the dominoes slid to make his path and then dispersed behind him.

I looked down at those which were keeping me afloat, the same which had drowned Ali, and I wanted no part of them. With the cane still firm in my grasp, I crawled my way across their mocking domino faces to the pier, and I did not stop to bid the limestone goodbye, for fear that they were laughing at me, too—that it should have taken this place so little time to make a pawn of me.

As I learn more, I will write.

Good night,
Gus

TEN

PELAGIA'S MONASTERY

The Friday before the reading of the doctor's sixth letter, Allesimone Gradycakes paid a confidential visit to the chess garden. A broad-shouldered Irishwoman in delicate hat and gloves, with a thin, dainty mouth and a thick, determined chin, she found Mrs. Uyterhoeven by the east fence, troweling fresh peat underneath the beds of lavender.

"Mrs. Uyterhoeven."

"Mrs. Gradycakes." Mrs. Uyterhoeven raised her eyes just a moment from her digging.

"Mrs. Uyterhoeven, I was wondering if I might ask a favor."

Mrs. Uyterhoeven pitched her trowel in the dirt and looked up.

"I was wondering if it were possible I might see the letter which you were planning to read on Sunday?"

"See—now?"

"Yes."

"And why would you want to do that?" asked Mrs. Uyterhoeven.

"Well." Mrs. Gradycakes pinched a smile. "Mr. Gradycakes and I were . . . not entirely at ease with the doctor's last letter. His tale seems to have taken a dark turn."

"Yes."

"Yes. Well, we just wanted to make sure there was nothing in the next letter that might be upsetting."

"You and Mr. Gradycakes have been upset?"

"Well, it isn't Mr. Gradycakes and I so much as the children. We've been bringing our grandchildren, you may not know."

"Betsy and Arthur have been upset?"

"Well, I wouldn't be surprised. I just don't think it's appropriate for the doctor to be drowning people in his letters."

"Drowning?" Mrs. Uyterhoeven looked up. "But you saw, he appeared right here, the piece."

Mrs. Gradycakes smiled with patient impatience. "Yes, well, I was simply wondering if I could have a peek at the next installment."

Mrs. Uyterhoeven shook her head. "I'm sorry."

"Well, but you see, I'm not sure I can allow the children to attend unless I know what they will hear."

"I am sorry," said Mrs. Uyterhoeven again.

Mrs. Gradycakes glared down at Mrs. Uyterhoeven and waited a moment before speaking again. "I assume you have the next letter already."

"It has arrived."

"But you will not let me see it."

"No."

"If it is your worry that I will divulge any part, I can assure—"

"That is not my worry."

Mrs. Gradycakes paused again, stepped back, and took one last tack. "You understand, I am not the only guest who is concerned."

"Of course you are not the only one concerned, Mrs. Gradycakes, and that is why we shall all read the letter together, this Sunday evening." She put her gloves back on. "But if you are so interested in what is to come, there are some new pieces in the library.'' She picked up her trowel and began kneading the bed again.

Mrs. Gradycakes stood a moment looking down at her, stunned, if not exactly surprised. ''Well then, good day, Mrs. Uyterhoeven.''

''Good day, Mrs. Gradycakes.''

Mrs. Gradycakes had half a mind to go straight around the side path and let that be that, but for the sake of her grandchildren, she passed through the library first.

Miss Steele was presiding, from a divan at the far end of the room. Mrs. Gradycakes went to the candlestick table where the goatskin board was laid out. She saw the boy in the boat, the crane, the thimble, and Ali. ''Miss Steele,'' she looked up, ''Mrs. Uyterhoeven said there were new pieces.''

''Beside the map,'' Miss Steele directed.

Mrs. Gradycakes turned to the dictionary stand. There was a small glass case, one which Mrs. Uyterhoeven normally used for ribbons and lace, but which had three golden leaves inside, all of the same tree.

''Sugar maple,'' identified Mrs. Gradycakes.

Miss Steele looked up. ''Sugar maple to you.''

The next reading was held, as scheduled, that Sunday, the tenth of March, out beneath the patio arbor for the first time since November. The second half was read the following Thursday. The Gradycakes and their grandchildren were in attendance both evenings.

The Sixth Letter

February 21, 1901

Dear Sonja,

First, you should know, I have decided to go to Orzhevsky. Orzhevsky, you will recall, is the home of the vandal bishops, the ones who first recognised the significance of the goods, and who also conceived the plot to destroy them all at once—at least according to Eugene. I am going to find them, despite the fact that it seems like madness, confronting the authors of such widespread treachery, but then I think of poor Ali-Uthmar, how the dominoes drowned him and how they buoyed me, and I feel beholden to know more; to know when, where, why, and, of course, why me.

As I trust you can see upon the map, Orzhevsky is a ways away, closer to the east coast of the land, in what some of you might think of as the ghost's left elbow. There is no good direct route there from Gwyddbyl. One has either to go over or under the heart of the land, which is eclipsed by a black forest, which most of the civilised pieces here treat as an impassable thicket.

I chose the top route, along a road called Wibintu-itcha, and was joined for a certain stretch along the way by a dog; a Holstein terrier, I would call her, with regard first to her colour and then physique. I found her on the side of the road trying in vain to bury a pair of cribbage pegs. For all their sakes, I invited her to come along with me, and was happy for the company.

The second morning of our acquaintance, the beck of my still ailing hip for a moment's pause happened to coincide with our coming to a small, arched bridge, which passed over a very narrow babbling brook. We climbed down from the path to find a place along the banks to rest awhile. My new friend took the opportunity to doze, and I myself had been paying mind to nothing in particular when I chanced to notice a leaf come floating down the creek, the size of a woman's hand. It spun its way towards me, flat and golden in the water, and then passed gently by.

A moment later a second leaf appeared, very much like the first, light and yellow; it came twirling down the water's surface, high upon its spine, and so seemed newly borne upon the current; but like the first, it paused not a moment but kept on happily till it too was gone.

Odd, I thought—a tree up the creek must be shedding its leaves for winter, and yet the forest surrounding us could not have been more thoroughly evergreen. The floor was everywhere a soft bed of faded needles. But then a third and fourth of these golden leaves came floating down the water—and these I reached out with my cane to guide to the banks, that I might inspect them from up close. They were thick, and ripe. The tree would seem to have been nearby, then, but I had trouble picturing it, a golden broadleaf in the midst of so much pine.

Something was curious. At the very least I was, so I roused my new friend from her slumber to travel up the banks and see. It was not far. A mere two bends into the forest and we came into view, not of the tree, but of five figures: a circle of four altar boys standing restlessly on the other side of the creek and back a ways; and then closer to us a king, in a wooden crown and wrapped in a robe of golden leaf. To his left on the bank stood a throne, but he had chosen to sit upon the trunk of a tree which had fallen across our little creek, so that from its seat he could pluck the leaves from his robe and drop them one by one into the tumbling water.

He did not notice our emergence from the wood. Two of the altar boys looked across at us for just a moment, but returned straightaway to the business of impatient waiting, tossing rocks out into the forest. The king kept tearing the leaves from his robe and discarding them like the petals of a love-me-not, and would have gone right on until he was bare, I suspect, had one of the boys' stones not struck with a particularly loud tock off a nearby trunk.

The king looked up. He turned to the boys and gestured for them to take the throne away. The boys came over two by two and set the throne upon stretchers like a Chinese rickshaw. They knelt before the king and waited till he waved them away, then off they went listlessly, with the empty throne wobbling between them.

The king turned his attention back to the leaves of his robe. He had yet to see us, and I was uncertain if I should make my presence known—one doesn't normally go up and introduce oneself to royalty. Unless, of course, one is a dog, in which case one does not care. My terrier friend trotted up and offered the king a few friendly barks from our side of the creek. The king looked at her with a wan smile and held out his hand for her to lick, and I was prompted up the shallow incline between us. I was going to beg our pardon, but when the king turned his eyes to me, I was stopped short.

He was crying. Tears were falling from his eyes in streams which he seemed helpless to ebb. He looked tired, worn, and weary of sorrow. Still, he managed to offer me the same faint smile as he had my friend. I bowed slightly; he withdrew his hand from her consoling tongue and returned his swimming eyes to the strange leafen fabric of his golden robe.

The dog looked back at me and we shared a moment of helplessness. ''Come,'' I called, and after two or three more unrequited barks, she did. I bowed farewell to the king, unseen, and then the terrier and I followed the creek back towards the road, as a new file of golden leaves glided past us down the stream.

Back upon the road, with the image of this melancholy king well branded to my brain, we started once again in the direction of Orzhevsky. I wondered what could possibly have made him so sad, and then a mere quarter of an hour down the path, we came upon a short stone ledge which marked a well-shrouded lane. The dog entered first. She'd seen something, and when I joined her I saw it too, a clearing in the forest, and colour. Down at the end of the lane, the pine gave way to a small grove of broadleaf trees, a few of which had shed already, but most of which were still in a full autumn blush. I saw crowns of burgundy and amber peeking out from through the wood, yellow and crimson. The dog and I committed farther to the path, and I noticed that throughout the grove were altar boys, just like the ones I'd seen waiting for the king. They were all sitting on stools beneath the trees, and turned towards the center of the grove, where as I came yet closer I could see there was a chapel, with quarters behind. It looked to be a monastery of some kind.

The terrier and I followed the lane all the way to its end, and there entered the grove. All the trees appeared to be of the same family, though they differed in age and in the pigment of their leaves. The first we came to was a plum colour, with a glum altar boy sitting underneath, looking very bored, with his elbows on his knees and his long face rested in both hands. Beside him was a small pile of leaves on a canvas tarp.

''Hello,'' I said.

''Hello,'' he mumbled. A breeze stirred the grove and a single leaf came falling down from the boughs above us. It landed near the foot of his stool. Languidly he leaned over to pick it up by the stem and placed it on the pile next to him.

From my coat pocket I removed one of the leaves I'd fished from the brook, to compare. ''May I?'' I gestured to the pile.

The boy nodded dolefully. ''Careful, though.'' Without removing his hands from his cheeks he fingerpointed to the middle of the grove. ''The groundsman's out.''

Beneath one of the distant trees I could see a ladder leaning up against the trunk, and the feet of what I presumed to be the groundsman standing on the fourth rung, high enough that his face was veiled by the foliage.

Cautiously I took a top leaf from the pile and held it up against my golden one. They were very much alike but for the colour, stiff like playing cards, and with an uncommonly drastic outline, as much the effect of space occupied as space absent.

I set the boy's leaf back in his pile. ''And what do you do with them when they've all fallen?'' I asked.

''Give them to the bishops,'' the young man said with a spiritless nod towards the chapel.

I looked round. An odd building, it was made of stone, and shaped like a bin or a half barrel, with a domed roof. At the peak appeared to be a skylight, and all round the sides were porthole windows in two rows.

''Do the bishops allow visitors?'' I asked.

The boy gave what I interpreted to be an affirmative shrug, and I saw that my terrier friend looked quite content where she was, sprawled in the shade, so I excused myself and started for the chapel alone.

I could hear a boys' choir as I came to the door, so I tried to be quiet entering, but there was no service under way. In fact, the atmosphere inside was more studious than ceremonial, like a library. The choir was at the far end, a single row of eight boys singing a hymn of overlapping phrases, and of what seemed to me a purely ambient purpose. Otherwise, the room was occupied almost entirely by monks—the bishops of the set, I presumed, though they seemed well overstocked. There may have been two dozen altogether, all in brown canvas robes, with bowl-cut hair and bald caps, and all exuding very much the same air—of deep, deep concentration. None noticed my entrance; at most, the draft of the open door may have elicited one or two remote coughs, but they were all too evidently wrapped in thought to look up.

Now, the subject of their attention, though as yet unclear to me, was common to them all. I could sense this, that the monks were all engaged in the same problem, but that in order to solve it, they'd set themselves at several different stations throughout the chapel, the most prominent being an enormous round table at the center, surrounded by seven concentric ranks of pews. The purpose of the pews was evidently for rest; I could see several monks had so availed themselves, heads slung back and snoring. The purpose of the table was less clear. As I entered, there were three brothers pacing about the burnished top in cloth slippers, arms crossed, chins in hand, all studying what looked to me like mats or linens down at their feet, which they kept tamping, turning, and sliding from place to place with the bottoms of their slippers.

Above them, looking down with equal severity from the rail of a narrow wooden walkway that rounded the whole of the chapel, were a half dozen more monks, and they too seemed keenly interested in the placement of the mats on the centre table. Every so often one of them would rap on the bannister, a code to direct the slippered monks where to slide the mats, from there to here or here to there.

The last station in the chapel was tucked underneath the walkway: a set of ten arched tables had been set flush against the wall, each manned by two or three monks, who sat like clerks on wooden stools with their backs to the room. All had sacks of leaves beside them, and more leaves spread out on the tables in front of them, which they were treating almost like playing cards, as if they were all engaged in slightly different games of solitaire.

The first two monks I observed were simply sorting their leaves into three piles—according to colour, I think. At the next table, the brothers had divided the leaves into many smaller groups—like cookies on a cookie sheet—but it wasn't until I came round to the third table that I recognised their game, for here the monks were not separating the leaves. Here they were actually trying to fit the leaves together, and the second monk had in fact succeeded. He'd found three different pairs of leaves so well conformed to one another, they actually fit together like the pieces of a jigsaw puzzle—and this of course is what they were doing, I now realised, all of them: they were making a puzzle of the leaves.

The monks at the next table had managed to connect three and four leaves together, and the next monks down had done even better. Indeed, each monk along the row seemed to be working on a larger island of leaves than the last, so that far and away the most impressive belonged to the final monk in the row. He had an island of leaves in front of him which was the size and colour of a spilled glass of wine, I'd say, but with the space of just a single leaf still remaining to be filled in the middle. To his right was a pile of leaves from which he was taking samples to try in the open space. He tested them one by one, with equal consideration, and I watched him reject some fairly passable fits, in my opinion, before he finally did find the one. It fit the space perfectly, both in shape and colour, but the monk expressed no apparent satisfaction. He simply tamped down the leaf with a wood block, then knocked thrice upon the table.

Up stood the nearest altar boy. He'd been sitting on a little stool between the tables—a handsome fellow, with light pale skin, short black hair parted neatly to the side, and a slim, restless face. He had a thin board like a giant wooden spatula next to him, which he took and held up to the table. The monk slid his finished island of leaves onto the flat surface, but with such precious care, the altar boy actually looked over at me—he was the first in the chapel to have done so—and gave an oddly charming roll of the eyes. Then he hoisted the board up onto his shoulder, turned, and made his way towards the pews and the central table.

I followed him as inconspicuously as I was able, which wasn't very. The pews had been arranged in such a way that there was no real aisle to speak of. I suspect there easily could have been, if the monks had simply bothered to rotate the pews properly, like the tumblers of a lock; but as it was—by this more enigmatic arrangement—the route to the central table was practically labyrinthine, so I had to follow close behind the altar boy.

When we finally cleared the pews, he made his way directly to the central table and slid the leaves from his spatula onto the surface like a giant fried egg. One of the slippered monks came over to retrieve it, and the boy took a seat in one of the front pews to wait, chin in hand.

I myself took the opportunity to round the table, curious to see as the slippered monks at work. Their purpose I'd deduced by now: to fit together the various islands they were brought from the peripheral tables into a larger continent, as it were. And I shouldn't think it necessarily a reflection on the intrigue of their efforts, but as I rounded the table, watching the three monks slide the mats from place to place, I became more aware of the choir's song. I actually gave it a good listen, and what struck me—in addition, of course, to the loveliness of the boys' voices—was that I could not recognise a word of what they were singing. There was not so much as a refrain for me to hold on to, with the notable exception of one name I couldn't help remarking, it recurred so many times: "Pelagia."

As I finished my circuit, the altar boy was still sitting glumly in the front pew. He was looking up at me, in fact, and gave a very pleasant sigh of ennui before slumping in his seat again.

I sat down next to him and waited what I thought was a suitably discreet moment before leaning over to his ear. "What," I whispered, "is Pelagia?"

The boy nodded secretly and waited to make sure the slippered monks were not looking, then whispered back. "The queen."

Like a bolt, the image flashed to my brain of the king in the forest, discarding his golden leaves, and of the tears spilling from his weary eyes.

I nodded in the direction of the choir and whispered again: "What are they singing about her?"

The boy waited. He listened to the hymn and then discreetly recited the words. "Show us in the leaves / how to free you, Pelagia / that we might walk with you again—"

Thump, thump, thump came a stern stomping from the central table. One of the slippered monks was standing at the edge with his arms crossed, tapping his foot beside another sheet of leaves—a large one this, the size of whole spilt carafe of wine.

The boy stood up, bowed his head, and approached the table with his board. Very quickly the monk slid him the leaves, and, with a look of scorn, turned away. The boy shot out his tongue at the monk's back as he shifted the board up to his shoulder; then, with a final glance at me of simmering contempt for his bishop, he started back. He tacked his way through all the pews, and exited the chapel through an arched doorway between the last two of the border tables.

I waited a moment, but as soon as the slippered monks were once again engrossed with their puzzle, I also stood up and started through the pews to see where the boy had gone.

I left through the same door as he, and I'm not sure what I'd been anticipating—some sort of vestry or parsonage—but in fact as I crossed this little threshold, I passed from the dreary, incensed air of the chapel into a most brilliant glass corridor, hung from end to end with enormous finished puzzles. There may have been two dozen, all suspended like banners from shining copper transoms. The boy was at the far end already, turning left into another doorway there, but I did not go after him so fast, that I might take this moment to appreciate the fruit of his and his brethren's labour.

The puzzles had been hung smallest to largest, and each had a name which had been carved in capital letters on a wood plaque above its transom. The first was Cunegundes, whose colour with the sun pouring through was the same as a pitcher of tea left out in the sun, and of a size just a bit larger than the rug in the front parlour. Next came Bede and Bertile. Twins they seemed, who both were twice the size of Cunegundes, and who like her were of a single colour—more cranberry, though, and far more subtle in complexion; much more clear was the detail of seams and veins throughout their panels—like the threads of a giant spider's web in Bertile's case; or in Bede's, the leading of a stained-glass window.

There was no puzzle as yet below the next of the transoms, which had been reserved for the leaves of Cyprian; but then came Jude, whose puzzle was of two colours, golden and blackberry, and then Rominald, and Barnabas and Aristede, which were spotted here and there by eyes of crimson and blue.

The next several puzzles after Rominald were more like lace. One named Finbar was made of leaves which looked like the petals of a cherry blossom, and which joined together gave the appearance of a giant snowflake. Ildefousus was lace as well, but the colour of straw and much longer; she hung below two transoms like a wedding veil. And the shadows it cast were so long beneath the late-afternoon sun, I could almost see them slide across the floor and up the wall, overlaying the hues cast through the younger puzzles. Indeed, with the light streaming through the panes of glass and all the different sheets of leaf, I felt as if I had entered a great kaleidoscope, which was being turned ever so patiently by nature's hand.

I'd gone halfway down the gallery when the altar boy emerged from the room at the far end. His tray appeared to be full of leaves again, and he looked at me with a faintly mischievous but familiar smile as he approached. He did not slow his step, but as he passed, he nodded out beyond the glass.

I turned to see the groundsman down from his tree. His ladder was hooked round his shoulder, and he was making his way across the grove. He had an unexpectedly noble air, it seemed to me, despite his function here and the quality of his garb. For livery he'd torn one of the brethren's frocks in half and fashioned it into a smock of sorts, and his tool belt was one of their hemp ropes, slung low from his hips with trowels and gloves and clippers. His features, though, were fine and aquiline, his skin a healthy sunburnt hue, framed by grey hair, which he'd pulled back into a small pigtail, and a short white beard with a sharp, whetted point. He was slender with age, but his gait was long and firm and his chest held high. He seemed an incongruous figure somehow, and then as he passed by, I saw why. Beneath his smock were jambeau and solleret, the steel boots of armour. He was not by origin a groundsman, then, but a cavalier; not meant to carry tools from a makeshift belt but a sword in one hand, a shield in the other. He was a knight of court, I realised, now keeper of the monastery grove.

Beyond the far end of the gallery, he entered into the dappled shade of a tree much larger and older than all the rest surrounding. Its limbs were bare, but still majestic. The groundsman set his ladder down flat beside the trunk, knelt on one knee, and bowed his head. He remained there a moment, with his head upon his arm and his arm upon his knee; then he placed one kiss upon the roots of the tree and a second against its bark. Then he stood up again, took the ladder back onto his arm, and continued on towards a small shed which stood beyond the outskirts of the grove.

I watched him all the way until he disappeared inside, and then I looked back at the tree, the subject of his prayer and adoration. It was so much larger than the rest, I knew it must have been the first of the grove, the parent, and that if its leaves had yet been joined together by the brethren, they'd be hanging last in the gallery. I started down directly, but when I reached the final transom, much to my dismay, it looked as if it had been torn down like an enemy flag, rent from side to side. Only the top leaves remained, drifting slightly in the air, and yet I recognised them at once. They were golden—like the leaves which had beckoned me this morning on the creek, like the leaves in which the anguished king had wrapped himself. I stepped back against the far glass wall, and there above the transom was the name of this rent puzzle: Pelagia.

Now just to my right was the doorway where I'd seen the boy enter before. I peered through. It was a small room, strung with clotheslines and small sheets of leaf hanging down. Against the far wall was a tall slim monk sleeping on a stone slab, and then, as I poked my head round the door frame, I saw another monk standing before a large linen-covered board, ironing leaves.

He had a small school slate hanging from his neck with the name GREGORY carved in the frame, and he seemed a pleasant fellow. He was short and plump, with bushy eyebrows and a dimpled chin, and though he appeared to be clean-shaven, still there was an almost blue shadow of beard covering his pendulous jowls. He looked up at me pleasantly.

''May I come in?'' I whispered.

Gregory stood up his iron to welcome me.

''I have questions,'' I said. ''Is it all right?''

Gregory removed the piece of chalk from behind his ear and nodded.

''I think I may have seen your king this morning,'' I whispered. ''Out in the forest.''

Gregory nodded—it was possible.

''He was discarding the leaves from the last puzzle''—I motioned behind me to the gallery—''the one called Pelagia.''

Yes, confirmed Gregory.

''He misses his queen very much.''

Gregory nodded.

''But she is imprisoned, as I understand?''

Gregory gave this some thought, but then allowed it.

''Is it by a rival?''

The kind monk looked slightly surprised by the question, and shook his head, no. Then he wrote something on his slate and turned it round for me—three words: ''By the king.''

''The king imprisoned her?'' I said. ''What for?''

Gregory shook his head with pity. He wiped his slate clean with the sleeve of his robe and began again, and this time as he wrote, the sound of his chalk against the slate stirred the sleeping monk. He half sat up, in fact—a tall and slender figure, with a long, slim face. He also had a slate hung from his neck, with the name DONAL carved in the frame. Donal looked about, for a moment disoriented, then fixed me with an irritated squint just as Gregory turned round his slate. It read: ''She fell in love with one of his knights.''

''Not the groundsman?'' I said. Gregory nodded, and at this, Donal nearly leapt up to Gregory's side to read what he had written.

''And where did the king imprison her?'' I asked.

The two monks propped up slightly. They looked at each other curiously, then back at me, as if to remark how thorough was my ignorance. Finally Donal answered, in a much quicker but only barely legible hand. ''The grounds outside the castle,'' he'd scribbled. ''Our Majesty drove a stake into the earth and shackled her there by the ankle.''

''How awful,'' I said.

Gregory nodded sadly as Donal scrawled a quick postscript: ''Then he left the castle for one year.''

''But what of the knight?'' I asked. ''How was he punished?''

With a painfully compassionate nod, Gregory took this to answer, more deliberately and succinctly than his brother. He wrote: ''He was forbidden to help her.''

I looked at them both. ''You were all forbidden, I presume.''

Yes, they nodded sadly.

''And did the knight obey his king's command?''

The two monks looked down at their feet, almost too ashamed to answer. Finally, yes, nodded Gregory; but then as if in the knight's defense, Donal took up his chalk and began dashing something off. Gregory had to stand up on his toes to watch, but nodded faintly at what he saw, which when Donal turned around his slate to show me, I could only barely read. ''But he spent every moment with her,'' it said, ''kneeling at her feet.''

Gregory looked up at me, and the memory of the image lay anguished upon his face.

''But he did not free her?'' I said.

No, shook Gregory's head, but again Donal came to the knight's defence. He wrote: ''But she drank rainwater from his helmet.''

''And what did they eat?'' I asked.

Donal wrote: ''The birds brought her berries and seeds from the wood, which she shared with him.''

''And in the cold?'' I asked.

Gregory answered. ''We brought them blankets,'' his slate read, and the two of them grinned sheepishly at their disobedience.

''But what happened when the king returned?'' I asked.

Gregory smiled and lifted his hand to claim the answer from Donal. ''By then,'' he wrote, ''Pelagia had taken root.''

I looked to Donal for help, but he returned my question with a contented grin.

''I don't understand.''

Gregory looked up at Donal and tapped the tip of his iron for him to continue with the leaves. Then he came round the side of the board and took me by the shoulder. With a nod Donal bid me goodbye, and Gregory guided me back out to the gallery.

The colours and shadows had all transformed in the time I'd been in the ironing room. The brother and I crossed to the far side, and there he touched the glass to indicate the eldest tree, where I'd seen the groundsman place his kiss. Then he ushered me to the door at the very end of the corridor, opened it, and, with a gentle pat on the shoulder, left me.

The light was falling and the air was cooler, and as I started towards the tree, I could feel the attention of all the glum altar boys follow me like the eyes of tired dogs. And yet as I came into the scattered light beneath the limbs, I was so taken by the strange beauty of her wood, I lost sight of any other presence. The roots rose up like snakes from the ground—they did not combine into a single timber but twisted round each other like a braid, which in the dying light was tan and green and almost lavender in shadow. Then round the base of the trunk was a ring of scars—from axe blows, I could tell, hundreds upon hundreds of them, which at first I thought might have been to encourage her bloom, as one might girdle an apple tree. But there were so many, and they'd been so thoroughly blunted. I bent over to feel the cords, how cool and stony they were, and then I saw—

emerging from the grip of twisted roots was a black stake, and a chain grown into her wreathed trunk.

My heart began to race. It seemed utterly strange to me, this iron spike, but then as my eyes drifted up the tangled braid of wood, I saw something glint. There was an opening between the cords. I looked in, and there before my eyes was the hand of a woman, her palm turned down and open—just as still as the wood surrounding it, and therefore almost hidden, but for the band of gold round the fourth finger.

I pulled back, but even as I did, my eyes were drawn up to a second hollow in the cords, level with my shoulder, just wide enough for the golden rays of the descending sun to slant in and touch the pale skin of Pelagia's face—her lips as still as stone, her cheeks smooth like ivory, and the lids of her eyes, serene and undisturbed, closed softly as if to savour the moment's warmth.

ELEVEN

THE STAUNTON'S PROPOSAL

The second half of the doctor's seventh letter was read just four days after the first, on Thursday, March 14. No other pieces had appeared in the interim, but the warm spell had passed, so rather than all the pieces being moved from the library out to the guests, the guests had made their way from the garden back into the library.

The Seventh Letter

February 23, 1901

Dear Sonja,

My thanks to everyone there for coming. I hope the day is falling comfortably to evening and that you have a whole tableful of treats and tea somewhere near. You've no idea how it helps me to think of you as I make my way and I write what this evening shall concern the second chapter of my encounter with the pieces of Pelagia's monastery, now three days past.

As I left off, I had just discovered the queen inside her tree. It shames me now, the horror which this struck in me. My first reaction was simply to get away, to escape this horrid monastery as fast as I could, and I suppose if I'd been possessed of a younger body, I might well have—fled the orchard right there and not stopped running till I'd found a warm library somewhere, a soft chair, and a nice safe picture book to leaf through.

As it was, I was compelled by age and by the silent witness of all the altar boys to retain at least the posture of dignity. On seeing the queen's visage there inside her tree, I turned away and, with more reliance upon my cane than I had yet ventured, began hobbling back across the grove in the direction of the entrance lane. My travelling companion, the dog, must have sensed my disquiet and came trotting over from beneath her tree to escort me, but just as we were nearly clear of the orchard trees, there came a voice from behind: "Sir."

It was the altar boy from the chapel, the one with whom I'd spoken in the pews. He was coming after me with a white handkerchief in his hand. "You left this. In the pew."

I stopped. Strange, I thought. I couldn't remember having taken my handkerchief from my pocket, and then to leave it there so absentmindedly—it seemed unlikely, and yet the handkerchief was most definitely mine.

As the boy gave it to me, he noticed my hand trembling. "Are you all right, sir?"

"I've just had a bit of a start." I mopped my brow.

"Oh, you shouldn't worry about the queen. She's fine. She's got all her children here, and she teaches them how to grow the leaves for us." The boy looked round the grove, and then back at me with concern. "Can I get you some water, though?"

Strange boy. There was something about his face, a touch of mischief, and yet his presence had a distinctly calming effect on me. "That might be good," I said.

"You wait here, sir." He offered me a stool beneath the nearest tree. "I'll go get you some." Then he started back towards the chapel.

Nailed to the trunk of this tree was a small block with the name MARCELLUS carved on it. A son. I leant over to look at the leaves which had been collected in a pile on the tarp. They were a dark purple like eggplant and with a slight sheen on one side. I spread out my coat on the ground and scattered a few of the leaves about to see if I could put any of them together myself.

I had very little luck. Trial and error was my method, but I was unable to find a single match. In fact, I was in the midst of unjamming two leaves I'd forced together when the altar boy returned, cup in hand.

"Can I help?"

"No." He'd slightly startled me. "I didn't mean—"

"It's all right." The altar boy handed me the cup of water and nodded down at the leaves on my coat. "Would you like to take some with you?"

I looked up at him, surprised. "But wouldn't the bishops mind?"

The altar boy shook his head. "The king ends up destroying most of the puzzles anyway. Just as long as the bishops know which tree, and I could tell them."

He was smiling faintly. Quite a beautiful boy, really, and treating me very kindly, but for some reason I was having trouble trusting him. "You're sure?" I said again, and this time he answered by getting down on his knees and bunching more of the leaves from the monastery's pile onto my coat. "But don't you think we should at least ask first?"

The boy said nothing. He just kept shoveling over the leaves until they were all in a single pile, much too big for my coat.

"But I'm not sure they'll all fit," I said.

The boy stopped, thought, agreed, then dumped half the leaves back onto the monastery's tarp, and pulled up the ties to sack them.

"This is very kind of you," I said, "but I don't know that I will be able to carry them both."

"I will," said the boy, and before I could object, he buttoned my coat over the leaves and pulled up the tails and collar to close the bundle like a dumpling. A few leaves spilt out. He leaned over and stuffed them back in—rather carelessly, I thought—then hoisted the coat over one shoulder, his satchel over the other, and looked at me. "Which way?"

And that is when it struck me, what it was about this fellow—something in his movements there, the way his lashes caught the light, the shape of his eyes and the slim nape of his neck: he was not a boy at all, but a girl in disguise. And you shall have to believe me when I say it was only then, on realising this, that I truly consented to let her carry the leaves for me—just to see what other tricks she might be keeping up her sleeve.

So this cunning altar girl, the dog, and I all made our way up the lane, and when we reached the road, I pointed her left towards Orzhevsky. I offered to take one of the sacks, but she refused. She said she'd escort us as far as Quigley, the nearest board in that direction, a half day's walk.

I hadn't wanted to seem suspicious, so we passed few words to begin; such as we did, most were mine. I told her about all of you, about the garden and our puzzles, but then perhaps a quarter of an hour down the road I noticed she'd begun to limp. I hadn't seen her twist her ankle or step on a burr, but her discomfort was quite evident.

"Are you having trouble with your foot?" I asked.

She nodded with pain.

"Would you like me to look at it?"

She shook her head bravely no and continued on, her limp growing more and more pronounced with every step.

"Perhaps you should go back," I offered. "I'm sure that I can make it from here."

She bit her lip and shook her head again. "I'll be all right," she said.

I looked at her, clever girl, and weighed what I was to say next with great apprehension, for it was a reckless notion—I can only say in my defence that as it came to me by inspiration, I didn't feel I could deny it. ''Perhaps you should take my cane,'' I offered, ''and I will carry one of the satchels.''

She glanced furtively at my hand and then, with a most histrionic display of reluctance, agreed. She gave me back my coat and I handed over the cane.

She took two steps. ''Better,'' she said, and slung the satchel over her shoulder. She took three more steps then, each more certain than the last—another and another—then quick as a rabbit she dashed off into the woods, satchel in one hand, cane in the other. In a moment she was out of sight. Only the tall grass of the brush and the bush leaves evinced her fleeting presence, nodding at me in her wake with a deserved mixture of sarcasm and reprimand.

I did have to find her, though, that was clear—not only because of the cane, it seemed to me, but because she was carrying a whole sackful of Marcellus's leaves. I started off in the direction she'd fled, a touch less sure of foot than before, but assisted in my pursuit both by my willing terrier friend and by the fortunate happenstance that the young lady's path was bread-crumbed by the trail of leaves which had fallen from her satchel as she ran.

I picked them up as I went, and they led me fairly deep back into the evergreen forest. The trees were well spaced, the cover was thick, and the floor was a soft bed of faded pine needles, comfortable to the foot, but an even more ideal surface for what I discovered was the wood's most Antipodal feature, which was an abundant population of glass marbles. There were nests of small ones lying in the roots of the trees like mushrooms, and larger ones with feline eyes rolling across the needlebed, kissing each other as they went. Such perfect spheres, they moved more simply and with more elegance than any other piece I've seen here, round trees and off into the distance. They were like fairies or fireflies, quick and evanescent, the guards and eyes and children of the forest.

Still, I kept to my trail, leaf by leaf, until I came upon the satchel itself, dropped in haste, with the rest of Marcellus's leaves spilling out. I looked round for some sign of the girl, but there was none, and the dog seemed as baffled as I—no scent or tread to follow. My trail had ended, and I was lost.

Just then a marble appeared in the distance. It stopped between two trees as though it had caught us out of the corner of its eye and was staring now. As if called, the terrier started off towards it, so I took up the satchel and my coat and followed. When I arrived beside them both, a second marble farther off did the same as this first. It rolled in view from the opposite direction and, upon seeing us, came to a sudden stop. We made our way for it then. The first marble resumed its path behind us, and the second marble waited for us to reach it. A third marble then appeared, a bit farther along the way. We went for it, and so, in like manner, by following the marbles as they stopped out in front of us, my friend and I were guided along an invisible path through the woods, until we found ourselves in the midst of a distinctly civilised aroma there amongst the bouquet of pine—my friend could smell it, too—something of an almost chocolate air.

I looked round, but the wood provided no explanation. ''Hello!'' I called out, but there was no answer. My terrier friend trotted over towards a tree which had fallen in the arms of its neighbour. Its roots had been torn up from the ground, and my friend began sniffing at the hollow, sticking her nose beneath the drape of moss and sod which protected it from view. As I came up from behind, I, too, could smell the aroma more clearly: it was the smoke of a man's pipe, most distinctly wafting out from this little cavern.

Warily I peered round the curtain of sod. In the midst of the shadow I saw the tiny orange glow of a pipe bowl.

''Hello?'' I said. The orange glow ascended slightly and made its way towards me, till it was close enough that I could see, above the faint light of the bowl, the face of the young girl glaring back at me.

''You!'' I said.

''What do you want?'' She clenched the pipe firmly in her teeth, and her eyes were wide and daring, like a raccoon's.

''You dropped this.'' I held out the satchel. She reached up for it quickly, but I pulled back. "Oh no," I said. "No. For my trouble, you must invite me down."

She plucked the pipe from her teeth angrily. For a moment she disappeared, and there was utter blackness. Then "All right," she said. A match lit and then the tongue of a kerosene lamp.

She offered me no assistance, and the dog appeared to have no interest in climbing down with us, so by myself I slid on the seat of my pants down into the hollow of the tree's roots.

It took a moment for my eyes to adjust to the light. The space was roughly as large as my medical office. The floor was hard-packed clay, and my hostess was sitting directly centre in an easy chair, with a cherrywood candlestick table at her side. She had pipe in hand and her feet were crossed upon an ottoman with a deep crimson cover. She was wearing a man's smoking jacket with black velvet lapels, a dress shirt unbuttoned at the neck, oversized silk pajama bottoms, and a pair of brown leather slippers. Her cassock was hanging on the tip of a root sprig behind her, and there was a baseball bat leaning beside it with a tumbler hat propped on its knob. On the floor was a fielding glove, a musket, a flat cream-coloured mat, and on her side table she'd set a tobacco pouch, a snifter, a decanter of some thick dark liquid, and then a dish filled with what appeared to be six or so diamonds and another six silver marbles, again like those I'd seen in the hands of the lord chancellor and Umr Ben Abd.

"This is a very nice little hideaway," I said. "Did you find it yourself?"

"Together we did." The young lady relit her pipe and nodded out in front of her. I hadn't seen it before, but there was a Staunton pawn standing there very quietly in the shadows—a dark mahogany piece of classic design, the height of my waist, and slightly worn along the collar and the ridge of its skirt. Right next to it, standing up against the wall, was my cane. "Drink?" the girl asked.

"Please."

There was only one snifter, dry, with finger smudges all about the bowl. The girl filled it halfway with what was in her decanter, and then extended it to me. "What are those?" She pointed at the breast pocket of my vest.

"Cigars," I said.

"Are they from Eugene's?"

"No." I handed her one. "But they should taste better than if they were."

She ran the cigar beneath her nose approvingly and then tucked it alongside the handkerchief in the breast pocket of her jacket.

"Well then"—I raised the snifter to her and to the Staunton—"a toast to you both, for having me."

The girl took up her decanter, but just as I lifted the snifter to my nose—"Wait," she said. "You *have* tasted the nectar, haven't you?"

I sniffed the liquid. It smelled sweet. "I don't believe so. Is it strong?"

The girl smiled. She leaned down and picked up the musket from the floor beside her chair and placed it in her lap, then extended her hand to me. "Give it back."

I obliged. She set the snifter on her side table and looked up at me suspiciously. "What are you doing here?"

"Well," I said, slightly taken aback by this turn of events, "I suppose I would like my cane back."

She shifted slightly to remind me of the musket in her silken lap. "And what do you want with the cane?"

"I am keeping it," I said, "for a friend."

"Eugene?"

I paused. "Yes."

She lifted up her tobacco pouch and recrossed her slippered feet on the ottoman. "Keep it here."

Charming girl. The only flaw to her cunning was the humour which attended it. "But I fear what you might do with it," I said.

She dumped the ashes from her bowl. "And what's that?"

"I fear you might break it."

She refilled the bowl and shrugged. It was true. She was a vandal. But then, as if to put the matter behind her, she sat up and gestured for the leaves.

I handed her the satchel. ''But would you mind if I ask a question about that?''

''You can do whatever you want.'' She slid me the ottoman so that I could sit down, and then she spilt out all the leaves onto the cream-coloured mat between us.

''I'd be interested to know how soon you intend to break them''—I gestured round the room—''all of your goods.''

She shrugged. ''I don't know.'' Then she reached down and began turning over the leaves, so that they all faced the same side up, matte as opposed to shiny.

''Well, but how will you know?'' I asked. ''Is there someone who will tell you?''

''I don't know.'' She shrugged again, but then her eyes glanced up at the Staunton. ''We'll just know.''

I leaned over to help her with the leaves. ''Your friend will tell you?''

''Maybe.''

I looked back at the Staunton, standing tranquil in the corner. I don't know that it returned my attention, but as ever with its kind, I'd the impression that it regarded me with pity. ''And how is it that the two of you know each other?''

The young lady kept turning over the leaves, a touch annoyed at my intrusiveness, I think, but finally she could not help smiling to herself. ''I was going to burn him,'' she said.

''Burn him?'' I did not look up from our work. ''Had he done something to harm you?''

She shook her head. ''I thought he might be one of Eugene's goods.''

''A good pawn?''

She nodded.

''I wasn't aware there were good chessmen.''

''There might not be,'' she admitted. The leaves were all the same side up now. She slid the slippers from her feet and leaned her elbows on her knees to survey them. ''But it seemed like it was worth a chance.''

I gave her a moment. Her eyes cast about all the dark shapes beneath her as if they were moving, but finally I was too intrigued not to interrupt her. ''I'm sorry,'' I said. ''I'm not sure I understand. Why would it be worth burning another pawn?''

She looked up at me with a cocked eyebrow. ''Well, if it were the good pawn and I could destroy it, then we'd all forget what pawns were for.'' She looked back down and selected two leaves to tuck them between her toes.

I thought of it. ''Yes, I suppose that's true,'' I said, ''but you'll have to help me a touch further—what good would that do?''

Again she looked up at me as though I were something of a bother and a dimwit. ''If no one knew what pawns were, or kings or bishops,'' she said with exasperation, ''then we could do whatever we liked. I wouldn't just have to sing and collect the leaves. I could do the puzzles if I wanted. And the groundsman could sing, and the monks could talk to the trees if they wanted, or rake the leaves. We could do whatever we wanted, because why shouldn't we. Because if you've got a bald head, that makes you a bishop? Because if you look like a boy, that makes you a pawn? That's not fair.'' She shook her head and looked back down at the leaves. ''Isn't even true.''

''I see,'' I said, for it did seem unjust. In fact, it struck me as an unexpectedly noble purpose, hers. I looked back at the Staunton in the corner. ''And so what made you think your friend here was the good pawn?''

''He was a Staunton.'' She chose three more leaves from in front of her to tuck between her toes. ''Most people figured if there were good pieces, they'd probably be Stauntons.''

I looked at him another moment. It was an understandable assumption, I suppose—what could be more a pawn than a Staunton pawn? ''But why this one?'' I asked.

''No reason,'' she answered from the murk of her concentration. ''We were just going to destroy them all.''

''Destroy them all?'' I looked up at her, astonished, but she simply kept on with the leaves, saving those she wanted and tossing the rest off to the side. "And what stopped you?"

She reached for a small leaf at the far corner of her collection and held it beside one of those she'd tucked between her toes. They fit. "The Stauntons," she said.

"But how?" I gestured to the leaves she'd connected. "And good for you."

She picked out two leaves from remote parts of the map and connected them as well. "Tricks," she said.

"What sort of tricks?" I asked. "And good for you again."

She cleared a space in front of her for the leaves she'd connected. "Tricks like putting tastes in your mouth." She plucked another leaf from her toe and fit it to one of the islands. "If you came up behind them, all of a sudden your tongue would start to taste like castor oil." Her face soured at the memory. "And they could do the same thing with smell—like rotten milk—and the only way you could get rid of it was to leave them alone."

"So they controlled your mind," I said.

"I guess." She selected another leaf from the side and connected it to one of her islands. "But they could also make it so you couldn't get your torch lit, if you wanted to burn them. Or if it was an axe you wanted to use, you'd get up close to one of them and all of a sudden it would feel like a thousand-pound sledgehammer. You couldn't lift it." She chose another four leaves from the clutter beside her, picking them out seemingly at random, and fit them all together directly.

Indeed, at this point, her pace with the leaves—which up till then had been nothing short of miraculous—perceptibly quickened. Each piece she reached for, she seemed to know instantly what to do with, and was therefore making connections at a rate which, I can personally attest, all the monks in the chapel, all working together in rapt silence, could not have come close to matching.

"They could make you see things, too," she said, her hands working, reaching, and fitting without pause. "There were two Indians who said they found a whole bunch of Stauntons in the black clover one time, but when the Indians lit their torches to burn them, they said they saw serpents all around them with long tongues and giant chickens with lion heads and vultures with long, skinny necks and beaks dripping flesh and blood. The Indians got so scared they just dropped their torches and ran. Then the next day they sent the shaman back, and he said all the clover was burnt white except for where the bishops were standing—it was a perfect black circle. The fire hadn't touched them.''

She stopped to assess her puzzle. She had by now created two rather sizeable oblong islands and began selecting more leaves from the side to build them up.

''But the worst,'' she continued, ''the worst was one time when eight pawns from Middlebunn found a bunch of Staunton pawns in Anders. It was the middle of the night and they had torches, but when they got up close, all they saw was a whole bunch of little children sitting there in the grass, crying. One of them was a little girl with long blond hair, and when they went up close with their torches to try to calm her down, the girl's hair started floating round her head.'' She bristled at the image. ''That one, I hate,'' she said, by which I think she meant that she enjoyed it most. She took up her snifter and gulped down four giant swallows of nectar. Then, almost as an afterthought, she spun one of the islands she'd been working on and coupled it to the other; they fit exactly but for the space of a single leaf, open in the middle.

''Very nice,'' I said. ''But now what about your friend here? What trick did he use?''

She looked over at him quickly and then paused. She seemed suddenly bashful. ''I don't know.'' She grabbed for her satchel and reached down inside to see if there were any more leaves at the bottom.

''But when you went to burn him, did he put a taste in your mouth?''

She shook her head and picked up my coat to look underneath. There were no leaves.

''Did he make you smell something rotten?'' I asked.

"No." She looked round behind her now.

"He made you see something?"

"No." She looked up with a stumped expression.

"Then what stopped you from burning him?"

She shrugged. "Just couldn't, I guess." She looked at me. "Do you have any more leaves with you?"

I reached in my pants pockets, and indeed, I did find six or seven more leaves. I held them out to her. "So is that when you brought him here, after he did nothing?"

She nodded and chose one leaf.

"And that is when you began collecting goods?"

"Sure have a lot of questions, mister." Then she leaned over and fit the leaf directly in the open space.

"Remarkable," I said, and we both looked down.

The leaves appeared more black together, solved, than they had apart, all smooth and finished, and as I looked at them, I felt a wave rush through me—at first unsettling for the suddenness with which it occurred—but then all at once the knots in my body slipped and the tweaks untwined, the churnings calmed, and the pain in my hip took leave, all as I gazed upon the finished leaves.

Then I spoke, on a strange and sudden impulse, hardly knowing what it was I had to say until the words were coming from my mouth. "Forgive me," I said. "I don't mean to overstep my bounds, but I wonder—" I looked at her. "Are you aware the Staunton is in love with you?"

My words surprised the girl less, I think, than they did me. Indeed, they'd left me slightly dizzy, but the girl remained still. She did not look at me or at the Staunton. She stared straight ahead, with legs akimbo, her eyes dry and unblinking.

"I am sorry," I said, trying to collect myself. "I shouldn't have embarrassed you like that."

She shook her head smartly. "I'm not embarrassed."

"Well, good," I said. "I'm sure he wouldn't want to see you solemn."

The young woman pursed her lips and slipped her feet inside her slippers again, unaware of my failing condition. ''He can't *see* me,'' she said. ''He doesn't have *eyes*.''

She had not finished saying this when suddenly the swell of well-being which had overtaken my body and the strange compulsion which had caused me to broach the subject of the Staunton's affection rose up at once and subdued me. And it was as if I were seeing everything in the room for the very first time. The impression was fleeting but so powerful that even as I wanted to answer the girl and tell her that she was wrong, and that the Staunton could see her very well now, I could not open my mouth to speak. I could do nothing but let this innocence and wisdom come and occupy me whole. And so from that moment, the moment she slid her feet back into her slippers, I saw what was before my eyes as a mere witness. What my hands touched, I felt only faintly, as if I were wearing thick mittens, and the words which came from my mouth I merely overheard.

''Is there more light?'' he asked, slow and clear, a voice like mine in register but different in tone, of wonder with itself.

Still, the girl assumed it was I who'd spoken naturally, and she was cordial. She turned up the lantern and hung it from one of the ceiling roots.

''Better?''

The light flickered on her face, a warm gold. ''Better,'' he echoed. ''Is that you?''

She looked at me, confused, then reached up to the lantern to improve the light, a response which, though unsolicited, I know was pleasing to my incumbent. For the first time he felt the blessed coercion of happiness upon a human face, and smiled.

The girl looked impatient at this. ''What?'' she said.

''You are exactly the same, but for seeing.'' She stood still beneath the lantern, with her arms helpless at her sides. ''It's the very same,'' he said. ''But look how clear the edges are.''

Poor girl, she must have thought I'd gone completely mad, but she did not let her confusion show. Even as I was lifted toward her by the Staunton's intention, she did not flinch. Then there was my hand upon her cheek, which was warm. ''You *are* embarrassed.''

''I am not,'' she said.

''Don't be. Look.'' The Staunton moved to face her. ''Look. The old man is gone,'' he said. ''It's only me.''

Finally, her eyes met mine. She searched for madness or sincerity, and when she found the latter, her face lit. ''Only you who?'' she teased.

''Me.'' My eyes glanced at the Staunton.

She looked over, too, then back at me to compare. ''It doesn't *look* like you.''

''No.''

''Looks like the old man.'' She took my hands and inspected them. ''Old man bullied his way down; and these look just like his old-man hands.''

''They do,'' he agreed. ''Very old.''

She stepped back. ''And these look like his dusty old clothes.''

''Yes.''

''Well then, if it is you, you don't look anything like you. You look like the bully old man.''

''I know,'' he said. ''But this—'' The whole room swept by, and then its discrete parts stopped one after the other at the center of his vision, everything which the light of the lantern touched directly—the decanter, the table, the chair, the roots hanging down, and then the girl, her hair and her clothes, her slippers, her wrists, her neck, her chin, her lips, the tip of her nose, and finally her eyes. ''And you. It's a miracle how much the same it is, and how well put.'' He continued looking at her shamelessly. Such a strange sort of attention, which she could not answer but by being, so finally she diverted it.

''What about this?'' She took down the lantern from its hook and held it out for him. ''Is it the same as you thought? It's the good lantern.''

''The lantern.'' My palm was against the glass. ''For warmth?''

She tilted her head generously. ''For warmth a little, I guess, but mostly for light.'' She held it out in front of her as though she were entering a haunted attic. ''For lighting dark places.'' She turned the knob, and as the flame increased, a few stray giggles wriggled up from my throat. The Staunton took the lantern in my hand and tried the knob himself. He lowered the flame, down very low, and out it went. For a moment the room was black, and then the whole of my chest and abdomen exploded with laughter. A match struck; the girl took the lantern back and lit the wick while the Staunton continued his laughing. Not the laughter of ridicule, though. It was more as though the very process whereby experience was sifted through the sieve of my civilized perception was unbearably, uproariously ticklish to him, and nothing more so than the dimming and brightening of light, which the girl effected at some length for his pleasure until the hilarity was too much. I fear they believed they might kill me, and so she replaced the lamp upon its root and offered a new subject for his attention—the tumbler hat.

She put it on her head and stood in the middle of the room. "For rain." She turned round. "To keep your head dry, and for being seen in." She strode back and forth with her arms extended behind her, and now I will allow that the Staunton's glee had more the quality of finger-pointing, but only in the friendliest way, and soon he fell, with great good fortune, into the good armchair.

"The chair is for sitting," she said.

"Ohhh," said the Staunton, calming himself. "Very peaceful."

"Yes, and this is to rest your feet on." She got down on her knees and lifted my legs onto the ottoman. Then she took the pipe from the side table and placed it in my hand.

"And this?"

"This is the pipe," she said, raising it to my mouth. She lit the bowl. "Breathe in," she suggested, and soon the smoke was inside me—without trauma, owing to the fact that it was my accustomed throat and lungs which he'd borrowed. Still, I'm not sure the purpose of this intake was readily apparent to him.

"It is for . . . ?"

She picked up the decanter and touched the top against her chin to think. "Changing," she concluded, then she poured three fingers of the drink into the snifter.

The whole room drifted into my eyes. ''I suppose,'' he agreed. ''It become a part.''

''Right.'' She held out the snifter to me. The glass was cool. ''For drinking,'' she advised.

''The nectar?''

She nodded.

''But what about the old man?''

She stood up and looked at the ceiling to think, and I assume the Staunton's pause upon her figure was to regard the physical presence of grace, and how simply it was achieved. The hat fell down past her ears and the coat was too broad for her shoulders. The cuffs of her pants were dirty from scuffing the mud floor. But she was like a ballerina, with the jut of her hip and elbow, the bow of her left leg, the crook of her right.

''Let him,'' she decided, and the glass was tilted against my lips, the nectar was on my tongue, tart and quite strong, I assume, for I don't think I'd have been able to taste it otherwise. The liquid slid down my throat, and the girl took a sip herself, from the snifter. ''Mmmmmmmm,'' she said. ''Try. Take a sip and then say mmmmmm.''

There was a second mouthful down my throat and then the resonant return, ''Mmmmmmm.''

''Better?'' she asked.

''Better.'' My voice sounded not completely convinced. ''The drink is just to taste?''

''To taste and quench your thirst.'' She took my left hand in both of hers and began studying all the lines and wrinkles.

''And what is that?'' He held up my hand to show the string tied round my finger.

''That?'' She touched the knot. ''It's for remembering things.''

The ceiling curved above me. The pipe was in my right hand, her hand was in my left, my feet were crossed upon the ottoman and my back was resting comfortably against the chair. My eyes touched all the goods again, one by one, and finally, for just an instant, the Staunton. ''There's much, much more, isn't there?''

''Oh, there's everything,'' she said. ''Candlesticks. I've seen the good one in Pickinwheel. I could get that easy.'' She pointed to the puzzle. ''And a rug and a couch. And a brass tub beside a fireplace for logs, and a bookshelf, and bookends, and bowls and ashtrays, bannisters and plates, and a rocking chair and a teakettle, and teacups, and a tray—just as long as I can get enough leaves to trade.''

My head rocked back and forth against the rest. ''And how have you imagined it?''

She paused, and I know that she was looking towards me. She pointed at the corner where the Staunton was, but my eyes remained upon the ceiling roots. ''You will be there.'' She touched the armrests of the chair. ''And I will be here.''

''But how?''

She looked round the room slowly. ''I could burn them,'' she said. She looked up at the ceiling. ''Or I could try to bury them.'' She paused. ''Or we could flood them, I guess.''

He closed my eyes and listened to the quiet, how loud it was, and then it was silenced again by the girl's voice. ''When?''

All remained black, but I could feel her hand fold inside mine. ''Soon.''

I felt her open my hand and then her fingertips faintly tracing lines. ''He is so old,'' she said; a moment passed, and then I felt her lips against my palm.

In a flash the room raced past and my hand pulled away from hers.

''I'm sorry,'' she said.

''No,'' he said. ''Don't be. But I have to go.'' She was before me, looking up. ''This is not what I came for.'' He touched her cheek. ''I have felt you already, much better that this—just as you feel and think, just as you are. But these hands—this is not how I am. And that''—the Staunton stood vacant in the corner like a bedpost, stiff and limbless—''that only holds my place. All of this is temporary. This is flesh and wood, and it's not why I've come, to drink or to smoke your pipe. I am only here to tell you, tell you so you can hear it with your ears—'' Her eyes were brown on green. ''What the old man said was true. From the moment you appeared, I have been in love with you, and I grow more so every time you return.''

She pressed my palm against her cheek, and I could feel her tears.

''Here.'' He opened my hand, and rolled the thread from my finger. ''If strings are for remembering, then I want you to wear this.'' He hooked the thread over her ring finger, which was so small he had to loop it twice. ''So that you will always be reminded, when all these things are ash and dust, you and I shall be together.''

He tried to pull my hand from hers, but she held to it fast. ''*Please* don't go.''

He stroked her hair. ''But I am not going anywhere,'' he whispered. ''I will be here.'' Her forehead was warm. ''And I will be here.'' Her heart was beating.

Then the spirit of the Staunton withdrew. My body was returned to me. The girl could feel the difference, I know, but she did not raise her eyes to mine, where she'd have found only me. She placed her head against my knee and then began to weep. I stayed with her until her eyes were dry and she was fast asleep. I lifted her onto the chair. I took back the cane and left her there, curled up in its seat, while the Staunton stood motionless in the corner, waiting silently.

Tomorrow I make straightaway for Orzhevsky—no more diversions. There is much I must discuss with the bishops there.

Sleep well,
Gus

P.S. I have not forgotten, be sure. I have torn a new thread from my inside pocket and shall tie it around my finger now.

Three days after the reading of the doctor's seventh letter, a six-year-old girl named Antonia Zehring arrived at the garden at 8:00 a.m., as usual, for her morning game, which she preferred to play alone, against herself. As usual, she marched straight back to the games shack and took down her set of Stauntons from its shelf. Like the older men, Antonia disdained the more figurative pieces, because she considered them distracting.

So she took her usual set back to her usual table, the one with shorter legs near the apple tree. She opened the box, and there inside, in among all the expected Stauntons, she found two other pieces: one, a beautifully carved figure of a slim man with broad shoulders, dressed in overalls; and the other, of an entirely different make, who was shorter and more egg-shaped, and whose face and clothes had all been painted on: Eugene she recognized, and his scribe, Egbert.

Antonia was a precocious girl who several years before had entered a perfectly normal phase of skepticism, rather liked it, and had remained there ever since. She had not missed any of the readings, of course—in fact, she was far and away the youngest child at the garden to inspect the doctor's letters themselves—but she had taken a quiet pride in not believing them for a moment. She knew the doctor was in South Africa—she'd made her father tell her, after having displayed a withering shrewdness about the rest of the Uyterhoevens' ruse. She knew that the doctor was making up the whole story, and she knew that Mrs. Uyterhoeven was putting the pieces out, so she considered it a fairly generous gesture, but also the only real alternative, when upon finding Eugene and Egbert in her box, she quietly and without anyone's seeing took them into the library and set them on the Pretorian board herself, in pawns' squares. Then just as quietly she returned to her table out by the apple tree, to play her matutinal match alone, against herself, and never said a word to anyone.

PART FOUR

The Shadow of Klipdrift

TWELVE

SOUTH AFRICA, 1867

In 1902, John Bigelow sent copies of all twelve of Dr. Uyterhoeven's letters from the Antipodes to Rudolf Virchow for his eightieth birthday. Bigelow was a longtime friend of the Uyterhoevens, an ardent Swedenborgian, and also a distinguished public figure in New York—he was among the founders of the public library, and also co-owner of the New York *Evening Post.* He had met Virchow only once, in 1892, when their visits to the chess garden coincided, but still thought of him ten years later when he received his own copies of the doctor's letters from John Patterson.

Bigelow sent the letters all at once, with a brief message of good wishes on top, and then at the end, beneath the last page of the final letter, a more personal note:

> It has always seemed to me that our friend's life could well be viewed as a long Continental corridor, followed by an equally long and distinguished American corridor, with one room between them—Klipdrift—that no one but he ever truly passed through, and whose significance we can only measure by the difference

which it yielded between the man who entered and the man who left.

I wonder if you would agree, however, that with these letters the blinds have been opened, and that the little room of Klipdrift, wherein the doctor's life may be said to have taken its turn, is finally shed some light.

Gustav had just returned from meeting with the head of appointments at the Faculté des Sciences when he received word of Larkin's death. There was a dispatch awaiting him at the hotel desk, an envelope from the Friedrich Wilhelm Institut with two notes inside. The first was just a single word, in Sonja's hand—"Come." The second was on Virchow stationery, and it was nearly as brief. In German, Virchow had written: "Courage. Your friend, R."

Gustav left for Berlin at once. Virchow was there when he arrived home, and Sonja, dressed in black. Larkin's body still lay in the bed where she'd found him. Virchow had been the one to assess the cause of death—a massive seizure, suffered in his sleep. He had found signs of an ear infection, but told Gustav that Larkin probably hadn't felt any discomfort beforehand. He hadn't been ill, and probably had not awakened.

Sonja did not speak until Virchow was gone, and then asked only that Larkin be buried in the Netherlands, at the cemetery in Workum, near the canals. The following day they left, with Larkin's body in a casket. Koos and Mirjam, Mattijs, and Elsa met them in Ijilst. Isabel came from London. Menno conducted the ceremony in English, and then Gustav and Sonja returned to Berlin.

The doctor decided not to take the position he had been offered in Paris. He left open the possibility of going in the spring or the following year, but he wrote the director that he didn't want to "taint my new start with mourning." Virchow offered him an indefinite grace period to do as much or as little as he pleased. The fall semester he taught one class in pathological anatomy and oversaw the research of a few select students, but conducted none of his own, and by winter an eerie stillness had settled around him. For the first time since most of his colleagues had known him, he seemed lost. "Not just drawn and pale," Karl Löffler described him, "but slightly bewildered by what has happened, that his child who had endured so much already should be taken from life so quietly, so swiftly, and at such an unthinkable age—five."

Löffler's opinion was typical of those who knew the doctor less well, who believed that Larkin's death had somehow staggered the doctor's well-known and vested romantic orientation. "It seems even more cruel, the irony," Buchheim wrote Virchow, "that the one among us who has made such a point of insisting on the obscurity of cause should now be subjected to such a brutal and enigmatic effect."

Those closer to Uyterhoeven observed something different. It was true he'd stopped working and could seem disoriented at times, but not because he felt remotely confused or betrayed. "God save poor Gustav from his own repugnance," wrote Schleide, his first tutor in biology. "I have never seen a man turn upon himself with such violence."

Lebert concurred. In a frankly concerned letter to Fechner, he described the doctor's "spells."

> In grief, he is revealed to himself a hideous creature, and it is literally as though a demon has entered the room when the creature visits. He says it squats in the corner, mocking him with its presence—a hateful and odious thing, in whom all the qualities that even his adversaries have come to admire are transfigured—the self-assurance, fear; the boldness, hubris. An arrogant, puny charlatan, he sees, a hideous and pathetic creature, so repugnant to him that he is reduced variously to insane terrors, helplessness, uncontrollable despair, but above all, such profound loathing for his own mind and self as causes him to regurgitate whatever he may in peace have had the strength to eat or drink.

Only Dr. Geddes in London took a hopeful view of such behavior. He quickly diagnosed the doctor's suffering as a "vastation." "A very common and beneficial process,'' he wrote Uyterhoeven, ''literally, a purification by burning, the subject of the flame in this instance being the damning and damnable self. No cause for worry, though. Be assured that when what needs consuming is consumed, you shall find yourself the better.''

Geddes's analysis brought Uyterhoeven little consolation. To him, his torment seemed a hopelessly self-perpetuating condition—evidence of its own necessity, that he should respond to the death of his son in such a selfish and self-pitying way. ''He loathes himself for loathing,'' wrote Lebert, ''and therefore cannot seem to stop.''

As best he could, the doctor tried to confine his spells to the laboratory, ''not to suffer Sonja such foolishness.'' Indeed, their differences had never felt more vast. She did not grieve outwardly but with her sister. Otherwise, she maintained an emotional continence—''a straight-backed, willful stoicism,'' he wrote Menno, ''belied by quiet words I hear from around corners, and by nightmares she will not speak, but from which she wakes to a horror yet worse, of finding me and never Larkin.''

''Their home is too grim,'' Virchow wrote Lebert. ''They pass each other in silence, like two shadows. I tell him he should sell, but in his state he could no sooner lift a tree. I suppose that he shall wait until he is convinced the boy is gone and not returning.''

In the spring of 1867, having by then watched his old friend hurtle between numb indifference and terrorizing self-abhorrence for six months, Virchow caught wind of an opportunity that he believed might be of benefit. The Dutch East India Company had become interested in the possibility of establishing a cinchona plantation somewhere in the African subcontinent. The bark of the cinchona tree was still at that time the essential ingredient in the production of quinine, which had been known to relieve malarial fever ever since the sixteenth-century Jesuit missions into Peru. When malaria found its way into Europe in the 1850s, the Dutch had established cinchona plantations in Java, but with the continued spread of the disease over the course of the next decade, the DEIC had foreseen the need for a yet more convenient source. South Africa was closer, was itself rife with the fever, and, if it was true what the prospectors were saying about diamonds in the hillsides, was due for an economic and demographic explosion which would provide their tree bark with an instant local market, in addition to the one already taking shape in Europe.

Initially, the DEIC had wanted to open talks with the local governors and landowners of the Transvaal, simply because they were Dutch. For the purpose of these negotiations, they had wanted to assemble a team of experts, including financiers, prospectors, botanists, and, of course, a medical consultant, to investigate further the benefits of quinine—whether, for instance, its use should be primarily remedial or prophylactic—and then, in suitably medical terms, persuade whoever needed persuading of the unique value which cinchona bark represented. In the spring of 1867, the DEIC had come courting all the top medical schools of Europe, of which the FWI was the finest, and in May Virchow recommended Uyterhoeven.

The reaction among the rest of the faculty was predictably harsh. They feared such a venture might blemish the school's reputation, first because of the compromises involved in lending their scientific imprimatur to a patently commercial venture, and second because of what they justifiably perceived to be Dr. Uyterhoeven's incapacitation. Virchow was not so concerned. He admitted that sympathy had played a part in his decision. It had pained him having to watch his friend sink deeper and deeper into his morass, and he had wanted to offer him some prod or a brief escape, a puzzle in which he could either lose or seclude himself, but he did not see that he was placing the school's name at risk. Frankly, it seemed to Virchow that Uyterhoeven was unusually well suited to the task. He was Dutch. His family name was known and highly respected in commercial circles. His integrity was beyond question, and as result of his now notorious homeopathic foray in London, he was probably more familiar with the uses and effects of quinine than any other doctor at the school or, for that matter, in all of Germany. The South African expedition had seemed like just the thing, then—an assignment whose investigative half might resuscitate Uyterhoeven's interest, but which also, if his spirit should prove to be too low for research, would be justified by the more administrative and wholly redeeming task of helping to start a cinchona plantation in a region which would soon desperately need one. So the recommendation stood, was accepted by the DEIC, and then submitted to Uyterhoeven himself, basically as a *fait accompli.*

The doctor was to be gone for no more than four months. Sonja decided that she would return to the canals while he was away, to be with her family. In early June they went up to The Hague together. Sonja boarded her father's barge, Gustav met with the other members of the expedition, and then, on June 9, left for South Africa.

There were two Dutch provinces in the region at this time—the Orange River Colony, which was currently engaged in border disputes with the native Basotho, and the recently unified Transvaal. The DEIC had set their sights on the latter, considering it to be the more stable. In late May, their negotiating party, including Uyterhoeven, landed at the port of Lourenço Marques and made their way east to meet with the Volksraad and examine the viability of their venture.

The prospects looked grim from the very start. The deeper they entered into the bush, the more clear it became that they had vastly overestimated the civilization of the region. If the Transvaal was stable, it was only by virtue of its total disarray. Politically, there still existed hostilities between the three former quasi-republics of Pretorius, Joubert, and Schoeman. The land was still largely a frontier, settled only intermittently and seemingly by whim. There were no roads, no railways, and no trustworthy common currency. Whatever hope existed of overcoming these obstacles depended on the openness of the local farmers and governors, and yet the incumbent governing body, or Volksraad, was a loose, makeshift outfit with no economic agenda and a fundamental distrust of outsiders. Their response to DEIC's cinchona proposal was, in Uyterhoeven's phrase, "barely audible." They had no interest in speculative capital ventures, and they did not, for that matter, consider malaria any great problem. To the extent they even acknowledged the disease, they regarded it as an almost quaint initiation to the land—"a process of 'climatization,' " the doctor quoted, "which, if it should happen to fend off Uitlanders, is perfectly fine with them."

In the face of such strange indifference and muffled antagonism, the DEIC party hadn't known quite what to do. Uyterhoeven suggested they talk with one of the native African tribes such as the Pedi, who had already proven themselves more agriculturally capable and fiscally ambitious than the Boers. For precisely these reasons, however—a queasiness about leveraging the natives—the DEIC would not consider it. Furthermore, the commission's agricultural advisor began expressing doubts about the soil of the bushveld. The cinchona tree needed a much more tropic environment, he said, and so the financiers turned longing glances toward the British colonies at the Cape and Natal, where they suspected the ground—and the minds in charge of it—might be more fertile.

Uyterhoeven chose not to accompany the rest of the team south. Out of equal parts frustration and disgust, and also simply for the opportunity to be alone, he made his way into the eastern bushveld, unaccompanied, to see what he could learn about the disease which had brought them all so far afield.

At the outset, he intended committing no more than two months to the investigation, at the end of which he had promised to submit his findings to the DEIC representatives either at the Cape, if they'd found any takers there, or back in the Netherlands. With the assistance of a local Afrikaaner doctor named Luka DeVries, he stationed himself in a town on a slope of the Steelport Valley called Lydenburg, or "town of suffering," so named to commemorate the devastating malaria epidemic which in 1848 had decimated the population just a few miles lower in the basin. He rented the annex of a dry-goods store and filled it with just the instruments he'd brought with him from Berlin and whatever else he'd been able to forage and improvise from local materials.

The prospects for constructive study were not particularly promising. There was no medical library in Lydenburg, and no trustworthy record of disease in the region. Malaria had gone by too many different names, and in truth, the local community seemed no more interested in controlling it than had the Volksraad—he noted that "the principal and most debilitating symptom of the disease is clearly apathy." The only factor playing in the doctor's favor as he began his study was the abundance of cases at his disposal. If he could not crack all the microscopic secrets of malaria, he could at least track the more broad-scale characteristics. He kept his own record of who was contracting it and who wasn't, where they worked and where they didn't, and within two months had deduced what a great many doctors in Europe and in North America had failed to, which was the role of the mosquito. Which type of mosquito he did not know, nor had he been able to say for certain whether it was the mosquito itself that carried the fever or, rather, some parasite that was achieving its destiny through the mosquito's bite. For that he would need a real laboratory, so he spent the final part of his stay outlining several more practical programs of response, which he left with DeVries. He recommended a study of quinine's use as a preventative rather than an antidote. He recommended wire cloth for doors, porches, and windows, better systems of drainage, and the elimination of mosquito breeding places, offering that, for exterminative purposes, nothing was better than a rain barrel filled with kerosene, which also served as an effective larvacide.

None of this had much interested the Lydenburgers, however, and frankly, after three months in their company, Uyterhoeven wasn't very interested in them either. He was ready to go home. First, he had promised to meet with DEIC representatives at Natal, where they had indeed found a friend in the British. Unfortunately, the only southbound traffic out of Lydenburg were ox-driven caravans of Boer and African fortune-seekers headed for Griqualand West, where diamonds had been discovered in greatest abundance. Uyterhoeven hooked up with a twelve-wagon cavalcade and found a place on the cart of a Swedenborgian missionary named Christian Liepoldt, who had promised to take him as far as the Vaal River. From there he had been assured that he could travel by coach the rest of the way, on the Gibson Brothers Red Star Line, four weeks to Port Elizabeth.

Liepoldt was good company, as it turned out—sympathetic but

not prying, and not overly insistent about his mission. He had been a minister in the Dutch Reform Church for twelve years before coming across the religious writing of Emanuel Swedenborg. He'd promptly quit his order and spent two years at the New Church College in Manchester, England, before dropping out from the official auspices of the church and coming to South Africa in 1865 to distribute Swedenborgian literature and wisdom along the frontier. In his wagon he kept a traveling library of Swedenborg's entire spiritual folio, thirty volumes worth, all in their original Latin, as well as pamphlets and fliers. He respected his guest's captivity, however. It wasn't until the second week of their trek, in fact, after a political discussion, that he offered Dr. Uyterhoeven Swedenborg's *Heaven and Hell* to look through.

Swedenborg was not unknown to Uyterhoeven, of course, though he would later note that his feelings toward Swedenborg's life and work were still surprisingly unformed at the time he and Liepoldt were making their way south. As an undergraduate he had read parts of *Economy of the Animal Kingdom,* one of Swedenborg's scientific treatises, and, in fact, during his two years in London he had daily passed by the New Church in Argyle Square, but had never once been tempted to enter. Concerning Swedenborg's biography and the religious endowment for which he was best known, Uyterhoeven knew roughly the same as any well-educated European. Swedenborg had been a Renaissance man of sorts, at least through the first half of his life—an assessor for the Board of Mines for King Charles XII of Sweden; he was also a physician, an engineer, an economist, a student of mathematics, chemistry, astronomy, geology, anatomy, physiology, and psychology. He was a philosopher and an inventor of high esteem and humble bearing, who would have occupied a highly reputable place in the Continent's intellectual history for these efforts alone, but whose life and notoriety were both transformed in 1744, when at the age of fifty-six he began experiencing, by his own account, free and open contact with the spiritual world.

Thereafter until he died in 1772, Swedenborg claimed to have led a basically dual existence, traversing comfortably between the realms of nature and of spirit, conversing with angels as openly and easily as with humans. The majority of his time he devoted to recording the arcane, spiritual meaning of the Scriptures which had been revealed to him by God, a divine assignment in the course of which he was also compelled to provide other insights regarding the practical, ethical, and cosmological implications of the correlation and correspondence which he perceived to exist between the natural, spiritual, and celestial worlds, life and afterlife. Over the course of twenty-eight years he published thirty volumes of such material at his own expense, and distributed them for the most part privately and to libraries, for the public at large to find when fortune and interest permitted. After his death, a Christian church was established in accord with his ideas, the Church of the New Jerusalem, but his influence was hardly confined by the New Church walls. Uyterhoeven was aware of those such as Blake, Balzac, Baudelaire, and Emerson who unashamedly counted Swedenborg among the greatest European minds of the millennium, but just as many, if not more, who dismissed him as a lunatic. If Uyterhoeven's own feelings leaned one way or the other, it had less to do with his assessment of Swedenborg's vision than with his own reflex to defend the seemingly absurd against the fascism of ''progressives.''

Liepoldt's company offered him no such opportunity, obviously, and the doctor was not in a particularly receptive mood during their passage south. When Liepoldt offered him *Heaven and Hell,* Uyterhoeven was civil. He leafed through it one night before retiring, and although he found nothing in its logic to which he could immediately object, after several days he put it back on Liepoldt's shelf without comment, and there it remained, for the balance of their trek, undisturbed alongside the rest of the library.

The final week of August, their caravan entered Griqualand West, where small settlements had cropped up along the Vaal River, near the most abundant digs. The caravan's number dwindled as it proceeded, but Uyterhoeven remained with Liepoldt, who was still the only ride to the nearest coach stop in Victoria. At an exasperating, evangelical pace, they made their way from dig to dig, spending at least a day or two at every one, so that Liepoldt could share some meals with the prospectors, offer an informal sermon, and then leave some literature for them to look through.

It took them two weeks to travel a mere ten miles along the river, but finally, by the third week of September, an end was in sight. They had just one more stop to make before Victoria, a small dig called Klipdrift. Liepoldt promised they wouldn't spend long, and the doctor was prepared to hold him to his word. On the night of September 22, they entered town, intending to stay no more than two days, but were informed upon arriving at the local hostel that they had driven directly into an epidemic of yellow fever.

In 1867, territorial rights to Griqualand West were still partially claimed by the Orange Free State, which was apparently more careful than its Afrikaaner neighbors to the north about containing regional diseases. Quarantines were not official policy, but it was understood, especially along the digs, that the fortune-seekers should not traffic their diseases. There were several instances in which whole towns had died out in self-imposed seclusion, and such were the prospects for Klipdrift when Dr. Uyterhoeven and the Reverend Liepoldt unwittingly entered. No one was being permitted—nor was the majority expected—to leave.

❧

It is, of course, in Klipdrift that the doctor's life "took its turn," as John Bigelow put it in his note to Virchow decades later. Unfortunately, as Bigelow's comment also suggests, Dr. Uyterhoeven never left a literal account of what actually transpired there, so the legend of his quarantine has come to rely almost entirely on secondhand accounts, which may be divided into two basic camps: those which are European in origin and those which are American.

Of the two, it is interesting to note that it is the European version—that is, the account of the Continent's rationalist elite—that is the far more sensational. As they understood it, Dr. Uyterhoeven had been in Klipdrift for less than a week when he himself contracted yellow fever. In the coming days, his temperature was said to have soared well into the hundreds. For two days he apparently hovered very near death, and at some point in the midst of that pendulation, he experienced a vision of his late son, Larkin.

When that vision and the fever that caused it finally passed, Dr. Uyterhoeven was said to have called for the Reverend Liepoldt, who had not fallen ill, and asked for the book he'd shown him back on the cart, Swedenborg's *Heaven and Hell.* Liepoldt did better. He moved his entire library into Uyterhoeven's room, and over the course of the next seven weeks served as a kind of human concordance while the doctor plowed his way through the better part of Swedenborg's religious folio. In fact, according to the notes compiled by Johann Lukas Schönlein for a never-finished biographical encyclopedia of the Berlin revolt, Uyterhoeven was purported to have polished off *True Christian Religion, Divine Love and Wisdom, Divine Providence, Heaven and Hell,* both volumes of *Apocalypse Revealed,* and all eight volumes of the *Arcana Coelestia.*

Whether this last detail is true or not—and probably it is not, given the magnitude of the works mentioned and fact that Liepoldt's editions were all said to have been in Latin—the point of the story was still fairly clear. Dr. Uyterhoeven had developed a passion for Swedenborg almost literally overnight, and the fact that that night had included a hallucination of his departed son seemed to speak for itself. Swedenborg's picture of the afterlife was very concrete, after all. His heaven and hell were just like life in sensibility, with tastes and smells and a landscape and so forth, all of which the doctor's colleagues had justifiably assumed would be very consoling to a bereaved parent, particularly one who believed he had just seen his late son. The German doctors took note, in other words, that Uyterhoeven had turned to Swedenborg at a time when he could not have been more emotionally and physically vulnerable, and had thus been taken in by his own worst impulses.

Certainly nothing they learned of Uyterhoeven's life in America, subsequent to his conversion, ever caused them to revise this impression. He was known to be living somewhere in the Midwest, running a chess shop, translating the writings of Swedenborg and other esoteric religious thinkers, and indulging his interest in "kitchen medicine." Wrote Buchheim: "It would seem that our friend has finally let go his interest in this realm, and directed his energies at the Unseen Other upon which his medical opinions have always, in fact, relied." Mitscherlich's opinion was even more spiteful. He put it that the doctor had "obviously abandoned his good senses" to become a "full-fledged, mush-headed agent of the occult."

What took place in Klipdrift to prompt this flight from reason—and in particular the hallucination of his son—was therefore deemed in retrospect to have been the decisive, though inevitable, moment of Dr. Uyterhoeven's fall, when, in the words of Schönlein, one of the most promising scientific minds of the century had been "derailed once and for all by the concurrence of a perilously high fever, a nagging spiritualist yearning, and a staggering personal loss."

The story was understood somewhat differently in American circles. In the first place, whatever may have happened in Klipdrift, it was thought to have been a good thing. As Mrs. Conover put it, Dr. Uyterhoeven had "entered the bush in the winter of 1868 a distinguished man of science and emerged six months later a distinguished man of faith." Second, the circumstances surrounding this transformation were not understood to have been particularly dramatic. There is no mention in any of the letters or journals of the garden's guests that the doctor ever came near death in Klipdrift; nor is there mention of his having read Herculean servings of Swedenborg; and perhaps most noteworthy, there is no mention of his having seen his dead son.

Simply, it was known that the doctor had been in South Africa conducting some sort of research on malaria, had stumbled upon an epidemic, was quarantined, fell ill, and, while bedridden, read the only literature available to him, which happened to be the work of Emanuel Swedenborg, which happened to excite in him a slightly more evolved appreciation of the world surrounding him than he had previously enjoyed.

Not an event on the dramatic scale of a human apparition certainly, but not a trifle either, when one took into account the intensity of the relationship that ensued. The doctor continued reading Swedenborg for the next thirty years, after all. Of all the most instructive voices he encountered in his work, Swedenborg's had been the one to provide him what he called ''the most reliable assistance in reminding me of what it is that I hold in faith, and know to be true,'' and he evidently felt no compunction about seeking this assistance in full view of the garden guests. According to Mrs. Conover, for instance, it apparently was not rare, when passing by the tables underneath the peanut arbor, ''to hear the doctor engaged in what sounded like a perfectly normal, if animated, conversation, only to find upon peeking through the hedge our host seated alone, with one of Swedenborg's books in his lap.''

Precisely what these ''conversations'' entailed was a subject of some debate and widely varying degrees of interest. Still, most all the guests would have deemed an insult the suggestion that a relationship which was as involved and enduring as the one their host enjoyed with Swedenborg could possibly have been inspired by a hallucination, the need for condolence, or some mystical fetish. The reason the doctor got along with Swedenborg was that they thought alike, that was all, and among those who took a more active interest in the doctor's beliefs, the ways in which he and Swedenborg thought alike were all fairly clear.

They agreed, quite simply. They agreed on no less than the identity of God. God was Cause, and Cause could not be shown. Before coming to Swedenborg, of course, Uyterhoeven had always been discouraged by this—or at least discouraged from any overt ''religious'' pursuit—uncertain, as he once put it to Fechner, how one was supposed to go about ''devoting one's attention to something that does not show itself.'' On reading Swedenborg, though, he finally found a way. Cause never showed itself, true—but Use did. Use was fairly evident, in fact—in nature, in the ''growth of seeds into trees, which bore fruit which, in turn, laid seeds''—and it was in observing such Use, said Swedenborg, that man came closest to seeing God. ''More in the verb than the noun'' was the doctor's slight modification, ''more in the feeding than in the food.''

However the doctor chose to express it, many pointed to this—the indication of God in Use—as being the great transformative insight that he took with him from Klipdrift. Use cast his favorite subject—the moment in front of him—in a divine light. It provided him the means to do what he'd never thought possible—''to witness God in Presence,'' as Bigelow put it, ''and so welcomed him to a life of devotion.''

And yet, of course, those who knew the doctor best agreed that something more had happened in Klipdrift as well, something more authentic to the doctor's own experience, and many even went so far as to suggest that a revelation of sorts had occurred. They simply did not think that what had been revealed was Larkin's spirit. What had been revealed, rather, was the spiritual essence of everything he laid his eyes on. Years later, in a more general context the doctor wrote:

> It has always been my experience that most instances of real understanding aren't so much a result of seeing something *else* or something *new*. They are the result of finally observing what has been there all along . . . So in matters of faith, most revelation refers in no way to having been granted some previously hidden view of spirit; it refers rather to the understanding finally of what spirit is.

What spirit was, in the doctor's phrase, was ''that which afforded all things the aspect of being.'' It was ''the abiding presence from which the moment emerges in space and time.'' Spirit was everywhere surrounding him, in other words, and in him and through him. It was the heat in fire, the Life—indeed, spirit turned out to be precisely the vital force which had always been the latent assumption of his thought and work but which had apparently needed the proper time and place to emerge in full clarity. In the first journal he kept after leaving Klipdrift, he wrote:

If nature is the realm of effects, then strictly speaking it is not a realm circumscribed by physics or chemistry. Nature is not comprised of what collides, mixes, joins, dissolves, sparks, and intersperses. Rather, it is a realm circumscribed by the limitations and attributes of human sensibility, which is comprised of five apparent faculties capable of five distinct estimations of being, all of which harmonize in space and time.

Obviously, conditions which are so easily enumerated can no more be thought to comprehend all reality than language can be thought to comprehend all expression. Inference, that the ever fleeting appearance of presence registered within these specific conditions is but a limited and definitively human apprehension of a more Abiding Presence, an infinite realm of cause, or spiritual world, that is contemporaneous with, provides for, and which is also evinced, exiguously, by a limited realm of effect, or natural world.

So it is that everything which we perceive can be understood as the resultant effect of some spiritual impetus of which it is the perfect sensible evidence, and without which it would obviously not appear to exist. Not a single puff of smoke rises, not a toenail grows, not a stone sits in its place, but by the encounter of spirit and sensibility, spirit and nature, that is—which are bound to one another in man.

Whether one ultimately agreed with him or not, no one ever questioned the doctor's loyalty to his own ideas, and this was equally true after Klipdrift as before. Once having come to his new understanding—in essence that the natural world emerged from spirit, and that its most divine attribute was "useful action"—the doctor more or less dedicated the rest of his life to the sole purpose of preserving and honoring these insights, and it was in this regard that Swedenborg probably played his most significant role. More than serving to inspire the doctor, that is, Swedenborg's writing helped elucidate the whole of the confounding relation that he had perceived between nature and spirit. Swedenborg pointed out the differences between the two, the similarities, and, perhaps most important from a practical perspective, the spiritual instruction that could be derived from nature on that basis.

Swedenborg claimed to have entered the spiritual realm, after all. He'd gone there quite often, in fact, and in the course of these excursions had come to see that it was comprised of a more pure, more primary and inward substance than nature, whose features he described as being more crude, secondary, and outward. In this respect, each individual person could be seen as a meeting place of these two realms—the border, the point of connection, and the difference between an infinite world outside, comprised of natural elements which bore upon the body, the senses, and behavior; and then an equally infinite world inside, comprised of spiritual elements, which bore upon the mind, discernment, and intention.

Of course, there was nothing radically new in this. Swedenborg's was a fairly classic dualist picture. What was so distinctive, inspired, and potentially ridiculous about Swedenborg's vision was his contention that these two realms corresponded, that for everything which occurred in nature there was a comparable feature in the realm of spirit. Both had gardens, in other words, and forests, animals, minerals, suns, moons, shade, and so forth—the difference being that while the features of the outside world were nothing more than appearances, really, comprised of a crude material and ephemeral substance, their correspondents in the spiritual realm were constituted by divine elements of heavenly, eternal, and what we might think of as abstract concepts—what Swedenborg called variously affections, pleasures, or guiding loves. The light of the spiritual sun, for instance, was God's Wisdom, and its warmth God's Love. The eye, in heaven, was Discernment. Black clouds were false elements arising from what was Evil. Sheep were Innocence. Caverns were Secrecy. Belches were Greed. Everything, the whole heavenly landscape, was like a very grand, very complex and interwoven metaphor for these concepts, except that its features did not merely stand for the truths they represented; they were these truths in essence.

But now, given this fundamental difference—that the spiritual realm was constituted in Truth while the natural world took the more deceptive guise of coagulent matter—one needed to understand that when these two realms encountered one another in the life of a given individual, they did not *necessarily* reflect. That is, the environment in which a man's friends might find him in the natural world was not always the same as where angels would find his spirit in the spiritual world. A man of Greed, for instance, might well in his worldly existence dwell in a mansion surrounded by all kinds of finery, while his spirit, according to Swedenborg, would be found in a hovel filled with "dirty things fit for pigs, and the kind of reeking vapors that undigested foods in the stomach give off," since hovels and belches corresponded to this man's guiding love, Greed. Alternately, the spirit of someone whose guiding love was Knowledge, Insight, and Intelligence and "who at the same time acknowledged the Divine" would by angels be found in gardens, among "beautifully laid out flower beds and lawns, surrounded by rows of trees and gateways and walks," since all of these corresponded to Knowledge, Insight, and Intelligence.

Of course, the amount of personal expectation that the doctor brought to bear upon such descriptions—uncanny as they may have been—was not so great. Of much more practical interest to him was the insight upon which these descriptions relied—simply, that men and women were not rewarded with heaven or condemned to hell on the basis of faith, predestination, or obedience to moral law. Rather, when a man died and shed his external, material being, all his affections and intentions remained with him, and he therefore found his spirit wherever it had been dwelling all along, where it was used to being, surrounded by whatever his guiding loves had been, whether good or bad, right or wrong.

This the doctor believed absolutely. He thought it fairly obvious, in fact, and the prescription equally so: to see to the state of one's spirit forthwith. The best way of doing this was to make oneself as useful as possible, of course—"One's spirit cannot be better served than by serving," he once wrote—but secondary to this, the doctor had seen the possibility of "cultivating one's inward, spiritual sensibilities." It had seemed to him a matter of simply learning to recognize and understand the elements that comprised the spiritual world—that is, the guiding loves, pleasures, and affections. And to do this, one needed simply to refer to nature, or to the Uses of nature, whose spiritual significance Swedenborg had basically diagrammed with the correspondences. The Use of caverns, secrecy; the Use of Eyes, discernment; and so forth. So long as one addressed his attention to Use, Uyterhoeven believed that the natural world was an ongoing illustration of all the elements which form one's spiritual life.*

> I look at the light of the sun, and I see that it serves that same purpose in nature as God's wisdom in heaven, to illuminate; I observe the warmth of the sun and see that it serves the same purpose in nature as God's love in heaven—to nurture; and when I do this, when I see how the spiritual affections and natural elements are the same in Use, it is difficult to know sometimes if I am being told more about the truths from nature, or more about nature from these truths.
>
> But it is of no matter, for what should I mind if someday I lost sight of the difference? Mind? That should be my goal, I think, not just to remember this, but to see it every day—that nature is spirit, and spirit nature, such as I have been given to know either.

Such passages make clear that though the second half of the doctor's life was obviously very different from the first, it did share one important element in common: his empiricism. For even as much as

*"One must be careful always to regard the elements of nature in their Use, as opposed to dispensation," wrote Uyterhoeven, "for if one does otherwise—if one regards the elements of nature in the nominative, rather than active, aspect, in their dispensation rather than their Use—one is driven to absurd conclusions, such as that the people of the Caribbean must be more loved by God than the people of the Aleutians, simply because they feel so much more of the sun's warmth. They are not more loved by God, of course—for it is only the Use which is of spiritual significance, and the Use of the sun's warmth in St. Thomas is the very same as its use in Unimak."

old adversaries such as Buchheim liked to believe that the doctor's voyage to America betokened a final surrender to the allure of the ''Unseen Other,'' the truth is that Uyterhoeven's interest in ''what could be shown'' remained as steadfast and as exclusive as ever. ''The doctor seeks no revelation that is not provided naturally to his senses,'' wrote Bigelow. ''Rather, he accepts that God's thought is expressed to him moment to moment in the only language he can understand, and further trusts in Providence that what he is given to understand and what he needs to understand are one and the same.''

If such a faith erred one way or the other, it wasn't for being too mystical, then—it was for being too carnal. ''Like a violin with but five strings, the doctor strives to tune his various senses as well as he is able''—Miss Steele once wrote—''to see and smell, to touch and taste and listen with all the mindfulness he can bear, the better to appreciate the sacred offering of human experience, every part and moment of which he understands, in its Use and its exquisiteness, to be the native shape of something else divine.''

Little wonder, then, that Miss Steele, Mr. Bigelow, and the rest of the garden guests took the view of Dr. Uyterhoeven's ''conversion'' that they did. With no firsthand account to draw on, they were left to assume that a faith which was as thoroughly invested in common sense and sensibility as the doctor's must have been inspired by the same.

This is not to discount the European reports, however. As different a moral as they may have taken from Dr. Uyterhoeven's experience in Klipdrift, and as distinct as their version of events there may have been, it is not entirely incompatible with that of the Americans. That is, the doctor may well have seen Larkin while under quarantine, and he may also have recognized the presence of spirit in everything surrounding them. The two perceptions are hardly irreconcilable, and there may be no better indication of that fact than that Virchow and Bigelow, leading purveyors of the Continental and the American views respectively, both agreed that the doctor's letters from the Antipodes pointed to Klipdrift. In his note of thanks to Bigelow for having sent the letters, Virchow closed with the following:

Regarding your suggestion that [the letters] might represent a figurative account of Dr. Uyterhoeven's experience the first time he traveled to South Africa, I will admit to having taken a skeptical view at first, of suspicion that you might have been unfairly disposed to your opinion by your own experience, if I remember,* and by the simple fact of their [the letters] also having been written in South Africa.

As I read on, I found myself not much more persuaded of your view until coming very near to the end—or the end itself, I should say—at which point, I must confess, Mr. Bigelow, I am not merely persuaded that your opinion might have merit; I know that it is so, and am slightly ashamed at myself for not having seen it sooner.

It was mid-October by the time the quarantine in Klipdrift finally lifted, having claimed the lives of fifty-one prospectors, or roughly half the town's population. The Reverend Liepoldt took Uyterhoeven to Victoria, and there they said goodbye. Liepoldt gave the doctor his own copy of *Divine Providence* and also a diamond that one of their less fortunate bedmates had left behind. The doctor then boarded the Gibson Brother Red Star coach and headed for Port Elizabeth, which took another four weeks. The DEIC representatives were already long gone. They had left back in August, and reported to Virchow as soon as they arrived in the Netherlands that they had lost track of his doctor.

There was no telegraph service extending between Port Elizabeth and Germany, so Uyterhoeven arranged a place on the next trade ship bound for England. From there he made his way to The Hague, where upon arriving he immediately telegraphed Virchow that he was well, had been detained in Griqualand under quarantine, and needed to know if Sonja had returned to Berlin. Virchow answered that he had

*Bigelow, too, had first come to read Swedenborg while under quarantine—not in South Africa, but in Haiti, in the winter of 1854.

heard nothing from her, so Uyterhoeven made his way straight to the canals.

Gustav and Sonja had anticipated difficulty finding each other when his South African business was done. There had been no way of knowing precisely when he would be returning, or where along her father's routes Sonja would be, so they had agreed that, starting in August, Sonja would leave word at each of her father's stops as to when she had been there and when she had left.

It was now December. Gustav was four months late. At the first of their drops, a tobacco shop near the Rijks, he found two notes both tied to jars of *boerejongens*—the first had been marked in late August and a second in November. She'd come round twice already, then, and he had missed her last return by a little more than a month. Koos's next stop would be in Haarlem, according to Sonja's note, and after that Gustav supposed they would probably go to Delft, but there was no way to be sure. The question was whether to try racing them down by the lead of Sonja's messages or to wait in The Hague in the hope that they would complete their circuit soon.

He spent that first night in the home of an old family friend, Eric van den Bergh, and by morning he had his answer. It was an unusually cold winter that year, and while he slept, the North Sea blew such a chill wind down on south Holland that he wakened at dawn to the happy, playful cries of children coming from the street—the canals had frozen.

Gustav went straight down and purchased a pair of skates. He packed a satchel, with a change of clothes, the Swedenborg book, and the Vaal River diamond that Liepoldt had given him. By afternoon he was skating down the canals, past families and racers and ice sweepers, under bridges and by barge after barge, determined to find where in all the Netherlands the ice had been generous enough to trap Sonja for him.

He skated for three days straight, too exhilarated for sleep, until on the third day he spotted a little girl with straight bangs beneath her hat sitting on the slope. It was Elsa, Mirjam's daughter, now eight years old. When she recognized her uncle she called out, but Gustav put his finger to his mouth. He whispered to ask if she knew where Sonja and her grandfather might be, and Elsa said they were just down the way. So Gustav asked if she would do him a favor. He took the satchel from his back and removed a diamond from the bottom. He held it out to her and asked if she would be so kind as to take the diamond to Koos's barge and leave it on Sonja's pillow for her, as a secret. Elsa agreed. She took the diamond and with her mittened finger against her lips she started in the direction of the barge. Gustav bought himself a basket of food and then went to wait by the chestnut tree where they'd once met when they were courting.

At dusk Sonja appeared in her boots and bonnet. She walked toward him with her blue eyes set firmly on his, and smiling.

"Mrs. Uyterhoeven?" he greeted her.

She nodded. "I am not going back to Berlin," she said.

"And neither am I," he answered.

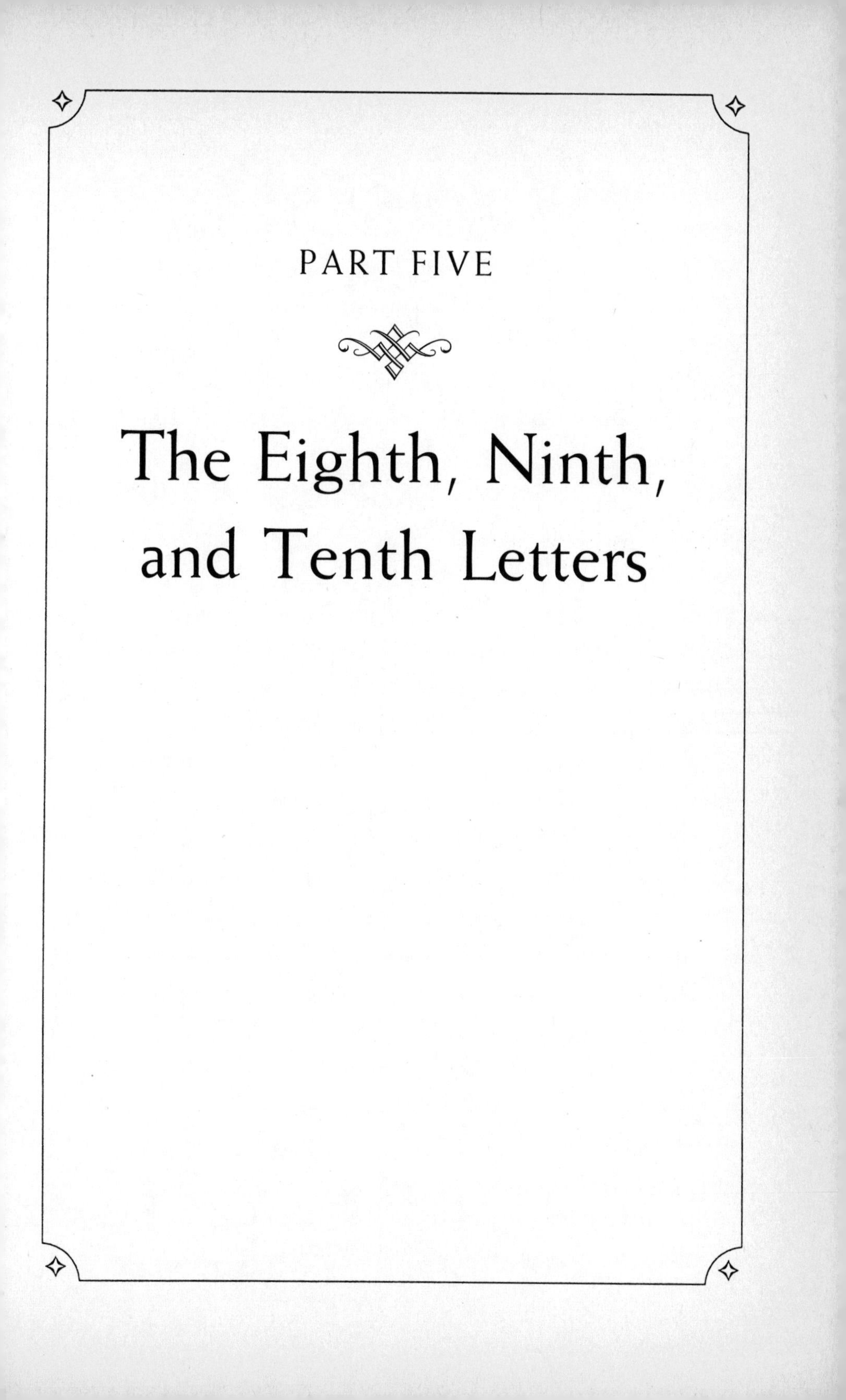

PART FIVE

The Eighth, Ninth, and Tenth Letters

THIRTEEN

JOHN EDWARD

Credit for finding the next two game pieces went to Miss Steele. She was said to have come across them at the bottom of her teacup one afternoon at the garden, which was not true, strictly speaking. Only one of the pieces was found in the cup, and the cup had not been hers, in fact. It had been her editor's, which anyone who knew her well would have known, since Miss Steele did not take sugar in her tea.

Tea was how she'd first come to know the Uyterhoevens. Back when the doctor and Sonja were still new to Dayton, the doctor had, as a favor to Miss Steele's father, Richard Steele—founder and first principal of Steele High School—formulated a tea remedy for his daughter Margaret, to treat a nervous condition that she had suffered from since she was a little girl. There was some question as to just how effective the doctor's potion had been. Some complained of its tarlike smell, and Miss Steele was still forced by her condition to live her days in repose, but she herself had highly praised his blend, and drank it ever after. Most considered it was not so much the tea as the Uyterhoevens' company that she'd felt strengthened by. She adored them both, and was one of the doctor's most challenging intellectual companions, as well as custodian of his library. Most days of the week she could be found either there or in the garden, though she was never a chess player.

She was, in fact, one of the Midwest's first women of letters, and in very late March of 1901, when the doctor's tale was seven stories old, she invited her editor, Wallace Dysart, to meet with her at the garden to discuss the book she was just then finishing, *Happy Life.* They took tea out on the patio, and Miss Steele had her usual therapeutic blend, without sugar. Dysart preferred a breakfast tea with two lumps, and that is how the first piece was found, as only one of his lumps dissolved. The other remained a small cube at the bottom. He spooned it out to show her—it was creamy white, like chalk or bone, and all its corners were equally rounded—then Miss Steele found a second, very much like the first, in the sugar basin.

The doctor's next letter was read one week later, on Sunday, April 7.

The Eighth Letter

March 12, 1901

Dear Sonja,

Well, I am in Orzhevsky, finally, home of the vandal bishops. I have crossed this land from west to east in getting here, and for these efforts I find myself now roundly, if silently, mocked. This place, these Antipodes, I should have known—the more faith I place in them, the more I try to grasp and master them, the more they escape me.

For I should say, not since leaving all of you have I been more determined, more certain of my purpose, than as I approached this cursed board: to find its two bishops and know their aim. Since last

I wrote, the imperative has grown in my mind from a whisper to a wail, for reasons which I suspect my letter may have intimated. But if not, then let me make perfectly clear: since my encounter with the altar girl and her adoring Staunton, I have found that my sympathies regarding the vandals' plot have begun treacherously to waver in the wind of my meditations, my experience, and even—dare I say—my affection.

For I'll make no bones. I very much liked that young lady, and I liked the Staunton, too. I like to think that someday soon their courtship shall be fulfilled—indeed, I would get down on my knees right now and pray therefore, but for the fact that to do so, I'm quite sure, would entail praying for the ruin as well. It troubled me. What was I to make of their open allegiance to a cause which seemed so inherently odious? How was I to reconcile the fact that this horrid scheme, which up till then I'd been free to envisage in any number of different monstrous guises—of devious lord chancellors, frightened sheiks, and murderous dominoes—had now managed to show me such a pretty, such a brave and tender face? Perhaps these vandals were not as bad as I'd thought. Perhaps there was some method to their madness. Perhaps I'd been too quick.

I wasn't sure anymore, and I will tell you, it is a strange process to feel one's mind changing, allowing ideas into your brain which it had once considered unthinkable. I cannot say it's painful, or particularly pleasurable, but that it requires a certain relaxation of the hold one keeps over oneself, and is to that degree both a thrill and a horror, and has furthermore left me convinced that all these questions regarding the fate of Eugene's goods—what should or should not happen to them, and what one should do in that event—these are more than matters of one's opinion; they are matters of one's soul.

Well, you can imagine my reaction, then—having recognised this changing tide within me and wanting more than ever to find some resolution—when upon finally reaching this board, Orzhevsky, home of the vandal plot, I should discover it as I did: vanquished, all the streets bare, the houses empty, the church bells silent. It seemed some other team had come and pillaged the board, but not even to take hold of the land. They'd done it simply for the sport, apparently, and a sport they'd played quite well. Orzhevsky appears to have been a town of Slavic persuasion, skirted by dairy farms, but with a sizeable merchant district as well, a palace, and a cathedral. All now abandoned, the stores and shops all gutted, and the homes like hollow tombs. They had taken everything and everyone—or so it seemed to me until a good hour into my search I finally came upon a lone survivor.

She was standing in the middle of one of the side streets near the central square, a stout and square-shouldered woman in a peasant dress—a pawn. She wore a red kerchief on her head tied round in back. She had a sickle clenched in her right hand, a milk pail in her left, and as I approached her from behind, I could hear she was muttering something under her breath, shaking her head furiously and spitting at the ground, in a posture still braced for attack. Her feet were planted in the ground like stalks, and I could see there were trails in the dirt surrounding her, of either friends who'd been dragged away or foes who'd been fool enough to challenge her.

I waved my handkerchief as I came close. ''Excuse me.''

She turned with her sickle raised above her head, a very severe-looking woman with red cheeks and a single dark brow.

''No, please.'' As I came round to show her my white flag, I caught a quick whiff of the milk in her pail and realised she must have been standing there for some time. ''I mean no harm.''

''What?'' She spoke in a thick Russian accent. ''You have come to mock? Come to take what is left? Well, there is nothing. They take everything. Swine!'' She spat at the ground.

''Who?'' I asked.

''Who.'' She shook her head. ''Who is . . . Espanish team. Shiny Spanish—team we fight many times, but always before we can defend. Always before we are full team and ready. But this time they come with their flags and shiny metal for clothes, and we are not ready. We are waiting here like ducks for them.''

''I am very sorry,'' I said. ''You hadn't a full team, then?''

''No full team. No bishops.''

"No bishops?" My selfish heart sunk to my belly. "Neither one?"

She shook her head. "First is gone for a long time—the good one." She touched her temple with the tip of her sickle to indicate his intelligence. "Would never let this." She looked around at the vacant streets. "So we are left with his coward brother, John Edward!" Her face flashed red and she swiped madly at the air with her sickle, then spit three times at the ground, as if the coward brother were lying there now, eviscerated. "Hides like mouse!" she barked. "Like bug! Hides from tsar. Hides from sky. And while he can hear horses in the street, while we are all defending Orzhevsky, he stays in his little hiding place."

"He is here, then?"

"*Da,* is here! Is in same place ever since his brother left." She jerked her head around to where the golden cross and green dome of a Russian Orthodox church peeked out through the building tops.

"But I have just come from the cathedral," I said. "There was no one."

"Oh, he is there," she simmered. "I promise." Then she tilted her head and looked at me slyly from the corner of her eye. "Why are you so interested?"

"Why? I have a message for him," I confess I lied.

"Message for coward bishop?" She seemed doubtful. "And where from is this message?"

"From . . . Eugene," I said.

She approved. "And you would like for me to tell you where he is hiding, so you can deliver your message from Eugene?"

"I'd be much obliged," I said.

She nodded slowly. "I will tell you, but you will take message for me as well, yes?"

I looked at the cathedral, and thought of all the quarters and cubbyholes; it seemed a worthwhile bargain. "Very well."

"*Da.*" She nodded. "So you would like to know where is our coward bishop, where he is hiding like mouse ever since his brother leaves.'' She folded her arms, the sickle and milk pail crossed. ''You have been inside cathedral?''

''Briefly.''

''You know where is Orzhevsky's tomb?''

I shook my head.

''Is on right side,'' she said. ''You follow up aisle, is great stone tomb. Then beyond, against the wall, there is little booth. You know what this is?''

''The confessional?''

''*Da,* confessional, where we go to tell our sins. And do you know who you will find inside confessional?''

''I have a suspicion.''

''*Da,* Mr. Messenger!'' Her teeth clenched in fury. ''You are right. You will find our coward bishop in the confessional. But do you know where in the confessional you will find him?''

''No,'' I said.

''On confessor's side!'' Her grey teeth flashed. ''Kneeling like little boy, like little baby crying, ever since his brother leaves. And while all his people is taken from their homes, is dragged away through streets, he is in there crying; while tsar and tsarina are taken in carts right down this way, and I can do nothing—coward bishop is kneeling in confessional like scared little boy!'' She looked up at me with tears of rage in her eyes.

''I am very sorry,'' I said. ''And what is the message you'd like me to deliver to him?''

''My message?'' A bitter tear spilled down her cheek. ''My message is this!'' She thrust out her pail of rotten milk. ''You take this to our coward bishop! And you tell him is from the members of his team, what is left. You tell him he can confess to this, the rotten milk of Orzhevsky! Let the rotten milk hear him weep and wail!''

I covered my nose and accepted the pail. ''I will,'' I said, and I wished there'd been something I could do to console her, but she was in a planted rage. As I started for the cathedral, she kept calling after me, twisting round as if her feet were bolted to the ground. ''You tell him, Mr. Messenger! You tell him what you see! Tell him what he should confess!'' she cried, and her cussing and spitting did not fall quiet until I'd ascended the cathedral steps and closed its doors behind me.

The space inside was ornate and very colourful. A shaft of white light was streaming through a shattered stained-glass window to notify the altar and the pews of Orzhevsky's fall. I paused at the back to listen, but all was silent, so just as the milkmaid had directed, I took my pail of sour milk up the right-hand aisle to the confessional and stopped at the confessor's door. Still silence, and so I entered the auditor's side. I redoubled my handkerchief over my nose, set the milk upon the floor, and took the seat.

''Hello,'' I spoke, but I could sense no movement from the other side of the screen. ''I am looking for the bishop,'' I said, and waited again, but still there was nothing—not a stir or a whisper—and I wondered if the bishop had perhaps been taken by the Spanish as well.

Then suddenly, in what I suppose was the time it took the stench of sour milk to sift through the screen, there came the sound of someone gagging on the other side.

''Is that the bishop?'' I asked.

The confessional fell quiet again. ''I know you're there,'' I said, but still there was silence, silence growing in tension, until finally he burst out.

''It wasn't me! I'm not to blame!'' he cried and, with the release, began to sob, which caused him to sniffle, which caused him to gag again. ''Tell him,'' he retched. ''You must tell him.''

''Tell who?'' I whispered through the screen.

''The Staunton,'' he choked.

''What Staunton?''

''Don't be coy.'' He gasped for air. ''Do you think I can't smell him judging me?''

I looked at the pail of rotten milk. ''Why would he be judging you?''

The bishop paused, and I could hear his open mouth breathing.

''Is it about the ruin?'' I asked.

"Who are you?"

"No one to fear," I said. "Just a visitor. But is it the ruin for which you feel wrongly blamed?"

He waited. I waved the vapors of the milk through the screen until he blurted out again, "Stop! Stop! Yes, of course it's the ruin! But I had nothing to do with it. That's what I'm trying to tell you." He muzzled his mouth with his hands. "I never said that anyone should break the goods. I said they should be taken care of and protected. Tell him. It isn't right that he should judge me so."

"But then whose—"

"Tell him!" the bishop barked.

Again I looked at the yellow milk, curdled in the pail. "I have told him, and he appears not to be listening. Perhaps if you helped me understand: if destroying the goods was not your idea, am I to assume it was your brother's?"

"Yes, yes, of course, it was my brother," he cried. "He's the one who said we should let the people use them. John William. I never wanted that. I said I thought they should be kept in stone vaults, but John William said no," the bishop wept.

I gave him a moment to calm himself. "And you believe he knew they'd be destroyed eventually?"

"I—" He gagged. "I don't know," he moaned. "I don't know what he wanted. He left. He went to serve them."

"The vandals, you mean?"

"Yes, but I stayed, can't you see?" He doubled over in his chair. "I am still here."

"I am not doubting you."

"Yes, but *he* is—your stinking judging Staunton friend!" He slammed his fist against the side of the confessional. "You have to tell him! I would never—I hate what they are doing! It frightens me." He placed his head against the screen and began openly weeping. "It frightens me."

"And is that why you are hiding here?" I asked.

"Yes," he whimpered, which obliged him to inhale, which caused him to gag violently, which in turn prompted a quick retraction.

''No,'' he confessed. ''Yes, I am hiding here because I am afraid of the ruin. But I am hiding because of pieces like your friend there, too, who seek revenge; and also—'' His whole frame began to shake. ''Also, I am hiding because I have heard that Eugene is spreading word that my brother and I are the good bishops.''

''So you fear the vandals as well.''

''Yes,'' he sobbed. ''I fear everyone.'' His bishop's crown rolled against the screen as he whimpered.

''Then is your brother hiding as well?''

The bishop dismissed the suggestion with a sniffle and a snigger. ''My brother has nothing to fear.''

''But if he is the one responsible—''

''If he is the one responsible it doesn't matter, because no one will find him.''

''But didn't you say he was serving among the vandals?''

He hesitated, and then answered curiously, ''Yes.''

''Well, then *they* must be able to find him.''

At this the bishop's head lifted, as with the dawn of suspicion. ''No,'' he said, bringing his face up closer to the screen to get a better view. ''He finds them—and what makes you so interested in my brother?''

''Nothing,'' I said. ''I was only trying—''

''Who are you?'' he asked.

''No one.''

''No one?'' he said. His face was now hovering just opposite the screen, trying to see through. ''You're a vandal, aren't you? Yes, you and your friend.'' He tried looking down toward the pail of milk. ''No wonder he smells so much. You're nothing but a pair of stinking vandals looking for my brother.''

He shook his head in disbelief, and I thought he might be on the verge of some violent attack, but then he began to laugh. The giggles wriggled up from his belly like bubbles. ''Oh, and tell me, sir, where have you been looking for him?'' He sniggered. ''Under beds? Up in the bell tower? Have you been checking under the porch steps?''

He laughed out loud, and then his mirth fell suddenly dead.

''Well, you're not going to find him. What, do you think my brother is a fool? You think he's going to let a couple of bunglers like you catch him? He'll catch you, my friends, and I've got news for you: if you're vandals, I'll bet he's done it already. I'll bet he got to you before you even knew, and twisted your twisted minds even further than they were twisted before!''

He jammed his face up against the screen to try to see us, and I could feel his breath. ''And neither one of you fools even knows it. That's the sickening part, is you have no idea.'' His eye passed behind the screen like a mad dog's. ''Tell me, have you been keeping track of the time? Hm? Can you think of an hour you might have lost? Or a day? 'Cause that's the only way you'll ever know you've found your precious John William, stinking vandals—is if you can't remember it!'' He began laughing again, caught between the evident pleasure he took at our farce and revulsion from the stench of rotting milk. ''But by all means keep looking!'' he sneered. ''Go and look as long as you like. Go check up in the tower or the broom closet! Just get your stinking stench out of my confessional, because he isn't here! He isn't here! He isn't here!''

At this point, the bishop's vituperation was cut short by an unspeakably disgusting attack of gagging, grunting, laughing, snorting, and heaving. I could take only so much. I did as he asked. I stood up, set the pail of milk on the stool in my place, and exited the confessional.

The cathedral was still echoing with his retching when I came outside, now rather daunted, I will confess. I descended the steps and started towards the side streets. I wanted to tell the milkmaid that I had delivered her message to the bishop, and also to ask if she had any idea where his brother, John William, might be—the ''good'' one, as she'd put it so innocently; the ''sane'' one, as I was now inclined to think, or hope.

And yet when I came to the spot where she and I had spoken before, she was not there. Only her footprints remained, deep where she'd been standing, and then fainter as they trailed off—where to, I could but wonder, and I wondered the same for myself. All this way to find the remaining bishop of Orzhevsky gone completely mad, and the other one, the one I should want to speak with, who knows where?

Not since coming here have I felt so utterly in irons, but I promise I shall write just as soon as I feel a breath of wind or catch a scent.

Good night,
Gus

FOURTEEN

JOHN WILLIAM

The next piece to appear at the garden was found by Paul Laurence Dunbar. First known to the people of Dayton as the young black boy who pulled the elevators at the dressmakers' building downtown, Dunbar had since risen to the status of resident poet laureate. For several years in high school he had also worked at the chess garden, helping run the grounds, making sure there was always enough food and drink for the guests, and keeping the plates and cups and saucers in clean circulation. He wrote some of his first poems there as well, and in 1892, upon the publication of his first "fugitive verses" in *Century* magazine, he held his first reading out beneath the oak.

The years since had seen the publication of two books, and a fair amount of public attention. He had given readings in Toledo, in

New York, and then in London, at the Gridiron Club, but in the summer of 1900 he returned to Dayton just in time to say goodbye to the doctor, and the following year was among the most loyal followers of his letters from the Antipodes. Not only did Mr. Dunbar attend every reading, he also, as a matter of course, would visit the library a day or two afterward, to take the doctor's most recent letter over to one of the leather chairs and read it himself, napping intermittently.

The eighth was no exception. Dunbar had come by the Tuesday following the reading. He shared some tea and finger sandwiches with Mrs. Uyterhoeven in the garden and then retired to the library. He did not emerge again until dusk. Most of the guests were gone, so he went out to the garden to see if there was anything that needed bringing in.

He had been clearing a small tea service from one of the black-iron Parisian tables when he found the milkmaid of Orzhevsky. She was standing right there between the cream and sugar, a lead piece painted in bright colors, but otherwise was just as the doctor had described, with the sickle still clenched in her left hand and her right fist free.

Dunbar took her to the library and set her on the Pretorian board with all the rest of the pieces. He looked for Mrs. Uyterhoeven to tell her, but she was nowhere to be found, so he finished bringing in all the cups and plates from the garden. He searched the house again for her when all the tables were clear, but still she was not there. He washed all the cups and saucers and then he dried them, but when the upstairs chimes rang eight o'clock and still Mrs. Uyterhoeven did not appear, he filled the creamer and took it into the library. He stood it next to the board, beside the milkmaid, and left a brief note under her feet. "In the garden," it said, "on the Parisian table, standing up beside the silver creamer, nostalgically. P.L.D."

The doctor's ninth letter arrived quicker on the heels of its predecessor than any other so far. It was read just one week after the eighth, on Sunday, April 14, outside.

The Ninth Letter

March 20, 1901

Dear Sonja,

I am giddy, giddy with glee and gratitude, and perhaps a touch intoxicated by the murmur of the landscape nearby. A reward, finally, I know not what for—not for my own cleverness certainly, nor patience, but something. I have met him! I have met John William, lost bishop of Orzhevsky. Ha! is what I say to John Edward. I have met his brother, and I remember it, and I am writing it here. I have met John William, and I found him to be a perfect gentleman, sober and exceedingly pleasant, this vandal—a man whom I would have every confidence in inviting to the garden and introducing to you in person. But I am here, not there with you, so to the beginning.

As I'm sure you will recall, I'd been very much in irons when I finished writing you last, following my encounter with John Edward in the confessional. The remainder of that evening I spent in Orzhevsky, scrounging round for dry food, but the following morning I decided I might find at least some consolation in the company of strangers. The board nearest by was a place called Bumbershoot, home of an English set whose pawns were all I ever saw. They wear a contemporary costume, black or grey suits with high starched collars and bowler hats and moustaches, and all carry umbrellas open above their heads. Bumbershoot is a suitably rainy place, so. It rained for two days straight upon my arrival, which I therefore spent indoors trying to see if I could find some instruction in all that had happened.

My third day the rain abated to a misting, and I had settled myself beneath the striped canopy of an outdoor pub, which had been set up on a foot-high wooden platform to keep the patrons' feet clear of any puddles or mud. I ordered myself some warm beer and cider, and had taken out my notebook to share with you the lesson I had gleaned during my indoor meditation, a lesson which had seemed fairly clear to me at that moment: I had expected far too much in coming to Orzhevsky. Even as well as it had served me as an eventual destination, I should never have imagined I'd find all my questions answered there. I had turned from the humble almsman of Providence into its predator, and look what it had yielded me. One mad bishop, hiding in his own confessional, and another whom it appeared I'd no chance of finding, despite the fact that he would seem to be the very one I needed to see.

I should have known—one is always best served by innocence of purpose. The question now was how to recapture such a thing? How to win my way back into the good grace of Providence, to fly as Timothy, on whichever wind should choose to carry me? How, I wondered, does one stalk serendipity?

Well, I am almost embarrassed to write it now, for shame at admitting the boundless generosity which Providence has shown me since I have come here, but I was in the very midst of posing this question to all of you, actually writing it down in my notebook, when an answer came and offered itself so conspicuously that even I, in the murk of so much deep deliberation, could not fail to recognise it.

From the corner of my eye, two white streaks flashed across the street towards me, and then sounded with such a loud crack against the pub's platform that several of the other patrons were compelled to let out whistles of admiration. As I happened to be sitting very near to where this collision had taken place, the pub's attention momentarily focused upon me. I answered by putting down my pen and looking over the rail to see what it was that had caused this rather startling interruption, and there observed two dice, one still quivering excitedly at the quality of its strike, the other perfectly still and apparently unconscious.

Now, I should say, my sense of compassion in this matter was not without its limit, as I have in the course of my stay here become familiar with the conduct of dice. Dice are not rare. As often as one sees a squirrel there among you, one is liable to witness here a pair of dice rolling by, and what I have observed of their behaviour is that it is very much as you yourselves know dice to be: reliably unpredictable. They neither stop nor go for any discernible purpose—other, I would submit, than to feel contact or action. That is, to the extent that dice can be ascribed predilection at all, they do appear to enjoy a collision, any kind of collision, which goes to point out that these two who'd come and struck our pub's platform were hardly the victims of some accident. No doubt they had sensed its façade from across the street and made for it with all their might. Hence the bridle upon my sympathy: if dice should insist on tumbling recklessly about, they are bound every so often to do what these had apparently done—or the motionless one in particular—which is to say, knock themselves senseless.

Still, being a doctor—though admittedly not a specialist in the field—I felt an obligation to do what I could. With my cane I scooped them up onto the stage and took them both in hand, for it was clear that the second die—the one apparently uninjured—had shown no wont to leave without its friend. The pub's attention returned to their bangers, mash, and warm beer, and I set about examining the two dice as best I could.

They were a fairly normal pair, black-spotted bone-white dice the size and weight of two grapefruits, but as I looked at them it suddenly struck me, the propinquity of their nature and my need. Had I not just written it in my notebook? Had I not this very moment been complaining to you of the breathless air which my feeble, nearsighted intentions had rendered? How better to recover my innocence, abandon my will, and offer myself back to Providence than to roll these two dice—once they'd recuperated, of course—and simply follow?

To all of you, in the comfort of each other's reassuring company, I know it may seem something of a reach, but I closed my notebook right there, the idea seemed so inspired. I pocketed the dice and made my way directly to the local bicycle shop. In exchange for one of the miniature Staunton bishops I'd brought with me from the garden, I purchased a suitable black model, and even as I walked it out to the street, I could feel the stunned die come to life inside my pocket and start roughhousing with its sibling. So I mounted my bicycle, removed the rambunctious dice from my pocket, and cast them on the lane.

They started instantly, in what seemed a perfectly pointless direction, and I followed as best I could, which was not so difficult to do within the confines of Bumbershoot. Such a civilised place offered any number of inviting obstacles for the two of them to strike and strike again, so it was actually a fairly tedious pursuit at first, waiting for them to finish bumping into this storefront here so they could cross the street and bump into the galoshes shoppe there. Once or twice I actually took the liberty of kicking them away from tight corners or alleys, which can preoccupy them literally for hours—but eventually, with a bit of assistance on my part, we did clear Bumbershoot and all the impedimenta of town life, bound north.

Now, I cannot say that I recommend chasing a pair of dice through the countryside as one's first venture at bicycle riding after so many years afoot. I did not have an easy time of it, particularly with my ailing hip and having to balance my cane upon the handlebars. I did, however, barely manage to keep up, and at length our chase brought us tumbling and joggling onto a vast expanse of meadowland. We were making our way at a somewhat heedless pace, when suddenly I saw that we were coming with dice-like recklessness upon a rather sizeable chasm. It stretched in both directions like a deep, deep river, and was a good stone's throw across. Very near the line of our approach, however, there happened to be a long wood-plank rope bridge, which for one very foolish moment I thought must be the destination of my two otherwise indiscriminate guides. I stopped pedaling well short of the bluff, therefore, knowing very well that if I tried following them across such a rickety pass I could by no likely means have survived. So I came to a quick halt, only to watch the dice that I'd been following miss the bridge by several yards and go flying over the edge, gleefully disappearing into the canyon below.

Not very clever, I thought to myself, but hardly surprising for a pair of dice. I looked round at the meadow. They had led me nowhere, and for a moment I wondered what else I had expected—following a roll of dice! How actually pathetic, I thought to myself. How desperate. And I had even begun to contemplate the way back to Bumbershoot when I was suddenly distracted by a very strange sound.

It was like a brook or a river, but not quite. It was more sharp than that, more as if a bucket of marbles were being stirred by a massive arm. But where? I listened closer, and it seemed to be coming from the ravine. Gingerly I dismounted my bicycle, walked it up to the chasm's edge, and peered down.

Perhaps one hundred feet below and covering the canyon bed in a blanket of mostly white, were thousands and thousands, perhaps hundreds of thousands, of dice, stretching as far down the cleft as I could see. They were all tumbling together, all flipping and jumbling, rattling, and bouncing off one another like jumping beans or as though the floor were piping hot sand—though, of course, I'd no sense of their being in any pain. Indeed, the overall effect was actually an extremely happy one, like a celebration taking place among the bricks of a fallen white city—tusk white, pearl white, bone white, with every so often a ruby-red die thrown in, or ebony or emerald green; and everywhere the dots, black and white, punched across their faces in patterns one to six—for every tumbling die twenty-one spinning dots.

And yet as I looked again, I saw this wasn't quite so. There were some hopping high up into the air, some scrambling over the top in circles, some only twittering in their places, and these I saw were bare of any mark; they'd been rattling in the canyon so long their edges were soft and their corners rounded. Some were hardly cubes anymore but more like pieces of chalk, hewn smaller and smaller by their heedless shaking kin, for whom no doubt the same fate awaited. All would lose their spots someday, and then their shape. They'd become little spheres, then whittle down to babies' teeth, then smaller yet until there was nothing left of them but dust like flour. I imagined this whole simmering white mass below me churning on a bed of their own ancestors' dust. But lest I glamorise and conceive the place as some sort of burial grounds to which every die was ultimately cast, I reminded myself that it was also, and no less, the result of a landscape such as this, strewn with frenetic dice and deep, dry runnels.

Whichever, it seemed a happy fate to them. I held my hand out over the edge of the ravine and I could feel their bliss rising up like a wind, but finer than wind. It seemed to pass right through my hand, and there it occurred to me, the significance of dice in this land. Indeed, I wondered why it hadn't been plain to me before, the reliance so many pieces here stake on the roll of dice? Not chess or checkers pieces, it is true, but the backgammon counters, cribbage pegs, or pachisi markers. Why, a good half of the population here—all the pieces of Kubeia—cannot move but by following a roll of dice. I suppose the reason it hadn't dawned on me before was how free they all seemed, how utterly at liberty to do as they pleased. Well, here it seemed I'd found the reason why: the dice—what I'd thought of as the bothersome dice—tumbling through the streets of villages, knocking into things, and here—here below my hand doing the very same, providing every roll that one could ever need. I could feel the energy wafting up a whole world of consent, as this galaxy of dice slowly, happily, pulverised.

I put down my bicycle and made my way over to the bridge. It was a ramshackle dilapidation. It sagged and groaned beneath my weight, but I walked out to the very centre and sat down with my feet dangling over the edge. I closed my eyes and listened: first to hundreds of thousands of dice all playing together—the sound coming up was soft and remote and seemed to resonate throughout me. I heard a river tumbling, and then voices, like happy voices in a ballroom, all distinct but speaking at once. I was like a child hiding in the highest windowsill above the princess's cotillion, and then it was as though the voices had begun to carry me. The bridge was gone and I was floating weightless upon the chasm's voice, which then became the sound of flapping wings, the soft and constant drumming of all the seraphim, which itself resolved to just a single sound, repeating—*kadosh, kadosh, kadosh.*

I have no idea how long I floated there, buoyed by this prayer. All I know is that I was finally lifted from its spell by the undulation of footsteps upon the bridge, walking straight up to me and stopping, a shadow cast upon me, and then the voice of a man, very pleasant and distinguished and melodic: "Are you the gentleman who broke the good hand mirror?"

I opened my eyes and looked up. Standing above me in sandals and a canvas robe was a man with a long black beard and a bishop's hat, smiling at me. I recognised his face and his voice as well, but couldn't place them. ''Excuse me?''

''Are you the gentleman who broke the good hand mirror?'' he repeated.

It was the bishop I'd met my first evening in the Antipodes, at the sunset at Ludo—the one with whom I'd spoken about my cigar. ''We've met,'' I said.

''We have?'' He smiled.

''I was dressed as a ghost.''

He thought back. ''Yes, who was eating the sun?''

''The very one.'' I extended my hand. ''Dr. Uyterhoeven.''

''John William.'' He bowed.

Strange as it may seem, I was not surprised by this. *But of course* was more my feeling—*of course he is John William.*

I started pulling myself up to greet him, but he waved me down. ''No need,'' he said. ''I am in something of a hurry. I'd like to find the person who broke the good hand mirror. You would not be he?''

''No,'' I said, without much consideration.

''You are sure?''

''Fairly sure,'' I said. ''I was not even aware that goods were being broken already.''

The bishop looked down at his feet and shook his head. ''Yes, unfortunately. It was found at the candletree in Shatranj. The glass had been shattered.''

I was ready to express my regret at this, or whatever seemed appropriate, when suddenly, and with enough might that I nearly fell from my place, it struck me—the candletree at Shatranj?

''Doctor,'' said John William, ''you've gone white.''

''*That* was the good hand mirror?''

''Hidden in one of the dripcastles,'' he said kindly. ''Are you the gentleman who broke it?''

My mind began to reel. ''But is that why the dominoes carried me?'' I asked.

John William smiled. ''Shall I take that to be a yes?''

I was too stunned to answer, but he sat down beside me and swung his legs over the side. ''I have been looking for you.''

I looked at him blankly. ''And I you.''

''Well, it appears we have killed two birds with one stone,'' he said cheerfully. ''Who would like to go first?''

I shook my head in a daze.

''Well, let me, then,'' he said. ''I am interested to know why you did it.''

I shook my head again, as I'd yet to gather my senses back. ''Well, I am not sure,'' I stammered. ''The truth is, I hadn't even known there *were* such things as goods back then. It was only that the original knight asked me to.''

''Timothy?''

''Yes, Timothy.''

''Hm.'' John William nodded and looked out over the railing. ''And you wouldn't know why Timothy asked you?''

''Well.'' I tried to remember. ''I suppose because he wasn't able to himself. He had been fighting for it with another origami knight, and he'd been burnt, and I suppose he must have been afraid that others might come, so he asked me to break the glass, which I did, and then he unfolded, and refolded to a crane, and then he flew off.''

''Hm,'' John William said again, swinging his feet gently.

''But is that why the dominoes carried me?''

''Could be.'' The bridge began to rock.

''But that doesn't seem fair, do you think?''

''Fair?'' The bishop stilled his legs and looked at me curiously.

''Well, that I should be held accountable.''

''How do you mean, 'held accountable'?'' His eyes narrowed kindly.

''That the dominoes let me walk upon them.''

John William's face remained both kind and humorous. ''But that would seem to have been very good of them.''

This gave me pause, for it seemed true. ''Yes, but to make me feel that I had done something wrong,'' I said.

''Who said that you had done anything wrong?''

I thought. ''Well, no one,'' I replied.

''Is it that *you* feel you may have done something wrong?''

I considered it. ''Well, yes, if I broke the good mirror. Yes, I suppose I do.''

''You needn't,'' he said. ''Of course, we might have preferred waiting, just for the fun of it, but that's all right.'' He looked at me kindly and with good humour. I didn't know quite what to say, so finally he broke the silence. ''So,'' he said, ''what is it that I can do for you?''

''Well, I suppose you've done it already, somewhat—I mean, if the mirror is really the reason I've been included . . . but also I suppose I'd simply wanted to find out more about the ruin, and why anybody would want such a thing in the first place.''

John William nodded thoughtfully. ''Might you be willing to meet me here again?''

''I don't know. What for?''

''Well, because I think that you're right. It isn't fair that you should have been drafted without your knowing why, and I would like you to understand more.''

''And what would happen if I met you here?''

His eyes widened. ''We would go see the king and queen.''

''The king and queen of what?''

John William's eyebrows jumped. ''The King and Queen of Vandals!''

Of vandals, I thought. I did not know what to say. The prospect was more than I could fathom.

''Well, you don't have to decide right this minute,'' he said, ''but I have been gathering together a party to go, soon, and we would be more than pleased for you to come along. Just say you'll consider it.''

He took hold of the rope above our heads to bring himself up, but then he looked at me with concern and paused. ''I don't like to think of you worrying too much about what you've done, though. Would you mind if I left you with something to consider?''

I shrugged. ''I suppose not.''

''Very well, but then I do have to go.'' He settled back into his seat. ''It's about how I learned the good mirror was broken, and I think you'll see, you've nothing to feel so wicked about.

''The board for which I was originally conceived was taken not so long ago, I am afraid.''

''Yes, I know,'' I said. ''I have just come from there.''

''You have?''

''Yes, I spoke to your brother.''

''You did?'' He winced with a combination of pain and compassion. ''Is he still in the confessional?''

''He is.''

John William shook his head and was for a moment distressed, but then recovered. ''Well, in any case, then you know that most of the pieces were taken, the tsar as well as the tsarina.

''Now, the tsarina of my native team is a very intriguing young woman—a very beautiful woman, I believe—with raven hair, green feline eyes, and white skin. And she has always been very kind to me and my brother. She likes to keep her bishops close by, I think because she feels protected by them, and because she believes that we are able—owing to our office, I suppose—to see angels and speak to them, angels who keep the team safe and sound.

''She always used to ask me what these angels look like, how they speak, how they move, and whether I would ever introduce her. She asked me this so often, in fact, that some years ago at her birthday celebration, I said that I had a very special gift for her. I told her that I had an angel friend who would like to meet her, and I led her blindfolded out into a meadow where I'd set up her dressing mirror. I sat her down in front of it. I held a candle to her face and then removed the blindfold from her eyes.''

'' 'Oh, but that is no angel,' said my queen. 'That is only me, John William.'

'' 'No,' I said. 'It is one of my very best angel friends,' and I pointed at her reflection, but she would not see it, and returned to her birthday celebration, unhappy with my gift, I am afraid.

''Now, disappointed as she may have been, this did not stop my queen from continuing to pester me about my angel friends. Sitting at her vanity in the morning, she would say to me, 'When, John William—when will you show me one, and let me see how beautiful they are?' And I would always say, 'But there is one in the mirror now, the best of my angel friends.'

" 'No.' She'd shake her head. 'No, John William. You still owe me my gift.'

"Now, to jump ahead—I was away, unfortunately, when Orzhevsky was taken. I am afraid I have been quite remiss in my duties, but I suspected the team responsible was Il Pisarro, as they have come before and tried to take us. I saw that most of the pieces were gone. I went to the tsarina's chamber and found that she was gone, too. So, loyal servant that I am, I decided to go see her, to make sure she was well. I retrieved some things from her chamber, things I thought she might need—some gowns, her brushes and powder and a mirror—and then I made my way to Il Pisarro.

"She was indeed there, being held in the captives' tower. I told her guard that I was her bishop, that I had merely brought her some of her belongings, and he allowed me to see her.

"Captivity did not seem to have treated her well. Her spirits seemed very low, but she was happy to see me. She told me what had happened. I apologised for my absence, and then when she'd forgiven me, I prepared to take my leave. She began looking through the things I'd brought her, and I had just set my hand upon the knob of her door when—'Oh, John William!' she said. 'Thank you. She is beautiful.'

"I turned to see what she could possibly be referring to, and she was holding the hand mirror up in front of her. 'Look at her,' she said, and her face was glowing.

" 'Who?' I asked.

" 'Why, you have finally brought me my angel friend, and she is beautiful, John William. She is most extraordinary.' And she gazed upon the glass as though she held a vision in her hand."

Here the bishop paused and looked at me with bright, smiling eyes. "Of course, I didn't presume to disagree with my queen, but thus did I surmise that somewhere someone must have broken the good mirror." He nodded surely, as though the logic in this were self-evident. "And you may be happy to know that I have since brought mirrors to all the captured men and women of Orzhevsky, so that they, too, might be consoled by the company of their own angels."

The bridge rocked as though for me to consider this.

"Now, I would not think that was a bad thing," he said.

"No," I allowed, somewhat boggled by the reasoning.

"I would think that my team is much in your debt, Dr. Uyterhoeven."

"I suppose."

"So take heart." He pulled himself up by the railing ropes and then looked down at me, with the sun behind him. "And if you are here when I return, then in exchange for a promise we shall go see the king and queen."

"What promise?" I asked.

John William pointed at my hand and smiled. "You shall tell me why that string is tied round your finger." Then he turned and started off for the far side of the bridge.

I looked down at the string—I'd clear forgotten it—and when I looked back up at the bishop, he had nearly reached the far bluff. "But when shall I meet you?" I called after him.

"Soon," he said over his shoulder. "Soon." Then he stepped from the bridge and made his way off, and he was not gone from sight before I had taken out my notebook to write you this, which having done, leaves me nothing now but to wait—to send this off and then return here to the chasm, for I should not want to risk missing his escort to the king and queen. The prospect excites me uncommonly.

Good night,
Gus

FIFTEEN

PO'S TAPESTRIES

Because of its length, four separate readings had to be scheduled for the doctor's tenth letter. The first week of June, Mrs. Uyterhoeven posted a sign on the inside gate saying so—the first would be Sunday, as usual, then Tuesday, then Thursday, then Sunday again.

Most guests took the sudden rush as reward for their patience. Seven weeks had passed since the last reading and no new pieces had appeared in the meantime. There were still just the seven: Ali, Eugene, Egbert, the milkmaid, the good thimble filled with ash, the paper crane, and the boy in the boat. That made four pawns, two knights, and a rook. The most powerful squares of the board—those belonging to the bishops, the king, and the queen—remained vacant as yet, a fact not lost on any of the guests. Theories abounded as to which was coming next, and the children were all slightly more alert than usual as they made their way about the garden, quietly on the lookout for strange new pieces that might be construed as either royal or clerical. There were none, however. Right up to the night before the reading, the four middle squares of the back row still yawned for tenants.

The last two guests to leave the chess garden that evening were Peter Willicker and Mary Raintree. Peter was then seventeen years old, and Mary had just turned sixteen. They'd been coming in later and later the last few nights, and this evening it hadn't been until the nine o'clock chimes that they made their way back, hand in hand.

Mrs. Uyterhoeven was sitting in her chair on the terrace. Peter nodded graciously to her when he and Mary entered the light of the terrace lamps.

"Who won?" she asked.

They dropped their hands from one another, and Mary blushed. Peter smiled. "Tomorrow, then?"

Mrs. Uyterhoeven nodded, and for a moment the young couple stood in front of her awkwardly.

"Do you need any help?" asked Mary.

Mrs. Uyterhoeven shook her head. They waited.

"And have you set out the next piece?" asked Mary.

"Pieces," said Mrs. Uyterhoeven. "And no."

Mary looked up at Peter with a congratulatory smile.

"Is it the king and the queen?" he asked.

Mrs. Uyterhoeven nodded.

"Mr. Patterson said he thought the bishop was coming next," said Mary.

"I know," said Mrs. Uyterhoeven, and once again an awkward silence fell.

"Can we see them?" asked Mary finally.

Mrs. Uyterhoeven looked up at them both, patted her knees, and then stood up. "Yes," she said, and led them both into the library.

Peter and Mary kept a respectful distance as they entered. Mrs. Uyterhoeven crossed to the doctor's desk and lit the lamp. "Come," she said, and they crept closer as she opened the drawer and took out a small unsealed envelope.

She removed two small rectangles of black velvet and folded them square on the doctor's blotter. Mary took Peter's hand as Mrs. Uyterhoeven reached back inside the envelope. This time she took out a small silver ball and placed it on the first of the velvet rests.

Mary looked closely. It was the size of a small plum pit, and the surface was flawed. "Is it a marble?"

Peter leaned down beside her and touched the velvet. "May I?"

Mrs. Uyterhoeven nodded, and he held it up for both of them. "It's a musketball," he said.

Mrs. Uyterhoeven smiled. "King."

Peter and Mary both swelled slightly, and as Peter set the bullet and its velvet rest in place, Mrs. Uyterhoeven removed a second piece from her envelope and set it on the remaining rest—a clear diamond, the size of a pearl.

"My goodness!" said Mary. "The doctor sent this?"

They all three leaned over to look at it, and Mrs. Uyterhoeven touched Mary's back lightly. "He brought it from South Africa many years ago."

Mary looked at the diamond almost plaintively. "Well, I've never seen such a thing."

"No." Mrs. Uyterhoeven smiled. "And you may put it in the queen's square."

The Tenth Letter

April 27, 1901

Dear Sonja,

After I finished writing you last, I went back to Bumbershoot briefly, to send my letter and pick up some rations, but returned as fast as I could to the chasm of dice. I'm sure that's not what John William had intended I do, but we'd set no formal date, and following our discussion, my meeting with the king and queen of vandals was all that truly concerned me. I didn't want to risk missing my escort, so I camped out on the bluff near the rope bridge. I waited there perhaps a day and a morning before deciding to go out above the chasm again. It was too maddening just waiting, particularly with the constant drone of pulverising dice. So I went and took a seat out at the middle of the bridge. Once again I felt the happy charge of all the tumbling dice wafting up at me, and in a matter of moments I was whisked back into a state of deep, deep sleep by the soft drumming of ten thousand seraphim wings.

I've no real sense therefore of how long it took the bishop to return, but he did. I was awakened—or, I should say, diverted from my meditation—by a gradual transmutation of the chasm's voice: from wings back to the ballroom party, a thousand voices chattering happily in a marble hall, and then to a distinctly smaller chorus: the sound of perhaps twenty voices humming like humming bees—and also the mewing of a cat—but all coming so distinctly from my right that the orientation itself seemed to reassert the bridge beneath me. I turned my head and opened my eyes to see John William standing on the bluff, surrounded by an assembly of pieces too eclectic for me to comprehend at once but which I now can say were: an ebony counter, two smaller counters made of wood, a fierce-eyed Staunton knight, a stack of four checkers, two dice unaccountably resisting the plunge, a Burmese cat, two Pente stones, two tiddledywinks, and a pawn who looked like a gargoyle, with a pale green complexion, a stooped posture, improbably small wings sprouting from the top of his back, and a pleasing grimace, as though he were at all points witnessing some spectacle passing directly in front of the sun.

All of them were looking at me, and as their humming quieted in my ears, I had the sense that they'd been waiting quite some time for me to awaken. So I gathered myself up as quickly as I could and for the first time crossed the bridge to the far side. John William introduced us all, and without further ado the group of us started off.

The far side of the chasm is a landscape like a moor, with rolling hills of soft teal, scattered low mist, and broad grey skies. Where precisely we were headed and how long it would take us to get there I had no clue, but we made our way in such contented peace and quiet, I didn't want to ruin the mood by asking.

Indeed, not a word passed between us until well into the afternoon, we came upon a very inconspicuous creek amidst the knolls and gullies of the northern landscape. Most of the totem hopped in to ride the current gently downstream, and only then did John William slow his stride to walk with me; there, as we trudged along the banks, he asked me about the string round my finger.

I was more than happy to oblige. I told him from the beginning—of the young mystific and Mrs. Anna, and then of Mrs. Anna's son, the mercenary, which required I tell him something about you, for I'd never have met the mercenary otherwise. I told him about the garden and the map, about my trip aboard the *Vestima,* how the mercenary slept all day and night when there was no fight to fight, of how Diggery Priest had taunted him in his sleep, of how the mercenary had saved us all from the throat of the maelstrom and then left us in his dinghy. I told all as best I could, and quite enjoyed the opportunity until I came near the end, to the matter of the string itself. I explained to John William that it was to remind me of Mrs. Anna and the young mystific, and of the vow I'd made to him—that if I should learn anything of her son, I'd find her and tell her.

It saddened me, actually, to think of it. John William asked if I'd come across anything worth telling them, and I had to say no, that with all the business of the vandals, I'd quite neglected my promise. After all this time, with this string tied round my finger to remind me, I had nothing new to tell them, and I didn't suppose there was much chance I ever would. The bishop could only shake his head from sympathy. "One never knows" was all he could say, and there, with a whimper, our conversation ended.

Not long after we'd resumed our silence, the creek that we'd been following split into three fingers running alongside each other like the prongs of a very long fork. Our totem friends chose the one nearest us, of course, so we could stay together—and not long after, like an apparition there appeared through the mists the only edifice that I have seen upon the northern landscape: a series of three stone carriage bridges with peaked roofs tiled in soft green and purple slate, the colour and tone of unpolished, weathered metal. They were all lined in a row like the cars of a steam train, joining the spits of land which the creek divided. Just past the last of the bridges stood two trees, a flat grey in the mist, but slender, the silhouette of two small cottonwoods, and again the only trees I'd seen since coming north of the chasm.

No sooner had these bridges and these two trees appeared than the dice and checkers all floated to the banks and tumbled up to our feet. The gargoyle bounded up ahead with the knight beneath his arm, to wait by the door of the first bridge.

John William did not hurry, though. While the gargoyle shifted anxiously from foot to foot, the bishop dried off all the totem with the sleeve of his robe; then, when all were clean and dry, he pulled open the first bridge door by its heavy black iron latch.

The room's breath wafted out at us, wet stone, and we all entered in line. There was a door at the opposite end of the bridge as well, closed, and in the far right-hand corner there stood a spartan stone totem bishop, waiting. Two large tapestries hung facing each other on the long walls, each with a marble bench beneath and six brass sconces mounted above, all burning low flames.

I took a seat on the right-side bench, as all the rest of the pieces settled in and took their places about the floor or in the corners, where diamond-shaped nests of straw, sawdust, sand, or pillows had been strewn. The cat leapt up to the sill of a porthole window above the door at the far end. She sat looking out, a perfect black cutout but for her tail, which draped over the ledge like the cauda of a capital *Q*. The gargoyle climbed up into the window opposite, poised there with his feet together and his fists to the side, his wings fluttering ever so gently from excitement.

John William went to greet the stone bishop in the corner, and as they spoke in silence, the candles above the first tapestry flared higher, the better to light the woven scene below. The scenes and figures it depicted were to me a nearly indecipherable constellation of characters and detail. Time and the moors' air have worn the myriad colours of the silk and wool. They are quieter blues than they have been, paler pinks and a softer burgundy. There is mustard also, blots of purple, deep Sherwood green, and in several places silver has been woven in.

There is a lone star at the top, and the image of an infant recurring throughout the landscape underneath, but as I looked upon it for the first time, I could make out little else before John William took his place at the centre of the room and began to speak.

He spoke to just myself and to the gargoyle, whose name I learned was Simeon, and who, I'd the impression, had been here at least once before.

''Neither good nor bad,'' said the bishop, ''history progresses day to day. If the ruin should come, as most who pass this way hope, it shall bring a new dawn with it, by ending this day in which we find ourselves.'' He looked round at all the pieces in the room with fondness. ''The day of effigy and totem together, but apart, as neighbours sharing the land.

''So, too, this day could not have come to be but at the sacrifice of another day previous. These tapestries, and all the tapestries in the bridges to follow, tell the story of this advent, when the original effigy, who were the people of Muroq, first encountered the original totem, which were the silver stones of Petteia.

''Our friends the totem cannot see the tapestries, of course, or hear my voice. What these bridges provide for their benefit, I leave to Constantine.'' He bowed to the stone bishop in the corner. ''But you may hold in faith that they are here to remember the same event as we, and that as we pass through these bridges, our thoughts shall share in common with theirs this child.'' He pointed to the infant whom I had already recognised on the tapestry. ''And also another, whom we shall meet later. For now, simply know that for every moment and in every way that our thoughts cannot be with him''—he nodded once again towards the infant in the tapestry—''the thoughts of the totem are and shall be.''

John William then came and sat beside me on the bench. ''The setting pictured is a place called Muroq, which is the ancient name given the whole upper peninsula or head of the Antipodes, as divided from its body by the river Guerin, which the dice have since soaked dry.

''The doctor''—he glanced at me and winked—''shall be pleased to find the inhabitants of Muroq very much like the friends he's left behind—blessed with eyes and ears and noses and throats, hands and thumbs, and all the things that follow naturally therefrom, such as clothes and tools and homes. They were born, grew from children to men and women, bred, and when they became lost were lost to this world utterly, so much so that their empty bodies were buried underground.

"Unlike most of the doctor's friends, however, the Muroquoi were devout stargazers, owing to the lay of their land. Where the royal palace of Muroq stood, still well north of here, the ocean was said to sweep the sky so clear at night that the stars shone by the thousands, so bright and so many that their progress could be discerned. Thus, the people who lived beneath understood their lives to be the coincidence not merely of the elements and circumstance which affected their experience immediately but of these elements, these circumstances, *and* the presiding stars, and ascribed to life such faith in its integrity that they bestowed royalty and political influence not according to bloodlines or ambition, as the doctor might be more familiar with, but rather in accord with the dictates of celestial motion."

John William paused one final moment before beginning the narration of the tale depicted in the tapestries, and how I wish you could have been here with me to hear him speak, and see the images he gave life, so you might appreciate how exact and careful was his reading, and what a labour of love for him to share. But alas, John William has gone off to meet other vandals, so we shall have to make do with the more rickety loom of my memory, but the finer silk, I trust, of your imaginations.

To the first tapestry, then, which I should call:

THE PERTURBATION OF QUORDIRO

Long, long ago, when the Muroquoi still thought of themselves as the lone creatures of heaven's attention, death came to the beloved King Charoneus. All the bishops and governors convened at the palace to attend the ceremony of his burial, and then after seven days of mourning sent word throughout the land that, in keeping with ancient tradition, the king's star, Quordiro, would choose as its next son and heir to the throne the first male child born the dawn of its ascendant night—the night that Quordiro passed highest over the peninsula—when its distance from earth had been measured by the great astronomer Caleb, long since dead, at precisely one year.

As this day drew nigh, the governors sent deputies out into the countryside to find as many of the land's expectant mothers as they were able and escort them to the palace, so that the governors could witness their labours and see whose child was first-born. And for those mothers who could not be moved, notaries were sent to observe their childbirth and then report back to the palace as to the time of their delivery.

Of course, there were many many mothers who wanted their child to be king, and so some tried withholding their labours until dawn of the appointed day, but they could not and their children were born too soon; and when the ascendant day finally arrived, there were just as many mothers who still had not given birth, many of whom tried inducing their labour earlier than nature willed, but they also could not, and their children were born too late.

That evening, however, at midnight, a black coach entered the palace gates and stopped in the middle of the courtyard. Several of the governors had noticed from their windows and came out to the king's balcony to see who it was. They watched as the footman descended from his seat and unfurled a long black carpet from the door of this coach all the way to the palace steps. The footman then took in his arms a large goosefeather pillow and a folded quilt and walked them to the steps as well. There he spread out the quilt for all the governors to see its crest—a willow tree and a five-pointed star—then he lay the pillow down beside it and returned to the coach to wait by the door.

This willow and this star—it was the crest of Lispenard, all the governors recognised. The Lispenard, who had long been one of the wealthiest families in the kingdom, a clan of silver-haired conjurers who lived among themselves in a castle at the edge of the Dai-kyrie forest, which many believed was home to spirits who haunted the wood like wind.

The governors all waited to see what purpose had this black coach of Lispenard, which had parked itself in the middle of the courtyard, but the footman gave no sign. He stood by the door, perfectly still, until the first light of dawn appeared above the horizon to the east. Then the coach door opened and out stepped a woman whose hair was the colour of the moon.

''Marthanella,'' said the governor of Bamph. ''The eldest daughter.''

''And look, she is with child,'' observed the governor of Gillem.

As so she was. So full and round was her womb, the footman had to take her hand as she started from the carriage. With the eastern light still rising, she proceeded towards the steps, with her silver hair trailing behind along the black velvet carpet, all the way from the coach to the palace steps, like a silver stream flowing across the courtyard, or like a fallen moonbeam.

And when she reached the steps, she lay down upon the quilt her footman had laid there for her and placed her head upon the pillow. She looked up at all the governors and smiled, then, at the very moment that the high tip of the sun crested the horizon, gave birth to two twin boys, right there at the steps of the royal palace.

The governors sent down the palace handmaidens at once, to take the firstborn of these children and prepare him for the throne, but Marthanella would not give the child away. As they reached out their hands for him, she removed two long pins from her silver hair and held them to the soft pink throats of her two newborns. ''No,'' she called up to the balcony of governors. ''You shall not have one unless you take the other and let him rule as well.''

The governors all looked at one another, astonished. ''We cannot risk losing the king,'' said Bamph. ''Or kings,'' warned Graham, and so it was agreed.

''Take them both,'' the bishop called down, and Marthanella

smiled. She replaced the pins in her hair and handed the maidens her firstborn, Puntamin, and his younger brother, Teflo.

As a matter of form, several days were given for the palace deputies to come in from their various posts and offer their reports, and several did come with infants who they testified had also been born the morning of Quordiro's descent, but none so near the crack of dawn as Marthanella's, and therefore none with a claim to challenge for the throne.

So the twins were prepared for their consecration. They were draped in the king's purple robes and put to bed beside each other in the king's crib. They were presented with the gifts that the people had brought to the palace for their new king; a second crown was beaten by the royal smith for Teflo. Then, when seven days had passed, all the people of Muroq journeyed to the palace to celebrate the anointment of the twin kings in the royal courtyard. They gathered outside the gates to wait, while all the governors, the bishops, Marthanella, and the twins convened on the palace steps inside to rehearse the evening's ceremony.

They had come to the bishop's blessing when a horse-drawn carriage bolted in the palace gates and raced for the steps. All the guards stepped up. They raised their spears to fend off the intruder, but then the bishop called out, "Hold! I know this man." He pointed to the driver. "It is Harold, notary of Borus."

So the company waited until the carriage reached the steps. The driver, Harold, descended from his seat and knelt before the bishop. "Forgive me, Bishop Thomus. I do not mean to intrude, but I have reason to believe I bring you the king."

"The king," scoffed Marthanella.

"You have the child with you?" inquired the governor of Bamph.

"And the mother," answered Harold.

"And where have you come from?" asked the governor of Muurh.

"The fishing village of Lewissa."

"Lewissa," hissed Marthanella. "I have never even heard of such a place."

"I know it," said the governor of Muurh. "It is a fishing village on the eastern Sea of Borus."

"And who is the mother?" asked the governor of Althos.

"Her name is Therese," said Harold, standing. "She strings beads and makes bracelets to sell in the markets."

"And the father?" asked Bishop Thomus.

"The father was a fisherman," Harold answered, and he gave the fisherman's name, which is no longer known, as it was later forbidden to be spoken. "But his boat capsized at sea," said Harold, "and he never surfaced."

"And is the child a boy or a girl?" asked the governor of Althos.

"He is a boy," answered Harold.

"But when was he born?" asked Marthanella with impatience. "Ask him that."

The bishop turned the question to the deputy.

"At dawn, your excellency, the morning of Quordiro's ascendance."

"At dawn," Marthanella sneered, turning to the governors. "But you saw for yourselves, not a moment passed between the sun's appearance and that of my first boy."

The bishop nodded to calm her. "Did you see the sun, Harold?"

Harold nodded. "I did. The child was born at the coast, so I could see—as the child drew his first breath, I looked to the horizon and saw the sun's peak kiss the morning."

The bishop and all the governors bent their heads to consider.

"But this is ridiculous!" Marthanella burst out. "Surely you don't believe him."

The bishop nodded to her and then looked back at the notary. "I assume you are telling us the truth, Harold?"

Harold bowed his head. "I am."

"And the mother is in the carriage?"

''She is,'' said Harold.

The bishop stepped to the door of the carriage and opened it. Inside was a woman of just sixteen years, with straight black hair and bronze skin, nursing a newborn infant. When she looked up and saw the bishop standing there, her young brow furrowed.

''And what is his name?'' the bishop asked.

''He has his father's name,'' said Therese, and she told the bishop. ''But you will not take him from me, will you?''

''Do you not want your child to be king?'' he asked.

Therese shook her head.

''But all the people of Muroq will praise his name.''

''I do not want a king,'' said Therese. ''I want a son.''

The bishop looked at her, and at the child suckling her, and his heart nearly broke. ''I am sorry,'' he said, ''but Quordiro has chosen him.''

''But Quordiro can choose another.''

''I am sorry,'' said the bishop, and he lifted the child from her breast.

When Marthanella heard Therese crying inside the carriage, she turned to all the governors smiling, for she assumed the bishop must have refused this pretender, but when he turned round with the little infant in his hands, all the governors fell to their knees.

Marthanella looked in disbelief. ''No!'' she cried. ''You cannot do this. I was here!'' But the bishop did not look at her. He blessed the children in her arms and then started up the steps to prepare the new king for his consecration. ''No!'' cried Marthanella. ''You saw for yourselves. I came here and presented you with your kings!'' She followed him to the steps, offering her children, but the bishop did not turn. He continued up the steps with the new king in his arms and entered the palace.

''But you cannot do this!'' Marthanella turned back to the governors. ''You saw. Not a moment passed between my boys and the sun.''

''Which first appeared on the Sea of Borus,'' answered the governor of Bamph.

"No! But then the mother is lying," cried Marthanella, looking at them all frantically. But as they could hear Therese inside the carriage, weeping, they knew the mother was not lying, and one by one the governors all started up the steps as well, to meet the new king and prepare him for the evening's ceremony. The governor of Bamph offered Marthanella the second crown they'd made for Teflo, but Marthanella would not take it. She spat on it and cursed them all. "You will pay for this," she cried. She stuck her head through the window of Therese's coach. "You will pay!"

Then she summoned her coach. She took her children and raced back through the palace gates, through all the people waiting there, all the way back to her family's castle in the forest of Dai-kyrie.

Puntamin and Teflo were taken straight to their bedchamber and locked inside. Then, as evening fell, Marthanella entered the woods outside the castle. Alone she walked to the edge of her family springs at Dai-kyrie, stripped off her gown, and entered the water, and while all the happy people of Muroq gathered miles away inside the palace gates to celebrate the crowning of their new king, Marthanella lay floating in the moonlight of her family springs. All night she stayed, and bled the silver from her hair into the water, until by dawn her mane was grey and the surface of the springs was like a perfect, shining mirror.

(This is shown in the tapestry. The silver which is woven into Marthanella's hair at the palace courtyard appears again in Dai-kyrie Lake, and from this point on, though Marthanella's hair remains exceptionally long, it is a dull grey like dirty string, as is the hair of all her children, save for that of her great-granddaughter Adriane and her great-great-grandson Bela.)

Following his anointment, the new king's reign progressed without disturbance. He was taken into the guardianship of the palace. He was bathed and fed and cared for by all the servants there, and every night the high bishop, Thomus, sat by his crib and read him the stories that the stars inscribed. Weeks passed to months, and the infant grew more and more beloved by the governors and his subjects. He was regarded as a good choice by Quordiro, a sweet and temperate child with a wise disposition. So months passed to more months, and when these numbered twelve, the palace held another celebration lasting seven days, from the anniversary of the child's birth to the anniversary of his consecration. Every night there was a feast in the courtyard. Parades marched beneath the infant's balcony, with acrobats, clowns, and all the paladins on horseback, and on the final night, a year to the day from his anointment, once again all the citizens of Muroq gathered in the palace courtyard to praise Quordiro, to sing for its attention, that it might look down and see its son, who was to be brought out upon his balcony at midnight and blessed by Bishop Thomus.

And as the kingdom of Muroq rolled by that evening, Quordiro did look down from its place in the heavens, but not because it heard the people's song or to see its chosen son. The reason Quordiro cast its eye in earth's direction was the brilliant light shining back up from the waters of Dai-kyrie Lake. Quordiro had never seen itself before, and was so enraptured by its own image, it wrested from its natural course to stay above the silver lake and not lose sight of its reflection.

At this very moment, back at the palace, as the nursemaids came to dress the little king for the evening's ceremony, suddenly he began to cry as though his gown were fire. No one had ever seen the child act this way. The bishop was summoned instantly, but he could not see what the trouble was either. So they waited. While the people in the courtyard chanted to see their king, Bishop Thomus and the nursemaids waited, but the king cried on and on until Thomus decided he could wait no longer. He held the child up to the window to let the people see their king, and they all cheered happily for just the glimpse. They clapped and hollered and threw their caps, and some began a song to him.

But as they raised their voices, the gates behind them opened wide, and once again the black coach of the Lispenard entered. It cut through the crowd and took its place at the center of the courtyard, then from its door emerged Marthanella, her silver hair now grey and held in baskets at her hips. She stood upon the dasher of the carriage and raised her finger to the window where the child was held. ''See the child!'' she howled, and all fell silent. ''He weeps. He wails because he knows.'' Her finger turned up to the sky. ''Quordiro has cursed your choice for king and will not let him grow.''

''Silence the hag!'' called out the royal guard, but Marthanella turned to him and stilled him with her eye. ''Let those who doubt behold the child, and those who ask for signs, let them consult the kingdom's star—a year from here, in one year's time.''

She held her finger there—one year—for all the crowd to see, then turned and climbed inside her carriage once again. All watched in silence as the horse turned and pulled it from the courtyard, and when the people turned to see their king up in his window, he was not there.

The bishop had withdrawn. Thomus took the king back to his crib and sat beside him all night while he continued wailing. The child cried until his voice was gone, and cried for three more days in silence, and even when his fever lapsed and he was peaceful once again, the bishop remained with him and held him in his arms, much concerned.

The bishop waited nine days before calling together all the governors to tell them of his fear, that what Marthanella had said was true.

''But this is madness!'' said one governor, Pioline. ''The child was only teething, Thomus. You shall see. The Lispenard are bitter—and rightly so, perhaps—but she cannot keep a child from growing. You will see, he will be walking in a week.''

The bishop looked at Pioline and shook his head. ''But I have been watching,'' he said gravely. ''His teeth are still barely through his gum, and as he was crawling on his hands and knees two weeks ago, he still is crawling. You may look yourselves, but you will see the same, not his hair, not his nails, not an ounce of flesh has he grown.''

''Then you believe?'' asked the governor of Althos in a panic, for there was no more sober head among them than the bishop. ''Do you believe Quordiro isn't pleased?''

''I do not know,'' said the bishop. ''We can only wait and see—watch the child, and watch the star—''

''And if it is true?''

''If it is true,'' said the bishop, ''if in a year's time the child has not grown, and there is this sign she speaks of, then we shall know . . .''

''That we have made a grave mistake,'' said the governor of Althos anxiously.

''That we should consider another king,'' said the bishop with more calm.

''The twins?'' said Pioline.

The twins, they all agreed.

The governors and the bishop all still prayed for the present king, that Quordiro would look kindly upon him, and yet as days passed to weeks, it became more evident that what Marthanella had predicted was true. The little king's teeth did not grow. His hair did not grow. He could pull himself along the sides of tables, as he'd been able to for weeks, but he could not walk. Six times a day the governors themselves fed him the best fruits and vegetables and the richest milk, and every morning they would take the child, place him on their scales, and measure his arms and legs, but every morning their measurements were the same. It was kept a secret from the people, lest the knowledge turn to panic, but the child remained balanced on the cusp of his thirteenth month, and every night the governors looked helplessly at the heavens, wondering why.

They are so pictured in the tapestry, a group of bearded men in golden robes, weeping. Two raise their hands to the sky in prayer. One holds calipers. One holds scales, and one of them, who is the Bishop Thomus, holds the child sleeping in his arms.

Finally, as Marthanella had foretold, on the second anniversary of the king's anointment, the sky replied. No celebration was held this time, for fear of what the people might think if they saw the child still small and wrapped in swaddling. But all the governors gathered in the balcony that evening. The bishop held the child in his arms, and they all looked heavenward together. They watched Quordiro climb into the sky above them, as it had every night, but then as it reached its peak, they saw, while every other star continued on its way across the sky, Quordiro stopped and stayed suspended there, like a lantern fixed at the end of a long, long pole.

''Look,'' said the governor of Bamph, his voice trembling in fear. ''It is not moving.''

''It's true,'' said Althos, his eye against his sextant. ''It has stopped above us.''

The bishop shook his head, for it was as he'd feared. ''Quordiro is perturbed,'' he said sadly, and then he took the child inside.

The governor of Bamph sent envoys to Dai-kyrie that very night, to the castle of the Lispenard, where Marthanella and her boys were waiting for their royal escort to the palace.

Of course, it wasn't only the governors who'd seen Quordiro pause. Throughout the land the Muroquoi had looked up in horror at the still and eerie beacon, so the palace sent word at once, admitting to the governors' mistake, telling of the child's spell, but then inviting all to come and celebrate the passing of the crown, or crowns, to the rightful heads of Puntamin and Teflo, the twins of Marthanella Lispenard, who everyone would see were sturdy young boys, now two years old.

In the weeks following the consecration of the Lispenard, there were many calls throughout Muroq for the sacrifice of the spellbound infant—even some of the governors, desirous of the new kings' approval, spoke of ridding the cursed child from the land—but Bishop Thomus interceded. It was not their place to take the life of one so innocent, he said, and perhaps when Quordiro observed the crowns upon the heads of Puntamin and Teflo, it would be appeased and loose Therese's son from its spell. So the child's life was spared, but Marthanella still decreed, as regent, that his name should never again, upon penalty of death, be spoken.

Thomus himself returned the nameless child to his mother in Lewissa. He told her not to fear but to pray, as he would, that Quordiro would see her child's head was bare and let him grow again, for he was a good child, said the bishop—good and wise, and would have made a very fine king.

Therese took heart as best she could, but was not consoled, for she knew there were those who cursed her son. Whenever a fire or a crop was ruined by storm, she saw how the people would look up at Quordiro and blame the child, and when she carried him to the markets, she saw how they would look at him, as if he were a blasphemy. No one would come near her stand, except to spit at him and upon her jewelry, and every evening when darkness unveiled the heavens, she saw Quordiro hanging there, staring down on her, and she began to feel that she herself was cursed.

When a year had passed and still her son had not grown, and still the star remained fixed in the sky, Therese's grief and fear became too much for her to bear. She left her son in a basket at the bishop's door and took her husband's boat to sea. She put great stones in the pockets of her dress, and so that Quordiro might be appeased and allow her son to grow, she cast herself into the water, where she sank down beside her husband on the ocean floor.

Therese had chosen well the man with whom to trust her son. Thomus had come to have great affection for the child during their two years together, but he too was aware of how the people blamed the child for their misfortune, and he feared that if it was discovered that the boy had survived, there might be some who would demand his life again.

So one evening Thomus smuggled the spellbound child in his basket down to the river to meet the boatman Raspagnetto, who is shown in the tapestries as a short, stout man with a loose tweed cap and a bushy red moustache which gives the effect of a perpetual grin. Raspagnetto had lost his wife and child to fire years before, and ever since had travelled the rivers of the land on a houseboat, collecting orphans along the way and then giving them to lonely couples.

The bishop showed Raspagnetto the child in his basket. He told the boatman who it was, that it was Therese's boy, the former king who would not grow, and then he asked if Raspagnetto would take the child on board with him to live among the other orphans.

"But what if he should be discovered?" asked Raspagnetto. "The palace will not look kindly on the man who harbours the former king."

"It's true," the bishop replied, "and that is why you must keep the child with all the other orphans and never give him away. Then no one will ever know."

Raspagnetto considered again. "But what if the child is cursed, as they say? I cannot have a cursed child upon my boat."

"This child is not cursed," said the bishop. "But if you are worried, then I will make this offer: take the child for just three days, and if you feel a curse upon your boat, then leave him on the banks. Be rid of him. But you shall not, my friend. You are a good man, and you shall see, the child returns what he is shown, and you will show him good."

At this, Raspagnetto was so humbled and obliged, he did not feel that he could refuse. He took the child, and Thomus returned to the palace straightaway and delivered the news to Marthanella that Therese and her son had drowned at sea. Marthanella pretended grief and announced a day of mourning for the unfortunate child, but let it be known that the people should look to the heavens with hope, for if the star Quordiro should keep its place above their kingdom, then its purpose must be to bless the reign of her two boys, a conclusion which their subjects had no cause to doubt, since Puntamin and Teflo clearly were not spellbound, but growing and flourishing like two normal little boys.

On the orphan boat, meanwhile, Raspagnetto came to find that what the bishop had said was true. The former king was not a curse at all, but a blessing to him and to the other children. Raspagnetto hid the spellbound child among the other orphans, just as the bishop had said, and none of the lonely couples who came down to the banks ever suspected he was the former king.

What neither the bishop nor Raspagnetto had quite anticipated, though, was how the couples would covet him. When they came down to look at all the children, more often than not they would ask for the little one here—the one without a name, they'd say. And to every one of these couples Raspagnetto would have to say no, he could not give this one away, as he'd promised this one to a woman down the river—his true mother. Raspagnetto would have to tell this lie almost every time he stopped, and soon became reluctant even to let the lonely couples see the child—or ever, *ever* hold him—for then when he took the child from their arms and told them of the mother down the river, the women would always leave the boat despondent and not even consider the other orphans. Raspagnetto began hiding the child down belowdeck, therefore, and only took him up again when the couples had gone, or at night, when he would sing songs to the little boy as he poled his boat along the moonlit rivers.

For seven years the spellbound child lived with Raspagnetto this way, touring all Muroq. He saw every town and alley, all the gardens and festivals, and he was very happy. Then the seventh spring of the little king's tour among the orphans, Raspagnetto stopped his boat near a town called Balmenisha, and a couple named Pietro and Gertrude came down to the river to see. As usual, Raspagnetto kept the child below while showing them the other orphans, but when Gertrude and Pietro returned to the banks to consider their desire, they noticed another little child standing at the porthole window of the boat, looking out.

''What about that one?'' Gertrude pointed.

''That one,'' answered Raspagnetto. ''That one I am delivering to his true mother down the river.''

''Where down the river?'' asked Gertrude.

''In Linnaeus,'' said Raspagnetto.

Gertrude was suspicious. ''But if his mother is in Linnaeus, then why is he with you?''

Raspagnetto could not think so quickly to lie. ''Because,'' he said. ''Because she has been ill, and the child has been living with his grandmother.''

''How ill has she been?'' asked Gertrude, peering through the window at the child.

''I don't know,'' said Raspagnetto.

''And if she falls ill again, what will become of this child?''

''I don't know—''

''Will you save this child for me?'' she asked. ''Will you bring him back?''

Raspagnetto did not know what to say. ''But his mother is better, I am told,'' he stammered. ''Why not look again at the other children?''

But Gertrude would not. She turned plaintively to her husband and then left the banks, while Pietro followed after, with his arm upon her shoulder.

He had seen how much his wife desired the child, and he wanted to make her happy, so unbeknownst to her, Pietro followed Raspagnetto's boat down the river to Linnaeus that night and observed that there was no mother waiting there. He saw Raspagnetto hide the child belowdeck when the couples came down to the banks, just as he had done in Balmenisha, and he saw Raspagnetto take the child up on deck when evening fell and sing to him. Raspagnetto meant to keep this little boy to himself, thought Pietro. So for three more days and three more stops along the river, Pietro lay in wait. Then the third night, after Raspagnetto had gone to bed, Pietro crept on board the orphan boat, snatched the little king from his crib, and raced back to Balmenisha.

When Raspagnetto awoke the following morning to find the child gone, he was horrified. He asked the other children what had happened, but they all shook their heads, they didn't know. With the help of all the fishermen he dragged the river, but they found only fish in their nets and no little boy. So Raspagnetto began to trace his way back up the river, along the route he'd taken, town by town, asking everyone he passed if they had seen the little child whose mother was waiting down the river—whose mother was dying of heartbreak, he told them, whose life had lost its meaning without him. But all the people shook their heads, and Raspagnetto fell into despair—for having lost the child, for fear the child was in peril, and for knowing that even if his little friend was well, if he had been stolen and was being cared for, soon enough his spell would be revealed, and then his true identity.

It took but a fortnight. Gertrude had been overjoyed at first when Pietro returned to Balmenisha with the child. She'd named him Alexander, and invited all her friends to come and see, and they agreed that Alexander was a beautiful child and counted Gertrude lucky to have found him. But soon her happiness subsided. As beautiful a child as her little Alexander may have been, he turned out to be awfully sullen and cranky—even their friends had seen. When after only days, one of Gertrude's neighbours mentioned it, Gertrude burst into tears, for it was true. Ever since coming to their home, the child had turned sour, she'd said. He was angry and strained to be free of her embraces. A horrid, selfish child, she said, and stupid. He'd been crawling about her floor, but he wouldn't learn to walk, and she'd wanted to put ringlets in his hair, but his hair wouldn't even grow. "He is a horrid child," she finally told Pietro, and so they took him to a doctor. They told the doctor of their troubles, and the doctor hadn't needed to lay a hand on the boy to give his diagnosis.

"This child is not named Alexander," he said. "I have seen him at the royal court. This is the former king, the spellbound child of Quordiro."

"But that child drowned, I heard," said Pietro.

"As did I, but this is he, I'm sure," the doctor replied. "And as you say, he doesn't grow."

Gertrude became suddenly frightened. "But what should we do?" she asked. "It is not our fault. We did not know."

"And so I will attest," said the doctor, who was a good and loyal subject of the throne. "But you must show him to the kings and let the kings decide."

So that very day, while Raspagnetto continued working his way back up the river in vain, Gertrude and Pietro took the spellbound child to the palace. They offered him to Puntamin and Teflo, who were nine years old now, with long grey hair like their mother. Gertrude told them that she and her husband had meant no harm or disloyalty. They had only wanted a son to raise, but that this child they'd found refused to grow and was, they feared, the spellbound child of Quordiro.

The kings did not quite understand. They had never been apprised of the scandal which had preceded their accession, so they took the question to their mother—how they should rule upon the little child's fate. That evening at dinner, they told her of the little baby boy who had been brought to them, whose parents said he wasn't growing, and when Marthanella heard this, she flew into a rage. She stormed to the chamber where the child was being kept and recognised him at once.

"Who brought this child?" she demanded.

Pietro and Gertrude were summoned.

"And where did you find him?"

"On Raspagnetto's boat," said Pietro.

"Then bring Raspagnetto here!" Marthanella ordered her first officer. "And whoever else has harbored this child. Find them and bring them to me!"

Then Marthanella returned to her two sons. She sat them down in their twin throne and, in as calm a voice as she could summon, spoke: "My dears, on the same day that the two of you were born, so was the little child who has been brought to you this morning, and by mistake he was given your crown.'' She touched the coronet on Puntamin's head. ''Fortunately, Quordiro noticed this and would not let the child grow. And when the governors saw, they realised their mistake and awarded the throne to both of you.''

''And was Quordiro pleased?'' asked Teflo.

''Yes, of course Quordiro was pleased.'' She touched her son's cheek. ''And you know why.''

''Because he likes the silver of our hair,'' said Teflo.

''That's right. He likes to drink it from the springs, and that is why the two of you must always remember to keep the water silver.''

''Yes, Mother, we know,'' said Puntamin. ''But will the child ever grow?''

Marthanella looked at them both gravely and shook her head. ''Not as long as Quordiro hangs in the sky to bless us,'' she said.

''But is there nothing we can do to help him?'' asked Teflo. ''It doesn't seem fair.''

Marthanella looked at him with compassion and pity. ''Do you see a way?'' she asked.

''We could pray,'' suggested Teflo.

''Yes, we could pray.'' His mother smiled, and the two boys thought some more.

''We could sacrifice him,'' suggested Puntamin.

Marthanella turned to him. ''Is that what you would choose, my son Puntamin?''

''If the star which blesses our kingdom will not let him grow.''

''But what then if Quordiro moves?'' asked Teflo.

''Then it will have been appeased,'' said Puntamin to his brother. ''Obviously.''

''But then what if it remains?'' asked Teflo.

''Then it remains to bless the Lispenard,'' answered Puntamin, whose mother, on hearing this, stood to kiss his forehead, and whispered in his ear.

''And your first child shall be the one to inherit the throne.''

So the kings decreed. Gertrude and Pietro each were given chalices for their service and belted calves from the royal stock, then word was sent throughout the land of what had transpired: that the spellbound son of Quordiro had not died with his mother, as had been thought, but had been in hiding these seven years, first with Bishop Thomus and then with the orphan's boatman, Raspagnetto. By two loyal subjects, who'd been richly rewarded, the child had been discovered in Balmenisha, still a captive of his thirteenth month, and so the palace in its mercy had determined to put an end to the child's cursed life, and upon the same altar to execute the ones who'd harboored him, as traitors.

When the day of execution arrived, the entire court was called to witness. Raspagnetto, Bishop Thomus, and the little child were all brought out upon the church altar. The two men were given vials of poison made from the petals of a cherry blossom, and the baby was given a bottle of the same. When each had finished his, the little child crawled up on the bishop's knee and Raspagnetto began to sing to him, the song that he had sung to him by moonlight on the orphans' boat, but before the verse was halfway done, the lethal blossoms silenced the boatman and turned the bishop's lap cold.

The child, however, continued crawling. "He is not dying," whispered Teflo to his mother.

"Taste the potion!" ordered Marthanella. The first guard drank from the child's bottle, and there upon the altar died.

Again the child was given his bottle to drink, but again it took no effect. "You, taste the potion!" Marthanella ordered the second guard, who did and promptly died.

A third time the child was given the poison to drink, a third time without effect, and a third guard was made to prove with his life that the contents of the bottle were lethal.

The court was now dead silent. There wasn't a sound or

movement in the cathedral but for the little child crawling about the five fresh corpses on the altar.

Then Puntamin stood up from his throne, walked to the altar, took the child in his arms, and spoke.

"It is a blessed day," he said. "Let it be known to all Muroq that today Quordiro has made clear its desire, in refusing the sacrifice of this child, to keep its place in the sky above us and to bless our kingdom."

The court listened to the boy as to an oracle. "The star's decision does pose a question, though: the governors and elders have taught us that it has always been Quordiro's office, and Quordiro's alone, to appoint the kingdom's king; that upon the death of every sovereign, the successor shall be the firstborn child on the day of Quordiro's ascendance. But look." Puntamin placed the baby upon the altar step for all to see. "Quordiro does not ascend. Quordiro does not move. Quordiro prefers to remain above us and cast its light directly upon our heads. And so it is that I conclude, as long as Quordiro defers its former office to watch us and bless us, there is no king's star. There is only king's blood, which is the blood of Lispenard."

Puntamin picked up the child, handed him to the fourth officer, and then resumed his throne beside his brother. All was silent as he looked out upon the court, until the new bishop, Allory, stood up and called, "All hail the Lispenard!"

"All hail the Lispenard!" an officer seconded, and then the whole court echoed their praise. All hailed the Lispenard, and as the hall resounded with their cheer, Marthanella stood behind the throne of her two boys and smiled, her will now fully done.

To celebrate Puntamin's proclamation and convey it to the people, the spellbound infant was carted through the streets of every town in Muroq, with the three dead soldiers as well as the bodies of Bishop Thomus and Raspagnetto laid round him on the platform, that all could observe the strength of Quordiro's spell and understand that now the throne belonged to Puntamin, to Teflo, and to all of their descendants. When every street had witnessed this, the bodies of Raspagnetto, Thomus, and the soldiers were buried in unmarked graves on a hillside, and Marthanella had the child taken as deep into the forests of Dai-kyrie as her guard dared go and left there, never again to disturb the throne of Lispenard.

So end the tapestries of the first bridge, with the child in the wood, the star suspended, the waters of Dai-kyrie silver, and the grey-haired Lispenard upon the throne. Now is time for rest, before coming to the second bridge.*

April 29, 1901

John William finished narrating the tapestries of the first bridge long before the stone bishop Constantine was through with the totem. The totem's meditation very often take longer than the effigy, John William said, and he hadn't wanted our idle thoughts to interfere with their meditation, so the three of us—he, Simeon, and I—excused ourselves quietly and slipped out the back door of the bridge.

The skies had opened rather wide while we'd been inside. Simeon dashed across to the second bridge, unconcerned, and climbed up onto the roof peak, to sit in much the same position as he'd taken inside the first. The downpour was too thick for John William and me to brave, so we took seats on the stone steps beneath the eaves and I took the opportunity to ask a question which had been concerning me since the bridges first came into view. I told John William that I didn't mean to seem impatient, as I was quite enjoying the tapestries and

*No other letter posed quite the scheduling challenge that the tenth did, and it would not appear that Mrs. Uyterhoeven ever firmly established the pace or allotments in which it was to be read. The first year, in 1900, four readings were scheduled over the course of the week, but where exactly she chose to divide her husband's letter is not known, and in years to come, when all the letters were read again, all different manner of apportionment were tried. The tapestries could be read in as few as three sittings or as many as six, and in one instance nobly ventured by Mr. Dunbar, the entire letter was read on a single Sunday, starting at noon and not ending until dusk, with breaks between for tea and sandwiches.

looking forward to whatever more the other two bridges had in store, but just so that I could adjust my palette, as it were, I was interested to know: Were we to have audience with the king and queen here at the bridges, or were they only a stop along the way?

John William looked at me with a slightly skewed but pleasant expression as I posed this, what I believed was a perfectly reasonable, query. "You're not a proponent of crossing your bridges when you come to them?" he said.

"Well, it's not that," I replied. "I suppose I'm just wondering which bridges these are, and also I suppose I'd just like to be sure we'll get to the king and queen before"—I looked at him but he seemed not to know what I was alluding to—"before the ruin," I said.

John William turned to face me square. "You're very bothered by the ruin, aren't you, Dr. Uyterhoeven?"

"Well, yes," I said. "Of course." It seemed an odd question.

"I wish you weren't." He looked down at the soggy path to think. "I mean, I understand that the circumstances under which you've been drafted were not ideal, that the whole business may seem a bit devious to you—and let me say, if it does seem just too underhanded, you may feel free not to play. You may choose to think Eugene a madman and the rest of us poor, deluded fools. Think it's all a trick the totem are playing on us, and I personally wouldn't say you were far from the truth. But I, for one, would ask you to come along, because I think that what you call the 'ruin' might be something worth looking forward to. I think it might be fun."

"Fun?" I said out loud, for never has a word seemed more inappropriate to me.

"Well, I can't promise," the bishop replied casually. "That might take a good deal of the fun out of it—but for you certainly—I think if you actually considered the prospect directly, you'd see that you haven't very much to fear."

"But I don't see how you can say that," I said. "I mean, it isn't as if I haven't been thinking about it, or 'considering the prospect,' as you say—really, I don't think I've been doing much else—but the fact is, it eludes me. What your ruin holds in store, I haven't the foggiest.''

''But of course you do,'' said the bishop.

''No. That's what I'm telling you. I've tried. I've tried with all my might imagining what it shall be like, but I can't.''

The bishop measured me with a scheming and yet humorous expression. ''And what if you could?''

''Well . . .'' I thought. ''If I could—I would, I suppose. Certainly. Then I would know.''

''Do you have a map?''

''Excuse me?''

''Do you have a map?''

''Yes.'' I handed him the one from my breast pocket.

''And I'll need a pen as well.''

I gave him my pen, and he began to mark a route upon my drawing of the Antipodes. I looked over his shoulder to see where, but he hunched up to block my view. Then, as if to distract me from what he was doing, he spoke:

''You say that you have been doing little else than thinking about the ruin. I am afraid I'd have to disagree. I'd say that what you've been doing is dreading the ruin, Doctor, which is a different thing altogether, but perhaps that is where we should begin.'' He still did not look up from his work. ''Now, what is it about the prospect of all the goods being destroyed that frightens you so?''

I stammered. I confess, I have taken the treachery of this conspiracy so long for granted, it took me a moment to remember why. ''Well, I am afraid of simply not knowing, I suppose—of losing what I know.''

''Such as?'' The bishop scribbled away.

''Well, the things,'' I said, ''the cups and cupboards and hammers and things.''

''But they'll still be here.'' He looked up at me and smiled. ''You just won't know what they're for.''

I looked back at him, unsure if he was mocking me or if he truly meant to offer this as consolation. ''But that's enough, don't you think? I mean, one puts a good deal of time and trouble into understanding what these things are for. In some cases I've developed great affection for what they're for, and I fear missing that.'' I thought. ''Or not missing that.''

John William smiled with a shrug. ''If your feelings are truly as affectionate as you say, Doctor, then I wouldn't think you've much to fear. But let's see.'' He folded the map for the moment and surveyed my costume. ''Have you something upon your person now about which you feel so strongly?''

I thought. ''I have a pocket watch.''

''Very good. And you are fond of this pocket watch?''

''Yes, I am. It was given me by a close friend,'' I said, now taking Rudolf's watch from its pocket to show him. ''It reminds me of him, who is like a brother to me, and of the youth we spent together.''

''And do you ever forget to wind it?'' the bishop asked. He was looking down at the face, which had read 10:29 since I left the *Vestima.*

''At present it is not worth winding,'' I admitted, ''as it has not been working for several months.''

The bishop looked up at me happily. ''Well, there you are. Do you feel any less fondness for your pocket watch because it has stopped ticking?''

''No.''

''So what shall it matter to you if the good pocket watch is broken? Yours has been useless for two or three seasons now and you haven't seemed to mind.''

As I looked at him, I felt the sudden victim of sophistry. ''I suppose,'' I said, ''but the value of the watch to me is primarily sentimental. Suppose the value of the thing at question is its purpose?''

''The very thing that stands to be destroyed.'' The bishop raised his finger.

''Yes.''

''Offer an example.''

As I considered, the bishop opened my map again and resumed his work. ''Well, take a cider mug,'' I offered. ''Suppose it is the good cider mug which is broken, and suppose that I am someone who has always enjoyed the way it feels to sip hot cider from a mug?''

''Well.'' The bishop did not lift his eyes. ''If it is the case that you enjoy hot cider so much, then I would imagine that at some point after the goods have all been broken, if you happen to come across some hot cider and are attracted by its fragrance, you'll find that a mug is a very good thing from which to drink it. If not—if you find something better from which to sip your cider, then good riddance to mugs, I say.''

He looked up to see if I'd been persuaded, which I had not, so he put down my pen again. ''I don't mean to make light of your concerns, Dr. Uyterhoeven. Yes, it's true, there shall be a brief period of oblivion, but you shall not be abandoned there. You will still be you. What you fear, you shall fear; what you enjoy, you shall enjoy—but that is what you need to consider. When you look round, when you take all these precious things in hand, do they inspire anger in you, or fondness, jealousy, glee? For these are what shall greet you after the ruin—the same affections you've been practising all along. They shall be your guide, and if you wish, they will lead you back to all the things that you fear missing. The only difference is that you'll have discovered them by the light of your affections.'' The bishop's eyes sparkled at the prospect. ''I know a pawn from Scarecrow who puts it very well: he says, 'What matters won't change. What changes don't matter.' ''

He looked back at me with a smile, but still it seemed to me an unsettling notion. ''But not all of one's affections are good,'' I observed.

''True,'' he allowed with a nod. ''True, and those are the stakes, I suppose. The same as we reap the benefits of our kindness, our gratitude, and our charity—we shall have to suffer the curse of our selfishness, our resentments, our disdain.'' He tapped his temple, with a smile—''Whatever's there to work with.''

''But do you think that's fair?'' I said. ''Subjecting us all to the realm of our affections without warning?''

John William's eyes grew wide. "And that is what bothers you, isn't it, Doctor—that you haven't been warned?"

"Well . . ." I thought. "Yes."

He handed me the map. "Then consider yourself warned."

I looked down at what he'd drawn. It was a route, very well marked with little drawings to indicate what modes of transportation I should take, leading from where we'd met on the bridge above the dice chasm to an X he'd marked at the very centre of the Antipodes, and next to which he'd written a word which, when I read it, struck a sudden note of fear and excitement in my heart—"Teverin," it said.

"Teverin!" I exclaimed. "I have heard of Teverin."

John William didn't seem surprised. "Yes, well, I don't recommend everyone go see him. There are some I fear who find the experience a bit terrifying—"

"So I understand," I said. "He's the one who threatens to haunt people with their nightmares, is he not? If they don't join?"

John William looked at me and smiled vaguely to veil the barest hint of offence at this—not at me, but at the stupidity of the idea that I'd conveyed. "Yes, well, I suppose some might look at it that way. He also happens to be the one who found this place—it was Teverin who built these three bridges and hung the tapestries—and he is also the only one who can show you what awaits you—and by that I mean *you*, Dr. Uyterhoeven—if you should choose to face it sooner than later."

"You mean before the ruin?"

He nodded. "And I really *don't* think you've much to fear, but if you'd like to see for yourself, you can." He tapped the map. "But now for now."

He screwed the cap back onto my pen and folded the map for me, then very deliberately tucked them both in my right-hand pocket.

Just then the carriage bridge door groaned open behind us and out slid the cat, who, seeing the rain, climbed into John William's lap. A counter came rolling after, down the bank beside the steps and on towards the second bridge. "Oh, ye without nostrils," John William scolded, snatching two checkers who tried to sneak by and tossing them out into the rain. They landed smartly upon their edges and rolled the rest of the way.

At seeing them come, Simeon jumped down from his place atop the roof of the second bridge and came splashing back towards us to fetch the stone bishop and the Staunton knight. He actually jumped over our heads, in and then out, and we watched as he and the rest all reconvened at the next door.

Finally, we stood up. John William stretched and looked at me. "You will keep playing, though, won't you, Dr. Uyterhoeven? Or let me be the first to invite you formally: Would you like to play?"

It was more from the glee in his eye than anything else that I said yes. "Yes," I said, "if you will tell me—are we there yet?"

John William laughed at this. He looked up at the sky and then across the rivers. "No," he said, handing me a checker. "We are not there yet." Then we stood, John William with the cat beneath his arm, and made our way across to the second carriage bridge, holding the checkers on our heads to shield us from the rain.

The mood inside the second carriage bridge seemed more intimate than that inside the first. There were six much smaller tapestries hanging three to a side on opposite walls, with marble benches beneath.

The complexion of the first tapestry was comprised of earth tones, of clay and mustard, brown and yellow. There was a child in the arms of a farmer, but it was not the spellbound infant. Quordiro was in the sky, but off to the side; its light fell outside the panel. There were fields in the distance, a home, a well, and a snake lying in two long strips at the farmer's feet. The scene was more like an illustration one might find in a book than the tapestries in the first bridge, and as John William narrated its legend to me, he gazed upon it more dreamily, more as one might admire a concert hall ceiling while the orchestra is playing.

The story is of a bean farmer named Borbo, who lived in the southern fields of the Bricole fiefdom.

Borbo lived in a small house with his wife, Cristina. They had few neighbours, but to those with whom he dealt, Borbo was known as a simple, peaceful man who bothered no one and asked no favours. There had been nothing at all remarkable about him or his life until the planting season of his third year at Bricole, when he noticed that snakes began to follow him. When he went out to work in the morning, they would meet him at his gate and they would creep behind him out to the beanfield and watch him as he toiled from row to row all day, with their tongues flicking out of their broad, mischievous grins, and when evening fell they would follow him silently all the way back to the gates of his house and there leave off until morning.

Borbo did not mention this to his wife, as he did not want her to worry and the snakes had done him no harm. They just watched him and smiled—until one day late in the planting season. Borbo had gone to wash his face at the pump, and when he went to pick up his hat again, there was a snake coiled up inside, sleeping. It was smooth and black with a tan belly, and Borbo was ready to shake it to the ground when the snake turned up its head and spoke to him. "Can you hear me, farmer Borbo?"

Borbo nodded his head. "I can."

"You will be a father, farmer Borbo, and your child shall possess the gifts you do, but tenfold."

"What gifts?" Borbo asked, but the snake unwound from Borbo's hat, slithered onto his arm, wound down his body to his leg and then the ground. Then the snake snuck back away into the fields.

Borbo did not know what to make of this—for he did not consider himself a man of gifts—and the snakes withdrew from his fields soon after. But later that spring when Cristina came and told him that she was with child, he could not help but think of the snake he'd found in his hat and what that snake had said to him.

The child was a boy, whom Borbo and Cristina named Gilles, and he grew to be a perfectly able young man. Borbo taught him all he knew about planting and harvesting beans, and when he took Gilles out to the fields with him, he would always watch for the snakes, to see if they would come and follow his son, or sleep in his hat or speak to him, but none did.

There did come a day, however, after fifteen planting seasons, that Gilles came to his father and said that he had grown tired of the farm and wanted to go into Bricole and work in the markets there. Borbo had seen that his son had no gift for the land. He had seen how restless Gilles became in the fields, but still it pained him that his son refused his work, and so although he hadn't seen the snakes in years, he blamed them for luring his son away and tempting him with the corruptions of the city.

Gilles had been gone three seasons when the snakes returned to Borbo's field. Just as before, they followed Borbo to and from his labour, with their grins and darting tongues, and this time Borbo was not so patient. He cursed and spat at them, but their smiles did not fade. He began taking a pistol and a hunting knife out to the fields with him to wave at the snakes when they came too close, for he did not know why they had returned—why but to boast—until one morning that spring Cristina told Borbo that she was once again with child.

She expected this would be good news to her husband, to be blessed a second time so late in life, but Borbo said nothing. He took his pistol and his knife and went silently out to work, and that day, as all the smiling snakes followed him from row to row, he grew so frightened for the child in Cristina's womb that when he returned from the fields in the evening, he told her that she should go to Plumerais, where his sister Marguerite lived, to have the child there.

He hoped that then the snakes would retreat, but they did not. By planting season, they haunted Borbo's fields in greater number than ever, some as slim as shoelaces, others like a hangman's rope, some as thick as a halyard. They followed him inside his gate when he went home at night. They were sleeping on his pillow when he turned down his covers, and all day they curled round the posts of the empty crib in the second room. When he put on his boots in the morning, he felt braided snakes inside, and when at breakfast he went to take down food or dishes, snakes spilled out of the cupboards. None of them ever spoke to Borbo. They only smiled and darted their slim tongues, but he knew that they were waiting for his child.

Late that autumn, word came from Borbo's sister Marguerite that he was once again a father, this time to a girl who was strong and bright. Cristina had not fared so well, though, and Marguerite urged Borbo to come to Plumerais and see her. Borbo wanted to, but he feared the snakes might follow, and so he replied that he could not leave the fields with the harvest coming but that they should all remain in Plumerais and not risk moving Cristina in her illness.

Still, the snakes did not leave Borbo. They surrounded him even closer, in the field and in his home, and he could not wave them off or even shut his eyes to them, as their trails now led inside his mind and into his dreams. Now he tasted them and smelled them. He could feel them creeping in his belly.

Just once in all this time did they retreat; one morning he awoke to find his pillow bare and the snakes withdrawn from his cupboards, boots, and shelves, and he wanted to escape right then and go to his family in Plumerais. He took his bags and the dried flowers from their kitchen sill, but when he reached the road which passed his farm, a coach was there waiting, with Marguerite sitting beside a bassinet.

His sister looked at him, in his unwashed torn clothing, and she saw his house and the fields untended, and she spoke bitterly to her brother. She said that Cristina had not survived the winter. She had been waiting and waiting for him to come and see their new child, but she had been unable to last any longer. She had died, not from the strain of labour, said Marguerite, but from a broken heart, because of how bitter he had become after losing Gilles and the way he had forsaken them—his wife and his daughter. Marguerite said that if it were up to her, she would keep the child herself to raise in Plumerais and never mention her father, but that it had been Cristina's last request that her husband see his little girl, the child he had been so frightened of. He did not deserve it, scolded Marguerite—but she had promised Cristina. So she handed him the child from the bassinet and bid the coach driver take her away, that she would not have to look any longer upon her brother's disgrace.

Borbo was beside himself, and when he looked at his daughter for the first time, he saw what a beautiful little girl Cristina had given him—Evelin was her name. She was so innocent and beautiful he knew that the snakes could not resist her. Even as he stood there at the road, he felt them turning once more in his belly, and when he looked back at the house, he could see them slithering up its sides, through its shutters and in its windows, up the steps and down the chimney, and he did not know how he would keep the child safe, where to hide her that no one would know. In the house or in the fields she would be seen. The snakes would be waiting for her, so he carried Evelin to the well in back, which had been dry for years, and he placed the child in the bucket there and lowered her down, to keep her where the snakes would never think to look.

And every day he led them all out to the fields the same as before, and in the evenings he led them back into the house, and he did not mind their following him now, since he knew his daughter would be safe. Only in the very early morning, just when dawn broke, would he slip from his bed and sneak out to the well. He would slice a pear for her and lower it down in the bucket, and while she ate and the daylight lifted, he would sit on the ledge and sing to her.

Quiet, Evelin,
there's no need to be so scared.
There's a moon up, and it shines for you
with a man inside
who loves you more than he can bear.

It's a full moon, Evelin,
and on pretty days it's blue,
and when night falls black
and our moon fades,
go to sleep, and dream of when
my promise will come true.

That I will hold you to me
and wrap your arms around my neck
and feel your heart beat up against me
nevermore to fill the well,
nevermore its black eye
staring up at me,
and never howl from its throat again.

Don't cry, Evelin,
Papa knows you're scared.
Your moon is come to take good care,
and someday, I'll say,
you'll climb inside that bucket,
you'll hold tight to the ropes,
so Papa can pull you up from there.

One morning when Borbo had finished his song and the well was safe and silent, he went to take up his hat and found, sleeping there inside, the same snake that had appeared to him so long ago. It asked him, "Farmer Borbo, why do you sing and place pears in the bucket?"

Borbo answered, "I sing to keep the sparrows near, and I place pears in the bucket because it reminds me of my wife, who used to like the water sweet."

The snake considered this. "Well, I myself am thirsty," he said, "and I should like to taste your sweet water. Would you be kind and pull some up for me?"

Borbo did not move, he so feared what might happen if his lie was revealed and his daughter discovered. "What is it, farmer Borbo?" The snake smiled up at him. "Surely you've some water to spare. Pull up a bucket and let me drink.''

Carefully then, Borbo set his hat upon the ledge, with the snake coiled up inside, and he began to pull up the bucket by its rope, prepared when it appeared with nothing inside to tell the serpent that the well must be dry. But to his surprise, when the bucket came to light, he saw that there was water at the bottom. ''Mmmmmmm.'' The snake's eyes widened. ''I am so thirsty.'' Borbo set the bucket down on the ledge before the snake, who curled over the brim of Borbo's hat and flicked his tongue at the water. ''Hmmmm.'' The snake looked up at Borbo. ''This does not taste sweet to me, bean farmer Borbo, but I cannot be sure. You drink the water and tell me what it tastes like to you.'' Borbo took a cup of water in his palm and tasted that it was like salt. ''It isn't sweet, is it?'' said the snake, flicking his tongue some more to contemplate the flavour. ''Do you know what it tastes like to me?'' he said. ''It tastes to me almost like . . . tears.'' The snake looked down the well. ''Could they be a child's tears?''

Borbo's heart raced, the taste in his mouth was so bitter and the sight of this snake so horrible, leering down the well where his daughter was hidden. ''Hello,'' called the snake, unwinding its length from Borbo's hat. ''Is there a sad little child down there?''

Borbo watched as the snake slithered over the lip, curling its body round the sides and down into the shadow. ''Stop!'' He took his gun and pointed it into the well. ''Stop!'' he cried again, but he could hear only the snake's belly sliding across the stones, and at the thought of this serpent finding his daughter and taking her, his second child, his mind flashed from fear to fury, and he took his pistol and fired down the well. One shot, and then two more, two more, and then one last. Borbo fired six bullets into the darkness, and when his gun was empty he placed it on the ledge and began to weep. He began to weep for his Evelin and for Gilles; he wept for his wife, Cristina, and for the fact that no bullet remained for him. For his whole life Borbo began to weep, but was silenced by a sound, at first very faint, coming from the bottom of the well—the voice of a child rising up towards him. Borbo wiped the tears from his eyes and looked into the shadow, and he could see her, Evelin, just her head and then her shoulders, turning—spinning slowly upwards, with the snake beneath her, holding her as it wound its way up the well stones, an oily flesh coil.

"Look, Borbo," the snake was saying. "Look what I have found at the bottom of the well. It is a child." Borbo lifted her from the sleek cradle of the snake, and he held her. He kissed her cheeks and tasted salt. "But I should be surprised," said the snake, curling its body onto the ledge, "after so long in a well, if she were able to see." Borbo looked in her eyes and could see that she was blind. "And I should be surprised," said the snake, "after so many days in a well, and with the thunder of your bullets firing down, if she could hear." Borbo sang to her, but she could not hear, and as she stared by, with neither sight nor hearing, Borbo flew into a rage.

"This was to be my child!" he cried. "My gift, and now she cannot even see, and now she cannot hear, and it is you who have done this to her."

"Oh, not I," said the snake. It lifted up its head skyward, hissing and laughing. "Not *I*, farmer Borbo." At seeing the snake's mouth wide open before him, hissing ridicule and blame, Borbo took the knife from his belt and killed the snake. He ran its blade down the length of its body, from its jaws to its tip, and then fell breathless, for there inside the snake, where it lay open in two long strips before him, six bullets were lined in a row.

So ends the tale of the first tapestry of the second bridge. I was given a moment to observe that indeed six bullets did line the open gut of the snake at Borbo's feet, and then the image fell dark. The candles above the tapestry spontaneously snuffed, so John William and I stood and crossed to the opposite bench.

Before the candles above the next tapestry had fully lit, I whispered to ask if Evelin was the other child he'd spoken of, who joined our thoughts with the thoughts of the totem. The bishop smiled and nodded, and then referred my attention to the next tapestry, for us to continue.

But I must take a moment here to rest my hand and mind, and you may well have to do the same, to rest your mind's eye. If so, good night, and we shall continue directly with the history. Sleep well.

Welcome again. I remain in the second bridge, but have crossed to the second bench, to observe the next tapestries. From the moment I first set my eyes on them, I could tell that we had rejoined the history of the spellbound infant. The palette is the same as of the tapestries in the first bridges, and Quordiro is at the top, still entranced. Of the story which the images beneath portray, this is my memory.

The reign of the twin kings had long since passed. They had served well. Puntamin had seen to it that the waters of Dai-kyrie remained silver, as his family's gift to Quordiro—and to ensure the water's brilliance for generations, he slew those of his children and his brother's children who were not born with silver hair, to purify the line.

His first son, Paulin, to whom the throne was passed, was neither so ruthless nor so cunning. Against his father's and his grandmother's wishes he married outside the Lispenard clan, and his firstborn, who by decree was to succeed him, not only was a girl, whom he named Adriane, but possessed black hair like her mother.

What Paulin lacked in guile he balanced with good fortune. There were no great droughts during his reign, and no wars, no scandal, or pestilence, or great fires. All the rest of his ten children inherited the Lispenard mane and, along with their cousins, were endowed with more than enough silver from their hair to keep the waters of Dai-kyrie silver. In fact, the only record of Paulin's reign is a small dark tapestry, which depicts him and all his white-haired brood, all the Lispenard children and nieces and nephews bathing under moonlight in the silver waters at the inlet bridge of Dai-kyrie, while his daughter, Adriane, sits above them on the bridge, looking down through her raven hair.

Adriane was a clever girl, though. If not the colour of their hair, she did inherit the cunning of her grandfather Puntamin and great-grandmother Marthanella. She ruled over all the games and contests of her cousins and brothers and sisters, who looked up to her in fear. Marthanella recognised this. She was very old by now and close to death, but she still saw that Adriane was strong and therefore did not object to her assuming the throne. She did set one condition upon Adriane's accession, however. On the midnight of her great-granddaughter's fifteenth birthday, Marthanella called the girl up to the balcony of her chamber at the palace, and they sat together, looking down upon the kingdom.

"You are a clever girl," said Marthanella. "The world does fear you with good reason. The Lispenard and all Muroq await your reign, but I trust that you understand by now, because you are so keen, it is not by wile alone that we succeed." She touched her great-granddaughter's raven hair with a quiet aversion and then looked out upon the kingdom, where off in the distance the silver gleam of their family spring rose up from the forest like a diamond mist. "I trust that you will understand the urgency of my wish that your firstborn be the son of your cousin Odelin."

Adriane scowled. "But Odelin is a silly, foolish boy," she said.

"Yes," replied her great-grandmother. "And Odelin's hair would be the colour of the full moon and all the stars of heaven if we did not bleed its silver to Dai-kyrie."

It was true, her foolish cousin's hair was brilliant, but Adriane still glowered, for the thought of marrying Odelin sickened her. "I hope you understand me, Adriane, and let there be no mistake—if you should refuse and threaten to pollute the line any more than you already have, I will see that you are buried beside me this very year."

"I do understand," the girl replied, and it was done. Her sixteenth year, Adriane gave birth to her successor, the son of

Odelin, a moon-haired child named Bela. Marthanella passed away that winter, pleased. Then at seventeen, Adriane ascended her rightful throne.

Adriane served well, just as Marthanella had expected. She protected and expanded the kingdom year by year, and she was feared and respected by all.

Her reign was on the cusp of its third decade when just outside a small country village called Claudile, a child emerged from the wood. A barmaid named Lucille found him. Lucille was a great round woman with a broad smile and black braids which she bunched over her ears like buns. She and her pig had been out looking for mushrooms when she came across the little boy, sitting there alone at the forest's edge. He appeared to be no more than a year old, but his parents were nowhere to be seen. Lucille searched and searched the wood for them, calling out into the weald, but when darkness began to fall and still she'd heard no answer, she took the child home to an old pub she ran in the middle of the village. She prepared a dish of banana pudding for the child, and then put him to bed in a crib she made out of gin crates and sackcloth, which she beat to make soft.

That night when her customers arrived for their pints and mushroom stew, Lucille took them back to see the sleeping boy, and told them she'd found him at the wood's edge. "Hard to imagine any parents leaving such a little one alone," they said, "he looks so dear." And Lucille agreed. "Oh, many, many lives has this child led—you'll see tomorrow in his eyes; he's wise, this little one."

The next evening, all of Lucille's patrons came earlier than usual to see the little boy up and awake, and to find if any parents had come to claim him. None had, said Lucille, and so they posted signs about the town and circulated word, but the days became a week and still no parents appeared. The patrons all shook their heads from sympathy for the boy, but Lucille was not quite so disappointed. She wanted what was best, of course, but she did enjoy the child's company. She'd never felt so blessed as by his presence, and her pub and life had never seemed so bright. Indeed, now when strangers entered her door, her heart would faintly sink, for fear that they might be his parents and take the boy away. And every night in bed she'd say two prayers—the first for his sake, that they come soon, and the second for her own, that they never come at all.

Then one night, after she'd said her prayers and fallen asleep, it came to Lucille in a dream why the little boy had touched her so, and why she needn't fear. When Lucille was a little girl, her mother had told her the story of the little boy who lived beneath Quordiro's light, a child who'd once been king but who had never grown and then been sent to live among the spirits of the forest. As a girl, Lucille had always said a prayer for him, the little king, and often dreamt of him alone in the woods, surrounded by all the quiet spirits there. As time passed and she grew older, Lucille eventually convinced herself it wasn't true and forgot all about such things, until one night, after putting the little boy she'd found to bed. She'd dreamt of the little king again—she'd seen him in the forest, with all the quiet spirits surrounding, and she saw that it was he, the little orphan.

When her patrons came for breakfast in the morning, she told them of her dream and said that she believed it was true—he was the little king, Lucille said, spooning pudding in his mouth. He was Quordiro's son.

Her patrons scoffed. "He is a dear," they said, "and we all do treasure him, but the little king?"

"The little king," Lucille replied, and to show them, she took the child from his chair and marked his height upon the kitchen door with a carving knife. "You will see," she said. "No parents shall come, and in a month's time he shall be no taller. You will see."

"I see only that Lucille wants a little boy," said Magnus, the miller. "She wants to keep him to herself!" and all the patrons laughed.

But Lucille, to their surprise, said no. She said she wouldn't keep the child. She said the child had no need for their protection—Quordiro saw to that. Of course, she would always have some pudding ready, and milk and carrots and split pea. She said she'd always leave her door open and have bedding if he should choose to stay the night, and they should do the same, she said—but never try to keep him. The little king had been alive and free too long, and too long in the company of spirits for anyone to try to keep him.

The patrons rolled their eyes at this. They believed that Lucille was fooling herself, but in the days that followed, they did see the child about the town, crawling out by the mills, and every time they would take him back to the pub. "You need to pay more attention, Lucille, or we shall have to find someone else to care for him."

But Lucille remained steadfast. "Quordiro cares for him," she'd say. "You needn't fear." So, she would feed him pudding if he liked, or sing the child a song, but then she'd let him go. Time and time again, the villagers would find him crawling about their doors and shops, and they wondered at Lucille's carelessness at first, but when they held him in their arms or kept him for the day, soon they began to feel the same as she, that though he was small like an infant, and though his skin was soft, though he gripped their fingers in his palm, and though his innocence was undisturbed, still he carried in his eyes a serenity they'd never seen in one so young, nor in any one at all.

More telling than this, of course, was the mark on Lucille's kitchen door. When several months had passed, it couldn't have been more clear. Lucille would stand him next to the mark she'd made, and everyone could see—he hadn't grown at all since he'd first appeared, not a hair. Eventually most everyone agreed, the child was blessed. They called him "little king" and considered it an honour that he'd come to stay with them so long. For this, they credited Lucille's law, and paid it heed—like the spirits of the forest, to let the child be. Wherever he chose to go, they treated him with kindness because he was a child, and with esteem because he was a king—but they never tried to keep him. At any time of day he might be seen crawling along the green, or in the arms of a storekeeper, playing with other infants, or having his hair brushed by little girls. He wandered where he liked, content to eat and drink what the villagers of Claudile offered, or to curl up on their beds if he was tired.

Most often, though, he could be found at Lucille's, as he is pictured in the third tapestry of the second bridge. He sits up at the bar. Lucille is there beside him, and all the patrons are standing round with smiles on their faces.

Only one among them does not look so happy, a man dressed as a minstrel, sitting at a table in the corner with a suspicious eye upon the little boy; and this one, according to John William, was Tuppence.

Tuppence was Queen Adriane's first bishop, and elsewhere in the tapestries he is more characteristically shown, with his cap and crosier, posed beside the queen, whispering in her ear. The minstrel's costume is a disguise he'd worn, to see in secret if the rumour was true about a little child in Claudile whom all the villagers had taken in, the one who'd come in from the wood and was said to not be growing.

Tuppence saw that it was true. In his disguise, he observed how the child made his way from place to place in freedom, how wherever the child chose to go seemed a blessed place therefore, and that the most blessed place of all was Lucille's pub. Tuppence saw how the villagers would go there just to see him and hold him in their arms, how they fed him at the bar and called him "little king," and how honoured they all were by his presence, pleased just to be wherever he was, as if by choosing to be there, in the company of the "little king," they had chosen to be good.

Most menacing of all, however, Tuppence had seen the mark upon the kitchen door. The child wasn't growing, it was true, and so Tuppence returned to the palace to deliver his queen the news. He met her privately in her chamber and told her what he'd seen:

that the son of Quordiro had returned from the forest and was living in Claudile.

"Is he still spellbound?" the queen asked.

"As the presence of Quordiro would attest, the child is not one day matured from when your beloved grandmother banished him."

"Then let him be," said the queen. "He is no threat if he is but a child."

"True," said Tuppence, "but I have observed this child and how the people treat him. They call him 'little king.' They believe the things he touches and the places he goes are thereby somehow blessed; and though I'm sure that it means little in comparison to your dominion, I believe you should be aware that by the freedom he enjoys in Claudile, the child's curse appears to have become a blessing."

"Yes?" said the queen with derision. "And what do you suggest, Bishop Tuppence? Constraining such freedom?"

"Oh no, my queen," said Tuppence in a soothing voice. "Merely that we show the child kindness too, merely that we win his affection, so that the people know that your palace is a blessed place as well, and that their queen is just as blessed as the barmaid of Claudile."

"Merely show him kindness?" asked the queen, with only the barest interest.

"That is all."

"Very well, then," said the queen. "Do so."

Bishop Tuppence acted at once. He dispatched envoys to Lucille's pub, inviting the child to the palace at the queen's behest. Then he sent out word to all the toymakers of Muroq to bring their finest toys to the palace, to offer the spellbound child when he arrived.

At Lucille's, everyone, with the exception only of the child and the barmaid herself, was very excited by the queen's recognition. Their son had been invited to the palace. When the day of his introduction finally arrived, they all preened him for his presentation. They bathed him and combed his hair. They dressed him in the finest infant clothes, and then he was taken to the palace in a chariot drawn by black and white horses. He was greeted at the palace gates by servants and given a chamber with a bed of roses from the queen's garden. He was served the finest strained vegetables, and then placed in a room filled with pillows to observe the presentation of gifts.

The line of toymakers extended all through the palace halls and out into the courtyard. One by one they offered him their toys—toy boats and trains, stuffed animals and puppets, tops and whistles, slingshots, mobiles, mechanical monkeys with cymbals, little bears who played lullabies from their tummies, toy soldiers and horses and horns and xylophones, kaleidoscopes, and Easter eggs with snow scenes inside. They brought puzzles and bouncing balls, wood blocks, hoops and slides, hot-air balloons with kittens inside—all the toys and playthings one could ever conceive of, but the child showed no interest. He was too young for such things, and also much, much too old.

When the last of the toymakers had come and gone, the door of the infant's chamber was opened and Tuppence watched as he crawled out and down the palace halls, down the great staircase, and out the gates. Returning to Claudile, the bishop thought—to Lucille's pub. So he picked the child up and returned him to his chamber, next to offer him candy.

All the bakers and candymakers of Muroq were summoned. They brought chocolate and gumdrops and ice cream and maple men, puff biscuits and raspberry tarts, angel-food cakes and custard, peach and rhubarb pies, lollipops, candy canes, meringue, and caramel-covered apples, crullers filled with whipped cream and jelly, butterscotch drops and marzipan, sugar-coated orange peels, dried sheets of apricot, and bowls full of icing and cookie batter. All the sweets that one could ever think of were brought to the palace and presented to the child, but once again he chose none. He would not open his mouth to any of it, and once again when his chamber door was opened, he started for the great staircase to leave.

Tuppence returned him to his chamber and next invited all the clowns, magicians, and acrobats of Muroq to come and perform for the child, and they danced and juggled and flipped and tumbled. They made coins vanish and birds appear and eggs hatch bouquets of flowers. They played shadow games with their hands and carved pumpkins into jack-o'-lanterns. They built gingerbread houses and held puppet theatre. They brought ponies for pony rides, and mimes and minstrels, and bears who rode tricycles, but no matter the entertainment, it met with the same reaction as all the toys and candy. The child took no interest, and, as soon as he was able, tried to leave his chamber.

The bishop found all this very frustrating and humiliating. He came to resent the little boy for spurning his efforts, and he did not enjoy having to report his failure to the queen. A month into his visit, Adriane had come to see the child, to observe his happiness, but when she found him sitting glumly among all his toys, she called to her bishop.

"He does not appear very happy, Tuppence."

"No," the bishop replied reluctantly.

"Why is that?"

"I am afraid that I don't know, my queen. We have brought him everything the country has to offer, but he takes no interest."

"You are telling me that you have given the child no reason to prefer the palace?"

"It does not appear so," said Tuppence.

"So when the child returns to his freedom in Claudile, he shall at no point exercise that freedom to come and visit us?"

"No, my queen," said Tuppence, "I would not imagine."

"Was this not the purpose, though?"

"Yes, my queen," said Tuppence meekly.

"Then we are worse now than if we had never taken such interest?"

"My queen," said Tuppence, "I understand your thinking,

and I assure you, no one regrets more than I our failure to win the favour of this infernal little beast, but I might suggest to you that we do not *have* to return him to his freedom in Claudile. We can, if we decide, merely tell the people that the child is happy and has chosen to remain here."

The queen considered this with great agitation. "I am not pleased, Tuppence."

"I know, your highness."

"But it is true. It will not do for this child, having been shown so much of our attention, to eschew the palace."

"No, my queen."

"Very well," she said, and it was done. Word was sent throughout Muroq that the spellbound infant of Quordiro had very much enjoyed his visit with the queen, was very happy at the palace, and had chosen to stay there.

When these tidings arrived in Claudile, the patrons of Lucille's were divided in their feelings. They were happy for the child, of course, but they also missed their little friend. Lucille in particular had not been well since he'd been away. She'd taken to bed for days on end and the colour was gone from her face. Everyone had hoped for her sake that the child would return soon to lift her spirits, but when the queen's announcement came, she did not complain. She told the patrons that if the child had chosen to stay at the palace, then the palace must be a blessed place, and they should be happy for him, and for themselves, to live in such a blessed kingdom. Three days later, she passed away of heartbreak.

Of course, the child had chosen no such thing. He did not ever rant or rave, but in his room at the palace, with his bed of roses, so many toys and so much candy, he waited quietly by the door for it to open, and every time it did, for feedings or for baths, he would try to leave. He would crawl out into the hallway, and the guard would have to lift him up and return him to some plaything, some rattle or toy train that held no interest for him.

His only friends were one guard named Gigot, who was from Claudile and had first met the little king at Lucille's, and the queen's only child, the son she'd had by Odelin—Bela, whom she'd not shown a moment's kindness in his twenty years. She disdained him, in fact, for though his hair was ample and bled a full moon's silver to the springs each time he bathed, she thought him a simpleton—which he apparently was—and an embarrassment—which he was not.

Bela had very little to do with his days, however, except to bathe with his cousins at the spring and await his mother's crown, which she had no intention of relinquishing until her death. One day he'd come across the infant's chamber, as it had been his own when he was a little boy. He knew nothing of the child's curse or blessing, only that he'd been brought all the land's toys and all the land's candy and that he'd rebuffed them each and every one.

Some of the toys Bela had quite enjoyed, though, and every so often he would come by the little child's room to play with them, or sometimes after meals he would go to have a bite of the child's candy. Bela and the spellbound child became friends this way. Bela learned how to feed him and play with him. He would ride the child on his back and let him tug his long grey braids as if they were reins, and soon it happened that at least once a day the queen's son was coming by the spellbound infant's room to play.

One day as he was leaving after just such a visit, Bela mentioned to the standing guard, who was Gigot of Claudile, how strange it was that the child disliked candy. Gigot had answered that the child was too young for such sweets but that he used to like banana pudding. So the next day Bela had Gigot show him how the pudding was made. Together they mashed bananas with milk and eggs and butter, and Bela offered it by spoonfuls to his little friend, who did indeed enjoy the blend.

"But how do you know this?" asked Bela of the guard.

''I know because I am an old friend of the child,'' said Gigot, ''from before he came to the palace.''

''Where was that?'' asked Bela, for he'd been told nothing of the infant's past. He only knew what the guards had told him, that the child hadn't any mother and wouldn't grow.

''That was Claudile,'' answered Gigot, ''where my family lives.''

''And the child is from Claudile?'' asked Bela.

Gigot shook his head. ''I'm not sure where the child comes from, but for a time he lived with us in Claudile.''

''And you gave him pudding?''

''We did.''

''And what else did you give him?'' asked Bela.

''Well,'' said Gigot, ''he liked to be sung to, by my sister Elsbeth.''

''Do you think your sister could come here to sing?'' asked Bela.

''I'm sure she'd like to,'' considered the guard. ''But you'd have to ask your mother first.''

Bela thought better of it. ''What else?'' he asked.

''He liked the mills,'' remembered Gigot, ''and pots, and pans and spoons, and bags of beans.''

''Well, that's not hard,'' said Bela.

''Yes, but I don't think it was the things he liked so much as being able to crawl about and see.''

Bela considered this. ''Then we should let him crawl about and see, too.''

Gigot shook his head. ''I don't think we can, your highness. I think the bishop is afraid he'll leave.''

Bela knew that this was true—he'd heard the bishop's tantrums—and left the child's chamber that day in a puzzle. That night, as he lay in bed, he kept thinking about the things Gigot had said, and of how unhappy his little friend was, sitting glumly in his room all day and night.

The next morning, he went first thing to the child's chamber, and after feeding him some pudding, he called in Gigot.

"Gigot, do you know where the royal cemetery is?"

"Yes," said Gigot.

"And do you know how to get from there to Claudile?"

"I do as well, but why do you ask, sir?"

"I want you to take me and the child."

"The little king?" exclaimed Gigot.

Bela nodded. "I don't think his chamber makes him as happy as he was with you and your friends back in Claudile, so I'd like to take him there."

"But your highness!" Gigot whispered, and he was going to remind him of the bishop's orders, but then he caught a glimpse of the little king; it pained him as well, seeing the child so lonely in his chamber, and he knew what Bela said was true. "Why from the cemetery?" he asked.

"When I was younger, my cousins and I used to play in passageways beneath the palace, and I know that they come up in the cemetery. Will you meet me there and take me to Claudile?"

"I would, my prince," said Gigot. "There is nothing I would like more, but I am afraid that when they find the child gone, Claudile is the first place they'll go to find him."

Bela thought. "Then the countryside," he said.

Gigot clapped his hands excitedly, for he'd never been so sure of a good thing, or party to such intrigue. "When?" he asked.

"I thought tomorrow," said Bela.

"But wait a day," said Gigot, "so I may warn my neighbours."

Bela agreed, and that night Gigot returned to Claudile and told his sister to gather everyone together at Lucille's old pub and tell them what was taking place—that the bishop had been keeping the little king captive and that he hadn't been happy at all, but that the queen's son, Bela, had decided to free him.

The following evening, on Gigot's guard, Bela entered the child's chamber. They shared a small serving of banana pudding;

then Bela took the little king into his arrow case and they escaped the castle underground.

Another day passed before the child was reported missing. The morning guard made the discovery and told Bishop Tuppence, who that same day raced alone on horseback to Claudile to see if the child was there. By the time he reached the village, though, it was deserted—even Lucille's pub, which once had been so alive with people and song, was silent and empty. He checked every kettle and cupboard and found nothing but a fresh grave in the back lot, with Lucille's stone.

So Tuppence returned to the palace, and with much dread reported his news to the queen, that the spellbound child had escaped and that all the people of Claudile were gone.

"You presume they are with him?" she asked.

"I do, but we should not have trouble finding them."

"And then?"

"My queen, such a community cannot be tolerated within the kingdom!"

"Are you suggesting the kingdom should make them pay in blood?"

"No," said Tuppence, wringing his cloak. "My queen, I do not know what I am suggesting."

Adriane smiled as she looked at him. "It is amusing."

"It is not amusing, my queen. How can you say such a thing?"

"That whereas our throne has always rested upon the child's life, it now would appear to rest upon his death."

"Oh, if only, my queen, but you know as well as I"—he pointed timidly at the sky—"the child is immortal!"

"No one is immortal." She cupped the bishop's cheek. "Call the family."

Tuppence did, he knew not what for, but that same evening all the Lispenard, all the grey-haired children, the cousins and nephews and nieces and uncles—all but for the fool Bela, who was nowhere to be found—gathered in the queen's court and bowed their heads before Adriane, who walked along the line of them, touching their heads one by one as she spoke.

"It has come to my attention how loyal the people are. Lo, these hundred years, have our subjects not been loyal? Florismart?" She turned up the head of a nephew.

"They have, Aunt Adriane," said Florismart. "There is no doubt."

"And do they not deserve some reward for such loyalty? Is it not time we gave them something in return? Roland?"

Her cousin Roland raised his head. "Yes, Adriane."

"I have decided it should be the castle in Dai-kyrie," she said. "And all the property surrounding. Would that not be generous? Orlanda?"

"It would be very generous," said the girl, who was a niece and did not raise her head to speak.

"Yes, I think so." Adriane turned her back to them and walked towards her throne. "We shall make our homestead a gift to the people. The castle shall be theirs to explore, the paintings theirs to look at, the china theirs to eat from. The grounds shall be theirs to wander, and the springs shall be theirs in which to bathe. Would that not be lovely?" She sat upon her throne, and all the Lispenard nodded their bowed heads and murmured how lovely it would be.

"I'm glad we agree, and just so that there is no misunderstanding, if I find that any of you has trespassed on the gift I am giving to our subjects as reward for their loyalty these past hundred years—and if, in particular, I find that any one of you has dipped so much as a single strand of your precious white curls in the springs, I shall have all the hair shaved from every one of your heads, and hang you by it. Am I understood?"

Odelin, the fool, looked up, father of her absent son, the only bigger fool. "You will hang all of us," he asked, "or just the one who bathes?"

"I will hang the one who bathes," answered Adriane, "and you, cousin Odelin."

All the Lispenard but one bowed their heads, a little niece at the end of the line named Nami. "But what of our gift to Quordiro?" she asked.

"Our gift to Quordiro," answered Adriane, "shall be to set it free and send it on its way."

So ends the final tapestry of the second bridge. So ends my day. In the morning, tomorrow, the final bridge.

Good night,
Gus

I had been careful when I first entered the third bridge not to look at the hangings on the wall, lest the figures pictured there might divulge the end of the story before I was ready to hear it. We took our seats in silence and expectation, and then John William directed my attention to the next tapestry. Neither by image nor by palette could I tell which thread of the story we had taken up—the little king's or Evelin's—until John William began, with her name.

Evelin did not remain with her father long after being lifted from the well. Had it been a virus which stole her sight and hearing, or an accident, perhaps Borbo would have endured the hardship of raising her, but he could not bear the knowledge that he was the one who had done this to her. When he held Evelin in his arms, all he could think of was the darkness and the silence, and he would have to turn away. He would escape to the beanfields, leaving Evelin in the care of the Sisters from the convent at Gilbert, Anjelique and Gadireau, who came every day to help.

One evening Sister Gadireau brought the child out to Borbo to say good night and found him kneeling in the rows, pounding the dirt with rocks to crush the snakes he saw, and she decided that night to take Evelin back to the convent, where all the Sisters could then care for her.

The convent at Gilbert was hidden in the forest of Thalen, south and east of Dai-kyrie, and there Evelin grew to be a young woman. She was cared for mostly by Sister Gadireau. Sister Gadireau taught her to cook and to cut flowers. They grew vegetables together in the convent garden and felt the tadpoles swim through their fingers at the fountain. They picked grapes from the arbour and made jelly, and often they took walks together through the forest, to feel the leaves and smell the wildflowers.

Evelin was thirteen years old when word came that Queen Adriane had made a gift of the Lispenard castle and the forest surrounding to the people of Muroq. Several of the Sisters had gone to visit and returned with stories of the Lispenard riches—their plates and paintings and quilts and such—but most remarkable of all, they said, were the family springs. They'd been discovered in the forest near the castle, and the Sisters said they had never beheld anything more glorious, for the waters weren't transparent but silver, and at night they shone with such a radiance that some believed that they had healing powers.

When Sister Gadireau heard this, she thought of Evelin, of course, of her dark eyes and silent ears. She borrowed the little boat the Sisters kept for when heavy rains would flood the cutting garden and left with Evelin the next afternoon.

The springs were a half day's journey by carriage, so it was evening when they arrived. Sister Gadireau had seen the light first. It was shining up above the forest and through the trees as if a great white fire were burning in the forest. The horse wouldn't go near. The Sister had to get down from her seat and lead him on foot, and when they finally reached the banks surrounding, she'd had to shade her own eyes, too, the light reflecting up was so intense. Still, she could see it was as they'd said: the whole surface of the water was like a great flat-looking glass laid upon its back, but emanating a clear white light and warmth, even as the night hung black and cold above.

Up until then, the springs had attracted more fortune seekers than anyone else. The Sister saw them all along the shore—panners panning the water skillet by skillet and reducing it above their campfires to just the silver dust, which they then scraped into bags to sell in town. And there were fishermen as well, with fishing poles and paper pinhole masks to shield their eyes from the light. They cast their lines over and over, telling stories to one another of the fish beneath the waters and how they would taste. They spoke of cleaning the silver backs of their catch and offering them to the queen—but this was only talk, for when the Sister asked, the fishermen confessed that not a single one of them had felt a nibble.

And when in turn they asked what business the Sister had in coming, she said she'd come in hope that the springs might heal the eyes and ears of her dear friend, and she introduced them all to Evelin, who stood quietly by the water's edge. The fishermen helped haul the convent skiff to shore, and then helped Evelin aboard. They sat her at the prow, and then the Sister climbed aboard herself and rowed out to the middle of the springs.

There were no other boats out on the surface, just the Sister and the girl, floating above their own reflections. The panners and the fishermen couldn't help chuckling at the sight of them—of the girl sitting up at the prow, stroking the water with her fingertips, and the sound of Sister Gadireau singing to herself.

The two stayed out until dawn and then the Sister rowed them in. The fishermen asked if the water had healed Evelin's eyes or ears, and the Sister said no, but that they'd surely had some effect, and she pointed to Evelin, who sat on the strand with her feet in the water and her hand upon the skiff rope.

They spent the day there. The fishermen shared their bread and fruit with them, and then when evening fell, when darkness spread above them and the water once again began to shine, the Sister and the girl rowed back out to the middle of the springs and spent a second night basking in the warmth and light.

Sister Gadireau decided they should return to the convent in the morning. The fishermen offered them food to stay, but the Sister said they couldn't impose again. "But I suspect that we'll be back soon," she said. "Yes," said one of the panners, "and perhaps next time you can teach the girl to fish; perhaps she'd have more luck than our friends here." All the panners laughed.

As Sister Gadireau took Evelin back around the forest, this seemed less and less a joke to her. As soon as she and Evelin arrived at the convent, they went to see if the Sisters kept any fishing poles anywhere. They didn't, so several days later she and Evelin attended the birthday party of Sister Monserrat. They brought her jars of grape jelly, and when the party ended, Sister Gadireau asked if she and Evelin could have some of the string which the Sisters had used to wrap their presents. Sister Monserrat let them have it all, so Sister Gadireau and Evelin took the string to the library and tied it end to end, then wound it into a ball as big as a cantaloupe.

The following day they returned to the springs with their ball of birthday twine and a jar of the convent olives. The Sister bid hello to all the fishermen and the panners, then rowed Evelin out to the centre of the springs, where it was most warm and light. Together they threaded olives onto their string and then cast the line into the water.

The olives had hardly disappeared beneath the silver when the twine suddenly snapped to attention. Evelin dropped the ball in fright, but the Sister gave it back to her so she could feel its life. It seemed to want to play with her, so she let it have more line, this playful thing, and it became more playful. It swam away and Evelin could feel the ball spinning in her lap. She held the twine between her fingers, and she could feel it turn and dive down deep—like a kite, but underneath her. It could pull beneath the skiff, or fly away and hide. It looped and dove and danced with Evelin, all the way till morning. Then when the sun came up, the line fell slack. Her friend had said goodbye, and Sister Gadireau rowed them in.

Back on shore, the fishermen in their pinhole masks all smiled and asked Sister Gadireau if they'd had success. The Sister told them yes, that Evelin had been playing with a fish the whole time they'd been out. ''Well, let's see, then,'' said the fishermen. ''If the girl has caught one of Dai-kyrie's silver fish, show us.'' ''Oh, but Evelin didn't pull it in,'' explained the Sister. ''Evelin had only meant to play, but then she let her new friend go.'' All the fishermen's faces steamed with laughter.

The next day, after returning to the convent and taking a nice long nap, Evelin appeared at the Sister's door with the ball of birthday string in her hand, ready to go again, but Sister Gadireau said no. She had decided that they shouldn't go quite so often, so as not to spoil the child. They waited seven days before returning, but just the same as the week before, when they'd threaded their line with olives and cast it over the side of the skiff, it came to life almost at once, as if her friend beneath the water had been expecting her. The fishermen could hear Evelin laugh all the way from the strand. Sister Gadireau shrouded her end of the boat with a blanket and lay down underneath to sleep while Evelin and her friend played together till dawn.

The following week they returned, to none of the fishermen's surprise, and the week after that as well. This time, however, Evelin cast a second line alongside the first. Sister Gadireau had told the other Sisters of Evelin's success, and they'd been bringing her little bits of string from their packages and rags, which Evelin kept together and tied end to end. In just four weeks it had grown as large as a cantaloupe, and so she'd brought it to the springs.

She cast both her lines together, and the first sprung taut at once, as usual. It swam far off, and then upon its return, the other line tugged as well. A second friend had come to play with her, who was like the first but different—like brother and sister. They swam slightly different sorts of designs. They scuffled and played. They twisted round their lines, pulling them as far as they could go, and then raced back. They danced and played all the way to morning, and this time when Sister Gadireau rowed the skiff back to shore, she boasted to the fishermen that Evelin now had two friends beneath the surface of the water.

The fishermen could only shake their heads, reel in their lines, and cast again.

From that point on, like clockwork, Sister Gadireau brought Evelin to play at the springs once a week. They kept the skiff there, tied to a post at the strand, and in the days between, they went to all the Sisters' birthday parties, giving presents of olives and grape jelly in return for string. And every time the string tied end to end was the size of a cantaloupe, they would bring it to the springs and cast it with the other lines, and another friend would come to play with Evelin.

In time, she cast a third line and then a fourth, and when her lines numbered five, her friends beneath the surface of the springs were strong enough to pull the skiff. The fishermen and panners could see the little boat turning circles back and forth, and gliding across the surface like a sleigh.

Its reflection in the water was not as clear as it had been before, however, all the fishermen and panners could see: the water had begun to lose its lustre. They could point to where the glow above the surface used to rise back when the springs were first opened and how low it had fallen since. Some blamed the panners for panning all the silver away, and others suggested that it was the girl and her boat somehow stirring up the water, but either way, the effect was very clear. By the time Evelin cast her sixth line, there was hardly any glimmer at all coming up from the surface. So fewer and fewer fishermen began to come, and fewer panners as well. The panners couldn't find enough silver in their pans to sell, and the fish, what fish there were, all seemed interested exclusively in Evelin.

In time she cast a seventh line and then an eighth, and by then the air was cool above the water. The light was dim, but Evelin did not mind. She could feel her friends weave braids for her and play cat's cradle; she'd tie the strings onto her fingers. And when she'd collected enough string to cast another line, her ninth, she made a cross-frame from tomato stakes and tied the lines all along, so that she could feel them all at once and pull at them like a puppeteer.

But a strange thing happened that night. A ninth friend had come to join the others, and they had all been playing together just the same as the weeks before, teasing and racing and tangling and untangling, when all at once and well before dawn they all pulled out as far as they would go, and then fell slack, one by one, in order.

Sister Gadireau was awakened by the idleness of the skiff, and when she pulled down her cover, she could see that the sky was still dark. Perhaps the olives had gone sour, she thought, so she helped Evelin pull in the lines and then rethread them, but when Evelin cast again, still the lines only hung limp over the side of the boat. All night long Evelin and the Sister waited, threading and rethreading the lines, but when the sun grew full and round above the treeline and still her friends had not come back, finally they gave up.

When Evelin got back to the convent, she slept that day and woke up crying. She would not eat the following morning, or garden or help with the vegetables. She would not even attend the Reverend Mother's birthday later in the week. But every morning she appeared at Sister Gadireau's door with all nine balls of twine in hand, cradled in her arms, begging to go.

The seventh morning Sister Gadireau finally did relent. All week she'd been praying that Evelin's friends would return, so they took the carriage to the springs and rowed out to the middle, but when Evelin cast the lines again, they only drifted with the current, as they had the week before, all night long.

Evelin wept the whole ride back, and after that Sister Gadireau decided they shouldn't go to the springs anymore. When Evelin appeared at her door in the mornings with her lines all wound and ready, the Sister refused her. Even after seven days had passed, she still said no, and Evelin grew resentful. She stomped her feet and pleaded. She called out at the top of her lungs and threw the balls of twine. As the days passed she finally grew so willful that the Sister had no choice but to take the twine away. She took the balls from under Evelin's bed one night and buried them behind the tomatoes in the garden.

When Evelin discovered that her lines had been taken, she forswore the Sister's company. She would not garden with her or eat or walk with her. She would not bid her good morning or good night. She spent her days alone, and all the Sister could do was wait for her forgiveness.

She brought peace offerings—flowers and little porcelain dogs, pastries and pillows made of all different fabrics—but Evelin would have none of them. Then one afternoon, the Sister took two goldfish from the convent pond and put them in a glass bowl for Evelin, but when she came to the girl's room to offer them in truce, Evelin was gone. The Sister searched the convent, but her young friend was nowhere to be found. The Sister did not know what to think until she came to look in the garden and found nine little holes behind the rows of tomatoes.

The Sister dashed to her carriage and raced it round Dai-kyrie to the springs, and there she found Evelin. The girl had walked the whole way herself and rowed out to the middle, in just her nightgown and a sweater.

The Sister waited on the strand for her all night, and when Evelin rowed in in the morning, the Sister went to help her, but Evelin would not allow it. She tied the skiff line to its post herself and then sat down on the strand, clutching all the lines to her. The Sister begged her to come back. She tried pulling her to the carriage, but Evelin would not budge. She waited there all day, and then when evening fell, she headed out alone again. She sat in the middle of the springs with her nine lines slack in the water, and she did the same the following night and the night after that. She slept in the forest shade during the day, and she would not let her old friend near. All Sister Gadireau could do was bring food from the convent—baskets of grapes and pears, olives and bread, and cheese and water. She left them in the boat for Evelin to take out at night, and when the weather turned cool, the Sister brought scarves and blankets as well.

But Evelin would not give up her vigil. Even when the water turned to ice and trapped her skiff at the banks, she sat up at the prow, with her nine frozen lines in hand, and every night Sister Gadireau watched her from the strand, wrapped in blankets, praying the child would come in and bury the lines herself.

But Evelin waited out the season, and when in spring the ice did melt, she rowed her way back out to the middle.

Then one evening when the moon was full and round, the Sister was sitting on the strand, fighting sleep, when she heard a sound which startled her. It was a baby crying, and it seemed to be coming from somewhere near the springs. The Sister stood to peer around the water's edge, but from her enclave on the strand she could not see where. She looked out at Evelin again and suddenly her heart leapt up. The girl was leaning forward on her knees, and in the moonlight the Sister could see that all the lines were moving; they were sliding round the side of the boat like threads of light shining down from Evelin's hands. They pulled out in front of her, and slowly the boat began to turn; then the little skiff started gliding in the direction of the inlet bridge.

The good Sister stood up and started round the water's edge to follow. Beyond the strand she clambered past the rocks and bushes, and the farther along she went, the clearer she could hear the child crying. Then, as she passed round beyond the widest bend in the treeline, she saw that there were strangers coming through the forest—not fishermen or panners, but bakers and children and millers and grandparents—a whole village worth of people making their way towards the edge of the springs, all with their eyes set fast upon Evelin as she glided towards the inlet.

Onward beat the good Sister, past the gentle villagers, but when the inlet finally came into view, she stopped in wonder at the sight. A man with long, gleaming hair the colour of the moon was standing waist high in the water underneath the bridge. There was a little child in his hands, a baby crying as though it had been wrapped in a fiery blanket. Above them more villagers were leaning over the rail of the bridge—half looking out at the girl sliding towards them in the skiff; half looking down at the moon-haired man as he cupped handful after handful of water onto the belly of the child.

The moon-haired man turned up his head as Evelin's skiff came near, and all the lines which had been pulling her fell slack and then tugged her gently to a stop before him. Evelin held out her arms, and the moon-haired man handed her the child, who fell silent at her touch. She cradled him against her breast, and as he tried to suckle her, while all the villagers stood in wonder, a silver tide emerged from the water; thousands upon thousands of gleaming stones rolled from the floor of the spring up to the banks, and from the banks they carried the starlight with them past the villagers into the forest.

And when the last of these silver stones had made its way from the water to the land, all the villagers, the Sister, and Bela looked back at Evelin, in whose arms the body of the little king now hung slack. She turned and laid it down upon the bottom of the skiff, then held out her arms to Bela. He lifted her up and stood her elbow deep in the water. Then her nine lines all slid out before the prow of the skiff and began to pull the little king's body underneath the bridge and up the inlet.

Before the skiff was gone from sight, Evelin started from the water to the banks, then entered the wood herself. The first to follow her was Bela, then Sister Gadireau, the guard, and then all the villagers of Claudile followed Evelin into Dai-kyrie. And only the good Sister was aware the child was sightless, for she led them without misstep, as if she'd walked these woods many times before, as if they were like the woods which lived inside of her. And as she made her way, the silver stones came out from behind the trees to meet her. Where she stopped to place her hand upon the ground, a silver stone would come to rest. The first she gave to Sister Gadireau, and the next to Bela. Then she knelt upon the needle bed and more of the stones came out to see her. They rolled onto her lap, and she gave them one by one to the villagers, for them to hold and greet.

Then, when all the stones had come and shown themselves, and all the villagers had seen, they returned to Claudile; Bela went with them as well, Sister Gadireau returned to the convent, and Evelin chose to stay in the forest. She lived there the remainder of her days, walking along its pathless bed, sleeping in the boughs of trees, and living among the spirits there. Sister Gadireau came and visited her often, and the other Sisters came as well, and the fishermen and panners who'd watched her in the skiff. They all would go and see her, the woman of the wood who'd finally let the little king free—Evelin, whose eyes and ears had long since died, but by whose incandescent spirit totem first met effigy, and effigy totem.

The last of the carriage-bridge tapestries is only the size of a picture book. It shows Evelin sitting among the silver stones, touching the habit of Sister Gadireau, so this is where John William ended. He looked back at me.

''And so what became of Quordiro?'' I asked.

John William nodded. ''When a year had passed from the little king's death, Quordiro's light was seen to move from its place above Muroq and to return to its own journey as if it had never paused.''

''And did it ever appoint another king?'' I asked.

John William shook his head with a general regret. ''When it was seen the star had finally moved, the kingdom divided between those who honoured the heavens and those who honoured blood, and the heavens warred with heavens, and blood with blood. More totem came to light and more divisions divided till it became as you see today.''

''And what of the infant's body?''

Again John William smiled at my concern. ''Where the nine lines drew the skiff is a mystery. There are some who believe that Evelin's friends took the child's body out to sea, where Therese's and his father's bodies lay. Others like to think that the skiff continues on its journey even today, and claim to see it every now and then, floating along the rivers.

"Still others believe that when Evelin felt the end of her life at hand, she went down to the springs and was met at the water's edge by her friends with the skiff. She lay down upon its bottom, and as the warmth withdrew from her breast, another tide of stones emerged from the spring, clear like diamonds. They rolled from the water to the banks and then into the wood. Then the skiff carried Evelin's body to the infant's side, a place which was never known for certain but which those who come this way have reason to believe is nearby"—John William stood to open the final door of the bridges, and pointed at the trees in the near distance—"is there, in fact."

Upon sensing the exit, all the totem started out. Simeon took the Staunton knight and Constantine beneath his arms and followed, then I, then John William.

The rain had passed and the ground was soft. We all made our way in a line to the trees, which stood beside each other on an oval peninsula of land, rounded by the third finger of the creek as it set off in its own direction—north.

The trees were both of slender stalk and arching branches, but strong enough to bear fruit. As we came near, Simeon set down the knight and Constantine and began leaping up at the boughs to pick the ripest. John William withdrew three tin cups from the pouches of his robe and handed them to me. I took them to the river to fill with water, and by the time I'd returned, Simeon had picked us each two fruit, one from each tree: the first like a plum, the other like an apricot. John William served his and mine on the wooden counters as though they were bread boards, but Simeon did not bother with such formality. He put both fruits in his mouth at once, and then rolled back on his hind to eat them, kicking his feet in the air like a Chinese umbrella juggler and tossing the marbles in the air.

I first tasted the one like plum, and like plum its flesh burst sweet in my mouth, its skin more bitter—I recognised the taste, though I couldn't think where from.

I took a bite of the second fruit, the one more like an apricot, and it was milder, but its flavor combined with that of the first served to recall even more vividly a taste I had tasted before—this very combination, but I could not imagine where or when. "Do such trees exist elsewhere?"

John William looked doubtful. "I am obliged to think there is but one body of Evelin and one of the infant, to bear such fruit."

Just then Simeon sat up and smiled a very broad gargoyle grin at me, set to burst with laughter.

"I believe Simeon has something to show you, Dr. Uyterhoeven." John William held his hand beneath Simeon's chin, and I could hear his wings flapping with excitement. Then from between his lips appeared a diamond, which fell into John William's palm. "The queen," he said, extending the jewel to me. I set it on the wooden counter, and John William placed his hand beneath Simeon's chin again. A second jewel appeared on the gargoyle's lips, this one like silver and perfectly round. "The king," said John William, catching it. "The seeds." He set it beside the diamond.

I looked down at them next to one another, the same pair as I'd seen in the lord chancellor's palm, and the sheik's, and then in the altar girl's dish—and then it came to me, the very time and place I had tasted this fruit before, or its nectar: with the altar girl and her Staunton, from her snifter.

"Well, thank you, Simeon," I said. Simeon acknowledged my welcome graciously. "But are they mine to keep?"

"Of course," said John William.

I folded the gems into my handkerchief. "I know just what I shall do with them."

"Send them to your friends?" asked John William.

"I'd thought so."

"And do you think that you shall be writing them as well?"

"If it is allowed."

"Certainly," said the bishop, "and if you need the assistance of the tapestries, I'm sure Constantine will be happy to light them for you again. Then when you're done, if you leave the letter and the jewels in his cap, when I return I'll see that they reach your friends."

"You're not staying?"

"I'm afraid not." He looked down the river. "There are too many others I need to see. But the dice will stay as well, I think, and then if you're still interested in Teverin, you can follow them back to the chasm. It's easiest."

He smiled and silence descended. We finished our fruit, drank our cups of water, and then he clapped his hands to call the others. He stood up and tossed his two shining seeds into the water, and the totem all scurried in after, all but the dice and Constantine. I walked John William to the banks and we shook hands goodbye. I thanked him as well as I could. "It is my pleasure," he answered, and I could see that this was true. Then Simeon took the bishop on his shoulders and carried him into the water. The kind gargoyle took a seat on one of the checkers floating there, and so my final image is of them gliding down the river, one atop the other, spinning slowly and waving to me. "Just look closely at the tapestries!" the bishop called as the gargoyle inconsonantly mimicked him. "Keep to the tapestries and you'll do fine."

So I have tried, and true to John William's word, the stone bishop Constantine has been most kind to light my way a second time through the bridges. You shall have to trust as to the rest, though, for my letter is done. I shall pluck two more fruit for myself, that I may have the seeds, and entrust the bishops to send you these. Then I suppose I shall take John William's advice and follow the dice back to the chasm. As ever when I finish writing you, I have begun to feel weary with loneliness; I suspect a night above the pulverising dice shall do me good.

Good night,
Gus

PART SIX

The Contemplation of Cause 1868–1900

SIXTEEN

THE FOUNDING OF THE CHESS GARDEN (1868–1884)

In February of 1868, the Uyterhoevens returned briefly to Berlin to settle their estate and to make official the doctor's resignation from the Friedrich Wilhelm Institut. Dr. Uyterhoeven offered the faculty no real explanation as to why he was leaving. They asked if he was going to join another university; he said no. They asked if he was going to pursue his homeopathic avocations; again he said no. He had scheduled a brief speaking tour throughout Europe, to lecture on the conflict between empiricism and allopathic theory, but other than that, he seemed to have no plan and no appointments, nothing but an avowal of faith that he expressed only to his closest friends.

He and Sonja left Berlin in late April of 1868. Gustav was forty-five years old and Sonja thirty-three. Money was no concern. Gustav had inherited a good deal of his father's fortune, as well as his flair for sound investment, and he did not expect to live extravagantly. The host colleges and universities housed them during their stays, fed them, and, in a few cases, fêted them. They saw Austria, Switzerland, France, and Italy, and they found a certain comfort in always knowing that they were to move on. Their only frustration was more Gustav's than Sonja's. Wherever they went, he felt that he'd been preceded by a disturbing reputation—as that of a once brilliant scientist who'd lost his way. "I am treated gingerly," he wrote Virchow, "as if I were a relic of myself . . . My lectures arouse more curiosity than interest."

London was more receptive. The doctor's lectures were well attended, and then purchased by the Cambridge University Press, which credited him with setting out "a lineage both illuminated and illuminating of the two legacies which Western medicine inherits." The Uyterhoevens stayed there eight months, from the fall of 1870 through the following summer, not only because Gustav felt less intellectually stigmatized, but because he still had family there, including his mother. Furthermore, London turned out to be a much more favorable environment in which to pursue his new avocation, of tracking down Swedenborgians wherever they were hiding to plumb their various spiritual impressions.*

Uyterhoeven's best find and principal companion in London was a physician named J. J. Garth Wilkinson, a leading proponent of Swedenborg's ideas, the premier English translator of both his scientific and theological writings, and recent author of several essays on the relationship between Swedenborgian and homeopathic theory. Needless to say, Wilkinson and Uyterhoeven became fast friends. In fact, Uyterhoeven's fresh enthusiasm prompted Wilkinson to dust off an old commission he'd struggled with years before, a Swedenborgian reader for the blind that he'd long promised a sightless cousin, a chaplain from Kent.

Wilkinson and Uyterhoeven worked on it together for a brief period, going over Wilkinson's old manuscripts, but they didn't get far. As accommodating as England had been, it was never a place that Gustav and Sonja imagined taking root. Sonja was hardly English, and the doctor's religious convictions had by then developed to the

*The doctor noted at the time that his Swedenborgianism held much in common with the two interests which had distracted him the first time he'd lived in London—chess and opium. All were equally "marginalizing," and their votaries displayed "the same barely restrained giddiness when revealed to one another, at the almost certain prospect of mutual indulgence for hours on end." The difference was that "those with an appetite for chess and opium were all pale and invalid, whereas Swedenborgians all strike one as red-in-the-cheek, healthy, and healthy-minded."

point of demanding compliance from more and more diverse and fundamental aspects of his life, including the society he chose. England was "much too class-bound," in that light, and the Continent "too tribal." Uyterhoeven wanted to find a place more encouraging to the individual, which he had come to consider "the current frontier of spirit."

Such a place was said to lie across the ocean, and Wilkinson encouraged the doctor to go and see for himself. He warned of a deep-seated puritanism, but otherwise the land was vast, the laws liberal, and the population diverse, all of which the doctor and Sonja found appealing. So, in the summer of 1871, the decision was made.

The Uyterhoevens landed in New York in November. To make sure before leaving they'd have at least some impetus, Gustav had scheduled several speaking engagements. Probably, given his new spiritual ardor, his precautions were unnecessary. Literally the day they arrived, Gustav went directly to the New Church in Brooklyn and made the acquaintance of the pastor there, Dr. Bush, who had edited one of the secondary books he'd read in Klipdrift, *Documents Concerning Swedenborg*. Bush soon introduced him to several other prominent theosophists and Swedenborgians, including John Bigelow, H. P. Blavatsky, Joshua Hunt, and Sampson Reed. That winter and spring the Uyterhoevens lived on Eighteenth Street near Gramercy Park, and the following summer they moved on to Boston, where the doctor conducted a seminar at the medical school of Boston University, which was then still primarily a homeopathic institution. He also delivered lectures at Harvard, and there befriended Theodore Parker, Bronson Alcott, and an old friend of Wilkinson's, Henry James, Sr., also a devoted reader of Swedenborg.

James informed Uyterhoeven that Newbury Publishers in London had scrapped Wilkinson's Braille reader, which Uyterhoeven took first as a disappointment and then as an opportunity. He wrote Wilkinson to express his condolence and then to ask if he would mind his taking a crack at the project himself. Wilkinson gave his blessing. In fact, when Uyterhoeven proposed the Braille idea to his friends at the Swedenborgian Foundation in New York, Wilkinson sent a ringing recommendation, and by the fall of 1872, as the doctor and Sonja embarked on a more nationwide tour, once again underwritten entirely by the doctor's lectures, he had himself a deadline, a stipend, and a provisional commitment to publish.

They visited the Universities of Pennsylvania, Maryland, Virginia, and then made their way up through St. Louis, Louisville, and Ohio, and from there quickly to Chicago. The Midwestern swing of their tour began in the spring of 1873, and it was late March when they first passed through Dayton, between lectures at the University of Cincinnati and Willoughby University on Lake Erie. They lodged in the house of Martha Hunt, the widow of Colonel Thomas Hunt, who'd died in the Battle of the Wilderness a decade before. Since then, Mrs. Hunt had supported herself and fended off the loneliness of widowhood by turning her home on Middle Street into a boardinghouse, mostly for teachers. A frail, petite woman, she had begun at the time of the Uyterhoevens' visit to complain of coughs and fatigue so enervating that she could not tend the acre of flowers and vegetables behind her home. The Uyterhoevens had been on one of the more hurried portions of their schedule, unfortunately—they spent just two days in Dayton the first time through—but the doctor still had time to diagnose Mrs. Hunt with pulmonary phthisis, or tuberculosis, and prescribe her a new diet and daily regimen.

From Dayton they went by train up to Willoughby, then the University of Michigan, and then finally Northwestern University, the last stop on Gustav's speaking tour. Where they would go from there was not yet clear. Upon arriving in Chicago, however, Gustav had discovered several folders missing from the translations he'd been working on for the Braille reader. It had been months since he'd been touched the missing sections, so he had no idea where he might have left them, but Sonja suggested they might be back at Mrs. Hunt's. The doctor didn't think so, but wired Mr. Beales at the Dayton post office nonetheless, and through the efforts of his secretary, Mrs. Thomas, he learned that, sure enough, Mrs. Hunt had found the chapters the day after they'd left, underneath a rock on one of the picnic tables in the garden. She offered to send them wherever the doctor wanted, but

Sonja persuaded Gustav that since they had no further engagements, perhaps they should return to Dayton to check on Mrs. Hunt's health and pay a more extended visit, maybe even as long as it took him to finish his commission. Gustav saw no reason not to. He wired Mrs. Hunt that she should keep the chapters and asked if she would mind their spending a season or so at the house. Of course she didn't. "It would be a pleasure and a help," she wired back, and so, the second week of May, Sonja and Gustav returned to Mrs. Hunt's boarding-house.

From the very start, Dayton seemed an answer to their wishes. If the Uyterhoevens had left Berlin with no real intention in mind, they had come to see over the course of their travels that they desired a different situation from any that they'd previously known. Between them, they had ample experience with cities, universities, manors, and canals. Neither had ever lived in a town, however, and in 1873 Dayton was still just a town, thirty thousand people in seven square miles, its roots firmly planted in a rural, agricultural pasture, but primed for its share of industrial development and expansion as well. Dayton was on the cusp of a golden age, in other words. "The people spend no energy which does not bear obvious fruit," wrote the doctor soon after their return. "The day proceeds from one prayer to the next, from school, to play, to mill, to cow, to store, to garden, to supper, to reading, and then to prayer itself."

In addition to being both ripe and simple, Dayton also sat at the basin of the Miami River Valley, its downtown district marking the confluence of four rivers, all of which in the 1870s were larger than the single channel they became. It was a site extremely prone to flooding, in other words, a feature which tinged not only the air but also the minds of those who chose to breathe it with an essence familiar to both the doctor and Sonja. Daytonians were stubborn people with an almost ferocious sense of community, driven by the very particular blend of defiance, acquiescence, and resignation that follows from tempting fate so openly, so constantly—what the doctor once called, in comparing the people of Dayton to those of Holland, "apocalyptic goodwill."

To his surprise, he also found himself to be much more at home in this atmosphere than he had ever known. By the early fall of 1873, he had finished the first draft of his reader and Mrs. Hunt was almost fully recovered. She was feeling so well, in fact, that she'd been tempted to accept her sister's invitation to come live at their childhood home outside Cincinnati. Her sister had recently been widowed, and Mrs. Hunt wanted to be with her; her only reservation was leaving her beloved flowers. She'd said so to Sonja one afternoon in the garden, and that evening, after consulting with Gustav, Sonja returned to Mrs. Hunt and offered to run the boardinghouse for her. Mrs. Hunt accepted right there, and the first week of October, for an undisclosed amount and the promise that her garden would never go untended, Mrs. Hunt turned over the deed.

From the point of their moving from the guest room into the master bedroom on Middle Street, the Uyterhoevens' life became one with the life of their home. On occasion they traveled, but never for long and never again to Europe, never to divert their attention for too long from Mrs. Hunt's modest acre and their promise to continue cultivating it. In the years to come, they would plant new trees and bushes. They grew new vegetables and bedded new flowers to bloom according to a slightly different calendar. They tore down the back fence and cut new paths into the grass. They extended the patio, laid shell walks and slate walks, erected trellises, dug ditches for stone pools with fish. They pruned limbs, built birdhouses, bought dogs, and built doghouses. They pitched night lamps and standing candles, stood sculptures and urns, hung hammocks and then swings. But most important of all, they set out chess tables.

The first appeared in the spring of 1874, as much at Sonja's behest as Gustav's. Twelve months before, when the doctor was still in the thick of his first draft and Mrs. Hunt was still in his care, his custom had been to take a walk alone after a good afternoon's session with his manuscripts and perhaps a nap. On one such occasion, his nose had led him to the lobby bar of the Phillips House, and he had been quietly enjoying some lemonade and beer when Richard Forrester, former principal of Steele Elementary School, unwittingly invited him to a five-minute game of chess.

Forrester was the local champion. Upon his retirement in 1869 he had commandeered the lone chess table near the front window of the Phillips House, and on Saturday afternoons he welcomed all comers, some of whom would travel overnight from as far off as Columbus and Cincinnati to try to dethrone him. The only stipulation he placed upon his defenses was that the game be played with a clock, and that neither player should have more than five minutes total in which to make all of his or her moves. If their moves should last, cumulatively, more than the time allotted, he or she would lose. With this provision—that is, more for his blustering tactics and sheer physical quickness than his command of the board—Principal Forrester had never been beaten.

At the time he asked Dr. Uyterhoeven to a match, sometime in the early spring of 1873, it had been over two decades since the doctor had last played, having in effect forsworn the game upon his return from England in 1852. That evening, however, an ocean away and twenty years removed from such caution, and also softened by the combination of his shandy and lingering feelings of foreignness, the doctor accepted. He took the seat across from Principal Forrester, and after an opening game which came to a lightning draw, he reoriented himself and proceeded to take the next seventeen consecutive contests from the reigning town champion before the dinner bells called both of them, and the small crowd which had gathered to watch the slaughter, home.

So began a seven-month and thoroughly lopsided rivalry. They played just once a week at first, to give the principal time in between to practice and study, but soon it became clear that he was overmatched, and their games gradually converted to lessons. The doctor prevailed upon the principal that if he was interested in developing his game, they should play longer "natural" contests, without the clock and with increasing frequency. By midsummer, they were meeting three or four nights a week, now in the company of a fairly regular audience, and had established a close enough friendship that the principal broached the possibility of the doctor's teaching chess at the elementary school he had formerly run for over twenty years.

The doctor hesitated. He wasn't entirely sure he liked the idea of becoming a chess master—it struck him as a "rather dank" role. On the other hand, he found very appealing the opportunity of getting to know more of the children in the community. Forrester proposed to let their rivalry decide: they would play one match every night of the summer, and if in that time the former principal could manage to win a game from the doctor, then the doctor would be obliged to teach at his school. If not, they both agreed that the principal should give up chess and the doctor should give up teaching it.

Neither was so compelled, fortunately. Forrester did manage a victory—just one. It happened in late August, after thirty-nine consecutive losses, and even it had been more discouraging than heartening, as Dr. Uyterhoeven had been the one to notice the game was over and needed ten minutes to explain to the principal why.

Still, Steele Elementary had won its first chess master. The doctor's classes met once a week at first, at the school on Friday afternoons, after session. There were only nine students to begin with, ranging in age from six to thirteen, and through the fall, that is more or less the way it remained. However, when the warm weather returned with the spring, Sonja asked why the children had to be cooped up just to learn a game. The doctor had no answer, so in March, at her suggestion, he invited his students to come to his garden after school and have their lesson there.

The garden was not at that time well equipped for such use. The doctor had managed to purchase just two chess tables. Most of the students had to sit on crates and balance their boards on overturned planters or whatever else they could find. As the semester proceeded and attendance continued to grow, the Uyterhoevens acquired more furnishings from yard sales, auctions, and neighbors' attics. Every week new sets would appear, and tables with mismatched chairs. They paid twelve cents for a set of blue tin cups for juice, and also bought six hourglasses to use as timers. When the doctor wrote Virchow in

Berlin to tell him of his new office, Virchow sent back a lavish gift of seven chess benches with marble boards laid right in the seats, along with a note congratulating him for finally having found his true calling. The Uyterhoevens spread the benches throughout the garden, and gradually the rest of the tables followed them out, until they were all evenly dispersed among flower beds and tree shade.

By the fall of 1873, the regimen was more or less set. Lessons began with juice and cookies on the terrace. The doctor would talk his way through a game with Principal Forrester, demonstrating new alignments and patterns of attack, then the children would double up and head out into the garden to find a table. The rest of the afternoon the doctor would spend strolling from game to game, stopping momentarily to lend his insight and then moving on.

By this basic program, the class and the garden flourished hand in hand. Lessons continued through the summer, and when fall came around again, so many children wanted to join for the new semester the doctor was forced to split them into groups by age, and to hold Wednesday classes as well.

Of course, the quick popularity of the garden brought with it more public scrutiny than the Uyterhoevens were prepared for, and therefore the first rumblings of consternation. Churchgoing was an early rub. The doctor had made no secret of his interest in Swedenborg, but he had been forgiven this at first, both because of his candor and because of his skill at chess, quite frankly—one couldn't easily dismiss a man capable of throttling the territory at mankind's oldest and purest strategic game. In any case, most in the community had justifiably assumed that the Uyterhoevens were members of the Church of the New Jerusalem, an established Swedenborgian denomination which had a chapter not so far away in Urbana. They'd found it curious, therefore, that the doctor and his wife kept popping up at different services in and around Dayton. In fact, a quick poll among the parents of the chess classes revealed that the Uyterhoevens had paid visits to no less than eleven Sunday services in the county, prompting the question: Of which faith exactly did the doctor and his wife count themselves members?

The doctor was asked several times, by several concerned mothers and fathers, and every time he answered with regret: None. He had been raised in a secular home, he explained, and Mrs. Uyterhoeven had grown up on the canals, so neither of them had ever developed a strong allegiance to any particular sect. The Church of the New Jerusalem had its appeal, obviously, but Mrs. Uyterhoeven didn't share his appetite for Swedenborg or Swedenborgians, and also, in the end, he himself preferred to treat Swedenborg's offering for what it was, in his opinion—a body of thought and not fodder for ritual worship—all of which had left him and Mrs. Uyterhoeven free on Sunday mornings to look in on whatever services they liked.

If such explanations satisfied certain of the parents, others took the doctor's independence as an insult, to them and to their religions. Church was not a place for dilettantes and connoisseurs, said they, and some even withdrew their children from the chess classes as a result. The Uyterhoevens in turn decided it might be best to trim their Sunday morning itinerary and go only where they felt absolutely welcome, which, owing more to the personality of the various congregations and clergymen than the prevailing doctrine, included St. Paul's Evangelical Lutheran Church; the Church of the New Jerusalem, of course; the Reformed Church, which was German; and First Presbyterian Church of Dayton because the pastor, Dr. Thomas, was a friend and the town's most talented preacher.

In return for such restraint, the popularity of the chess garden did, after a brief stutter, continue to grow. The garden held its first tournament in April of 1874. First prize was a chess set that Virchow had sent from Bavaria, of bears carved in pear wood. It went to a ten-year-old named Michael Morse, who chose to keep it at the garden rather than take home. The garden was where he intended to do his playing, after all, and that way, all the other children could have the pleasure of seeing his trophy and at the same time be reminded of his victory.

The Uyterhoevens certainly didn't object. They were gratified that their students should think of the garden with such a sense of welcome, and the following summer, to further encourage this impression, the doctor installed a second gate in the front fence, with its own path around the house so that the children could feel free to come any time without fear of disturbing either himself or Mrs. Uyterhoeven. The children happily complied, and as a consequence of such liberty, all subsequent tournament winners observed Master Morse's reasoning and bequeathed their prizes to the garden, all chess sets donated by the doctor's old friends in England and Europe. The doctor put small brass plates on each one to note the year's winner, and eventually began to store them together in the toolshed at the back of the property.

Parents began to join in playing by the third year of classes—fathers in particular, alarmed at the ease with which their sons and daughters had begun to mate and checkmate them at home. Some came early to listen in on the doctor's lessons, and then invite each other to games. Others who'd never even played before would stroll through the second gate to visit and watch, and before long they too found themselves sitting across checkerboard tables from one another. The Uyterhoevens only welcomed the company, and soon enough, chess at the chess garden had become so popular and accepted a pastime that often when Mrs. Uyterhoeven went out into her garden in the morning she would find two players already locked in combat, and the same was true at night: when she looked out her sewing-room window, she would sometimes see candlelit games still in progress.

She did not object to this. Sonja never placed much stock in the privacy of their property, and she never begrudged Gustav his chess, but neither did she hold any strong allegiance to it. Her feelings were fairly firm and simple actually, at least as the doctor registered them once in a letter to Virchow: "It is Sonja's feeling that if the children should think of playing chess nowhere else than at the garden, that is fine. What would not be fine is if, when the garden came to mind, they should think of only chess."

Gustav heartily agreed. In fact, he was probably more wary of the game than she. As integral a part of his own education as chess had been, as much as it intrigued and enchanted him, he was by the same token well aware of "potentially insalubrious effects." "Like opium,'' he once wrote Menno, ''the rooms in which [chess] takes a bolted place all eventually assume the same decrepit air. They warp and begin to sag; complexions turn pale and sallow. A stench takes hold.''

To make sure that their home never succumbed to such a fate, and to honor Sonja's wish, the Uyterhoevens took several different measures, some more deliberate than others. They lent use of the garden to every public good that arose, for recitals and lectures, readings, discussion groups, benefits, auctions, and dances, including once for the centennial celebration, when they hosted a waltz with a half-orchestra. Of course, they never tried to disturb the gamesmen for too long—they remained the property's most enduring and predominant feature—but by the same token, certain ground rules were set. With the exception of puzzle making, which took place either in the library or, on rainy days, in the attic, all games were to be played outside, in hopes that ''nature might serve to ventilate the grim deliberation of the players.'' For much the same reason, the doctor often arranged to have music playing, either live performances by local players or later, after he'd purchased his beloved phonograph, recordings. He frowned on speed chess, or ''blitz,'' and encouraged other less ravenous games as well. He acquired rare and exotic sets of checkers, pachisi, backgammon, and other pieces, including marbles and jacks, all of which took residence in the drawers of a great cherrywood dresser he stationed in the games shack, to stand stubbornly in the midst of the perpetually expanding collection of chess sets. Dice was discouraged, however, as well as any game which in his estimation relied too heavily on chance. The doctor would not allow playing cards on the property, claiming their presence made him slightly ill. All forms of wagering were strictly forbidden. In fact, no money was ever to exchange hands at the garden, even to compensate the Uyterhoevens for their hospitality. All payments were to be made strictly in kindness, although the Uyterhoevens would accept new games as well, and artwork, drink, books, food, and music.

Just as important as any of these more deliberate gestures in helping expand the garden's role in the community was its perennial function as the doctor's place of business. In part, this entailed keeping a small medical stock, to serve as a kind of local apothecary and perennial second opinion. Primarily, though, the second half of the doctor's professional career was devoted to translating the religious writings and confessions of the world's most renowned men and women of faith. Swedenborg was first and foremost, of course, but there were many others as well, whose common link was what the doctor once called "a predilection for the immanent over the eminent God; those who see that earth is not apart from heaven, but rather stuffed with it."

He had an office and stocks for this work as well, a former sitting room which would eventually serve as the library, but his preference was always to work out among the players in the garden. Where in the garden did not much matter. The doctor had several different stations, some hidden, some out in the open, and he would gravitate from one to the next depending upon the time, the light, and his mood. He had no set schedule. He might just as well be found out by the oak at midnight as under the peanut arbor at midday. The important thing, in his view, was being at liberty to work whenever the mood struck. Hunger helped, and it was always better to be slightly cold than warm in his opinion, but never tired. He napped liberally, but never slept for more than five hours at a time and, with the exception of the occasional lavish affair, rarely ate a full-fledged meal, preferring to nibble through the day and night on whatever the guests had been kind enough to bring.

However unorthodox his methods, they were certainly productive. *The Swedenborgian Reader for the Blind* was published in 1877 and, because of its obviously limited audience, garnered little notice at first. The doctor followed it with a translation of Swedenborg's diaries, however, which was well enough received to reflect attention back on the *Reader*, which was subsequently published in English in 1881 and praised as the most alluring available collection of Swedenborg's essential writings. By that time, the doctor had finished translating a collection of Meister Eckhart's Latin sermons and the dialogues of Cassian, which together with the *Reader* established him very quickly as one of the most productive, and certainly the most independent, translators of European religious literature in the country.

In the years to come, he tried to choose from more and more diverse traditions, as many as his linguistic abilities would allow. He translated works from Dutch, German, French, Latin, and Greek to begin with, but then attempted other languages as he learned them. He had an Indian scholar come live at the garden for over a year to teach him classical Sanskrit and Vedic, and help him through the sacred texts of Hinduism. He studied Japanese and Hebrew as well, and by the turn of the century had succeeded in translating over sixty volumes of then esoteric religious literature into English. These included not only two dozen highly regarded renderings of Swedenborg but also the work of a great many saints, including Bridget of Sweden, Julian of Norwich, Catherine of Genoa, Augustine of Hippo, François de Sales, Bernard of Clairvaux, Gertrude, Jeanne Chantal, and Teresa of Avila. He introduced select writings of many uncanonized figures as well, among them Jean-Pierre de Caussade, Jakob Böhme, Dionysius the Areopagite, Suso, and Jan van Ruysbroeck; and he also helped oversee the first English translations of both ancient and contemporary writings from Eastern traditions such as those of Ibn Taifal, Patañjali, Al-Ghazzali, the Bhaghavad-Gita, the Upanishads, and several other less successful, unpublished attempts at selected Mahayanan sutras.

In the course of such work, the doctor established innumerable friendships with scholars, clergymen, Sisters, and students of all different faiths and denominations, most of whom at one time or another accepted his invitation to come and stay in one of the guest rooms. As the years progressed, the Uyterhoevens' list of boarders came to boast a cultural, doctrinal, and professional variety to match that of the games collection. They hosted poets, philosophers, artists, composers, psychologists, politicians, journalists, Western and Eastern scientists, and the occasional chess master. The greatest American player of the century, the then-retired Paul Morphy, stayed at the garden the year before his death and even consented to play a match with the doctor, which was said to have come to a draw. Emerson visited on several occasions, as did Bronson Alcott, Henry James, Sr., John Hay, Annie Besant, Abner Doubleday, and a whole slew of other luminaries among the various spiritual communities of the day, including those of the Transcendentalists, naturalists, Christian Scientists, Rosicrucians, and theosophists.

As with the day-to-day guests, the Uyterhoevens would accept no remuneration from their boarders, but as ever welcomed food, games, musical recordings, and above all literature, particularly that pertaining to God and faith. All guests were invited to leave copies of those books which had most influenced them, and so, in time, the Uyterhoevens were known to have amassed not only the finest collections of games and chess sets in the country but also one of its most comprehensive libraries of comparative religion and theology. The library actually began lending and borrowing books under the direction of Miss Steele in the mid-1880s, by which time the doctor himself had become something of an attraction as well. "The spiritual pathologist of Dayton, Ohio," he was called, regarded by many as one of the country's most distinguished and compelling men of spirit, not just for the quality and variety of his translations, but for the constancy of his interest in other people's faiths, and the certainty of his own.

Of course, the doctor was not without his detractors. Those who early on had taken issue with the Uyterhoevens' religious independence looked upon the growing prominence of the garden and its proprietor as something of a menace. "An unrepentant profligate," the Pastor Thomas Sty called him in a concerned letter to a fellow squire.

> He is a sensualist and an aesthete. He revels in liquors, coffees, essences, desserts, and other rich foods. He flaunts romantic music on unsuspecting ears. He relies for his livelihood upon the charity of guests, practices medicine without a license, translates arcane and apocryphal religious material for public distribution, and is furthermore responsible for bringing an unwelcome string of outsiders into a perfectly contented community, to promote discus-

> sion on matters which did not properly admit it . . . Bad enough that a man of such extreme and epicurean tastes has chosen ours as the community that he should settle in, but to have turned his home into a temple of low, earthly delights, and to have instilled in our youth precisely the excessive, carnal appreciation of life of which he is evidently himself a victim, I would agree—these are points of no small concern, and merit continued attention.

The doctor was vaguely aware of such criticisms, and it occasionally did concern him, the possibility that he might be promulgating a religion of leisure, but for the most part he accepted that given the nature of his work, he was liable to being tarred a hedonist. A menacing hedonist, no. He made it a rule never to traffic his opinions in places where they weren't welcome, and therefore spent a great deal more time turning down opportunities to promote his beliefs than accepting them. He let stand literally dozens of offers to teach and lecture at the university level—not in medicine or pathology anymore, but special courses in translation and Christian mysticism—and in more ecumenical circles there was an even stronger hunger for what the doctor had to say on his own behalf. He was under fairly constant pressure to take an active role in a number of different new churches and spiritual outcroppings, from Blavatsky's Theosophical Society to Mary Baker Eddy's Church of Christ, Scientist, to a short-lived utopian community outside Cincinnati called Wayfarer.

He never did succumb, though, or almost never. On occasion he gave talks at the New Church, in deference and gratitude to Swedenborg, and he also delivered an admittedly obscene number of eulogies, which he didn't feel that he could refuse. Otherwise he declined all offers which might even remotely cast him in the role of proselytizer. In comparing the doctor's mission to that of the original frontier Swedenborgian, John Chapman—better known as Johnny Appleseed—William Q. Judge wrote that "Chapman went to the mountain. Gustav is a bit more like Mohammad."

The most definitive explanation for this strange diffidence may be found in a letter the doctor sent one Constance Fowler, an infrequent garden guest who had been beseeching him to join the board of overseers at a regional Rosicrucian mission. In refusal, he wrote:

> The cumulative effect of my own failures has nonetheless led me to the conclusion that it is a colossal exercise in futility, foisting ideas on people who either do not already possess them or are not on the tip of the lip of the brink of doing so. Men only understand by agreeing, by listening to things they already believe to be true. It has therefore always seemed to me that any time a person stands before an assembly of any kind to express his most heartfelt conviction, he shall find himself either preaching to a choir, banging his head against a brick wall, or being sadly, appallingly, and dangerously misconstrued.
>
> Know that it is with no small shame that I admit to such an unbecoming and cynical view, but let me therefore hasten to add another—or two—much more cheerful opinions, which I assure you I hold in equal certainty: first, that the sky is not falling and that everyone shall find what they need in time; and second, that the Truth does not require a very aggressive champion. There always have been and always will be individuals attuned to it, and who have spoken it to one another over centuries and oceans and deserts, in voices neither loud nor strident.
>
> Best for me, then, to listen and to let them, to continue going about my business here, with the assurance that this shall entail not just the faithful rendering of more helpful books, but the firm resolve on both my part and that of Mrs. Uyterhoeven to make our home as hospitable a place as possible, and always keep the gate open. In this way, whoever is tempted may feel free to enter whenever they like and, in so doing, consent to suffer our influence, which we in turn may feel free to exert with greater candor and in the manner to which I, at least, am more inclined—that is to say, one case at a time.

SEVENTEEN

THE CASE OF AMOS AVERY BLODGET

Among the books that Mrs. Conover rescued from the great Dayton flood in 1912 was one entitled *The Literary Remains of Henry James, Sr.*, which had been published in 1885 and in whose leaves someone—presumably the doctor or Mrs. Uyterhoeven—had folded two brief letters from William James, who had compiled and edited the volume during the years following his father's death in 1882. The first was a note to thank the doctor for the help he'd provided in research, in particular for sharing several of the letters that James Senior had written him over the years. The second, written from Chocorua, New Hampshire, in 1887, was less formal and ended with this brief mention of a mutual acquaintance.

> Also, if perchance you've found the time to fix the roof of the shed in which you keep your games, I know that Mr. Blodget would be much obliged if you let him know. It seems that every time it rains, he still thinks of your garden, out of concern for the shed roof, which I gather is in disrepair.

The Mr. Blodget to whom James refers had visited the chess garden in the summer of 1885 while on leave from his second year as a graduate student of philosophy and psychology at Harvard. Then just thirty years old, Amos Blodget was already something of an academic journeyman, having devoted seven postgraduate years to anthropology, archaeology, and ethnology, the last of which he'd studied in Europe with Rudolf Virchow, who had taken up the subject in the natural course of his own intellectual evolution.

In 1884 Blodget had tired of sociological pursuits and returned to Harvard's integrated studies of philosophy and psychology. There he developed an apparently unrequited admiration for William James, who was still just an assistant professor at the time, and a good five years from finishing the psychological textbook that would make him famous. James had recently founded the first American branch of the Society for Psychical Research. Blodget signed on as one of the first, youngest, and most eager members, and in the spring of 1885, just two semesters after his return, he decided to take the coming summer and fall to conduct some fieldwork on the society's behalf. He met with the members in May to inform them of his intention, which was essentially to meet and interview as broad a cross section of American mystics as he could find—channelers, diagnosticians, automatic writers, and so forth. His interest was neither to verify nor to debunk their claims, but simply to observe and perhaps see what corollaries existed in conduct, psychological type, or background among those who purported to have been touched by psychic abilities.

The society members reacted positively. They listened as he outlined his itinerary; then, when he was through, James offered just one suggestion—that he add the name of Dr. Gustav Uyterhoeven to his list.

Blodget recognized the name. Uyterhoeven was Virchow's friend, the former pathologist, and he had a vague recollection of his living somewhere in the Midwest now, running a chess shop. James confirmed it was the same Dr. Uyterhoeven. Blodget said he hadn't been aware that Dr. Uyterhoeven was himself a man of psychic ability.

James said that he wasn't, but that Blodget might be interested in meeting him nonetheless.

To be polite, Blodget took the doctor's name and address, a touch chagrined at James's apparent misunderstanding. He said that he would keep the doctor in mind but that he wasn't sure that he'd have time to consult with what he called "secondary sources." James graciously conceded, and the meeting ended soon thereafter.

Blodget's final itinerary included twenty-two "primary sources." He did not expect to get to each and every one, but given the nature of the subject matter, he thought it best to keep his schedule as simple and elastic as possible, in case he found himself enthralled by a given individual or, on the other hand, unimpressed. From the full list of potential subjects, he made only three firm appointments. The second week of May he was to meet with Andrew Jackson Davis, more popularly known as the "Poughkeepsie Seer," who since the 1840s had been delivering, in trance, successful medical diagnoses of the ill, both near and far. In July he was to stay a week with Sister Mary Elizabeth Dupré, who bore wounds in her side which smelled of flowers and who for the past two years had been speaking with the Virgin Mary at the fountain of her convent in Louisville, Kentucky. The final of Blodget's definite appointments was with a prohibitionist doctor in Indianapolis named Levi Dowling, who was said to be composing, also in trance, a fifth Gospel of Jesus Christ.

As it turned out, Blodget met with almost everyone on his list. Through the first two months of his journey he conducted interviews with no fewer than fourteen separate psychics, the majority of whom he found at least sincere. There were some obvious frauds, and one alleged channeler in Virginia Beach who, in Blodget's opinion, was merely epileptic. Still, on the whole, Blodget found himself more credulous than he would first have thought, in large part because most of the people he interviewed demonstrated nowhere near the talent, imagination, or basic intelligence that their performances would seem to require. In fact, that was the reason he spent so little time with any of them—it wasn't that he doubted their candor; it was that he'd found none of them very interesting to talk to. The sixth week of his journey, he sent the society the first formulation of this opinion:

> It is becoming increasingly clear to me that the attraction of such talents, or illness, to the lives of these people has naught to do with their human magnetism or intellect. On the contrary, I have observed an inverse relationship: that the more inarticulate and passionless the subject, the more spectacular his gift is bound to be. Likewise, the more engaging the subject, the more likely his miracle shall be of dull, more nebulous variety.

James responded, swiftly and simply. Where Blodget next received post—in Lexington, Kentucky—there was a telegraph awaiting him, from Cambridge, with just the name and address, once again, of Dr. Uyterhoeven.

This was not the first reminder of the chess garden that Blodget had encountered since embarking on his research. If it had been, Blodget might well have paid it heed. He was not far from Dayton, after all, and he did not lack for time. And yet since leaving Cambridge, he had come across the doctor's name twice more. At the outset of his trip he had been dining with Madame Blavatsky in New York, and she, without prompting, had recommended he see Dr. Uyterhoeven. Pressed, she acknowledged just the same as James that the doctor had no psychic gift, but still suggested that he might make Blodget "feel better," to which Blodget had responded, with understandable annoyance, that he felt fine.

A month after that—and just five days before James's telegram greeted him in Lexington—Blodget had come across the doctor's name again in the work of Clara Bleeker, an astrologer and automatic poet from Bluefield, West Virginia. Bleeker's psychic gift was "to make plain the instruction of the universe to man," and her method was fairly simple. She would find a setting wherever the spirit moved her—but usually a common place, such as a town square or a schoolyard—induce a trance, and then, while her son-in-law, Jergen Bantham, faithfully recorded her every word, would very slowly turn in a circle, describing everything that passed in front of her. When her trance lifted and she stopped spinning, she and her son-in-law would then apportion the transcripts into stanzas, each representing a roughly equivalent number of degrees in her rotation; then they would publish these blocks together as a poem cycle, or ''revolution,'' along with a formula to which the reader could apply his or her own birth date and place, in order to calculate which of the stanzas was appropriate to him or her on a given day, to read and appreciate as some admittedly open-ended spiritual counsel.

Mrs. Bleeker's editions were simpler in form than in theory, and compelling enough in their own way to have inspired a fairly sizable and devoted following. Blodget spent three days with her in Bluefield, chanced to witness no poetry, but did, in the course of reviewing her library, discover that one of her most highly regarded cycles had been composed in the chess garden of Dr. and Mrs. Uyterhoeven, in Dayton, Ohio.*

Blodget couldn't help remarking the coincidence. He told Mrs. Bleeker that this Dr. Uyterhoeven had been recommended to him twice already. Mrs. Bleeker asked if he was intending to go, and Blodget told her just what he'd told James and Blavatsky, that given the nature of his research and the fact that the doctor had no apparent psychic gift, he could see no reason to.

Blodget kept to his schedule, then. In fact, he had been on his way to Louisville to see about Mary Dupré, the fragrant bleeder of the Sacred Heart convent, when James's telegram met him in Lexington.

Now the fifth mention of the doctor's possible interest to him—if one included Virchow's reference two years before—James's note inspired only Blodget's defiance. That night he wrote in his journal:

*Mrs. Bleeker's garden transmission took place in April of 1881, was published the following September, and was so widely heralded that it caused a subsequent boom in the garden's popularity to which many of the regulars objected. Miss Boydd was said to have commented that ''the Bleeker book has ruined the chess life of the garden with too much traffic.''

> I will not be bullied by mere coincidence and the stubborn refusal of others to recognize my purpose into an excursion which can offer me a service which, as I can see, could just as well be served by a pipe and some port.

The following week he met with Sister Dupré and then made three more stops—one with an automatic writer who, in Blodget's opinion, had contrived her gifts as a means to wrest her husband's attention from fishing—then finally, he came to Indianapolis, his last scheduled destination and home to Dr. Levi Dowling, medium of the fifth, Aquarian Gospel of Jesus, "the Christ," as he put it.

Dowling's specifically psychic gift was for reading the akasha, which he understood to be the binding fiber of all existence, so ubiquitous, constant, and fine it would bear the impression of all history, from the flight of every dandelion seed to the fall of Rome. Dowling's commission, as assigned by a vision which had come to him three separate times in his life, was to "build a white city," which he had taken to mean that he should transcribe from the akashic record a new Gospel of the life of Jesus, the purpose being to translate Jesus' teachings into terms more appropriate to the coming Aquarian Age.

Blodget arrived in Indianapolis the first week of August, and found Dowling to be a humble individual, if somewhat pious, and far more resentful of his imposition than any of his previous subjects had been. He was reluctant to show Blodget any of his work—reluctant, at times, even to speak—but, after three days, finally came to realize that the only way to get this intruder to leave would be to show his manuscript. He allowed Blodget one day alone in his office—Dowling would not be there—then Blodget would have to go.

Blodget took full advantage. He spent twenty-four hours without a break poring over Dowling's manuscript, and once again, on the whole, he was impressed by the sincerity of the labor. The "Aquarian" interpretations of all the standard episodes he found at least distinct and well wrought.

The most intriguing aspect of Dowling's efforts, however—and the most telling, it seemed to Blodget—concerned the "silent years";

that is, the nearly two decades that passed between Jesus' conversation with the teachers in the temple, which took place when He was twelve, and the establishment of His ministry, which did not begin until He was thirty. The four canonical Gospels hadn't very much to say about them, presumably because none of the authors were there with Jesus at the time. Dowling, however, because he was reading from the akasha, was able to account for the whole of Jesus' life, beginning to end. The silent years he depicted as a period of extensive travel. Jesus is shown throughout the Middle East and India, not dispensing wisdom so much as rendering opinions about the various religions of the day.

Blodget was less impressed with these sections. He sensed a certain more pedantic departure in tone from the more trodden paths of Jesus' life, and he noted several historical inaccuracies as well—one having to do with the extent of Buddhist migration in the year 20, for instance. There was one chapter, however, the thirtieth, that did impress Blodget both in its audacity and its beauty. He was so touched, in fact, that he copied the whole thing down in his own notes:

> One day as Jesus stood beside the Ganges busy with his work, a caravan, returning from the West, drew near.
>
> 2 And one, approaching Jesus, said, We come to you just from your native land and bring unwelcome news.
>
> 3 Your father is no more on earth; your mother grieves; and none can comfort her. She wonders whether you are still alive or not; she longs to see you once again.
>
> 4 And Jesus bowed his head in silent thought; and then he wrote. Of what he wrote this is the sum:
>
> 5 My mother, noblest of womankind: a man just from my native land had brought me word that father is no longer in flesh, and that you grieve, and are disconsolate.
>
> 6 My mother, all is well; is well for father and is well for you.
>
> 7 His work in this earth-round is done, and it is nobly done.

8 In all the walks of life men cannot charge him with deceit, dishonesty, or wrong intent.

9 Here in this round he finished many heavy tasks, and he has gone from hence prepared to solve the problems of the round of the soul.

10 Our father God is with him there, as he was with him here; and there his angel guards his footsteps lest he go astray.

11 Why should you weep? Tears cannot conquer grief. There is no power in grief to mend a broken heart.

12 The plane of grief is idleness; the busy soul can never grieve; it has no time for grief.

13 When grief comes trooping through the heart, just lose yourself; plunge deep into the ministry of love, and grief is not.

14 Yours is a ministry of love, and all the world is calling out for love.

15 Then let the past go with the past; rise from the cares of carnal things and give your life to those who live.

16 And if you lose your life in serving life you will be sure to find it in the morning sun, the evening dews, in song of bird, in flowers, and in the stars of night.

17 In just a little while your problems of this earth-round will be solved; and when your sums are all worked out it will be pleasure unalloyed for you to enter wider fields of usefulness, to solve the greater problems of the soul.

In keeping with his agreement, Blodget left Indianapolis as soon as his day with the manuscript was through. He had no more appointments to keep, however, so he traveled to Chicago to visit his cousin, an architect named John Root.

The second evening of his stay they went to dinner at the home of Root's partner, Daniel Burnham, and Blodget recounted his travels at length. Burnham entertained more than a casual interest in matters of the spirit—he was a Swedenborgian, in fact—so he'd been happy to listen. The three of them had finished dessert and retired to Burnham's library when Blodget finally came to Dowling's Gospel.

Blodget showed them his copy of the thirtieth chapter, and Burnham and Root read it through together. When they were done, Burnham excused himself and then returned a moment later with a clipping from a Chicago journal, *The Canticle*, dated November 7, 1883.

It was the text of a meditation that he and Root had attended together at the New Church in Chicago. Burnham did not impose upon Blodget to read the whole thing through. He explained that it was a story of seven people's journey, by gondola, through a labyrinth of tunnels, from one side of an island, where sat a town called Afgunst, to the far side of the island, where a town called Nut was said to be. He thought Blodget might find the very end of interest, though, and so he read it aloud.

> . . . They emerged from the innards of Cupertin, and it was as Peter had said. There was no town of happy people; just a stretch of land like that from which they'd come, but that where Nut would soon arise, the river cut through wider fields, and the sea embraced the sun.

Nut, noted Burnham—the place to which the tunnels were supposed to have led the party, and that would lie amid these "wider fields"—was the Dutch word for "usefulness." Was it not curious, he asked, the similarity to the phrase in the seventeenth line of Dowling's chapter, "wider fields of usefulness"?

Blodget could not deny a twinge of intrigue. He asked who had composed the meditation, and was both stunned and strangely unsurprised when his cousin answered that the speaker had been Dr. Gustav Uyterhoeven, the chess master and spiritual pathologist of Dayton, Ohio.

Enough finally seemed enough. That night in his journal Blodget wrote:

> If it might have seemed superstitious to me before, the idea of following such tenuous and uncompelling leads to the doctor's garden, it strikes me now as equally superstitious to resist them,

just to defy the illusion of a guiding hand. Furthermore, the doctor and I now have something to discuss.

The following morning, September 5, Blodget took the train from Chicago to Dayton. His cousin had assured him he needn't announce his intention; he could simply go. He arrived in the afternoon, secured lodgings at the Beckel House and there asked directions to the Uyterhoevens' chess garden, which the clerk seemed happy to give: take Jefferson to First, go west on First to Stratford and then across the river, follow Riverview left to Salem, Salem to Holt, then Holt to Middle. The Uyterhoevens' was just up the block on the right, first house.

First of only two, Blodget discovered, distinguished from the other not only by its larger size but by a second gate in the fence marked TO THE GARDEN. Blodget entered and walked around the side path to the patio. For a moment he stood there awkwardly underneath the grape arbor. He could see several chess matches under way out in the garden, but none of the players looked up at him. There was a table of drinks set up. Blodget lifted an empty glass to his nose and smelled port, but there was no apparent bar or bottle. He lingered just a moment longer, then ducked his head inside the glass-paned doors. Just to the left he saw a second door with a small plaque on the frame. TO THE LIBRARY, it said.

"Excuse me."

Blodget turned to find a Negro gentleman standing in front of him, and who, it appeared from the knees of his pants, had just come from working in the flower beds. "Can I help you?"

Blodget was slightly startled. "I was looking for the proprietor," he said, "Dr. Uyterhoeven."

"Dr. Uyterhoeven is eating with a class at the moment." The man smiled. "Would you enjoy a game of chess while you wait?"

Blodget thought, and then accepted. He hadn't played in years, but remembered being fairly proficient—not expert, but capable of beating any challenger who was not himself a genuine player. He and his host, a Dr. Burns, walked out into the garden and there met Mrs.

Uyterhoeven, who was weeding. "Found a game and leaving me?" she said. Dr. Burns introduced Mr. Blodget with apologies and she waved them both away. Burns led him deeper into the convolution of flowers and chess games, urns and slates and small statues. Finally they came to a table underneath a grand oak tree, from whose boughs at least a dozen swings and ropes and rope chairs were hanging, like a gallery suspended in air. Without a word Burns took their chess pieces from a bin beneath the table and set them up.

Their first game lasted twelve moves, and Blodget was spared the brunt of his embarrassment by the return of Mrs. Uyterhoeven. With a complete and tactful disregard for the board, she said that she was making a trip to the house and wondered if either of them would like something to eat or drink. Dr. Burns requested tea and some butter cookies, and Blodget admitted to feeling an urge for port.

Mrs. Uyterhoeven excused herself, and Burns set up the pieces again. The second game was another drubbing, of greater length but equally certain outcome. Burns won before Blodget could manage an endgame, and he found himself in the midst of an equally desperate third match when his confusion was mercifully interrupted by the emergence from one of the garden's hidden alcoves of eight or nine small children followed by an older gentleman of an elegant but highly amused bearing, stout from age, with a straight back, long white muttonchops, and a shad-bellied, swallowtailed coat.

"Is that the doctor?" Blodget asked, and Burns nodded. The children all surrounded him as he walked with a pleasant stateliness back to the rear patio, where Blodget could just barely see their mothers waiting. The doctor exchanged a cheerful sentence or two with each, then had a brief consultation with his wife, who handed him a small tray with a plate and two drinks.

With one of the children still by his side, the doctor then started out toward their table, but it was a ways and their progress was slow. They stopped by every game and dog and cat, so by the time the doctor finally arrived, Blodget had returned his attention to his king's doom. The doctor observed the game in silence for several moves, with the tray of drinks in one hand and the little boy's hand in the other. Blodget was soon undone by the attention. He blundered badly and in three moves tipped his king. Grudgingly Burns accepted the victory and introduced the doctor, who introduced the boy, whose name was Matthew Shulters. Burns then passed some words with the doctor about the shack at the back of the garden. He said that with the tree overhead, there was no way to keep the roof shingles from rotting. The doctor listened with a friendly but unconcerned expression, and finally Burns excused himself. He thanked Blodget for his game and then returned to the flower beds along the west fence.

The doctor invited Blodget to sit again, hoisted the boy onto one of the near swings, and then took Burns's place at the table. ''I assume,'' he said, glancing cheerily at the board, ''that you did not come here to play chess, Mr. Blodget.''

''No.'' Blodget smiled.

''What brings you?''

Blodget rushed to credentials and their friend in common. ''I have been conducting some research for William James, at Harvard.''

''William.'' The doctor smiled with a distinct avuncularity. ''Yes, we exchanged some letters recently. He is well, I take it?''

''Generally.''

''And he recommended you come?''

''Twice.''

''Twice. That's very generous. And what is it that you are researching?''

Blodget sat forward. ''Psychics,'' he said. ''Mystics—as many different varieties as I can find.''

The doctor nodded. ''You've seen the library?''

''I think—in the house, you mean?''

''Yes. Do you think it will be of service?''

''Oh, but I am not here for the library,'' said Blodget.

The doctor squinted curiously. ''But I'm sure Professor James understands, there is no one at the garden of extraordinary psychic ability, aside perhaps from Oren''—he gestured toward a dog who had settled at the foot of a nearby apple tree—''who seems to know when it's time for his drops.''

"Yes, Professor James made that clear."

The doctor tilted his head thoughtfully. "Then why do you think he recommended you come?"

His manner had been perfectly pleasant, but Blodget felt suddenly uneasy. He couldn't quite tell if the doctor was extending him a friendly hand or was preparing to peel him like an onion.

"Actually, I am not quite sure," he said. "To be frank, I am not here strictly speaking because of Professor James's recommendation. I am here because two nights ago I was having dinner with a cousin of mine in Chicago, John Root, and his architectural partner, and they happened to show me a meditation that you delivered a few years ago in Urbana. You were recounting a story from your youth, of a boatman bringing the people of one town through a mountain—"

"Menno's story."

"If it is about the boatman."

There was a pause as they looked at each other expectantly; then Blodget reached into his bag and took out his journal. "Well, you see, just before hearing this story I had come from meeting with a gentleman named Levi Dowling. Are you familiar with his work?"

The doctor shook his head.

"Yes. Well, he is at work at the moment on a fifth Gospel, which he claims to be reading from the akasha. Are you familiar with the akasha?"

The doctor nodded. "I believe it's mentioned in the Bhaghavad-Gita, as the subtlest of the five elements which the Hindus understand to comprise existence."

Blodget was suitably impressed. "Well, that would make sense," he said. "I was not aware that there were five, but in any case I suppose you know, then, that this element is considered to be very impressionable, so much so that it bears all history on its face, and that this history is legible to certain select individuals, of which Mr. Dowling claims to be an example."

"And he has chosen to translate a new Gospel," the doctor surmised.

"Exactly," said Blodget excitedly, "and because he is reading it from the akasha, you see, he has included all of Jesus' life. Not just the birth and the ministry, but the youth as well, and education.'' Blodget looked to see if the doctor found this at all intriguing, but the doctor merely nodded for him to come along.

''Well, there is one particular passage, when Jesus is a young man teaching in India. It isn't very long—'' Blodget opened his notebook and flipped to where he'd copied the chapter from Dowling's manuscript. ''Do you mind my reading aloud?''

The doctor shook his head, and so Blodget began. He read the entire chapter, and the doctor listened with encouraging attention. When Blodget finished, the doctor asked for the notebook, to read the passage himself, which he did more slowly. Then when he was through, he reached out with his cane and tapped the seat of the young boy on the swing, who'd been sitting patiently. ''Matthew.'' The doctor took a pen and paper from his pocket. ''Would you be so kind as to copy down the story which Mr. Blodget has brought for us?''

''Oh, I would be happy to myself,'' Blodget offered, as the child seemed much too young for such an assignment, but the doctor seemed to prefer that Matthew try. He promised the boy that he could play with the armored soldiers when he was done, which sparked quick obedience. Matthew took the work straight over to the table on the other side of the tree and started his transcription.

The doctor turned his chair slightly, and he and Blodget sat in silence watching Matthew write. They sat for close to a minute, and then finally the doctor spoke. ''So you have come here because of the phrase, 'wider fields of usefulness'?''

''Yes,'' said Blodget.

''And did you want to know if I have ever read the phrase elsewhere myself?''

''I would be interested to know.''

The doctor began tapping his finger on the chess table in rhythm with his logic. ''Because if I have read it elsewhere and I am quoting it from prior knowledge, the possibility exists that Mr. Dowling is doing the same?''

''The possibility exists.''

"And if Mr. Dowling's writing were shown to contain phrases we could find elsewhere, in more mediated prose, would that indicate to you that he was not therefore reading from the akasha?"

Blodget was slightly taken aback by the precision of the doctor's question, but rallied. "I do not think that it *proves* that he was not reading from the akasha, but it provides another possible explanation, which I shouldn't think impugns Dr. Dowling's integrity."

"Oh, I don't think that you are impugning his integrity, Mr. Blodget. I am only trying to understand why you are here."

The doctor then fell silent. He looked across at the boy copying from the notebook, and Blodget felt exposed. "You should understand, Dr. Uyterhoeven, I am only gathering information. It is not my interest to determine the legitimacy of these psychic phenomena, but surely you can see, the question of authenticity does bear some relevance."

The doctor kept looking at the boy, but his expression was deliberative; he literally seemed to be chewing on something, with his front teeth. "Are you a Christian, Mr. Blodget?"

Blodget sat up almost as if he'd been offended, though he wasn't sure why. "I was raised a Christian," he said sharply, "but whether or not I now believe that Christ is the son of God, I certainly recognize that Jesus the Nazarene was a source of much wisdom—or that the words attributed to him are wise, and I would be interested to hear more of those words, and more about his life, just as I would want to know more about the lives of Gautama, or Mohammad, or Moses."

The doctor nodded but did not turn his head. "Your answer is no, then."

"Yes, my answer is no."

"How are you coming, Matthew?" the doctor called.

Matthew that instant took up his pen and pages and brought them over for the doctor to see. "Very good. Now, as one last favor, would you be kind enough to take your copy over to Mrs. Uyterhoeven." Matthew looked at him with just a hint of impatience. "Then the soldiers," the doctor assured, and off the boy went.

The doctor watched him all the way until he reached the patio, then turned his chair to face Blodget. ''Would you say that you were an atheist, Mr. Blodget?''

Blodget's back curled. ''Do I appear to be an atheist, Dr. Uyterhoeven?''

The doctor smiled. ''You appear to me to be someone who might call himself an atheist. Do you?''

Blodget glared at the doctor with what he hoped was an expression of defiance. ''With due respect,'' he said, ''yes, I do.''

The doctor sat back in his chair and thought openly in front of his guest, and patiently, occasionally meeting his eye, expressing continued welcome but no inclination yet to speak. Blodget sipped his port, and had some bites of the cheese that Mrs. Uyterhoeven had left on Burns's cookie dish—a Stilton.

At length Matthew emerged from the house again and returned directly to their table. ''Soldiers,'' said the boy.

''Mr. Blodget''—the doctor turned to him—''would you like to escort Matthew to the shed? He knows where.''

Blodget hadn't particularly wanted to, but Matthew took his hand and he didn't feel that he could refuse. He stood up and was led to the very edge of the garden, where a small shed stood shrouded by willow leaves. Beyond was a tangle of overgrown shrubs and volunteers.

Matthew waited for Blodget to open the door, but rushed in before him like a dog and pointed to the set he wanted. Blodget took it down and handed it to the boy. Inside was a fearsome set of Arthurian knights in armor, all made of lead. Matthew picked five, handed the box back to Blodget, and then left the shack.

Blodget remained. The space inside was no larger than a walk-in closet, but it was entirely taken up by games, filling the shelves and stacked on the floor. Directly across from him was a large cherrywood dresser, with a hinged, rectangular mirror returning his reflection. There were two freestanding drawers on either side. One was open, and he could see stones inside, found on walks and brought back here, to keep. He pulled open the other and found seashells, and down below the drawers were full of stray pieces, standing figures and checkers. One was filled entirely with dice, and another with marbles. All along the walls were nothing but boards and sets, stacked on sagging shelves. There may have been two hundred altogether, but the most valuable seemed to be distinguished by small brass plates which bore the names and years of tournament champions. Blodget came across sets from Bavaria, Egypt, Korea, India, and China, with boards of all kinds—rosewood, walnut, sycamore, pear wood, leather, stained glass, stoneware, opaline, and moss agate. He found pieces formed from tortoiseshell and mother-of-pearl, rock crystal, alabaster, colored marble, ivory, horn, and some from Königsburg which were made of clear and cloudy amber.

Dr. Burns had been right about the roof, thought Blodget. Most of the sets were much too valuable to be housed beneath rotting shingles. He found a Tibetan board on a top shelf, one of several prizes won by William Deforest, and was ready to open it when it occurred to him that he was probably taking longer than was appropriate, so he took the Tibetan board with him, to see it better in the light.

The doctor was in the same position as Blodget had left him, and Matthew was down among the oak tree roots playing with the armored pieces. The doctor was saying something to the boy, but stopped when Blodget sat down.

Blodget showed him the board he'd taken. ''Do you mind if I look?''

The doctor turned his chair and glanced approvingly at his choice. ''You can touch them, too.''

Blodget removed the pieces from their pouches, and as he began setting them in their places, the doctor spoke.

''You should understand, Mr. Blodget, that one thing I have come to trust is that people find what they are looking for, what they believe on some level that they either need or deserve. I think this is proven moment to moment, so I take it as more than mere happenstance that you are here. I take it as a measure of your will, which honors us and obliges me to be honest.''

Blodget looked up from the Tibetan pieces to find the doctor's eyes directly upon him. ''Please.''

"Well. Something else I've come to trust is that truth is provided in precisely the measure and form appropriate to each of us individually. I find, moreover, that the disposition of truth is not, as it may sometimes seem, to withdraw and then appear. That is a function of our concentration. The disposition of truth is to remain constant. That way, when a man chooses to look directly at whatever happens to be surrounding him—whatever it may be—he will find the truth there, waiting. Am I clear?"

"I'm not sure."

The doctor considered. "You may continue looking at the pieces," he said. Blodget wasn't sure if he should, but the doctor waited for him to do so before he continued.

"Understand, I take no issue with your psychics, if they are sincere. For those among us who can read history from the akasha, it is fine for them to do so. For those among us who can feel unfamiliar spirits enter their bodies, I'd hope that they would welcome those spirits, and hear them, or transmit them in whatever way.

"For those of us who cannot, however—and I am assuming that you cannot, Mr. Blodget—I think we do better to address our attention to what is apparent to us; that we not try looking through things or behind things, I mean, or to see things we cannot see, or hear things that we cannot hear. I would think that in such vain attempts we only express our envy."

"Doctor." Blodget hesitated. "If I understand your implication, let me assure you, you cannot imagine how little I envy these psychics their gifts—"

The doctor closed his eyes and raised his hand. "Mr. Blodget, you have spent the last several months, if I understand you correctly, interviewing and observing people who have in common only the fact that they claim to experience things of which you have no firsthand knowledge. Furthermore, you are only here now, or so you have led me to believe, because you want to determine the legitimacy, or illegitimacy, of a Gospel whose chief point of interest to you is that it purports to fill what you perceive as gaps in the New Testament. Is this not so?"

"Very well."

"Do you not think it would be fair to say that you have demonstrated, at least in these ways, an interest in things of which you feel you have been deprived?"

"Deprived?"

"Deprived of the ability to talk with spirits; deprived of the ability to read the akasha; deprived of information regarding Jesus' life. Why do you think you are so interested in such things?"

Blodget fumbled a moment. "I suppose for the very reason you say, Doctor. They are mysterious. I shouldn't think one would have to defend one's interest in mystery."

"No, that's true. But perhaps one should be made to defend one's lack of interest in what's manifest." The doctor's tone then changed, became more musing and accelerated: "What's so interesting to me, Mr. Blodget, is that if you did not call yourself such an atheist, I'd be tempted to say that all you thought about was God. I'd say you were preoccupied with God, and that you wanted desperately to know what He was thinking, but that your curiosity has been stymied by the notion—who knows where it came from—that He is playing some game of hide-and-seek with you, that He is withholding His thoughts from you, in which case I would say to you—if you did not call yourself an atheist—that He is not. He is making himself very clear, Mr. Blodget, and is simply waiting for you to pay attention."

"You're not speaking of the Bible?"

"No, I am not speaking of the Bible." The doctor paused. "Not yet—but let's not go leaping to conclusions. Now, suppose you were not an atheist. Suppose, hypothetically speaking, you believed that there was one light and life which makes this so, this life in which we share, some infinite thing to our finite thing, some eternal thing to our temporal thing. Such as we bound creatures could possibly fathom the mind of such an eternal and infinite being, what would you expect us to find characteristic of it?"

"Of its mind?"

"Yes, such as we could grasp its wisdom."

"I don't know, Doctor."

"Well, I would suggest that whatever thought we could possibly perceive, or possibly share, with this infinite and eternal Being, would at the very least have to be true. Does that seem fair?"

"I suppose."

"But not just true. Not just true in the way it's true that the President's name is Cleveland, but true in a suitably divine way, by which I mean never-not-true but constantly true, and everywhere true. True not just to you but to Matthew and to me, and not just true to us today but true yesterday and tomorrow and the next day and thereafter. Wouldn't you think?"

"I suppose, Doctor, but I would also think that that was a tall order."

"Yes, a very tall order, but not one which cannot be filled. In fact, I would suggest to you a very simple possibility, that this"—the doctor looked around him and gestured generally to indicate the day—"this ongoing moment which conserves our existence might well be thought of as an expression of God's thought, such as we could fathom it. At least it appears to satisfy our criteria: it is apparently true." He rapped his knuckles on the table. "As it was yesterday, as it will be tomorrow. And not just to me but to you, and to Matthew as well. Yes?"

"Very well."

"Yes, and one of the things I would point out about the present moment and everything it contains is that you and I have ample means to appreciate it, Mr. Blodget."

There was a pause. Blodget and the doctor looked at each other, as affectionate combatants.

"And your point?"

"My point is that if you were not an atheist, Mr. Blodget, and if, therefore, you were to entertain the idea that the present moment is a faithful, if extremely limited, expression of God's thought, then you would not be inclined to try looking through it or around it or behind it. If you believed that this moment was an idea that God had been kind enough to share with you, you would attempt to comprehend it directly, as you have been given every opportunity to do."

Blodget looked at the doctor questioningly.

''You would listen to it, taste it, smell it, feel it, do whatever you could to occupy it.''

''Ah, but you make that sound like an easy thing, Doctor, which it is not.''

''Good heavens, no. Ask them.'' He pointed at the Tibetan pieces. ''Not an easy thing in the least, but still worth the effort, I would think, if there's a chance of grasping some divine wisdom there. Better to take the bull by the horns than wait for some visitation, or go asking someone else what's behind the curtain—that's what I am saying.

''And I say the same with regard to your interest in this Dowling Gospel. Or I would if you were a Christian, because you see, if you were a Christian—'' The doctor winked at Blodget, reached into his side pocket and took out a small black Bible, which he placed on the table beside Blodget's notebook. ''If you were a Christian, Mr. Blodget—which I understand that you are not, but if you were, hypothetically speaking—you would hold in faith that the Bible, including the New Testament, is God's word, and being God's word, merits the same degree of reverence and attention that one would apply to the moment, if he were not an atheist. That is to say that if you were a Christian, Mr. Blodget, you would most likely try to look at the New Testament directly—not through it or behind it or between the lines. You would not, for instance, travel all the way from Cambridge to Indiana to read parts that aren't included in your version. You would read the parts that *are* included—most of them four times over—and then it would become very clear to you, I think, that this is not a biography.'' He set his hand on the Bible. ''It is not the story of a young man who wrote his mother a letter from the Ganges, no matter how lovely that letter might be. The New Testament is a story about God becoming man in Christ, and what happens then. And if, as a Christian, you were to read this story with an eye toward its divine wisdom—that is, a wisdom which must be as pertinent and true and constant as the present moment—you might not be surprised to find that the New Testament and the present moment are actually expressing the very same thing: the same as happens here in God's word''—

he patted the Bible—"happens here in God's thought." He opened his hand to the day, then looked at Blodget expectantly.

"And what is that?"

The doctor lowered his hand. "Oh, Mr. Blodget, you know very well what happens. What happens when God becomes man, through Christ, is that He is crucified. He is crucified on Golgotha. And He is crucified here as we speak—in you, in me, in Matthew, and in this tree."

"But I am afraid I don't see that, Doctor."

Dr. Uyterhoeven nodded. "Well, I'll grant it may not be as obvious a notion, or as popular, but I promise you, if you look directly, you will see—" He leaned forward on his elbow and held up his hand between them, as if to display it. "In order that we may live, that we may have this experience, the Infinite has clearly taken a very finite, very limited form, a form which places such a tight yoke on its infinitude that it apparently must expend its captive energy by scrolling it out, so to speak, through time." The doctor closed his hand. "Or we may choose to look at it the other way: that Eternity has entered the moment—it has done this for our sake—but that this moment places such constraint upon Eternity that it likewise must expend its captive energy by spilling off this vast expanse of space."

The doctor smiled. "Either way, the same obtains for everything you'll ever know of this life, Mr. Blodget, everything you can touch and taste and smell—everything you can confirm—casts an otherwise infinite and eternal being, God, into a very limited, very fleeting and fatal existence. But such is man, alas. Such is our lot. Such is your lot, Mr. Blodget, that you should only ever seem to be where these vast planes of time and space intersect, here and now. That intersection would seem to comprise your existence, I know. It would seem to sustain you and distinguish you, but it also literally crucifies what is divine in you. Understand that much: man crucifies his Lord. He cannot help it. It is his nature, for man *is* his Lord crucified, as is this day, as is the whole of this domain—an infinite and eternal being, wrested into a finite, momentary world and pinned there, to live and die, over and over again.

"And if that sounds bleak to you, Mr. Blodget, or lugubrious, take heart. Think of it as a Christian, for you see, when a Christian observes the crucifixion—either in the Word, in church, or, if he should be so lucky, in the moment that contains him—he sees something beautiful, and blessed and necessary and sanctifying, for there on the cross he recognizes God, and there on the cross God recognizes him. That cross—which you may think of as wooden, or you may see as clear as day, right here—this is the moment we share with our Lord. It is the window through which God and man can see and understand each other. And so that is where the forgiveness begins, Mr. Blodget, and the redemption, and the ascension into heaven—all these so-called mysteries of faith: in empathy, in the fact that God has become man—and obviously continues to do so or we would not be here—and as He becomes man, He continues to recognize the nature of our condition, through Christ. He continues to see that we are crucified here, and we continue to see that He is crucified here as well. So we are understood, so we are welcomed to Him, so we are forgiven."

The doctor lowered his left arm and removed his right hand from the Bible. His voice had been approaching a fevered pitch, but now he calmed himself. He put both hands on Blodget's notebook and closed it. "But I go on. You are not a Christian, and you do not believe in God, whatever that may mean." With a confidential grin he slid the notebook across the table to his guest. "Have you a place to sleep?"

"I do, at the Beckel House." Blodget took his notebook and put it into his bag.

"You'll give my best to Professor James, then?" The doctor stood up.

"I will." Blodget stood up to shake the doctor's hand, much sooner than he'd expected to.

"You may stay as long as you like. I simply have a lesson I need to get to."

"Another lesson?"

"I'm afraid so, but this time I am the pupil." The doctor stood back and bowed. "*Arigato*, Mr. Blodget." Then he turned to Matthew and did the same—"*Arigato, Shulters-san*"—but the boy was so intent upon his pieces, he did not even see the doctor leave.

EIGHTEEN

THE FAREWELL PARTY

Hope Gray was two months pregnant with her second child when she learned the doctor had decided to leave Dayton in the summer of 1900. Her son Henry first mentioned something about it as they were walking home from one of his lessons at the garden. He'd said the doctor was getting ready to go to the Antipodes soon, but Hope hadn't given it much thought until the following week. She'd gone to pick up Henry again, and there was a sign on the inside gate. It read:

THE GARDEN WILL BE CLOSED
FROM AUGUST 28–30,
IN PREPARATION FOR THE DOCTOR'S
SEARCH FOR THE ANTIPODES

The words frightened her, actually. Hope had been going to the garden since she herself was five years old, and never once could she remember its ever being closed. She found Mr. Patterson and Miss Steele out beneath the chestnut tree and asked if they knew anything about the sign on the gate, so they had been the ones to tell her.

Hope was stunned. She asked when the doctor was leaving and

Mr. Patterson told her—September 3. She asked how long he was going to be away, and she was hoping Mr. Patterson would say that he'd be back by spring—her child was due in February—but Mr. Patterson said he didn't know. He supposed it would depend on the British and the Boers. But what about a farewell party? Hope asked. Was there anything she could do? She looked at Miss Steele, but Miss Steele only shook her head. There wasn't going to be a farewell party, she said. The doctor had forbidden it. She said Hope needn't worry too much, though. He had promised to write.

Hope was not consoled. She excused herself, numb, and when Henry emerged from his class, she didn't even go to say hello to the doctor. She saw Mrs. Uyterhoeven just as she and Henry were leaving, though. She was coming up the street with a basket of planting stakes, and for the first time Hope could ever remember, she felt angry at Mrs. Uyterhoeven. How could she? was all she could think. How could she let him go?

It took several days for the initial shock to wear off, but even then Hope still felt a lingering frustration over the fact that no formal observance had been planned. She understood why the doctor might not want an open discussion on the subject, for the children's sake, but that was no reason his friends should be deprived of the opportunity to acknowledge his leaving, if only to try to make sense of it. She'd half expected that someone closer to the doctor might step forward and hold a dinner, but no one did, so she decided to offer herself. She sent invitations to two dozen of the garden's most regular patrons—not people she would normally have gathered in her home, but who she assumed must feel as she did, a certain forsakenness at the doctor's going. She chose the night of the twenty-eighth, the first evening the garden would be closed.

The last days of August were treated, deliberately, no differently than most others at the garden. The doctor continued his lessons with the children, and the guests came to play chess, to talk, and to read. Then, on the twenty-eighth, the garden closed, just as the sign had promised. No child or adult entered. Some passed by to see—the gate had to be roped shut since there never was a lock. Then near 7:00, all the most loyal patrons of the chess garden made their way to Mr. and Mrs. Gray's for dinner.

The evening started out a sad and awkward affair, absent precisely the ease and comfort which it had been conceived to commemorate. Wine had helped some, and then dinner, but the conversation remained spare and trivial. The guests offered toasts, thanked their hostess, and wished the doctor well, but without quite the special moment that Hope had hoped for.

Most of the company left soon after dessert. Hope went to check on Henry, and when she returned, she found just six guests remaining in the living room, including her husband, Paul, who hadn't said a word all night. There were Mr. Patterson, Captain Stivers, Dr. Thomas, Mrs. Conover, and Miss Steele, who had come out before dessert to lie down on the chaise.

As Hope joined them, Captain Stivers was quizzing Mr. Patterson about the logistics of the doctor's trip—when he was leaving exactly and how he was getting there. Mr. Thomas asked who was administering the camps, which led to the matter of Milner's policy and then the war in general. Preposterous, Mrs. Conover said, fighting about gold. But it wasn't just gold, Mr. Patterson clarified. It was the Boers being stubborn, not caring to join the twentieth century, and the British having to drag them, kicking and screaming.

Hope sat and listened, quietly and politely dismayed. Here were the doctor's closest friends, all sitting in her own living room because the garden was closed—closed!—and all they could do was discuss the madness of the war. Captain Stivers mentioned something about British entrepreneurs selling arms to the Boers, and finally Hope couldn't contain herself anymore. For the first time since dinner she sat up and spoke. "But do we think the doctor is even well enough?"

Silence fell as all the company's eyes dropped to the floor. No one answered, so she turned the question to Dr. Thomas directly. "Do you, Dr. Thomas?"

Dr. Thomas shrugged. "Dr. Uyterhoeven sees to himself."

"But he *is* very old," Hope said. "Does anyone know how old?"

"Seventy-seven," Mrs. Conover answered. "His birthday just passed."

"*Seventy-seven,*" Hope repeated. "Do we really think that such an old man should be going so far, with all the heat and pestilence?" She looked at them. "It just doesn't make sense. You've all said so yourselves—it's not as if the Boers are very appealing, or the British."

At that moment, Reverend McKinney, the reverend from the New Church in Urbana, entered from the kitchen with two mugs of tea. Odd little man, thought Hope. He always seemed too young to her to be a reverend, and too nervous. He sat down beside Miss Steele on the chaise, and as she accepted one of the mugs, she seemed to take life from the vapors. With her eyes still closed, she turned in Hope's direction. "A doctor doesn't need to choose sides in order to help."

Hope's face flushed. "Oh, help!" she nearly cursed the word. "He helps enough here. He's the one who makes your tea, isn't he? He's the one who teaches the children. And what about all the books? Isn't that help?"

"No one is saying he doesn't help." Mrs. Conover touched Hope's hand to calm her, and she felt very young all of a sudden. Only the reverend was looking at her. The way his eyes filled out his glasses, he looked almost like a little owl. "Well, have you spoken to the doctor about it?" she asked.

"About leaving?" McKinney's head shivered, no.

"Well, but doesn't it seem extreme to you?"

"It seems—yes, I suppose." He cleared his throat. "Extreme."

"Well, do you have any idea why the doctor might be doing such a thing?"

McKinney leaned forward with his arms on his knees, trying unsuccessfully to appear at ease. "Well, I'm not sure I've known the doctor long enough to say, but I can see how Miss Steele might have a point—I mean, in that it might be difficult for someone like the doctor ever to be sure he was doing enough. At least I could understand if he felt a certain ambivalence."

"Ambivalence?" Hope sat up. "How can you even say that? The

doctor isn't ambivalent. I don't think I've ever met a man who's more certain of what he thinks, or more at peace with his faith."

The reverend looked back at her, startled. He seemed to have offended his hostess. He wasn't sure how and he certainly hadn't meant to, but he was an intelligent man and not willing to sacrifice a misapprehension for the sake of mere cordiality. His head shivered again, to ready him to speak. "I'm not sure I see the connection."

"Well, I'm just saying it doesn't seem to me that going to South Africa is the sort of thing an *ambivalent* person would do."

All eyes turned back to McKinney. "Well, that's true," he nodded. "But the ambivalence I was referring to wasn't about what the doctor believes. The ambivalence I was speaking of had to do with the tension that exists for all of us, in all our lives, between learning to accept things as they are but also wanting to help and do good, and how the two can sometimes seem at odds."

Hope shook her head stubbornly. "I don't understand what you mean."

He looked around the circle of guests to see if they shared their hostess's interest in his opinion. Mr. Patterson apparently did not. He stood up and went over to the mantel to fill his pipe, but the others sat up expectantly; Captain Stivers even turned his ear horn directly toward the reverend.

"Well"—McKinney leaned slightly toward the mouth of the horn—"it's just something that the doctor and I spoke about once—about how it is that when one looks around at the world and sees the suffering and the misery, one wants to help, of course, out of compassion, but that one is also advised, in his faith, to try to take a more detached, more reflective view sometimes—a view of things as they are, and an acceptance that all creation is constantly changing, and living and dying, and that this is as it should be. And so what the doctor and I discussed was the problem of how one reconciled these . . . impulses, I guess one would say: the one which strives to mitigate the suffering in the world and the other which strives to see that all creation is perfect, as is." The reverend paused.

"And?" said Hope. "What did the doctor say?"

"Well," the reverend cleared his throat again, "the general wisdom, I think, is that these impulses actually approach one another. Perfect compassion will eventually learn perfect detachment and acceptance; and conversely, perfect detachment will learn compassion. This is what the doctor said. For practical purposes, until one reaches that point one just has to be careful, that is all—to be aware that acceptance can lead to idleness, and also that certain types of compassion can breed selfishness, or self-importance, and therefore misunderstanding."

The seated company all nodded at this faintly, except for Hope. "So what does this have to do with the doctor's going to South Africa?"

All eyes turned back to the reverend again, except for Miss Steele's, whose waited approvingly beneath her lids. "Well, I think we can all agree," said the reverend, "the doctor is more of a contemplative. He comes to his faith by way of acceptance, through being able to see that what is happening is part of something else which is fine and good and knows what's best. I think clearly that is the gift he brings, and what he attempts to cultivate in everyone who comes to the garden.

"But still I think there is always the fear, for someone who is so disposed—that he might therefore be liable to look at some injustice or some suffering and let it be because he trusts that it's nature's course, whatever it is, and needs to be happening—I'm not saying the doctor would ever actually do that—but I think he has that fear, or that wariness. And given that—" The reverend paused a moment at the precipice of his rationalization, and then dove. "Given that, isn't it possible that such a man, a man like Dr. Uyterhoeven, who knows his own particular strengths and nonstrengths, and also being a doctor, which is obviously so helpful and compassionate—wouldn't it be possible that on occasion such a man might look around at his garden and instead of seeing the children and the good use to which he'd put his energies—the truly good use, certainly—that instead he might look around and perceive only his own idleness? Mightn't he worry that he is ignoring the greater problems of the world—the sickness and disease and wars taking place—all because he'd been lucky enough to find his heaven and wanted to stay there?''

There was silence as all considered the reverend's suggestion. Much of it sounded reasonable, but Hope still wasn't entirely convinced. ''So you're saying he's going away in order to ease his conscience?''

McKinney looked at her blankly. ''I don't know.''

Hope turned to Mr. Patterson, who was in a cloud of blue smoke over by the mantel. ''Does it make sense to you, Mr. Patterson, what the reverend says?''

Mr. Patterson looked back at them all. He took a moment to repack his pipe before returning to the circle. Then he stood before them as if he were about to make a toast. ''I'm sure the doctor would be moved by your anxiousness for his well-being, Mrs. Gray, and perhaps what the reverend says does hold some truth, though it is a matter of the doctor's conscience, which he has not shared with me. But I think your care for him might have blinded you to one simple fact—''

''Mr. Patterson,'' Miss Steele spoke up with censure, but Patterson continued.

''Obviously the doctor does not go all the way to South Africa intending to return.''

He looked down at each of them, and they in turn looked up at him—all but Miss Steele, whose breast fell slightly from disappointment, slightly from relief, and Captain Stivers, who hadn't heard. He whispered to Mrs. Conover, ''What did he say?''

Mr. Patterson leaned over and spoke into the captain's ear horn. ''I said that the doctor won't be coming back. He is an elephant, returning to his burial grounds.''

Miss Steele's eyebrows lifted. ''Or birthplace.''

Hope looked up at Paul, and for the first time since she'd seen the sign on the garden gate, she considered Mrs. Uyterhoeven. Not Henry, and not the unborn child in her womb. And when everyone stood to say good night and thank her for her kindness, which was not long after Mr. Patterson's announcement, still she thought of Mrs.

Uyterhoeven. She thought of Mrs. Uyterhoeven as she and Paul cleaned up, and then as she lay next to him in bed, crying—she thought of the doctor and his wife alone in the garden, and wondered if this horrible compassion of hers would ever learn acceptance.

PART SEVEN

The Last Two Letters

NINETEEN

TEVERIN

The doctor's eleventh letter was read in the garden on June 30, a Sunday evening. No other pieces had appeared on the goatskin board to herald it.

The Eleventh Letter

May 22, 1901

Dear Sonja,

You will have to forgive me, but there remain certain elements at the outset of what I have to tell you this evening which are not yet clear to me. I hope they shall grow more so as I write. If not, not—but such as I can recall the series of events which have led me to my present circumstance, they begin the morning I awoke on the bridge above the chasm of dice.

There was a chill in the air of which the night before had seemed to hold no promise, and my first thought was of how quickly the seasons turn. I hadn't minded, though, for my second thought—or more a feeling, actually—was of great great, and what I even then recognised as an unwarranted, contentment. My pursuit of the dice had served me well, it seemed. Though they'd failed to lead me to John William—and such was my most firm conviction—they had given me something better; in just a single planetary semi-turn, they had conferred to me their mood exactly, of carefree vigour. The cold? So much the better to feel my lungs, I thought. And John William? John Who? was my feeling. What use had I for John William and his dreadful little ruin. I awoke with the caterpillar's confidence that if I simply went about my business in good and humble faith, I'd be ready for change whenever change should come, whatever change might bring.

I wanted to write you this. I wanted to share with you the peace of mind to which I had awakened, so I turned up my collar and made my way from the bridge. My bicycle was right where I had left it, if a bit rusted from dew, but perfectly serviceable. I pedaled back to Bumbershoot, braced by the morning frost, and at the same pub where the dice had so fortuitously interceded upon my thinking the day before—or so I thought—I found myself the very same table and had taken out my book to write you, to add my impressions to those which I recalled having written you before, of following the dice to the chasm and sitting on the bridge above them. Yet when I flipped to the last entry of my notebook I found no such description. Only the fray of torn pages.

But I *have* written you of the dice chasm, have I not? Of sitting at the pub and of the dice striking the platform—I told you that, I'm sure. And of my following them on bicycle out into the countryside until they fell into a ravine filled with thousands and thousands of other dice; and how I went out on the rope bridge above them and the sound wafting up was like the flapping of angels' wings. I know I have written you this, but it didn't make sense to me, for after the flapping wings I'd drifted off, and then it was the night, and then it was the morning I awoke to the chill and to my peace of mind. So I've no idea *where* I could have written you, but still I am certain I have—and I suppose you all know the truth better than I—but there at the pub I began rummaging through my coat and trousers to see if these pages were somewhere else on my person. I started checking all my pockets, and there in the right-hand pocket of my coat I did feel a strange piece of paper. I pulled it out, fully expecting that it would be my account of the dice and chasm and so forth, but it was not this. It was my map.

Strange, I thought—I don't keep my map in my hands pocket. I keep it in my inside breast pocket, where I know it will be safe. Still, I opened it, and there, to my utter bewilderment, saw that someone had written directions on it: leading from the bridge above the dice to a place in the very middle of the Antipodes, an X, next to which there appeared a most unexpected, most thrilling and disturbing word: "Teverin."

Teverin. Eugene's nemesis. Teverin. Keeper of the Sayyid Umr Ben Abd's nightmare. Father of the conspiracy. Teverin. And here, directions to him.

But who could have done this, I wondered. I didn't recognise the handwriting, though it was very explicit and precise, even suggesting what forms of transportation I might use in getting there, with little drawings. I wanted to see them closer, to see if there might be some clue, and so again I began rummaging through my clothing, this time for my reading glasses, and again was stopped by an unfamiliar find, what felt like two small stones in my right-hand breast pocket now. I took them out to see, and found they were not stones at all but a most extraordinary pair of jewels: a diamond and a silver one, very much like the ones I'd seen on the altar girl's dish in her hideout, like the ones the sheik had shown me and the chancellor had kissed on the road from Eugene's rook. In *my* pocket! But where had they come from? Was it the person who'd written on my map, I wondered. And was I to deliver them to Teverin? Was that the implication? I didn't understand. Who would ask this of me, and why couldn't I remember?—

And that is when it came to me—what John Edward had said to me in the confessional. He'd said that if I ever did meet his brother, John William, the only way I'd know is if I couldn't remember. I looked back at the map, and then at these two jewels. The sneak! This was John William's handwriting—I was certain of it. The scoundrel! Well, I shall not do it, I thought. I shan't do his bidding. No, I put the jewels back into my pocket. "I shall send them to the garden" is what I thought. That will teach him, the little bandit.

Well, needless to say—needless in the fact that you do not find these jewels enclosed in my envelope—I was on the road to Teverin's by mid-afternoon. It took me one fretful breakfast to realise that whatever peace of mind I had managed to glean from the dice had been utterly spoiled, and that sending these jewels to you would not do, not knowing so little of their significance.

I'd no trouble following the directions. I travelled to Chimeroo by checkers, where I made a raft of four wooden counters which carried me along the Kyrie River all the way to the Scrimshaw Valley. There, another team of checkers was kind enough to carry me to the ruins of a town called Hlique, which stands at the edge of the forest of Corwin. From there I made my way, as the map pictured, by cane and by ear. What this meant I didn't quite know till I was well inside the woods. The trail was marked at first by little scars and ribbons upon the trees, but as I entered deeper, there was music. I heard faint melodies, and when I followed, they led me to trees which had been carved to whistle like flutes, to a little mill in a brook which strummed a zither as it turned, to drumskins stretched beneath the dewdrops of a sweet gum. They were all throughout the wood, these musical instruments, all playing gently as the forest went about its patient day, and I followed them until at length I came upon a small log cabin.

It was sitting there, alone in the wild. There was one door and on every other side a single window, each of which was boarded shut. The roof was thatched and the stone chimney had been stuffed with sticks and mud. I went to the door, whose frame had likewise been packed with mud to seal it tight. A small stone was plugging a hole near the latch, and I was just about to remove it to see if I could look inside, when in the distance I heard wind chimes.

They were coming from around a bramble thicket, and I noticed a path traced by twine, strung from tree to tree. I followed it, not far, and it led me to a second cabin, evidently built by the same hand as the first, though this one was larger, with two windows to a side and a third higher up at the front and back, to light a lofted space. An incandescent gold was glowing inside. The chimney was open and puffing gently, and wind chimes were chingling from the eaves.

I crept to the window and peered in. Over at the far end was a man with his back to me. He was standing by a stove, a tall figure with a broad slim frame and an artisan's smock tied to his waist. Behind him looked to be a studio. There were two tree stumps emerging from a wood-plank floor, which was covered with wood shavings and sawdust and carving tools. All different sorts of wooden sculptures like totem were lined up against the wall, though I couldn't tell their caste, and at the center of the room was a chairmaker's bench and a spinning lathe, with a stool between them. On the stool was a lamp to work by, with what appeared to be an earthen cider keg for a base.

I looked back at the man. He was making himself a cup of tea, pouring the hot water over a spoon of leaves. His hands were large and broad-knuckled; then when he turned, I recognised the broad slim mouth, the square jaw, sunken eyes, and gunmetal hair. It was Eugene.

Quickly I rounded the corner and knocked upon the door, and when he opened it to me, I could see he looked well—not mad and shaggy, as Ali had said. There seemed more peace round the corners of his eyes. "Eugene," I said.

No, he shook his head. "Teverin." Then he examined the whole of my person until his eyes settled on the cane. "Come in."

He returned to the middle of the room, slid his spinning lathe to the side, and set a simple chair in its place for me, in front of his bench and to the side of his lamp. I took the chair, but he remained standing. "Do you know why you are here?" he asked.

"Not really." I took out the map, the diamond, and the silver stone to show him. "Some days ago I found these in my pocket, and someone had written directions on my map, leading here—John William, I think." Teverin passed over the jewels but took the map and examined it.

"Tea?" he asked.

"Thank you."

He went to the stove, and while he prepared my cup, I looked about the room, at the pieces. They were beautiful, but most definitely not chess totem—some other kind of creatures, waiting for life, it seemed.

Then suddenly the worklamp flickered, and from the corner of my eye I thought I saw something drip from the spigot of the keg underneath. I looked and saw there was a mug on the floor directly below, near to brimming with something very dark like black coffee. Another drip fell down from the nozzle, but it didn't appear to be liquid. It was like a thin trail of black smoke spilling silently down, but before I could examine it more closely, Teverin was before me, handing me a steaming cup.

"You saw the first cabin?" He straddled the chairmaker's bench.

"Down the path, you mean?"

He looked at me intently. "I am to warn you of what is inside, and you are to listen."

I sat back, and from the corner of my eye I could see another long trail of black fall silently into the mug, but I kept my focus on Teverin directly. "You have been to Eugene's rook?"

"I have."

"Then you've gathered that Eugene and I are from the same team, the Hlique." He leaned forward with his long arms resting on his thighs, and this was the position he kept through the remainder of our conversation, save for when he would reach down to take a sip from the mug he'd placed beside his foot. He spoke directly, without pause or much inflection.

"Long ago," he said, "before there ever was a rook, we lost our king, as happens. He was captured in ambush, leaving all the rest of us behind with nothing to defend and no purpose other than to keep from being lost, which was our greatest fear. So we remained together and went about our lives as if nothing had happened, all but for Eugene, who was the only one to admit that without our king we were lost already. He saw no reason to remain in Hlique, so he left on his own.

"Most of us who remained considered Eugene reckless and doomed. We assumed that without the rest of us surrounding him he would become disoriented soon enough, and then lose all purpose, and we commended ourselves that we had remained.

"In time, however, word came that Eugene had found the hill near Macaroni and built his rook. We were told that our old mate was a prophet, that he was finding goods for all of us, and that pieces from all around the Antipodes were lining up to see him. I could not help admiring him myself, though not for finding goods or commanding the respect of all the land. I admired that he had managed to find a life alone, and I sought the same for myself, but a place more solitary than Eugene's—no goods, no lines leading to my door. Just a cabin, small and square.

"Eugene's rook was in the open, on a hill. I chose the forest, nearer to Hlique. I found a tree, as Eugene had done, and I cut it down to make a cabin. I brought the tools I needed from Hlique, and sand to mix with tree sap for mortar, and I took stones from the creek. But I told no one. I did all the work myself, and while I built the cabin, it made me happy to think of the day when I could sit inside it, warm and undisturbed. I thought that I would find peace and contentment there, in the fact that I could be alone and not lost.

"But as the day drew near, I grew troubled. It was as though my contentment had rested wholly in the building of my secret, for the closer I came to being done, the more my contentment waned. The day I finished, when I had swept the floor and placed my chair in the middle, that was the day my contentment ended. I spent just three nights there, but found no peace, only solitude and loneliness, and I returned to Hlique.

"I did not desert the cabin, though. Whenever I felt the need to be alone, I would go there, to build a fire and sit in my chair, and in this way, the cabin served me.

"It happened one spring that my mates and I were building windmills for the neighbouring board of Vicar, and one evening after a long day's work, I decided that I would go spend the night at my cabin, to rest and be alone. I entered the forest at dusk, but as I approached along my secret path, I heard the sound of wind chimes, and when the cabin came to view, I saw them hanging from the eaves.

"There was no sign of who'd put them there, and otherwise the cabin was undisturbed. Still it troubled me. I sat up all night waiting for whoever had hung these wind chimes to return, but no one did. There was only the wind, the chimes, and I.

"In the morning I went back to the windmills of Vicar, but that evening I returned to the cabin. I found it just as I'd left it, with the wind chimes still hanging from the eaves, but now also a lamp on the floor inside. This lamp." Teverin looked down at the earthen keg between us, and its flame seemed to flicker in response, as the spigot drooled another long line of smoke down into the cup below.

"Once again, I waited up to see if the one who'd put it there would show, but once again he did not, and the following evening when I returned, I found not just the wind chimes and the lamp, but now a kettle on my stove. Just as I had the previous three nights, I waited up in vain. No one came, and the following night a basket of wool had been added to the collection, and then, the evening after that, a loom.

"That night, after a week's worth of sleepless vigilance, I could not stay up. I fell asleep in my chair and was awakened in the morning by the smell of tea. When I opened my eyes, there was a Chinese man standing before me, offering me a cup. He had a kind, round face, smooth like marble, and there was the faintest smile in his slim eyes and mouth. He said his name was Po, and he introduced me to his friend in the corner, a stone bishop named Constantine.

"Both Po and Constantine seemed gentle and beautiful pieces, but I told them nonetheless that this cabin was not theirs to live in. I told them I had built it for myself, and that while I did not go there often, I had intended it for my solitude.

''Po listened kindly to what I said, and bowed. He apologised for their intrusion and said that they would go and find another place in the forest, but that he could not take his things all at once.

''So just as Po had made his presence known to me, he withdrew, piece by piece, discreetly. First he took the loom, then the basket of wool; next he took the teakettle, and then the lamp, until all that remained were Constantine and the wind chimes. For nine days and nights now, they'd been hanging from my eaves, and as I lay in bed that evening, listening to them play, it occurred to me how I would miss them when they were gone. It occurred to me that in asking Po and Constantine to go, I was only protecting my loneliness. So the following day when Po came for Constantine and the wind chimes, I told him that I had reconsidered and that, if he liked, he and Constantine could stay.

''Po asked if a cabin made of just one tree wouldn't be too small for the three of us together. I said I would build a second cabin, of two trees. I told him that nothing would make me happier, which was the truth, so the three of us walked out into the forest and chose two trees side by side, to make our new home.''

Teverin paused to sip his tea and cast his eye successively upon the two stumps in opposite corners of the room.

''I built this cabin,'' he said, ''and Po and Constantine and I lived here together. I kept working in Hlique, but the cabin was now my home. Constantine and Po were both quiet and prayerful and never left the forest. Po grew herbs and flowers and vegetables, and he made musical instruments from things he found in the woods. He carved holes in trees, or strung their limbs with catgut for their leaves to strum when the wind blew. He stretched skins across jugs of water, and sat them under knotted threads, and when it rained the threads would drip and drum the skins. He hid his instruments throughout the wood, and when I came home in the evening, he would lead me and Constantine out to hear them play. Then we'd return to eat our meal and drink our tea, and after dinner I would go to bed and Po and

Constantine would go to the first cabin. Po kept his loom there, and his wool, and his lamp, and he'd weave his tapestries throughout the night.

"We lived this way together for three years. Then one day Po came to me and said that he had finished his tapestries. We went to see them. He told me their stories, and then when he was done, he said the time had come for him to go. He said he wanted to hear the forest sing, and he asked if I would keep his things. I said I would, and then he left. He walked off into the forest, alone.

"The first night he was away, it rained gently, and I couldn't sleep with the sound of all Po's harps and drums thumping in the dark, and the wind playing his chimes and flutes. I rose from bed and walked out through the rain to the first cabin. I'd wanted to look at Po's tapestries, but as I came round the bramble, I saw there was a light inside. I looked through the window and Po's lamp was on his stool, burning a flame. I called for Po, but there was no answer, so I entered, and that is when I saw it for the first time—all across the floor surrounding his lamp was a black fog, and there was a shadow spilling steadily from the tap in its base."

I looked at the lamp. As if on hearing its name, the light flickered and another trail of black drooled down from the spigot and vanished into the mug like a dark spear through a hole.

"That is shadow, then?"

Teverin nodded calmly and continued. "I took a cup and placed it underneath the tap, and then looked for some way to snuff the lamp. I tried turning the tap shut, but the threading was worn. I tried smothering the flame with a damp towel, but it began to smoke and burn. I plugged the nozzle with cloth, but the shadow seeped straight through. There seemed no way of extinguishing either the light or the dark, so I swept the drifting shadow out the door into the night, and took the lamp back here to the second cabin and to Constantine. I set it on a stool with another mug beneath the tap, and I watched the shadow as it spilt down, folding into itself blacker and blacker. I placed my fingers in to feel how cool it was. I dropped a pebble in the cup, and it made no sound. I stared at the flame all night, but it showed no sign of subsiding, for it consumed nothing; it simply shed its light by casting darkness in equal portion.

"By morning the cup was brimful, so I replaced it with a jug and took the cup out into the forest. I poured the shadow inside a rotting tree, but I could see it drift and spread, and I knew I'd have to find another way.

"It seemed all I could do with the shadow was collect it. I brought all of Po's mugs and cups back from the first cabin and made sure there was always one beneath the tap. I found they took a day to fill up before they'd begin spilling over, so I could go to Hlique and see to my work, but when I returned in the evening I'd always find another cupful waiting for me, and the same was true at night. Always before going to sleep I'd place a fresh cup beneath the spigot, and then when I woke up in the morning it would be filled to the brim with black. So mug after mug filled up with shadow. I dumped them into larger jugs and bowls, and when the jugs were full, I'd take them into the first cabin.

"Soon all the shelves and the whole floor of the first cabin was cluttered with pots and bowls, all filled to the brim with shadow. I could see it drifting above their open mouths when I entered, and the room growing more dark and gloomy. I couldn't keep the shadow still, and I had no other containers, so I'd no choice but to make a vessel of the whole cabin. I stopped the chimney and filled in the cracks in the walls, and when I brought my cupfuls in the morning or in the evening I simply poured them into the air and watched the shadows drift like smoke and join the rest.

"The cabin grew dark very quickly. I'd enter from a morning ablaze with summer and inside find it like dusk. If I called out, my voice would sound muffled, as if it were coming from inside a closet or an attic. There was so much shadow drifting, I had to be careful going in and out so as not to lose any, for the shadow had begun to seem precious to me. I wanted as much as I could gather in a single place, to see how dark the dark could be.

"Eventually I stopped going in for fear that too much shadow was escaping when I came and went. I bored a small hole in the door which I plugged with stone, so all I'd have to do when I came with my cupfuls was pour the shadow through. How black and silent it was growing inside I didn't know, but I could think of nothing else. When I went to bed at night or when I was in Hlique, all I could think of was returning to the lamp and feeding more of its shadow to my dark cabin, and how dark the dark must be inside. The cabin frightened me, but it also thrilled me. Every morning when I went to look inside the evening's cup, I felt both hope and dread at finding it all black inside, and I didn't know, if I'd found it clear, whether I would feel relief or devastation. When I carried a mug along the path outside, I wasn't sure if this was good what I was doing, confining the darkness this way for the sake of the forest light and song, or if it was dangerous. For what if the shadow should somehow escape, what if I should unstop the chimney, how high into the sky would my shadow spew? How dark and hushed a night could it cast upon the day? I didn't know, but it was all I ever thought of, and finally I realised I couldn't keep taking this chance, I couldn't keep feeding this thing unless I knew what it was, unless I went inside myself and saw.

''The only question was how to enter without losing too much of the shadow. I thought of digging a tunnel underneath or adding another entryway. Then one night it came to me—I should simply wait and go under cover of darkest night; I should enter the black from black, for then the shadow of my cabin would find nothing outside to cast itself upon, and stay.

''The blackest night here beneath the canopy of trees was the night of the new moon. I tacked a string along the path to guide me; then finally the night came. No moon appeared in the sky, and so I followed my string to the dark cabin and entered, unobserved by either the night or the black of Po's lamp.''

Teverin paused to take another sip of his tea.

''And?'' I asked anxiously. ''What did you see?''

He looked at me, and for the first time the hint of a smile curled at the side of his mouth. ''I saw many things, and every time that I return, I see something else, but what *I* have seen is of no matter.

What matters is what I have learned, and that is what I am here to warn you: The shadow is only as safe and open as the heart which enters it. A clouded heart shall find clouds; a light heart, light.''

He looked at me with a perfectly still expression, then stood up and took his cup back to the stove.

''But wait,'' I said. ''I don't quite understand. You keep telling me you mean to warn me. Why?''

He began to rinse the cup with water from the kettle and with his back to me answered, ''I take it from your presence here that John William thinks you might enjoy entering the cabin yourself.''

''Entering myself?'' I was flabbergasted. ''But I'm not sure I want to.''

''Then you do not have to.'' He turned round. ''In fact, if you've any apprehension, I'd strongly recommend you stay away.'' He took a towel and wiped the cup dry. ''But I also trust John William's judgement.''

He then walked back to the bench and waited for the spigot's latest trail to finish. Between the drips of shadow, he removed the first cup, which was by now full and black inside, and replaced it with the one he'd cleaned. ''Why don't you come with me.'' He held the cup of black out in front of him as though he were about to make a toast. ''It's time to add this day's shadow.''

My heart at this point was thumping like a jackrabbit, but I managed to stand. Teverin opened the door and held the cup out with a perfectly steady hand. In silence we followed the path along the string; then when we reached the first cabin, Teverin removed the small stone in the door and replaced it with his thumb. He raised the cup to his lips and drank the shadow into his mouth. He smiled at me with his cheeks full of darkness, then removed his thumb from the peephole and blew inside.

When he was finished, he plugged his thumb against the hole again and looked back at me. ''Would you like to try?'' He handed me the cup, which despite the length of his draft was only half diminished of its shadow. ''But be sure not to swallow.''

''What would happen?'' I asked.

His eyes rolled back in his head. "Dreams," he said. "Dreams, for days on end, and not for the faint of heart."

I put the cup to my lips and took the shadow into my mouth. It was cool and smooth. Teverin removed his thumb from the hole and I blew the shadow in; I kept my lips against the hole until my mouth was warm again and all the dark was out. It had been strangely pleasant.

Teverin took back the mug. I watched him finish off the rest of the shadow and blow it through the cork hole, and the inside no longer seemed quite so fearsome.

"When is the new moon?" I asked.

"Eleven days."

"Eleven days?"

That didn't sound right, but Teverin silenced me with a glance. "You have been with John William, don't forget." He meant, who knew for how long. "It is eleven days until the new moon," he repeated. "Also, should you choose to enter, there is one condition."

I looked at him, dazed. "Yes?"

"You will bring me a good." He glanced down at the cane. "That would do."

I looked down myself. "But this was given to me by Eugene."

Teverin smiled. "All the goods have been given to us by Eugene."

I took the jewels from my pocket to offer him. "You wouldn't take these instead?"

He barely looked at them. "Those are yours, sir, to keep. To me you will bring a good—that is, if you decide you want to see the shadow." Then he turned back toward the second cabin with his empty mug, leaving me eleven days to wait. Eleven days to find a good, I realised, for as mad as it may seem, I know already that I shall have to enter Teverin's cabin. Whatever is waiting there inside, I suppose I'd rather I found it than it found me.

Good night,
Gus

TWENTY

THE LAST READING
(The Dark Cabin)

On July 14, the Sunday following the arrival of the doctor's last letter, Mrs. Uyterhoeven emerged from the front door of her home at roughly 5:30 in the evening, descended the porch steps, and crossed the small front lawn to the garden gate. A shingle was hanging beside the latch, with the words charcoaled on:

READING SUNDAY/AFTER DINNER.

Mrs. Uyterhoeven lifted the sign from its hook and without pause carried it like a tray back across the lawn and up the porch steps. Inside, she placed it flat on a shelf in the front closet, which was otherwise filled with house tools, stray mittens, scarves and hats, some boots, and a number of coats and jackets which had been left at the garden and remained unclaimed. Mrs. Uyterhoeven lifted a three-pronged fork from underneath a canvas coat and took it with her out to the foyer and up the main stairs to the second floor.

At the far end of the hallway, on the garden side, was the trapdoor to the attic. Mrs. Uyterhoeven had to use the gardening fork to reach the finger clasp, but when she pulled it down, the stairs unfolded to her feet like a giant beetle. She hung the fork on the hallway banister and climbed up.

The attic was relatively free of clutter. At the far end sat the few items that Mrs. Hunt had neglected to take with her to Cincinnati. There was a trunk filled with tablecloths and old clothes that Gustav had gone through once or twice with the children before consigning it to this remote corner. There were some of the general's military coats as well, hanging from a clotheshorse, and a wooden cane hanging in their midst, with a worn handle and a brass ring around its neck. Mrs. Uyterhoeven lifted it up and took it back down to the second landing, hoisted the stairs, and then went to her bedroom.

There was a large, open envelope on the mantel, postmarked June 8 from Bloemfontein, June 11 from Capetown, and June 23 from London. From deep inside she pulled out something muffin-sized, wrapped in tissue, and put it in the pocket of her dress. Next she took the letter itself from her bedside table—the doctor had filled an entire notebook he'd taken from the British administrative office in Bloemfontein. She tucked it beneath her arm, remembered the cane, the gardening fork, and then headed downstairs again.

She returned the fork to its hook in the front closet, and then went into the library. She removed a box of dominoes from the bottom drawer of the doctor's desk and plunked them by handfuls into the pockets of her apron. Then she checked to see that the letters were in order. They were all stacked inside the cherrywood drawer on the doctor's blotter. She set the most recent letter on top and then turned her attention to the chess pieces. They were all in their places on the goatskin board. The crane was the worst for wear. Gently she pulled its wings to fill out its body, and then shook it to make sure the shards were still inside. She checked to see that there was still ash in the thimble from Eugene's rook. She took General Hunt's musket ball from the king's square and polished it with her dress, and then did the same for the Vaal diamond. The other pieces she checked for chips or smudges, and set them one by one at the center of the board. Last was the sleeping child. She placed him in his little boat for the trip outside, then folded over the goatskin and set the bundle on top of the letters. She closed the drawer, hooked the cane to her wrist, then carried them both out to the garden, with the dominoes clicking gently in her pockets.

It was a mild day, but only Mr. Geoheghan and Mr. Leo were out. They had been there since noon, and barely looked up from their game as she passed. She walked out to the oak, and there on the east table she set up the pieces again, on the goatskin. When they were all in their places and presentable, she took the cane over to the apple tree behind the oak. She chose the most welcoming limb and hooked it there, halfway out, so that it could hang freely.

Then Mrs. Uyterhoeven returned to the eastern table beneath the oak and sat quietly to wait for the guests.

Hope Gray was first. She came with a tray of cookies. Mr. Patterson arrived not long thereafter, with Mr. Drake and Mr. Collinsworth, who immediately set about moving chairs and benches out to the oak. Mr. Patterson helped Mrs. Uyterhoeven carry out the blankets. They lit the cans of citronella, and then on the way back they both stopped at the lily pond. Mrs. Uyterhoeven knelt down and took the dominoes from her pockets, and as she spread them out across the water, she asked Mr. Patterson if he would be willing to read this evening. She said her voice had not returned. He said he would, and they walked back to the patio together. Mr. Patterson poured himself a glass of bourbon, set up the bar, and then went to see if the lectern was still in the library, as he preferred to read standing up.

Sometime around 6:30 the rest of the guests came strolling around the path. Mrs. Uyterhoeven took her place on the patio to welcome them all, but kept her words to a minimum. Most of the children went straight to the oak to see the pieces, while the parents saw to their drinks first and then drifted out into the garden by twos and threes.

Finally, at around 7:00 or so, Mr. Patterson's bell sounded. The smallest children sat on the blankets surrounding the eastern table, and the rest all found seats. Mrs. Uyterhoeven took a chair next to Miss Steele's lounge at the periphery, away from the candlelight, and when everyone was settled, Mr. Patterson stood up behind the lectern.

He said that as most the guests had no doubt gleaned already, Mrs. Uyterhoeven had been feeling a touch under the weather that week and lost her voice, but that she'd been kind enough to ask if he would read for her. With apologies to the doctor's prose, he accepted. He thanked her with a slight bow, poured himself a glass of water, and, without further ado, opened the doctor's notebook and began.

The Twelfth Letter

June 12, 1901

Dear Sonja,

I hadn't much time—eleven days before the new moon, to find a good and bring it back to Teverin. I knew there were some at the altar girl's cavern, but I wasn't sure that I wanted to diminish her collection, nor was I at all certain I'd be able to find her hiding place again. I'd a better sense of how to get to the low-tide island of the duck pond in Gwyddbyl, and I suspected there might still be a few goods buried there. It was a ways away, but with no other options in mind and the sandglass decisively spun, I set off.

It turned out to be farther than I'd imagined. After six days of tireless walking, I was still barely a third of the distance there. The chances of finding a good and returning in time were growing increasingly slim, and I even began to wonder if I should give Teverin the cane. I knew if I turned back right then I could perhaps have made it in time.

Fortunately, I wasn't forced to make the choice, for just at the very moment that I paused to take the measure of my conscience, I was joined by one of my very oldest friends here. The red counter rolled up from the roadside and stopped in front of me.

It was quite a surprise, needless to say, and a very happy one, but we dispensed with any pleasantries, for it appeared that the counter was equally distressed as I and wanted my assistance for something. It kept rolling off the road for me to follow, and I in turn was trying to convey to it the fact that I hadn't time for such escapades. At one point it began swerving and wavering about the lane as if it had fallen ill, then spun down flat like a coin in front of me. But just as I leaned over to make sure it was well, up it jumped, bright as a pup, and started off the road again. A ploy, but obvious enough, and desperate enough to persuade me of the counter's urgency, and so, in light of my own quandary—and aware that I'd probably just as good a chance finding a good off the road as on—I let hope prevail and followed.

Just the same as when we first met, it led me to an orchard, this time of apples, in the midst of which we came upon another candletree, not near as large as the one we'd visited in Shatranj but still with its own healthy bouquet of candlebloom and the resultant alpine kingdom of wax drippings underneath.

As I came near, however, I saw that all the dripcastles had been pillaged. They had been stomped and trampled, melted and carved with blades. They appeared to have been looted of their insides, and that is when I realised—of course, the dripcastles! What better place to hide a good?

And yet it seemed I'd come too late. Clearly someone had beaten me to the punch, and I'm not sure why, but as I looked about the ravaged kingdom, the realisation descended upon me like a chill that time was even shorter than I'd thought. The final collection had begun, and I was still without a good for Teverin.

I wasn't sure what to do, but as I looked back at the counter, who'd taken its place just outside the tree's umbrage, I saw that one of the candles had lit on the lowest bough between us, and that its first drips were just now dripping down onto a small lump below. I stumbled through the cracked spires and thawed hills to see: there was a little untouched castle there.

Quickly, with my cane I pulled down the branch, plucked my friend's candle, and then applied its little flame to the castle spire. It melted like beeswax, and in moments I could see there was indeed something underneath, something hard and the shape of a cylinder. I pulled it out from the sticky goo—a jar. Not like Ali-Uthmar's, but a jar for preserves.

I turned to my red friend to thank it, but it was already starting back through the orchard, beckoning me to come quick, so I wrapped the jar in my kerchief and put it straight into my pocket. I followed my good friend back to the road and there found a stack of red checkers waiting for me. Their intention to help was obvious, if inexplicable, so with more gratitude to the counter than I could ever speak, I bid adieu, climbed aboard the higher stack, and off we went, the checkers and I, back in the direction of Teverin's cabin.

They carried me almost the whole way at a good but very comfortable clip, through day and night, and I am much obliged to them, for I'm not sure I'd have made it otherwise. In three days we arrived in Hlique, the dusk of the new moon. There the checkers left me. I entered the forest alone, with cane in hand and jar in pocket, thumping at my side. I followed the song of Po's fluted trees to a water mill–harp, and from there I could hear the cabin chimes. They led me past the dark cabin again, but I didn't dare look, for fear again that if I saw its windows, blind and boarded, I might turn back. I went straight to the threaded path and did not look up again until the second, larger cabin came to view.

There was light, as before, and smoke coming from the chimney, and through its windows I could see Teverin, quietly at work before his lathe, shaving his cords of wood to pieces as yet unknown. I announced myself with three knocks upon his door, and he welcomed me with neither surprise nor expectation. He merely looked at me and asked what I had brought.

"I have the good jar," I said, and I unwrapped it from my kerchief to show him. "For preserves."

He looked dubiously at my offering.

"I'm fairly sure," I said. "I found it hidden in a candletree drip-castle."

He held it up to examine, and then he peeled away a strip of the caked wax. There was something inside; I hadn't even noticed. Teverin looked at me stolidly, opened the jar and spilt out a small canvas pouch into his hand. He slipped the knot and then removed two things: a note and a silver pocket watch. He examined the watch first. He wound it to make sure that it was ticking, then read the note to himself, before handing them both to me. "It's for you," he said.

I read:

Dear Dr. Uyterhoeven,

Hello! and my best to our friend the red counter, if he is still there. Congratulations on your decision! I trust such gameness shall serve you well in what lies ahead, and so in recognition (and on a hunch that you will be wanting to keep your word to Eugene) let me offer you: the good pocket watch!

Your friend,
John William, Bishop of Orzhevsky

I looked up at Teverin, boggled.

"So," he said flatly, "would you prefer the cane or the pocket watch?"

"You mean to give you?"

He nodded.

I thought. "The pocket watch, I suppose," and I handed it back to him.

He set it down upon the larger of his two stumps, and then started a pot of tea. I took a seat, and when the pot began to hiss, he poured just one cup, for himself, and then set the day's mug of lampdark before me.

"To drink?" I asked.

He nodded.

"And swallow?"

Again he nodded.

"But what about the dreams?"

Teverin allowed a smile. "You are not going to sleep tonight," he said. "It will be easier if you've had some to drink."

I took my first sip of pure shadow, and I felt its cool flow down inside me. It was a pleasant sensation. We sat in silence as he drank his tea and I my dark, and the shadow seemed to cast a serenity through me until I was brimming. Then, when the basin of my cup was light again, Teverin stood and checked the window. The time had come.

"But is there anything else I should know?" I asked.

He opened the door for me. "*You* are entering, Dr. Uyterhoeven. I've no way of knowing what awaits you."

For some reason this struck me as amusing, his frankness. I stood, and I could feel an ease in my joints like that which had suffused my brain.

Night had fallen entirely dark, with no moon and the starlight hidden by the leaves. Teverin lead me straight to the string, and as we felt our way along, the trees and chimes seemed to be playing to our procession, encouraging me with flutes and strings and drum thumps. I was calm, but still very excited. The faint silhouette of the small cabin appeared before us. I felt Teverin's hand on my shoulder and let go the string, and as he guided me to the door, I asked, "How long?"

"Time should be of no concern."

"But where will you be?"

"I will be here," he said. I smiled at his sobriety. Then I heard the door open just a crack before me, felt Teverin's hand stiffen on my back, and I entered three steps in.

It was deathly quiet and deathly black. I didn't even hear the door close behind me, but the song of Po's trees and chimes suddenly hushed and the darkness was as if I'd entered a coffin.

But I had expected this, the silence and the dark. What I had not expected was that the cabin's air should be so fine, and so this is what most affected me. I could feel it seeping through my skin, as though the shadow were cool water and I a sponge, and again I was grateful that Teverin had me drink the day's mug, for it seemed to quell the shadow's interest to find some sympathetic air already adrift inside me. I shuddered just once, but less at the physical siege than the perception, which was that I had just been swallowed by a great black ghost, a ghost which was subsuming me now, lifting me slightly—I was breathless, but not requiring of breath—sustained, suspended, and then, as I stood there, steadily erased.

I mean that just as my sight and hearing had been taken from me, so my sense of touch was growing numb. The good cane slipped silently from my fingers. I raised my hands to my face, but it was like a foreign palm upon a stranger's skin. My fingers began to clench till I could not feel them anymore, nor my arms, nor now my feet against the floor, nor anything at all. No light. No sound. And now, no body. No difference between myself and what lay outside myself. All there was of me was mind, and now I knew very well why the sheik so feared this place, for it was true: What was I to do, bereft of any sensibility, if perchance some nightmares should discover my condition and occur? I could not wake. I could not run. I could not avert my eyes or call out for help. The very darkest of my demons could come and establish their domain in my brain—

But before even so much as letting this thought conclude, I intimated the danger and rushed straightaway to guard against it. It was a reflex almost, but the only way I could think was to occupy my mind as fast as possible with as safe and trustworthy an object as I could imagine. And what first occurred to me, in the midst of this deafening silence, was music. What better than music? And the music which occurred to me was the Romance by Dvořák. That is simply what occurred to me first, and I don't think it would have been such a bad selection in itself. I think it would have been quite nice, if I could have managed it, to summon a piece of such complexity from such thin, thin air. I tried. I listened, and the beginning was not so bad, the way it creeps in like light from round a window shade. Certain of the early phrases emerged quite clearly, in fact, but then the farther into the piece I ventured, I am afraid the quality of my rendering fell off rather dramatically. I had a great deal of trouble with the pace. I found myself rushing through the parts I knew less well and diving headlong into the more familiar, and then repeating these over and over. By the middle it was a hodgepodge, wanting in all the elements that make music music, or make it pleasurable—the patience, the dimension, the silence, the fore and aft in every moment. Perhaps Mr. Pierce could have done better—I'm sure he could have—but as for myself, I am afraid that I was hopeless, and becoming agitated.

So I moved over to images next, for my defenselessness remained. I tried to envision images that might bring comfort, but I hadn't learned my lesson. I aimed extremely high—for *Pieta*s and *David*s, which, for the same reasons as I'd failed the "Romance," weren't particularly impressive. I could manage only glimmers and shadows. In fact, so miserable were my attempts that I could not miss the reason why—that I was a novice in this atmosphere, it was very clear; a virtual infant, really, who being so new to the dark might do better to attempt simpler subjects first. Instead of symphonies and Sistine Chapels, perhaps some nursery rhymes and nursery shapes.

And here in fact I did meet with much more success. I was able to hear an entire verse of "Clementine" and a chorus of the children singing "Happy Birthday"—to Meredith Fitzgerald, I believe. As for shapes, I confined myself to those which one might find on one of Mr. Kelly's mobiles—stars and boats with full white sails, the silhouettes of cows and crescent moons—and I did not do so badly with these either. They stood out like cookies, in colours of their own apparent choice, all set fairly clear against a hazier, smoky-dark background.

But better than this, better than the improvement which my more modest attempts had yielded, was the tendency of these sensations, these simple songs and pictures, to change into other songs and pictures which I had not intended, but which for that very reason seemed to occur with an even greater clarity. Indeed, it seemed the less I tried fixing my attention on some selected target—the less, that is, I tried to conjure—the more vivid was the image which came to mind, and the one which followed from it, and the one which followed after. These visions within the shadow seemed to have a life of their very own, whose basic instinct was to change, so that my one task, if it was clarity I sought, was simply to let them.

Thus did I see a tunnel become tombstones become rows of clubs and rows of spades, become rows of stars, and Christmas trees, all absolutely clear and brilliant, and filling my mind with such colour and vibrancy that soon I'd lost all perception of the dark. The shadow was gone, and the same held true of the silence, for at its heart, if I listened, was not silence but music, to be sure—not my Bohemian romances or lullabies but melodies unknown to me, which nonetheless played flawlessly. I heard voices and strings, the choir of Pelagia's monastery and oboes and drums, and I was thrilled quite frankly, not just by the performance, but by the discovery as well: there was no silence. All I'd had to do was listen and I had heard. And there was no black either, no void, nor anything to fear. All I'd had to do was look and I could see—that was all the foolishness of the outside world, to think that there could be such things, for here inside the shadow was a pageant so bright and game and plentiful, it seemed to me that I'd had it backwards all this time. Everything I'd thought was real and lasting, that place out there where Teverin stood and Po's chimes chingled, that all seemed a mirror now, or a puppet stage—and all the things that I'd called figments were nothing of the kind, were here in front of me, as real as real could be. I'd had it backwards! And so like that, with that simple turnabout, my captivity inside the shadow turned into freedom; my sympathy with the fearful sheik was spun into envy for Teverin, for his chance to enter this shadow time and again, for with practice—oh, the things he must have seen, the music he must have heard.

But what of touch? I wondered. What of body? I'd almost forgotten—I'd been so enchanted by the flood of sound and light—and yet I'd still no sense of form, of what or where I was. But it seemed only fair that if the black should hold such visions, and the silence music, then surely this emptiness I felt must somewhere in its depths be keeping shapes for me as well, things for me to touch, and forms to take. It must, I thought, and now I wanted to feel them, whatever else this cabin had in store.

Ah, but I was an educated student of the shadow now. I knew better than to try imagining what they might be—refrain from thoughts of steeplechase and ballet. I knew that I would be best served if I let go my expectations and set my mind as best I could upon my seeming absence.

And so I did, but here I note the temper of the shadow discernibly changed. I felt it almost instantly. Whereas before, with all the sounds and shapes, it had seemed to me they'd come at random or by whim, as if the purpose had been to display the cabin's bounty, here as the shadow directed its attention to my sense of touch was no whimsy. No, I felt much more as if I was being communicated to, or being led.

So this journey began as a vague thunking at my side, very faint at first, but which grew more vivid with each return: it felt like a club of some kind, and then more like a hammer, a hammer with a blade at the end—an axe. Someone was chopping at my waist with an axe, and yet I felt no pain but rather that I was blunting these blows like stone; a good thing, too, as the second of my physical perceptions, such as I can discretely order them, was of being buried halfway underneath the ground and clutching to it. I felt born of the ground, in fact, and that I had limbs which spread as far and wide beneath the earth as they did above, in open air. I was a tree, but a tree of such hard and tempered wood that all this pounding at my waist could not have seemed more vain. The axeman hacked and hacked in growing desperation, but to so little effect that my attention turned to a warmth that I could feel inside, and not so far from my heart, a recurrent whisper grazing against my bark like someone barely breathing, some human body there inside me which my roots and vines entwined—the object of the axeman's desire—whose reply to his frantic blows was of a perfect and merciless restraint, simply to remain, to feel her roots and grow, drink water from the earth, and pull it up the vines embracing her, to imbue my higher limbs with such life and yearning that from one thousand shoots throughout her crown I sprouted one thousand leaves to feel the air.

And in the air I felt a warmth and light which both came from a single place, which I knew must be the sun. By my thousand palms I felt it at its height and then descending in the sky. I felt the air grow cool. The breath at my heart grew faint. My middle cooled to heartwood, and when the sun touched down upon the cold horizon, it shattered into a thousand shards, which rolled in through the grove to me like dishes. And as each one took its place to rest surrounding me, somewhere in my crown a candle lit. My crown became a heaven all of candles, dream by counterdream. And as the night fell deeper, the air grew cold, and all the candle flames were frozen into diamonds and silver stones, which wrapped themselves in fruit to keep away the frost. And there was no grove to protect me now. I was on a moor. The air began to sweep and stir, and then a wind flew down around me. It lashed at me and yanked my limbs; it flung my jewelled fruit away, and then began to twist me down. I could feel my roots tear up from the ground, but I was caught in the arms of another tree, and where we were was not the moor. It was a forest, all peaceful. The wind was gone, and in the hollow which my roots had torn, I could feel the drift of pipesmoke and the warmth of two young lovers making puzzles of my leaves. They felt like two warm bricks at the foot of my bed, and I was quite content.

But then the arms which had been holding me gave way. Down I fell upon the needle bed, and the puzzlemakers snuffed. There was no hollow anymore, but my stump and roots still clutching to the earth, and I beside, a timber—and then there was an axe again, but not the same one as before. It was a sharper blade, and the hands that wielded it were different, too. They struck with much more purpose and effect. They cleaved deep into me, but not to harm, and so there was no pain. I lay upon the ground and yielded like a sleepy child, serene and drifting, pretending slumber while his father dresses him in nightclothes. I could feel his hands and different blades—shearing me and splitting me, stripping my bark and sanding me, stacking me and fixing me with sap and mortar, fitting me end to end, and when he was through, there was still my base, my stump inside, but surrounding it was a different body than I'd known—no longer divided by earth and air but by a space inside, enclosed by me, and then the without—I was but their meeting place and their partition. I provided all their difference, and the difference was this, as I could feel:

Outside me was a moonless night, cool and dark, purring with chimes and hooting trees, and shifting in a breeze. And within me all was still and silent. Not the faintest whisper. I was Teverin's cabin, stored with all the shadow of Po's lamp, and though I couldn't feel it yet, I knew that my body must be somewhere in the black and silent air, hovering motionless like a puppet from a nail, and so I searched for it the only way I could. I felt every surface where the shadow touched—the walls and all eight corners, the cool smooth surface of the windows, and the boards nailed carefully across. I felt the beams along the ceiling and seven hooks screwed inside the wall, the head of every nail, and the stovepipe plugging the roof. I felt the mantel, three kerosene lamps along the top, the hollow of the fireplace, the bricks round the hearth, the cupboard along the wall, the cups inside the cupboard, a four-poster bedframe and the steamer trunk beside it. I felt the tree stump in the middle of the room and the rim and mouth of every jar across the floor.

Then three steps from the door I felt my cane. It was lying where I had dropped it, and I knew I must be standing right beside, but the shadow was so through and through me, I couldn't make it out at first. I tried with all my might, then gradually I did begin to feel the faint impression of a figure swathed in darkness, an old familiar frame, and I knew that it was mine, for slowly from the murk of my distraction the room began to emerge in light—only very dim at first, but on every surface where I'd felt the shadow graze, the image now appeared—all the cabin logs and cupboards, every hook and nail, and every jug across the floor—all from where I stood before the door. Bit by bit the light crept in on every nearer surface until the shadow hovered last of all above the tree stump.

But there was something sitting there, and I realised I was not alone. Someone was before me, sitting on the stump, who had been there all along, waiting in the shadow, waiting in all the colour and song. And as the room's light crept in closer, I could see it was a man, sitting with his legs crossed, and he was in a simple robe. His face was round and smooth like marble, with a small mouth and slim grinning eyes, looking back at me. It was Po.

And though his smile was kind, there was in the tilt of his head a hint of chiding. He seemed to be asking what I was doing there, and why, of all the things which were mine to find inside the shadow of his lamp, had I chosen the walls of Teverin's cabin? Clever, he seemed to say, but would I not prefer to see what was in my own heart?

He pointed to the cane at my feet. I reached down to pick it up, and when I looked back at him, now with the light more clear, I could see him close his eyes and wait. So I closed mine, and when I opened them again, Po was still before me, but with a much more pleased expression on his face, and I knew why—from the scent in the air and the hue of light. I was in the library. Po was sitting in the English chair, still cross-legged, and I was standing three steps from the door. There by the fireplace were my two globes, and the map of the Antipodes was still on the dictionary stand. There were our books along the wall, the smell of their pages and bindings, and of the rugs and draperies.

It was twilight. I looked out the window, and the garden drifted in the breeze, all different hues of blue. I wanted to go walk in it. I wanted to find someone, for there were only Po and I inside. I looked back at him, and with a nod he excused me.

On the terrace the drinks table was covered with plates and crumbs and half-filled glasses, but there were no players at the nearest tables, so I started out along the slates. I rounded the drift of lumen, and there was a team of dominoes floating in the lily pond, but I did not stop, as I could see, with the lavender night falling, a golden light coming from beneath the general's oak, and I could hear you now, hushing. The lanterns were all surrounding you, and I wanted to call out—you looked like angels in the light—but I couldn't. So I walked farther along the shell path, and when I reached the grass, I heard a whisper. Someone was calling my name from your midst.

I looked to see who, but my eyes fell first upon an unexpected guest. It was Timothy, the knight who'd folded himself into a crane, and I thought, How wise a wind to carry him here! And then I saw in front of him was Ali-Uthmar, not drowned at the bottom of the domino pond but here with you, and here was the milkmaid of Orzhevsky with the sickle in her hand, and beside her Egbert, and then Eugene, who looked neither mad nor shaggy but very well. He was standing before the good thimble and the ashes of his rook, beside which was a little boat, and then the one who'd called my name, a long-bearded bishop who was returning my gaze directly and very pleasantly. He was the only one who seemed to be aware of me, in fact. With a nod he invited me to his side, and then, as his contentment broke into a smile, the glimmer in his eye recalled to me my first night in the Antipodes, in Ludo—I recognised him; of all people, it was the bishop I had spoken to on the pier. I passed through the group of you, and as I sat next to him, he opened his hand and there were the two jewels on his palm, a diamond and a silver stone, just like those I'd found. I took mine from my own pocket, and I showed them to him in turn. He smiled and nodded. He looked down at my cane and whispered in my ear—had I found the pocket watch? I looked at him, he winked, and then it came to me—John William! It was John William. My friend, my best friend from the Antipodes, and in his hand the king and queen, the spellbound infant and Evelin, and he, John William, reading me their story from the tapestries—Po's tapestries. ''But Po is here,'' I said, ''he is in the library.'' John William only nodded. He put his finger to his lips and then pointed to the string on my finger. ''There is someone you should see,'' he whispered, and he gestured to the little boat beside us. Together we peered over the side, and there was a little boy sleeping, with his hands upon his chest, and all I could think was that my dream was true. Here he was.

But what story had you gathered here together to read him? I turned and asked the bishop in a whisper, and he looked at me with a very wide grin. ''You,'' he said. ''They are awaiting word from you.''

So I stood up straight to look at you, at every one of you, and I whispered in your ear, How I have missed you. I miss you every moment desperately, but I could not have been more consoled or felt more blessed than at this moment, to have looked inside my heart and found you there.

Then there was a hand upon my shoulder, and a voice at my ear. ''Light's coming,'' it said—Teverin's voice and Teverin's hand. He took me from your circle, and we started towards the games shed. I had no time to say goodbye, but I stopped us underneath the apple tree, and on the nearest branch I hung the cane for you. Then Teverin and I entered through the door of the shed, and back into the forest, to the song it sang for missing Po, on the darkest of nights in this strange and foreign land.

We were standing outside the cabin door, and Teverin asked if all was well. I told him yes. ''Good,'' he said, and then he turned and started back along the path, with his hand upon the thread he'd strung for nights like this.

I looked down at my hand, at my third finger, at the thread which all this time has tugged in so much vain for my wandering attention, and I slipped it off. Then, as dawn crept up, I made my way back through the forest from strain to strain, and when I reached the edge, I left my loyal thread upon a twig, for I knew that I should have no other purpose now than to go to the rivers and wait. I shall wait as long as it takes the mystific to pull his queen along the banks to me, so that I may tell her finally—I have seen her son, and he is in heaven.

For the better part of the doctor's letter, Mrs. Uyterhoeven sat perfectly still. Then very near the end, where the doctor had opened his eyes to find himself in the library, she excused herself quietly and made her way back to the house. She poured herself a glass of water from the pitcher on the patio table and carried it with her into the library, which was dark. She took the small piece from her apron pocket, unwrapped the tissue, and then set the figure on the English chair—an Asian man, carved in ivory, sitting cross-legged and smiling faintly.

Then she took her glass of water upstairs to her room. She did not light her bedside lamp but sat at the window looking down at the garden. The oak was far enough away that all the guests were blocked from view by the boughs of trees, but the candlelight still needled through. She could tell when the letter was finished. First, the children scrambled out from the circle over toward the apple tree, and then the adults followed more slowly. They all started back toward the house, some children running and others sleeping in their parents' arms. Mrs. Uyterhoeven sat back on the bed, and she could hear them taking in the plates, shushing each other and keeping the children quiet, for her sake.

A knock came at the door. ''Sonja?'' It was Charlotte Conover, through the crack, and then opening the door halfway. ''Are you all right?''

Mrs. Uyterhoeven nodded.

''Did they see the cane?''

Mrs. Conover nodded. ''Mr. Patterson made sure. He left it out, though—on the branch. He didn't know where you would want it.''

''Did they see in the library?''

''What?''

''In the library.''

Mrs. Conover looked back toward the stairs and spoke in hushed tones to someone there, then turned back to Mrs. Uyterhoeven with a smile. ''Yes.''

Mrs. Uyterhoeven touched the top button of her dress to show she wanted to be alone now, but Mrs. Conover paused in the doorway.

''Good night.''

''Good night, Sonja.'' Mrs. Conover closed the door and went downstairs. Mrs. Uyterhoeven could hear all the guests down on the patio, and then Mr. Patterson's bell ringing quietly for an announcement. She could hear them filing into the library, children calling out and being hushed by their parents. They didn't stay long. Just to see Po and rinse the dishes. Then, family by family, friend by friend, they made their way around the walk and said good night out on the street.

Only when all was quiet did Mrs. Uyterhoeven take her candle and make her way downstairs to see how Mr. Patterson had left the letters. Everything was in place. The cherrywood drawer was open and all the pages were stacked inside. The goatskin board was spread across the candlestick table, and all the pieces were in their squares, now with Po among them, sitting serenely in the bishop's. So Mrs. Uyterhoeven returned to her room and lay down on her bed, for the first time alone.

No mention was made of the doctor's death. For three weeks after the last reading Mrs. Uyterhoeven left the pieces and letters in the library. One night before bed she went in and put them all in the drawer—the pieces, the letters, the goatskin board, and even the map. She took them all upstairs to the top shelf of her closet, all but the cane, which she left out on the apple branch.

No formal service was ever held. The doctor's body was returned to the Netherlands and buried alongside Larkin's, at the cemetery in Workum. In Dayton, a stone appeared out among the wildflowers in the children's grove, with the doctor's initials and the years 1823–1901.

A year passed, and the box remained in Mrs. Uyterhoeven's closet. Then the following spring a number of the mothers came to Mrs. Uyterhoeven and asked if she would consider taking the letters down again. New people had come to Dayton, they said, and the children had grown, children who had been too young the first time.

Mrs. Uyterhoeven agreed. She brought out the letters but declined to read them herself. She set out the pieces in order, and welcomed whoever came to listen, but preferred that others have a turn telling the tales. Captain Stivers read, and Miss Steele, Mr. Dunbar, Dr. Burns, Dr. Thomas, and even some of the older children. It took them the six weeks of Lent to finish, and just the same as the year before, the number of guests who came to listen grew steadily from reading to reading.

The following spring, the letters were brought out again, and the spring after that as well. In fact, for ten years straight, the Lenten phase in Dayton was observed by the gradual appearance of the doctor's pieces, and the spring of 1913 would likely have been no different. The cherrywood drawer had already been taken down from its shelf and was poised for its eleventh trip downstairs when Mrs. Uyterhoeven fell ill. She took to bed the day before Ash Wednesday and there remained, in the care of Mrs. Conover, until she passed away, March 25, the morning of the great Dayton flood.

Acknowledgments

To all the following, my thanks, for the friendship they've shown me and my book:

First to my family, whose constant faith and support are my greatest fortune, and for which this work and all my work is a meager restitution.

To Mollie Davies, Chang-rae Lee, Annabel Wing and Adam Guettel, for their friendship and homes.

To my research staff, including Zachary Gleit, Steven Gross, Whitney Hansen, Eric Noter, Reverend McCluskey, the New York Public Library, The Writers Room, Stage Left, the Swedenborg Foundation, and the Virginia Center for the Creative Arts.

To Whitney Abbott, Maria Artemis, Helena Meryman, and Suzanne Weber, for the welcome boost of their various talents and enthusiasm.

For their help with the manuscript itself, my thanks to Peter Hansen, Hope Gray, Nick Davis, and Celia Wren.

To Amanda Urban, of course, for the uncommon reserves of experience, forbearance, and mettle which she summoned on behalf of this unexpectedly troublesome book. To Sloan Harris, for calling only when the news is good. And to Anne Taberski, for always making it a pleasure.

To Carol Welch, Miles Hutchison, and Sheena Walshaw, for helping spread the word.

To Ileene Smith, here and in perpetuity, for her founding faith and interest.

To Alane Salierno Mason, for her unrivaled commitment to the work itself, and for the talent, concentration, and severity that she applied to see that my words not flout my meaning entirely.

To Jonathan Galassi, for his judicious guidance through the end, and for the access he provides to so much more talent and expertise, that in particular of Paul Elie, Lynn Warshow, and Cynthia Krupat, who could not set my mind more at ease.

And finally to Virginia Medellin Priest, for her confidence throughout, her talent and example, her standards, her ear, her patience and impatience. I only hope I offer the same.

Brooks Hansen is the author (with Nick Davis) of *Boone* (1990). He lives in New York City.